THE NEXT GENERATION

CONVERSION BOOK FOUR

S.C. STEPHENS

This is a work of fiction. Names, characters, places, brands, media, and incidents are either the product of the author's imagination or are used fictitiously. The author acknowledges the trademarked status and trademark owners of various products referenced in this work of fiction, which have been used without permission. The publication/use of these trademarks is not authorized, associated with, or sponsored by the trademark owners.

Copyright © 2012-2017 by S.C. Stephens
Cover design by Okay Creations
Editing by Madison Seidler Editing Services
Formatting by JT Formatting

All rights reserved.
Without limiting the rights under copyright reserved above, no part of this publication may be reproduced, stored in or introduced into a retrieval system, or transmitted, in any form, or by any means (electronic, mechanical, photocopying, recording, or otherwise) without the prior written permission of the above copyright owner of this book.

First Edition: 2017
Library of Congress Cataloging-in-Publication Data
The Next Generation (Conversion Series) – 1st ed
ISBN-13: 978-1548793524 | ISBN-10: 1548793523

*For Lori, Sam, and Becky.
Thank you for all your hard work and support!*

CHAPTER ONE

Nika

MY PENCIL WAS tapping out a furious rhythm on a blank sheet of lined 8x10 paper. The dull thudding did nothing to remove my writer's block, but it mildly helped relieve my anxiety. A question was pounding through my brain, a question that every person in my English class was expected to answer by Monday morning. The question wasn't difficult; most of my schoolmates would be able to write up a response in twenty minutes. But me? I was struggling with the three seemingly simple words that I'd been asked: *Who am I?*

Well, that was the million-dollar question, wasn't it?

To the outside world, I was Nika Adams, an average sixteen-year-old human girl. I was best friends with my twin brother, Julian, even though we sometimes fought over stupid stuff—stuff we ended up laughing about later. I frequently chatted on the phone to my girlfriend, usually about cute boys at school that she had a crush on. I pushed the borders of my parents' household rules, but ultimately, I loved and respected them. I enjoyed animals and nature, hoped to make a difference in the world, and wanted to find the man of my dreams someday. I was experimenting with hair and makeup, wearing shirts that made my dad frown, and skirts that made my mom march me right back upstairs. While my brother and I lived with our parents in the heart of Salt Lake City, the rest of my family lived on a working ranch, and I would much rather spend a Saturday afternoon delivering a calf than aimlessly loitering around the mall. Pizza was my favorite food, followed closely by hot fudge sundaes. My grandparents were the best people in the whole world, and my aunt Ashley was my hero.

Yes, to the outside world, that was my life in a nutshell.

But that view was flawed, and missing several important details—details that I couldn't talk about. For one, I couldn't talk about my father to people outside my family, not with any sort of fondness anyway. The "story" that the world was being told was that my father was a deadbeat dad who'd left me and my brother at birth. I really hated that. I'd have preferred it if my fictional dad was a war hero, died in the heat of battle. But my "mother" had picked the story, and she preferred the deadbeat dad scenario; she'd even killed him off in a bar fight, so there would never be a question of him showing up in our lives.

Even though I disliked the lie, I understood why it was necessary. None of the men in my life could pass as my father. Besides my grandfather, they all looked too young. And they all looked too young, because they were all dead, every single one of them. Most of the rest of my family, too, for that matter. Because who I really was ... was a vampire. But no one could know that; it was vital that everyone believed the lie. Deception and concealment were practically family mottos in my home, ones I'd been taught since birth. *Hide who you are. Don't use your abilities in plain sight. Never show your fangs.* Yeah, just like every other vampire in my family, I had fangs. But unlike most of the rest of my nest, Julian and I also had heartbeats. We were still alive ... for now.

Born into this life, it was just the way we were, the way we'd always been. But being a vampire didn't make us evil or anything. My brother and I didn't spend our evenings trolling the city for young necks to rip open. Really, all it did was make the idea of a nice steaming cup of blood sound better than it did to a human. It was a tasty snack that we liked to indulge in on occasion, but that was about it. It was a little different for the undead members of my family. They lived on blood, needed it as much as a human being needs water. To an outsider that probably seemed barbaric, but it was just the way our species survived past death.

My real dad, Teren Adams, the one I couldn't talk about, was a third-generation vampire. He'd died and converted into an undead creature right before his twenty-sixth birthday, so, visually, he was still in his prime. My mother, Emma, had been completely human before being converted by Dad. The story was legend in our house. She'd been attacked, near death, a true death, and Dad had swooped in and saved her. And the babies growing within her—Julian and me. That was only *one* of the times Dad had saved our lives. Yeah, my *real* father was kick-ass.

Mom had ended up being just like Dad after he'd changed her. Vampires had certain restrictions on what they could do, depending on what generation they were. The negative side effects lessened with each generation, so the four of us—Mom, Dad, Julian, and me—frequently enjoyed things the others couldn't, like sunbathing. Dad's mom, Alanna, wasn't so lucky. Being second generation, she could be in daylight for short periods of time, but then it bothered her and she had to hide. I couldn't imagine living like that.

Alanna's husband, Grandpa Jack, was purely human and wanted to stay that way. Besides Dad, Grandpa was the coolest guy I knew. To the outside world, he technically owned the ranch. He'd also been remarried about a zillion times, all to the same woman, Grandma Alanna, of course. Since Alanna looked Dad's age, it was necessary for Grandpa to marry her every decade or so. Typically, it was done whenever the family moved to a new area; Grandpa brought his "new" bride to the "new" ranch.

Dad and the rest of the undead female vampires at the ranch—Grandma Imogen and Grandma Halina—were being sold in the story as Alanna's siblings. That one was weird, even for me, but Dad and the girls all looked the same age, and were eerily similar in appearance, so to group them as siblings was the easiest explanation. Even still, it was odd for me to hear Dad call his mom … sis.

Imogen and Halina were another story. They acted more like friends than mother and daughter, so it was easy to picture them as sisters. Imogen was a first-generation vampire. She tended to stay awake during the day, but couldn't go outside at *all* … too painful. Halina was the only pureblood vampire in the home—the one who'd started us all. She'd been pregnant with Imogen when she'd been turned, which was how Imogen had become half-human, half-vampire. While the vampiric nature inside of me was pretty weak, it was a marvel to behold in a pureblood. Halina could do things none of us could do. She was faster, had better hearing—and that was saying a lot—and she could trance humans ... basically make them do anything she told them to do. That skill was pretty handy. Especially when we needed people to forget certain things.

Halina's temperament was also different. She could seem aloof or distant to outsiders, even cold and calculating, but it was the pureblood in her, and not really her. Being turned hadn't made her a monster, hadn't made her start relentlessly slaughtering people, but it *had* changed her. It hadn't helped anything that Halina had been turned against her will. She'd had a certain grudge against her life for a long time, or so Dad had told me. But I'd only ever seen her happy and in love, so it was sometimes hard to picture.

Halina was in love with the smartest man I'd ever met—Gabriel. Gabriel was ... well, a hunk, with blond hair, green eyes, and movie star good looks. But he'd always been like a grandfather to me—my brother and I had even called him Grandpa Gabby until we were ten—so seeing him as sexy was kind of ... ew. But Halina sure did; I'd learned more about the birds and the bees from the two of them than anyone else.

The last two vampires in my life weren't related to me in any way, but they were still a part of my extended family: Starla and her boyfriend, Jacen. As Mom had grudgingly told me, they'd both followed Gabriel into our group. Starla got on Mom's nerves, but she was doing our family a huge favor, in one respect. Starla was taking medicine that prevented her from converting into an undead vampire, so she was just as alive as Julian and me. That allowed her to age ... and that allowed her to play the role of our mother to the clueless humans around us.

Starla wasn't thrilled about the situation, and she really hated being called Mom—said it made her feel old, which Halina only laughed about. But until the flaw in her blood that kept her from converting was fixed, a problem Gabriel was pouring all his efforts into, Starla had to keep aging. It was either age or die with her, die-die that was, so she had no choice.

The last family members in my life were all on my mom's side of the family. Grandma Linda lived out at the ranch with the vampire girls. She'd bonded so tightly with Alanna that when our foursome had moved into the city, she'd decided to stay behind in the countryside. Mom had been surprised by her decision. I hadn't. When my brother and I had been homeschooled by our many grandmothers, the bond between them had been pretty obvious.

Grandma Linda's second daughter, Aunt Ashley, was still living back in San Francisco with her husband, Christian. They were as happy as could be, even though her husband was completely clueless to the true nature of his in-laws. While we all tried to get together a couple of times a year, either going down to California, or them visiting us in Utah, I missed Aunt Ash. Mom did too. Between the two of us, we talked with her almost every day.

So that was my family tree, the bits and pieces of my life that made up who I was as a person. And I couldn't write down most of it. Here I was, living in the genealogy capital of the world, and I had to keep my genealogy as secret as possible. Sometimes deception sucked.

Sighing, I tucked a loose lock of brown hair behind my ear. It was the same shade as my real mother's hair, not that anyone at school knew that … one more thing I couldn't write down.

"What's with the incessant drumming? Having trouble with your homework?"

I looked over to see my best friend, Arianna, smiling at me. Well, as best of a friend as a secretive mixed vampire could have. Julian would always be my closest friend, but the perky brunette beside me was the closest female friend I had … who wasn't related to me. "Yeah. I'm just finding it a little … difficult … to get back into the swing of things."

Arianna sighed and leaned back on her hands. Dropping her head back, she let the full glory of the Indian summer sun caress her. It was a beautiful day for sunbathing, and that was what I should have been doing, instead of sitting on the edge of the football field, waiting for my "mom" to pick me up. Starla was late … again. It was only the first week of returning to school and she hadn't been on time once.

"Well, it's supposed to be a simple, one-page, welcome-back-to-school essay. Easy peasy." Lifting her head, Arianna pursed her lips in thought. "Let's see … You're Nika Adams, you live in the city during the week, then hide away on the weekends at a massive ranch in the middle-of-nowhere. You have an insanely gorgeous best friend." She paused to wink at me. "And a brother so hot it should be illegal."

I rolled my eyes as Arianna sighed and looked around the empty field. "Where is Julian anyway? Shouldn't he be waiting with you?"

Her hopeful tone matched her face. Arianna had had a crush on Julian since day one of our freshman year. I knew girls found my brother attractive ... my dad, too, when they saw him (Dad and Julian were practically carbon copies of each other), but they were my family, and when my girlfriends drooled over them it was equal parts weird and amusing.

I shrugged. "I don't know where he is. How would I?"

A small smile crossed my lips as I looked over to the gymnasium on the other side of the football field. I knew exactly where Julian was ... I could feel him. I could feel every member of my family. Most of them were just blurbs in my mind—a vague sense of their general direction that was calling out to me—but since Julian was so close, I could have extended my hand and pointed to the exact room he was in ... the far end of the gym, up on the bleachers. I wasn't sure why he was in there since he wasn't on a team, and he didn't have P.E. for his last period, but that was where he was.

Julian didn't really have to hang out and wait for Starla though. I could let him know when she was here. I could murmur it on the breeze and let the arid wind carry my message and he'd probably hear it. Well, no, that wasn't entirely true. We did have supernaturally good hearing, but being fourth generation, ours wasn't as great as the rest of the family's. And with how far away Julian was, and the pockets of noisy people loitering around the school, I would probably have to duck inside the building to whisper my message. And, even then, if Julian was preoccupied with something, he might miss it. If that were the case, I would have to yell for him, just like a regular human. Wouldn't be the first time. Sometimes Julian got lost in himself.

I blamed his moments of self-absorption on our childhood. It wasn't that our childhood hadn't been great, most of it had been awesome, but there had been a dark spot ... a *really* dark spot. And while Julian seemed fine 99 percent of the time, he did, on occasion, have episodes. It was something that the entire family helped him through...panic attacks or moments of unnecessary, paralyzing fear. Just thinking about it tightened my heart. He could be so fragile at times. Sometimes I wanted to wrap my arms around him and growl at anything that came his way. But I couldn't be his protector forever ... none of us could. Eventually I would have to let him go, have to let him sink or swim on his own.

Of course, the "special" bond between us made letting him go a challenge. It was difficult to ignore Julian's pain or fear when I could feel it slicing through my body as if it were my own. That was our connection though—an unbreakable, empathic bond—and it was a double-edged sword. We'd loved it when we were younger, loved knowing exactly how the other one felt all the time, but as we'd gotten older ... well, it wasn't always a gift to know exactly what someone else was feeling.

Squinting my eyes—a warm, brown shade that also matched my biological mother's—I examined the feelings I knew were coming from Julian. Whatever he was doing in the gym, he was happy about it—darn near giddy. Shaking my head, I tuned him out. It could be any number of things making him feel all lighthearted and joyful, but I was pretty sure I knew what it was, and if I was right ... I was going to have some serious words with him when we got home.

"I'm sure he'll be here anytime ... then you can drool all over him." I grimaced, and Arianna made an offended noise.

"I am *not* about to drool over him!" Arianna smirked as her caramel-colored hair bobbed around her shoulders. "Maybe pant a little ... but definitely no drooling."

Rolling my eyes, I shook my head. Arianna sat up and asked, "What about you? When are you gonna drool over some guy?" She sighed. "It's no fun if I'm the only one crushing on somebody."

Glancing over at her, I smiled. "Somebody? You're obsessed with half of the school."

She giggled, looking around at some of the boys lingering in the parking lot. "I can't help it if we've got so many hotties here, Nika."

Giving up on my impossible homework assignment, I shoved the paper into my backpack and glanced around with Arianna. A pair of long-legged, gangly teens were attempting to skateboard down the handrail of the steps that led away from the main building. I watched them fall time and time again, only to get back up and give it another try ... like they thought they were super-healing vampires or something. My enhanced ears heard a stream of cringe-worthy expletives coming from them, and I turned away.

Out in the parking lot was another group of guys; a couple of them were attempting to keep a small ball in the air. I could hear their conversation as well. It mainly seemed to be a discussion about the shorter skirt lengths on the cheerleaders' uniforms this year.

Turning my gaze away from them, I looked over to the football field. A couple of boys were tossing a football back and forth. There was some good-natured ribbing coming from them, but other than that, they were blissfully silent. It was a rarity among teenage boys. I'd overheard so much more than I'd ever cared to hear, and I knew more about what the male populace in this school thought than any girl should ever know. And the boys here mainly thought about sex.

It seemed horribly cliché, and I'd tried hard to find pockets of conversation that didn't include it, but unless guys were discussing sports or homework, girls and sex were the focus of most of their conversations. It made the prospect of dating one of them not that attractive. I didn't want to be looked at like a piece of meat. I wanted someone to look at me the way Dad looked at Mom—glowing, adored, worshipped, loved with every fiber of their soul. I knew I was too young to hope for such a thing, but still, I found myself looking for it, and none of these … youths … had it.

Shaking my head at Arianna, I shrugged. "Sorry, I just haven't found anybody who catches my eye yet."

Tucking her hair behind her ear, Arianna gave me a sympathetic smile; she knew what I was looking for in a man, and she also knew I probably wouldn't find it here. "While I totally understand, I just want to remind you … my mom will only let me go on dates if I double with a friend. No pressure, but my love life is completely depending on you finding someone." Leaning over, she playfully poked me in the stomach.

A slice of anger ran up my spine—I shivered with the strength of it. As I closed my eyes, intense, rolling hatred seared my body, tightened my muscles. I wasn't angry at Arianna's comment; I actually found it rather amusing. No, the anger scorching my soul wasn't coming from me, but from Julian. And it was strong. He was pissed.

My eyes snapped to where I could feel him in the gym. He was moving away from the massive room, hopefully coming out to join me. Curiosity and concern blossomed in my chest. I really wanted to know why Julian was so angry. Although, knowing him, I did have one guess …

"I'll work on that …" I murmured to Arianna as I felt Julian leave the gym and enter the boy's locker room. Frowning, I wondered what the heck he was doing. His anger had spiked as he'd left the gym, not diminished. My concern heightened. *I should go see what's wrong with him.*

Knowing Julian could feel me just as well as I could feel him, I tried to squelch the worry bubbling inside my stomach. I even tried sending calming feelings Julian's way, but it wasn't working. Whatever had him riled up wasn't letting go; he was getting angrier and angrier.

Arianna laughed, then she started going into elaborate detail about all the dates she wanted to go on, and which boy she wanted to take on them—she had about five or six mapped out already. Tuning her out, I tried listening for my brother. I couldn't hear him through the people and structures in the way though. My ears just weren't enhanced enough. It irritated me sometimes that my family's gifts were weaker in Julian and me—the two of us were much more human than vampire. But that allowed us to feel more normal than the others, and I did appreciate that fact. The limitations were just really inconvenient at times. While any of the other vampires in my family could have easily picked out the conversation Julian was having, all I was getting was low, husky murmuring. But his emotions were simmering, and that was all I needed to know.

Glancing at Arianna, I gathered all my stuff and zipped up my bag. She raised an eyebrow, but didn't pause in telling me all about her imaginary date rock climbing with Jake McKinley. Giving her a soft smile, so she didn't get too suspicious, I started to stand. "I'll be right back, Arianna, I—" Dread locked up my muscles, and I halted mid-sentence and mid-stance. Fear. Julian was feeling fear now. His anger had been rising to a boiling point, but now it had shifted to stark terror, and I had no idea why. Dropping my bag to the ground, I hauled ass across the football field.

"Nika? Where are you going? What's wrong?"

I ignored Arianna's concern and kept running. I had to get to Julian. I could have blurred to him in a split-second, but hampering my abilities had been drilled into me since birth, and I wouldn't go against that training unless the situation absolutely demanded it. And when Julian's fear shifted to panic ... I began to believe that the situation demanded it.

But knowing that Arianna was staring at me as I ran away curbed the desire to blur to Julian. I wouldn't freak out my friend if I could help it. And aside from extreme panic and lingering fear, Julian was okay. Well, he wasn't in pain at any rate.

Pulling open the doors to the gym, the metal singing in complaint at my force, I suddenly felt a rush of agony. Gasping, I paused in my step. The zing of hurt had exploded over me, almost like I'd felt it myself. I hadn't, though; it was separate from my own feelings of fearful concern. The pain had come from Julian … and renewed anger came right behind it.

Once I was inside the gymnasium, my hearing finally picked him up. He was cursing, and there was a lot of scuffling. It sounded like he'd gotten himself into a fight. Odd. Julian wasn't one to pick on people. But then again, if what had happened earlier in the gym to make him so happy was what I was afraid it was … then yeah, he might have started this fight.

Cursing under my breath as another bout of pain lashed Julian's body, I glanced around the empty halls. Seeing it was clear, I sped off after Julian. In mere seconds, I was at the edge of a group of people in the boy's locker room. They were all cheering on a couple of guys going at it in the center. Two bodies were sprawled on the tile floor of the open shower, wild punches being slung everywhere.

From the blood bond and our emotional connection, I knew Julian was amid the melee. Silence shocked me for a second as I stood on the periphery and watched my brother through the cracks in the teenagers surrounding him. He'd gained the upper hand and was straddling a senior: Russell Morrison. I watched in horror as Julian successfully landed a punch to Russell's jaw. So many racing heartbeats thudded in the room … it was nearly deafening. *What the hell?*

Knowing that our supernatural strength was superior to every other kid at this school made fear cut through my startled state. Julian could seriously hurt Russell if he wasn't careful, and with the amount of pain and anger Julian was feeling right now, he didn't seem to be worried about being careful anymore. He was completely out of control.

"Julian!" I screeched, an edge of panic to my voice. He could *not* get in a fight with a pure human. He'd accidentally kill him.

Feeling my presence, hearing my tone, Julian snapped his head up. Eyes as pale as a spring sky locked onto mine. He was panting, sneering, as adrenaline and hatred poured through him. I shook my head, sadness and disappointment washing over my fear and worry. Feeling my heartache and grief, Julian's face relaxed, and he averted his eyes from me. Still underneath him, Russell took Julian's moment of distraction as an opening. His punch was successful, landing right along Julian's eye. Pain flashed through my brother, and he tumbled back. With a vicious grin, Russell wormed his way free and sprang up to attack Julian again.

I elbowed my way through the people to run to Julian's side. Stepping in front of him, I shoved my hands against Russell's chest. "That's enough!" I yelled, careful to push him only as hard as a normal human girl my size would.

Russell moved back an inch and leered at me. "The little Adams to the rescue. Typical." Sneering at Julian over my shoulder, Russell added, "Gonna hide behind your sister, chicken shit?"

Julian sprang to his feet and stepped toward Russell. The punch Julian had received had opened his skin, and a bright red trail of blood was rolling down his cheek. I wanted to sigh in frustration. Men! Why did violence always come first with them? Twisting around, I put my hands on Julian's shoulders. "Stop," I whispered below human hearing. "One wrong move and you could kill him."

Julian's pale eyes flashed to Russell. "He deserves a beat down, Nick," he murmured.

Digging my fingers into his shoulder, I exhaled the words, "Dad wouldn't want you to do this ..."

Julian slowly returned his eyes to me. Then he sighed and hung his head in defeat. To Russell, it probably looked like he'd won, like Julian was whipped, defeated, but I felt the tension in my brother's body, felt the fire in his emotions. He could have easily knocked Russell into the next county if his conscience hadn't agreed with me ... and if I would have let him.

Slumping against the cool, tile wall of the shower, Julian kept his head down. Russell laughed, and the rest of the boys joined in with him. Releasing Julian, since he no longer seemed inclined to fight, I faced Russell. He eyed me up and down, mentally undressing me, and I lifted my chin in defiance. Feeling my own rage start to mix with Julian's lingering anger, I balled my fingers into fists and waited for the jerks to leave.

Russell looked between the two of us, shook his head, then spat at our feet. Considering Julian had landed a solid hit and his lip was cut, Russell's slimy gift was laced with blood; I could smell it. He pointed a finger at Julian. "You stay the fuck away from my girlfriend, or I'll do a hell of a lot more than cut up your face ... Julia!"

All the boys laughed at Russell's "clever" nickname, and Julian snapped his head up. His eyes narrowed as his lips curled into a sneer. The anger he'd been trying to suppress instantly flared up again, and my sharp eyes caught the subtle outline of fangs underneath his skin; Julian was about five seconds away from ripping Russell's throat out. Mom and Dad would be crushed if he attacked a student. Halina ... would probably be proud.

One of Russell's friends smacked his shoulder, telling him, "Good one," like Russell had just made the joke of the year. I wanted to roll my eyes, but I was too nervous about what Julian might do if they didn't leave.

My brother was normally a calm person, not easily ruffled or riled, but Russell was his exception. Consequences aside, Julian would fight him to the death in a bathroom, and drain him dry in an alley; he hated him to the core. And all because Russell was dating the woman Julian was infatuated with: Raquel Johnson.

Raquel was the girl Julian wouldn't shut up about. They were lab partners for a semester last year, and had developed some sort of friendship during class. But while they talked on occasion, and Raquel seemed to like Julian well enough, Russell was the moon and stars in her eyes. And he treated her like dirt. It was all very tragic, and sometimes I wondered if Julian was only attracted to Raquel because he wanted to save her. He wanted to be her knight in shining armor, wanted to be a hero, like our father. Only problem in this situation was that Raquel didn't seem to want a knight. Some damsels preferred being in distress.

Just when I was about to yell at Russell to leave already, he and his entourage finally backed away from the shower area. Julian's body was still tight with anger as the sounds of Russell and his gang started to dissipate. When the heavy door to the locker room banged shut, Julian opened his mouth, exposing his fangs to the boys who were no longer there.

Annoyed, I put my hands on my hips and faced him. "What the hell were you thinking, Julie?"

Julian stepped away from the shower wall; his eyes were still firmly locked on the locker room exit. "You didn't need to rush in here, Nick. I had everything under control."

I wiped a smear of blood from his cheek. Holding my red finger in front of his gaze, so he'd concentrate on me and stop staring at the door, I murmured, "Yeah, I see that."

He glanced at the blood and sighed. "Damn it." Tenderly, he touched his fingers to his face; when he pulled them away, they were red.

I momentarily considered sucking the swath of his blood from my finger—the vampire in me growled in delight at the idea—but I easily ignored the desire. Grabbing Julian's elbow, I pulled him to the sink.

Looking at the cut near his eye in the mirror, Julian grimaced. "Great." His face contorting around his fangs, he asked, "How am I gonna explain this to Mom and Dad?"

Turning on the water, I let the cool stream wash away the yummy goodness that a part of me yearned for. "Well, since *I'm* still waiting for an explanation, why don't you try out your excuse on me?"

Sliding his fangs back in, Julian shook his head; his pitch-black hair instantly reminded me of our father. Julian was right, Dad wasn't going to like hearing about him fighting. "It was nothing," he murmured, his expression sheepish. "Just Russell being a dick because I was *talking* to Raquel."

Sighing, I moistened a paper towel so Julian could clean himself up. "Didn't feel like nothing, Julie. It felt like ..." Remembering his fear and panic, I bit my lip and handed him the towel. That had been a lot more than Julian just reacting to Russell being a jerk. That had been ... primal.

As Julian took the towel, his light eyes silently begged me to not finish my statement. Knowing his feelings when he didn't want me to know them felt intrusive, so I decided to respect his reluctance as much as I could. "It just ... felt like something," I told him.

Julian hissed in a breath as he dabbed the towel against his cut. Unfortunately, since we were living vampires, Julian and I didn't have the fast-healing ability that our undead family members had. Julian's wounds would have to close the old-fashioned way. "I was just having a ... moment," he whispered, glancing at me in the mirror.

With sympathy in my heart, I nodded at his reflection. Julian's panic attacks had subsided over the years, but they crept up now and again if he was put in the right circumstances. Dealing with Russell must have put him over the edge.

I said nothing more about it as Julian wiped away the bloody evidence from his face. I could feel the lingering bumps and bruises Julian felt, shared the ache stinging his cheek. Pain wasn't necessarily an emotion, but our bodies processed it as such. Ever since birth, I had known when Julian was hurting, physically *and* emotionally. My long, lean limbs felt fine, but I was *aware* of his injuries, and was going to be aware of them for the next several days while he healed. Yeah, double-edged sword.

When Julian was as cleaned up as he was going to get, I nodded at the doors. "We should go. Starla is gonna be here soon."

Julian nodded and grabbed his backpack from where it had been haphazardly tossed to the floor. After we left the locker room, I felt a wave of hope wash through Julian as we walked past the open door leading into the heart of the gym. But as his eyes scoured the empty room, his hope shifted to disappointment. I clapped his shoulder. "I really wish you'd stop liking her. She's not worth fighting over."

Julian twisted to look at me and frowned. "Yes, she is." Like sunshine breaking through the clouds, warmth blossomed in his chest, and he smiled in a clearly love-sick way. "She's wonderful, Nick. You just don't know her like I do."

That I had to agree with. I didn't see anything overly wonderful about the woman Julian adored. But I didn't talk to her like Julian did, and by the feelings that sprouted in his chest whenever she was around, it was clear he had found something in her worth obsessing over.

Hating to burst his bubble, I cringed. "You know you can't date her, right?" Julian furrowed his brows at me in confusion and I let out a weary exhale. "Even if she left Russell to be with you, Julian, you can't date her. You can't tell her what you really are … so you can't be with her. It's as simple as that."

"Why couldn't I tell her?" Looking back at me, hope in his eyes and his heart, he said, "Dad told Mom."

Knowing the story well, I shook my head. "They were older, Julian, and Mom is … different than Raquel. I just don't think she would be as accepting as Mom."

Julian raised his chin. "But you don't know that. You're just assuming she'll react badly … and I don't think she will."

Shaking my head, I started heading for the front doors. "Well, it doesn't really matter anyway, since she's with Russell." I looked back at Julian silently following me. "And I don't think she's leaving him anytime soon."

Lowering his head, Julian kicked a rock down the stone steps. "Yeah, I know that, Nick," he bitterly stated.

As we reached the bottom step, Arianna began walking toward us from the field. "What happened, Nika?" she said, still perplexed as to why I'd run off.

Waving at her, I murmured to Julian, "You know, Arianna would date you in a heartbeat if you asked."

Stepping beside me, Julian smirked. "I know that too, Nick." There was no bitterness in his voice this time, just amusement.

Arianna handed me my backpack when she was in front of us, but her eyes were solely focused on Julian. "So, what was the emergency?" she asked. "Everything okay?"

I felt a wave of embarrassment flood through Julian as he was scrutinized by my best friend, a woman who clearly only had eyes for him, even if we both acted like half the guys at school interested her. Humor at my brother's uneasiness bubbled through me, and Julian glanced over and rolled his eyes. "Not funny," he murmured, too low for Arianna to hear.

Smiling, I shrugged and answered Arianna as best as I could. "I forgot a book in the gym ... had to go get it."

Arianna lifted a light brown eyebrow. "A book ... really? It seemed like ... more."

I shrugged. "It was a really good book." Arianna looked about to question me more, but I grabbed Julian's arm and tugged him forward. "Look what else I found."

Even more embarrassment flashed through Julian as he nearly collided with Arianna. The giddy girl giggled and put her hands on Julian's arms. "Hey, Julian. We were just wondering where you were."

Julian looked back at me, an amused smile on his lips. He knew I never wondered where he was. I didn't have to. Trying to distance himself from Arianna without openly offending the woman, he murmured, "Here I am."

Just as Julian successfully removed her hands from his body, Arianna noticed the red and raw cut beside his eye. "Oh my God! What happened?"

Arianna grabbed his face, angling his head toward her so she could examine the wound more closely. A feeling of extreme discomfort surged through Julian, and he quickly pulled his head away from her. "I ... uh ... fell."

Arianna sighed, her face heavy with compassion. "Oh, you poor thing."

Right when she looked like she might reach out and hug him, I heard the hum of a car that I knew very well. Julian and I looked across the football field at the exact same time. A silver BMW shone in the afternoon sun as it pulled to a stop. The horn honked twice, unnecessarily, since Julian and I were already aware of the vehicle.

Relief rushed through Julian as he gave Arianna an apologetic smile. "I have to go. Our mom's here."

Arianna frowned and looked back to the parking lot. A petite blonde had stepped out of the vehicle and was waving at us. It wasn't a *Welcome, glad to see you* wave either. It was more a *Hurry up, I have better things to do* wave. Starla didn't exactly enjoy being our fetching girl, but Gabriel had asked her to do it, so she did. There weren't too many things Starla refused to do if her "father" asked.

Arianna sighed and stepped back from Julian. "Well, I guess I should go home now, too." She looked over at me. "See you Monday, Nika ... Julian."

She gave me a swift hug, gave Julian a lingering gaze of longing, then headed off in the opposite direction. Arianna lived right behind the high school and always waited with me until I got picked up. Creepily enough, Arianna lived on the other side of a graveyard, and had to walk through it every day to get to her house. We sometimes scared ourselves silly by running though the cemetery at night. Well, Arianna was scared silly. It didn't bother me all that much. I was used to nighttime excursions with my family, and since Halina was the scariest thing around, not much in a cemetery frightened me.

"Would you two hurry up!"

Julian and I looked back at Starla. Shaking my head, I told her, "We're coming. Chillax." I spoke it at regular volume, but Starla heard me just fine. She popped a bubble with her gum and ducked back inside her shiny vehicle.

Smiling at each other in amusement, Julian and I started walking her way. "So ... why don't you just ask Arianna out, since you know she likes you?" I asked him. "I think you two would be cute together."

Julian smirked, humor flowing from him to me. "You think she'd be any cooler about what we are than Raquel?"

Biting my lip, I considered that. Arianna was cool, certainly, but was she *that* cool? It was hard to tell. She would handle it better than Raquel, though. I was pretty sure of that. "Yeah, I think so ..."

Julian was quiet as we continued across the field. The smell of fresh-cut grass nearly overwhelmed my senses. It reminded me of the ranch. Once we were climbing up the small slope that led to the parking lot, he finally spoke. His words matched his mood—subdued. "I just don't think I feel that way about her, Nika." He looked over at me with a regretful smile. "She's not the one I want to be with ... sorry."

I patted his shoulder in sympathy. "I know."

Starla honked her horn again. Visible through the windshield, she raised her hands in a come-on-already gesture. Rolling my eyes, I hurried the short distance to her car. Cracking open the door, I darted in the front seat while Julian took the back. Starla stepped on the gas before I even had a chance to fully close the door.

"Sorry I'm late," Starla muttered, snapping another bubble with her apple-flavored gum.

"It's all right," I muttered, glancing over at the woman. Starla was quickly approaching forty, but she still dressed and acted like she was much younger. Her light blonde locks were cut stylishly short, spritzed and sprayed into a rigid helmet of perfection. Her skin was tan and Botoxed to be as smooth as possible. Wrapped in a tight designer dress and sunglasses that were as large as they were round, she seemed like someone much more at home shopping on Rodeo Drive than hanging around Washington Square. And, in fact, she was exactly *that* person, but her nest was here, the love of her life was here, and, Gabriel, the man she eerily called father was here, so ... she was stuck in Utah, for now.

Smacking on her gum, she tossed a smile my way. "So, how was school?"

"Fine." Returning her smile, I relaxed into the seat. I didn't want her to suspect that anything out of the ordinary had happened today.

I felt tension coming from Julian and noticed him squirming in his seat, angling his head away from Starla so she wouldn't see his damaged skin. He couldn't do anything about the smell though. The fresh blood was faint, but it was still clear enough for a vampire; it even permeated the smells emanating from Starla.

She inhaled, then looked back at Julian. "I smell blood on you ... why?"

Starla eyed his face for a long time, a lot longer than someone concentrating on driving really should. "Are you hurt? What happened?"

Sighing, Julian stopped trying to avoid it and twisted to face her. "It's fine ... I fell."

Starla narrowed her blue eyes at Julian, appraising him. With a smirk, she shook her head and returned her attention to the road. "Sure, kid." Looking at him in the rear-view mirror, she added, "You might want to work on your story before you get home, though. Your parents are going to buy it about as much as I do."

Julian groaned and laid his head back on the seat. A wave of reluctance and anxiety went through him, and I reached behind my seat to pat his knee. He felt the sympathy pouring from me and sighed as his tension started returning.

Starla watched his reaction in the mirror, then said, "So, heard you talking outside ... who's the lucky girl you want to be with, Julian?"

CHAPTER TWO

Julian

CLOSING MY EYES, I tried to relax. This was turning out to be the crappiest day ever. Well, maybe not ever—I'd had some crappy days in my life—but today was rapidly moving up the list.

Focusing on steadying my emotions, so Nika would stop sending me waves of sympathy, I ignored Starla's question about who I liked. I was *not* about to talk to Starla about my love life. Or lack of one. Not that I had anything against Starla—I didn't—I just didn't want to talk about it with anyone. No one but Nika, and she'd made her feelings on the matter perfectly clear—stay away from Raquel. She was trouble, and would bring me nothing but heartache.

In my heart, I knew Nika was right. While Raquel and I had a decent friendship, she'd never given me any indication that she wanted something more from me. Russell was who she wanted. They'd been firmly attached to each other since Raquel's freshman year, and Russell didn't seem to be letting go of her anytime soon … as today's debacle had shown me.

A flash of anger ripped through my spine, opening my eyes. Nika removed her hand from my knee and twisted around to look at me. Concern momentarily overrode her sympathy. I ignored the question in her light brown gaze, and instead thought of the beady pair of eyes I'd been staring down this afternoon.

It had all started after school. Up until that final bell had rung, my day had been as normal as any other day. But once all the kids had shuffled outside, I'd caught a whiff of Raquel's perfume, and had followed the scent until I'd picked her out across campus. So attuned to her, I'd then heard the distinct sound of a sniffle being carried on the dry breeze. My sudden anger faded away as I remembered watching her walk into the empty gym. I'd known that I shouldn't follow her in there, especially since she always met up with Russell after school, so odds were good that I would run into him, but there had been something about the pain in her whimper that had made turning away from her an impossibility. Stupidly, I'd walked in after her.

Seeing Raquel sitting on the bleachers, her long legs exposed under her short skirt, her jacket folded in her arms, her thick, dark hair shielding her face as she sat with her head down, a burst of affection had exploded in my chest. A smaller version of that euphoria rippled through me now, and Nika grimaced. Shaking her head, she turned back to the front of the car.

Sighing, I turned to stare out the window; patches of brown earth and green lawn whizzed past, creating a blur of muted tones. It was frustrating at times that Nika didn't understand my feelings for Raquel. It wasn't like I could control them anyway. When Raquel was around I just felt ... lighter than air. For once, I wasn't a human-vampire mix hiding from the world in plain sight. No, I was just a normal sixteen-year-old boy trying to find his place. My feelings for Raquel were simple and beautiful, and I didn't see how anything so wonderful could be wrong.

Nika just hadn't experienced it yet, not for herself anyway; otherwise, she would understand. Once a boy had made her heart skip a beat, then she would get it, and she'd leave me alone to crush on the girl of my dreams.

Smiling, I watched the vegetation blur by as I listened to Starla's conversation with Nika. It revolved around moisturizer, from what I could tell. Blocking them out, I reminisced about my conversation earlier with Raquel ...

"Raquel, you okay in here?" After quietly asking, I cautiously walked over to the woman with her head hanging in defeat. I hated seeing her like that.

She lifted her chin and looked up at me. Her beauty was so searing, it almost made me stop in my tracks, for surely, if I stepped any closer, I'd be burned. Eyes as dark as night, skin golden and creamy, she was breathtaking. She made me ache in ways that I couldn't talk about to anyone ... not even Nika.

Raquel wiped underneath her eyes after my question and gave me an untroubled smile. I instantly saw the lie in the gesture. Setting my backpack down, I sat beside her on the bleachers. "I'm fine, Julian ... just waiting for Russell."

Studying her face, my enhanced vision picked out the wetness on her cheeks, the redness in her eyes. "You've been crying. What's wrong?"

Lip trembling, she shrugged. "Nothing ..."

I wanted to reach out and touch her skin; I was sure it would be the softest thing I'd ever felt. But I wasn't brave enough, and only gave her a friendly smile as I bumped her shoulder with mine; just sitting beside her made my soul soar. "Doesn't look like nothing."

Raquel gave me a genuine smile then, and my heart nearly swelled beyond capacity—thudding so loudly, I almost didn't hear her response. "It's just ... Russell ... he sometimes ..." *Sighing, she bit her lip and looked away.*

Warmth and good feelings overpowered me, and I found the courage to reach out and touch her cheek; it was as soft as I imagined. Fingers trembling, I turned her head so she was looking at me again. I always wanted her to be looking at me. Me. Not Russell. "I know I've told you this before, but you don't have to put up with him. There are ... other options."

Her mouth curved into a soft smile as she stared at me, and her eyes glowed with warmth as she searched mine. I never wanted to kiss a girl more than right then. I knew it was wrong—she was with Russell—but Russell didn't deserve an angel like her. He didn't treat her the way she should be treated. He didn't treat her the way I *would treat her. My heart surged uncontrollably at the thought of her lips on mine.*

I started to inch toward her, started to give her a kiss ... my first kiss ever. We were so close—she was leaning into me while I was leaning into her—and then everything changed.

"What the hell is this, Raquel?"

I broke apart from Raquel and spotted Russell and his gang entering the gym. Raquel's tan cheeks had gone completely pale, and she immedi-

ately stood up and stepped away from me, guilt as plain as day on her face. "Nothing ... it was nothing, Russell. Just ... waiting for you."

She simpered and bowed her head in a submissive way that fired me up. I hated how Russell beat down her spirit, made her seem almost a shadow of a person. She could be so much more, if I could just get her away from the creep. But she grabbed her stuff and walked down to him with only a fleeting, apologetic glance back at me.

Once she reached Russell, he jerked on her arm, squeezing it until she cried out in pain. "There better not be anything going on," he growled.

The hatred in Russell's voice, the fear on Raquel's face, it was too much for me. I immediately jumped up from the bleachers. "Leave her alone, Russell!"

Russell's eyes snapped to mine. "What are you gonna do about it, Adams?"

Honestly, I wanted to fight him, show him exactly what I would do about it, but I knew my parents wouldn't approve, and the thought of Dad's disappointed face gave me the strength to do something extremely difficult. Swallowing my pride, I grabbed my backpack ... and walked away. Raquel sighed with relief; it sliced me to the core to leave her with him.

But Russell wasn't okay with letting me be the bigger man. No great surprise there, really. He and his buddies followed me when I left the gym. I was seething with anger already, and that feeling only grew with each step I took away from the jerk. Maybe Russell saw that he was affecting me, maybe Russell was just a grade-A asshole, but he amped up the situation by shoving me into the boy's locker room.

And that was when things shifted for the worse ...

Looking down as I felt Starla's car crunch to a stop, I remembered my backpack falling to the floor, remembered the guys pushing me, backing me into a corner. It shouldn't have affected me the way it had—it shouldn't have affected me so negatively—but when they'd pressed me into the shower area, when they'd ... trapped me ... I'd started to panic.

A slice of that remembered fear shot through me, and I swallowed a few times to push it back. Nika started to bring her hand around to me, twisting her body in the front seat to face me again, but I opened my car door and stepped out. I didn't need to see Nika's sympathy right now, I could feel it oozing from her anyway. I had to learn to deal with this debilitating terror on my own.

Life had cut me a raw deal, but I'd been a toddler then, so surely I should be over the trauma by now. But as the wall of people had closed in on me, I hadn't felt over it at all. No, I'd felt like it was happening all over again.

Pausing beside Starla's closed door, I let the lingering tension of the memory slip away. I hated sinking back into the darkness of those age-old fears, but Russell's gang had pushed me over the edge. With all their bulk blocking the exit and my back against the cool tile wall, I'd felt like I was three years old again, trapped inside a dark, smelly trunk. The claustrophobia had kicked in full force, shifting my anger to instinctual fear and panic—I would have done anything to get out, and I had. I'd struck Russell.

As I'd attacked, the panic had subsided and rage had taken over again. Preferring that to fear, I'd gladly let it in.

As Nika stepped out of Starla's BMW, a voice inside the car addressed the two of us. "All right, there you are, safe and sound at home. See you guys Monday morning."

Smirking, Nika leaned down to look back at Starla. "Thanks for the ride, Mom."

Starla groaned and dropped her head back on the leather seat; if she used just a touch more of that floral hairspray, she'd puncture the leather. Pulling down her oversized sunglasses, she glared at Nika. "You don't have to call me that when no one's around."

Nika smiled wider. Amusement flashed through her and my spirit momentarily lifted. Starla hated being called Mom. Closing the door, Nika waved at Starla. The high-maintenance woman waggled her fingers and revved her engine. "Have a good night, you two," she murmured, her voice audible to us through the glass. Twisting to look back at me, Starla curved a painted lip. "And try not to fight anyone over the weekend."

My mouth dropped open in surprise as Starla stepped on the gas. Nika and I backed up a step so she wouldn't run over our toes or spray us with tiny pebbles from the road. Since Starla was playing the role of our mom, she lived a few streets over with her boyfriend, Jacen, so she could be on hand in case we needed a parental figure in our lives.

While Starla didn't relish her assigned task, the housing situation worked out well for her; Starla had no desire to live out in the dirty, dusty countryside with the rest of the vampires. It also suited Mom just fine, since she found Starla to be a little grating; she'd strongly protested Starla living at the house *with* us, which would have been the easiest way to keep up the appearance that Starla was our mother. We'd solved that problem though. To prevent our neighbors from becoming overly curious about Starla's frequent absence, the world around us believed that Starla spent an exorbitant amount of time with her boyfriend, leaving our "roommates"—Mom and Dad—to watch over us nearly every night. A nosy neighbor had complained to Starla once about her lack of parenting skills, but after a visit from Halina, the busy-body hadn't thought twice about it. None of our neighbors did now. The arrangement was a touch on the complicated side, but it was preferable for everyone.

After Starla's sporty taillights disappeared around the corner, Nika turned to me. "She's so maternal, it's almost smothering."

I cracked a smile and shook my head. "Yeah, she should cut the cord already. We're sixteen."

Nika laughed as she unzipped her backpack to get her keys. "You think Dad will let us get a car this year? Give Starla a break?"

I listened to her digging fingers scraping against the fabric of her bag, then heard the metallic sound of a key scraping against another key. Starting to walk toward the house, I shook my head. "Doubt it. You know how overprotective he can be." As we reached the door, I smirked at her. "We'll be married with kids of our own before we get a car."

Imagining Raquel as my wife, I let out a wistful sigh. Nika frowned as she opened the front door. "Please stop that."

Adjusting the bag on my shoulder, I sniffed and changed my thoughts. "Stop what?" I murmured, knowing exactly what she meant.

Nika gave me a wry look as I tossed my bag in the entryway, just a foot from the door. Ignoring my question, she instead asked, "What are you going to tell Mom and Dad?" She pointed to my face, to the tell-tale sign that I'd been in a fight.

Shrugging, I looked out into the living room. It was empty except for a very old, very tired collie. Spike wagged at us, his tail thumping against the long, white couch that he loved to lie on all day. I smiled at him and told Nika, "Maybe they won't notice?"

Nika gave me a crooked smile and walked into the living room to sit with Spike. Carefully setting her bag next to the couch, she nuzzled her head into his fur and murmured, "Sure, Julie."

I exhaled a frustrated breath. I knew they'd notice just as quickly as Starla had. It was the blood. Even healing, the wound exposed the scent into the air. It was a smell specific to me, and being undead vampires who existed solely on blood, my parents would pick up on it almost instantly. Shaking my head, I joined Nika on the comfortable, leather couch. Resting my head back, I waited for Mom and Dad to get home. In about an hour or so, I was going to be filleted.

My parents worked just a few minutes away, in the heart of the city. They both worked for a local magazine highlighting life in the great Salt Lake. Dad was the writer of the bunch; he enjoyed it nearly as much as ranching. Maybe more, I wasn't sure. Mom worked with him. She was his secretary or research assistant or something.

As I rested on the couch, I imagined my father's disappointment when he learned that I'd gotten into a fight. Then I imagined my mother's. God, this was going to suck. What would the rest of my family think? Most lived at the ranch, about an hour outside city proper. The sprawling place nestled in the mountain foothills was where the family tended the herd of cattle that we lived on. For food, and for money.

Before Mom and Dad had moved Nika and me to this house, so we could go to a regular high school, our family had lived much closer to the ranch, just a handful of miles really. Nika and I had spent almost every day there when we were younger. Our grandmothers had all taken turns home-schooling us until just a couple of years ago. I had some great memories of growing up there.

My family was tight, and I was sure they'd all know about the fight by tomorrow morning. They definitely would after this weekend. I could almost hear my various grandmothers' disapproval at the thought of me fighting. Well, except for Halina. Being full vampire, she was a little more tolerant of violence than the rest. She'd probably give me a sly grin and ask if I'd left my mark on the asshole.

About an hour later, I felt my parents' position begin to move; the pinging sensation of them in my head started shifting toward home. I wasn't looking forward to their arrival. At all. Nika was resting on the couch beside me, laid out on her stomach as she worked on her homework.

Whatever she was working on was frustrating her, but Mom and Dad approaching quickly snapped her out of it. Again, sympathy welled from her. Reaching over, I shoved her shoulder. "Quit worrying about me, Nick."

Tilting her head, she gave me a smile. "Not gonna happen, Julie."

Shaking my head at her, I stood up and stretched. "I'm gonna go take a shower."

Nika nodded and I felt her amusement. She knew that clean water and citrus-scented soap wouldn't really do anything; Mom and Dad would still see and smell my injury. Leaning down, I gave Spike a kiss on the head before I left; his tail slowly swished back and forth as his glossy eyes peeked up at me. Leaving Nika and Spike to their bonding, I trudged upstairs.

We all lived in a Bavarian-style house. As far as homes go, it was actually sort of cool. With creamy white walls and dark brown exposed beams elaborately decorating the outside of it, the place reminded me of a fairytale come to life ... Hansel and Gretel or something. I think that was one of the reasons Dad had bought it, the other being that Mom had fallen in love the moment she'd spotted it. Someone else had lived here then, but they had miraculously decided to sell the place to Dad just weeks later. It was long rumored in the family that Dad had enlisted Halina's "help" in getting the homeowner to sell the house to him. Whenever someone asked Dad about it, though, he'd get annoyed and say, "Do you really think I would do that?"

I wasn't sure if he had, but it wouldn't surprise me to find out that the rumor was true. There wasn't much Dad wouldn't do for Mom.

Nika had confessed to me before that she was sure she'd never find a man who would treat her like Dad treated Mom, that he set an impossible standard. But even still, it was a standard that I strived to reach. I wanted to be like that to someone ... someday. Maybe to Raquel? My heart started beating harder at just the thought of buying her the home of her dreams one day. God, wouldn't that be amazing?

Stepping into my bedroom, I shut the door behind myself and waded through the mess of clothes and crap to get to the shower. The bathroom that Nika and I shared was squished in-between our bedrooms and each room had a door that led to it. In a normal family, that could lead to some embarrassing moments, but since we could all feel each other's location, it wasn't a worry in our house. We generally didn't even lock the door.

Walking into the bathroom, I glanced through Nika's open door into her picture-perfect bedroom. We were a lot alike in several things, but in the realm of cleanliness, Nika had gotten most the genes ... much to Mom's dismay. Shaking my head at my neat-freak sister, I closed her side of the bathroom and turned to examine myself in the mirror again. I looked a little better than I had in the locker room mirror, when blood had been openly trailing down my face, but the ragged, red line was still with me ... and I was pretty sure my eye was starting to bruise.

Feeling my parents approaching fast, I shucked off my clothes and hopped into the shower. It was refreshing, if nothing else. As the relaxing water pummeled me, I noticed some bruising along my ribs, and was instantly grateful that at least my parents wouldn't see *those* marks.

I was lathered and rinsed when I felt and heard Mom and Dad come home. They were laughing about something as Nika greeted them. Sighing, I leaned my head against the shower wall and took a moment to collect myself. As I let my skin soak up an obscene amount of hot water, I heard Mom ask Nika, "How was your day?"

I tensed, waiting for Nika's answer, but I knew she wouldn't throw me under the bus. We'd never do that to each other. Nika sighed. "Fine, just stuck on this stupid English assignment."

"What is it?" Dad asked. "Maybe I can help."

I shut off the water as I heard Dad sit down. The two of them started having a conversation about what Nika could and couldn't say about our family history. I felt Nika's distress as she told Dad, "I can't talk about you like I want. It's so unfair."

Climbing out of the shower, I mulled over Nika's feelings. She had a point. It was a little unfair that we were never able to talk about our parents *as* our parents ... but it was just a part of our deceptive life. Nika would have to accept that one day. Me too.

I tossed my towel on the floor, next to my dirty clothes, and changed into some fresh ones. I felt Mom coming up the stairs as I slipped my shirt over my head. When she was almost to my door, I debated running back to the bathroom. No time.

A heavy thud sounded outside my doorway. "Julian, if you're done with your homework, can you please put your backpack away in your room ... not leave it in the entryway?" She knocked on my closed door when I didn't respond to her statement right away. "Julian?"

Inhaling a calm breath, I felt Nika tense as she waited for my secret to explode. Her conversation with Dad stopped as she listened to my response. "Yeah, okay, Mom ... sure thing."

Biting my lip, I waited to see if she'd leave. She started to twist the knob, and I stifled a sigh. She wasn't leaving. "Can I come in?" she asked.

Containing a curse, I turned my back to the door and found something to busy myself with. Unfortunately, all I could find was an old comic book on my nightstand. I didn't really read them anymore, but they were strewn throughout my messy room. "Yeah."

Mom stepped inside my room, and I heard her place my heavy backpack on my side of the door. I studiously kept my back to her—I didn't need her to see the jagged line across my skin. Hearing her sniff, I concentrated harder on my book. What was she smelling? My crusty socks in the corner, or the healing wound on my skin?

"Ugh, maybe you could clean up in here ... it's a little gross."

Dropping my book to the nightstand, I immediately started picking up clothes; anything to distract her. "Sure, Mom."

I felt her walking toward me, and I twisted to get a jacket that had been shoved under my bed sometime last spring. "You never agree to pick up your room that fast. Something going on?"

Closing my eyes, I shook my head. "No." My heart started racing, and from downstairs I heard Dad ask a suddenly silent Nika, "What is it?"

Hearing my heart surging, Mom knelt beside me. Her cold hand touched my shoulder, and a light shudder passed through me. "Hey? What's going on?"

Silence echoed throughout the house. Dad had finally figured out that Nika's quiet concern was for me, and he was listening for my reply just as surely as Mom was. Right when I was about to turn and face her, Mom inhaled a deep breath and exclaimed, "You're hurt!"

Her cool fingers were on my face then, shifting me to look at her. Warm brown eyes locked onto mine, then shifted to my wound. Those eyes widened as she examined the injury, and I sighed as I felt Dad speeding up the stairs. "I'm fine, Mom. It's no big deal."

Dad stepped into the room and Mom broke away from me to look back at him. Impossibly youthful for being my father, Dad and I were almost twins. Mom and Nika also could have pulled off being identical twins, too. When we moved to the next city in the few years, we were probably going to have to tell the world that *we* were brothers and sisters. God, that was going to be weird.

Dad's hands went to his hips as he stared at me. Cocking his dark head, he narrowed his sky-blue eyes. "What happened?"

Looking between the two of them, I shrugged and wriggled my way out of Mom's hands. "I'm a kid; I was clumsy and fell. I don't think we need to make a huge production out of it." Standing, I looked away from my father's suspicious eyes and my mother's concerned ones.

Dad stepped closer to me. "I've seen falls, and I've seen fights ... and that looks more like a fight."

I tried twisting my head even more, so he couldn't see the burgeoning bruise beneath my eye, but Dad grabbed my chin and made me face him. I felt my will power shrinking as I held my role model's gaze. "What happened, Julian?" he quietly asked.

Mom came up to stand beside him, putting one hand on my shoulder, the other on Dad's. "You can talk to us, Julian. We love you." Her smile was warm, loving, and a flash of guilt washed through me.

"Tell them, Julie," Nika murmured from downstairs. I frowned at her, but it didn't really matter anymore. Mom and Dad weren't stupid. They knew I was lying.

Sighing, I looked at the floor. "I got into a fight at school ..."

Dad let out a long exhale, and my heart broke a little. Even though I wasn't emotionally connected to my parents like I was with Nika, I felt the waves of disappointment radiating from Dad. Mom clenched my shoulder, silent. Nika's feelings turned supportive and I felt her presence zip up to my bedroom.

"They started it, Dad. It's not his fault. He was just defending himself."

I peeked up to see Nika standing in my doorway, her chin tilted up, her mouth in a firm line. She looked just as she had in the locker room when she'd been sticking up for me in front of a pack of bullies. Only now it was our parents she was shielding me from. Always my protector.

Dad looked over to her, then back to me. I tried to avert my eyes again, but the concern in his gaze held me. "I'm sorry," I whispered. "It won't happen again."

Dad nodded, then extended his hand toward the hallway. "Come with me. I want to talk to you ... alone."

Nika was still standing in the doorway. She looked up the hall, to where we both knew Dad meant for me to go. The only place in the house to have a private conversation was Mom and Dad's bedroom. They'd had Gabriel soundproof the room the moment we'd all moved in. And by soundproof, I meant vampire-soundproof. It was like being in an isolation tank once you stepped inside and closed the door—all outside sounds ceased. There had been similar rooms like this everywhere we'd lived, and anytime either my sister or I had gotten into trouble, it had usually included a visit to the "private" room. It wasn't something either of us enjoyed.

Biting my lip, I nodded. Mom leaned up and kissed my injured temple, her lips cool and comforting. As she patted my shoulder, she glanced at Dad. Some silent conversation passed between them, and Mom nodded. I was pretty sure their nonexistent conversation had been along the lines of, *Do you want me in there with you? No, you stay here. Julian and I need to have a man-to-man conversation.*

My heart fell as I trudged to the door, and I sort of wished Mom was coming too. I might have been able to play on her sympathies. Not that Dad was overly harsh—he was very fair, even I couldn't deny that—but sometimes I could wrap Mom around my finger. Maybe that was because I was the spitting image of Dad; sometimes my looks were a blessing. Also, I was pretty sure Mom still carried around a large amount of guilt over what had happened to me when I was younger. Dad too. I wasn't the type to use that guilt against them though, and I tried very hard to never bring up the incident. Another reason I wasn't looking forward to this conversation.

Nika gave me a sympathetic smile as I passed; her mood matched the look. Walking into my parents' room, I sat on the edge of their perfectly made bed. Dad stepped in a moment behind me and shut the door before twisting to face me. The absence of external sounds was both jarring and soothing. Living with a constant level of humdrum in the background—cars on the street, dogs in their yards, the neighbor asking what was for dinner—was a fact of life that I was used to. Having all of that suddenly shut off felt like being struck deaf; my heartbeat was the only thing that told me otherwise.

Inhaling an unnecessary breath, Dad walked over and sat beside me. Putting a hand on my knee, he examined my wound as he spoke. "You want to tell me what happened?"

I sighed and gave him a small smile. "No, not really."

Dad smiled too. "I wasn't really asking."

Pressing my lips into a firm line, I shrugged. "It was nothing, Dad." Looking away from him, I remembered Russell's snide face as he'd grabbed Raquel's arm. "It's just ... this guy ... he's such a ... jerk."

Leaning forward to get my attention, Dad asked, "A bully? Are you being picked on?"

I swung my dark head back to his. "No, not me ... but there's this girl ..."

Dad sighed, then nodded. "I should have suspected that it revolved around a girl." Smirking, he added, "It almost always does. Is she pretty?" he asked, raising an eyebrow.

My expression relaxed as the memory of her face washed over me. I felt my chest expand and my heart beat harder. Even though I couldn't hear her, I was sure Nika was sighing at me. "She's beautiful, Dad."

Listening to my reaction, Dad frowned as he watched my face melt into a dopey smile. "Is this boy you got into a fight with ... her boyfriend?" I immediately averted my eyes, and Dad sighed, my answer clear. "Julian, you can't fall for another man's girl."

I snapped my gaze back to his. "He's so disrespectful to her, Dad. The way he talks to her, the way he treats her. She cries all the time. She's miserable with him."

Dad looked thoughtful for a moment, his fingers coming up to stroke the stubble along his jaw as he leaned over his knees. "If she doesn't want to leave him, Julian, you can't make her. If she's not willing to stand up for herself, there's not much you or I can do. In the end, the choice to leave has to be hers. It's the only way she'll be happy."

Frustrated by his answer, I looked away. "So, I just leave her with this guy? Let him treat her like a dog? No ... worse than a dog."

"Julian, I know it's hard—"

Thinking of my family's many gifts, of the abilities that we had, that we hid, I twisted my body to face him. "No! It doesn't have to be hard at all. We have gifts that we can use to help people! That we can use to help *her*!"

Dad shook his head. "We're not super heroes, Julian. This isn't a comic book."

My cheeks heated with anger, and I knew they were bright red. "Grandma can force her to leave him! Grandma can fix *all* of this!"

Dad ran a hand back through his hair, his eyes sad. "Julian, we don't alter people's behavior without good cause. We don't use our abilities in the way you're suggesting …"

I instantly pointed at the wall of the home we now lived in. "Yes, we do! You used Grandma to get this house for Mom! Was forcing someone to leave their home a 'good cause'?"

Sighing, Dad shook his head again. "I know that's the joke around the house, but that's not what happened. I asked the homeowners at the right time, with the right amount. I didn't—"

Standing, I cut him off. "I want to help her, Dad. I want to be with her." Anger, fear, and confusion swam through me in a reckless cycle, and I felt Nika's emotions shift in response; she was worried about me.

Dad slowly stood up too, his hands out to placate me. "I know you feel for her, Julian, but if she doesn't return those feelings, we can't make her." I balled my hands into fists. Dad eyed my hands, then stepped toward me. "And would you really want her affections that way? Forced?" Lifting an eyebrow, he added, "Would that make you any better than him, Julian?"

My jaw dropped open in surprise. No, *forcing* her to like me would make me even worse than Russell. So much worse. Just the thought sickened me. My legs gave out, and I collapsed onto the corner of the bed.

Kneeling in front of me, Dad searched my eyes. "I'm sorry, Julian, but she has to see him for what he is, and leave him on her own. That's the natural order of things. But you're so young, you'll find the person you're supposed to be with one day. You just have to be patient."

I nodded with my head down, and Dad sighed as he sat beside me again. Putting a hand on my shoulder, he said, "Now … can you tell me exactly what happened today?"

Turning my head, I looked over at the man next to me. Strong, brave, and wise, Dad was exactly what I wanted to be when I was older. In a way, I understood Nika's feelings about guys—Dad set an impossible standard. Would I ever measure up?

Not wanting to admit that a fearful panic attack had made me lash out at Russell, I bit my lip, then whispered, "It's hard to talk about. Did you tell your parents everything when you were my age?"

Dad surprised me by laughing. Shaking his head, he murmured, "No. No, I kept so much from them." Sighing, he looked down at his hands. "And people got hurt because of it ... me included." Glancing back up at me, his eyes were sympathetic. "I learned my lesson the hard way, Julian. I know it's difficult, but talking about it is so much better than keeping it inside."

Nodding, I took a deep breath ... and told him everything.

It was well into our typical dinner hour when we were finally finished. As Dad put a supportive, chilly hand on my shoulder, my stomach rumbled. We both looked at the gurgling organ, then Dad laughed. "Come on, let's go see about some food for you." Smiling warmly at me, he added, "And I could use a little drink myself."

"Thanks, Dad," I whispered as we both stood. I'd been dreading this moment all afternoon, but I felt better after talking to him. I didn't hate Russell any less, and I *definitely* still wanted to be with Raquel, but my heart was lighter, and that was enough for now.

Twisting the doorknob, Dad told me, "Anytime, Julian. It's what your mom and I are here for."

Dad opened the door then, and the sound of the world immediately flooded me. It was overwhelming at first—my body had gotten used to the quiet stillness of my parents' bedroom—but with some effort, I pushed the cacophony to the back of my mind, where the residual buzzing of life always stayed with me, generally unnoticed. As I walked downstairs with Dad, I allowed Mom and Nika's voices to reach me. They were in the kitchen making dinner, and the smell of boiling pasta and bubbling cream sauce made my stomach rumble again. So did the tang of fresh blood in the air.

I couldn't wait to have a tall, steaming glass of it ... and that was exactly why Raquel and I would never work. Nika was right. She would never accept what I was. Deep down I knew that, but I still couldn't leave her with someone like Russell. She deserved better, even if better wasn't me.

CHAPTER THREE

Nika

I COULD HEAR Dad and Julian exiting the silent bedroom and paused mid-laugh with Mom. She was teaching me how to make Fettuccini Alfredo. The only problem was that Dad was a much better cook than Mom and she was struggling a bit. It didn't help the matter any that Mom couldn't taste-test her own product. Being an undead vampire, her body didn't handle food well anymore. I wasn't quite sure what would happen if she ate real food, but by the tender look of sympathy that Mom had given Dad when I'd asked, I figured it was bad.

So I was Mom's guinea pig as she carefully adjusted the seasonings going into the creamy sauce bubbling away on the stove. It had gone from too bland to too salty in just a couple of teaspoons and I was giggling at Mom's annoyed expression when Dad and Julian reentered our world.

We both paused and looked up to where we could hear them. I'd been keeping an emotional "eye" on Julian the entire time he'd been talking to Dad upstairs. I'd wanted to give him privacy, and I'd tried to not pay any attention to the feelings emanating from him, but when he shifted from one extreme to another it was difficult to tune him out. Much like the salt now coating my taste buds, Julian's mood swings were too overpowering to ignore.

Mom inhaled a deep breath, and I looked back at her. She had a dopey, lovesick grin on her beautiful face, and I knew it was because Dad was approaching her. Since Dad had "made" Mom into what she was, they shared a special connection. They were drawn to each other. More so than just a couple in love.

Dad had told me once that when a vampire sired another vampire, a bond was created so that the newly formed vampire and the creator would want to be together. I guess it was so that the newbie didn't die. Anyway, Dad said the extremeness of the bond depended on the connection the pair had pre-turning. If a stranger was turned by someone, they'd only have a mild interest to be around each other. Mom and Dad had been married at the time. Halina had once told Julian and me that Mom and Dad's bond had been almost pornographic in the beginning. Thank God it had diminished over time, and was much more subdued now.

Mom said it was like coming home.

Mom closed her eyes for a second, then reopened them when Dad stepped into the room. I heard him exhale at the same time Mom did. Ignoring Julian and me for a moment, they stepped toward each other. I glanced at Julian as our parents leaned together and kissed. He smirked at me, shaking his head in amusement. His mood was a lot mellower than it had been upstairs. Whatever Dad had told him had pacified him ... for now.

After a couple of tender kisses, Mom and Dad finally pulled apart. Dad glanced into the pot of pasta sauce and frowned. "That smells ... off." Peeking up at Mom, he cocked a dark eyebrow. "What did you put in there?"

Her full lip in a pout, Mom pushed Dad's shoulders away from her. "Just the stuff you told me to." She pointed to the pot, and Dad cracked a smile. While the tiny grin was full of amusement, the way Dad looked at Mom was unmistakably full of love. I hoped to see a look of such deep adoration directed at me one day. "I topped it off with a dash of salt," she said.

Dad looked over at me, his tiny grin growing. Knowing that he was asking me how it tasted, since he couldn't try it any more than Mom could,

I stuck my tongue out and made a "yuck" face. My answer clear to him, Dad twisted back to Mom. "A dash of salt?" he asked.

Mom shrugged. She had her hair in a ponytail today and one of the long, brown locks was starting to fall out. Dad tucked it behind her ear, then dragged his thumb over her cheek. "Well, maybe a couple of dashes …" she murmured, clearly distracted by his caress.

Dad chuckled at her admission. "It's a *pinch* of salt, Emma." He lightning-fast grabbed her waist, and she squealed in surprise. "Don't you know what a pinch is?" he asked, his fingers coming down to squeeze her bottom.

Mom started laughing and squirming, trying to get away from him. Julian groaned and dropped his head back. His wave of embarrassment matched my own. Good Lord, they'd been married forever, you'd think the honeymoon period would have been over by now. Not with my parents, though. They were still sappy and playful. Outwardly, I acted just as disgusted as Julian, but inwardly, I was filled with longing.

Covering my face, I peeked at the flirty pair through my fingers. "Uh … guys, impressionable kids in the room. Time to be good role models and all that."

Dad stopped kissing Mom's neck and glanced at me. "Sorry, sweetheart." He released Mom but gave her such a heated look that she smacked his shoulder and whispered at him to stop. I was pretty sure their bedroom door would be firmly closed tonight. *Thank you, Gabriel, for your miraculous vampire-soundproofing.*

Taking over for Mom, Dad made a couple of adjustments to the sauce and had me try it again. Whatever he'd done eased the saltiness, and I gave him a thumbs-up. Dad smirked at Mom, and she rolled her eyes. Chuckling to himself, Dad checked on the noodles while Mom slung her arm around Julian's waist. The two of them started in on a conversation about school. Mom avoided talking about the fight though. By the meaningful glance Dad gave her, I was sure he would fill her in later, when the two of them were alone. Normally, I hated being left out of the loop, but I already knew what Julian was going through, and I could pretty accurately guess what his conversation with Dad had been like. They were respecting Julian, by discussing the topic in private, and I let them.

As Julian and Mom moved their conversation into the living room, Dad twisted to look at me. "Okay, I've got one child's troubles under control for the moment. So, do you want to tell me what's eating you, Gilbert?"

Smiling at Dad's reference to one of my favorite movies, I rolled my eyes. "You're so embarrassing ..." I muttered, not really meaning it.

Dad laughed at the look on my face. "Me?" He shook his head; the kitchen lights made a ring of white in the pitch blackness of his hair. It sort of looked like a halo. "You know nothing about being embarrassed. Ask your mom some time about visiting the ranch for the first time." Mom laughed in the living room, and Dad smiled at her through the wall that separated them. Looking back at me, he asked, "Still mulling over your English paper?"

Knowing my problems sounded so insignificant compared to Julian's made me want to cringe. But they were my problems, so they felt big to me. Walking over to the stove with Dad, I lifted the lid on the last pot simmering on the stove. Taking the top off, I examined the deep red, viscous liquid. The small vat of blood was beautiful ... in a horror-movie sort of way. It also smelled amazing, better than the Alfredo sauce.

Turning off the burner, I looked over at Dad watching me. "It's just ... this assignment is supposed to be easy. It's supposed to be a getting-to-know-you piece, and I have to lie."

I ran my finger along the edge of the warm pot, carefully gathering a sample to taste without burning myself. When the edge of my finger was nice and bloodied, I stuck it in my mouth. My fangs immediately dropped. Normally, I had a firm handle on them, holding them up at a more respectable "human" level, but just a small drop of blood in my mouth made them impossible to contain. Blood meant drinking. Drinking meant down. I could stop the reaction about as much as I could stop my heart from beating harder when I exercised. I could, however, immediately pull them back up. But since we were home, I left them down for a bit. It emphasized my point anyway.

Fangs fully extended, I looked Dad square in the eye. "I'll always have to lie."

Dad's light blue eyes washed over my face. "Not always, Nika. You don't have to lie with us. And you won't have to lie to the person you eventually marry, if you choose to tell him everything, which I hope you do. It's much easier on your marriage if you're free to be yourself with your spouse."

I gave Dad a crooked smile, an odd thing to do around fangs. "Whoa, who said anything about a husband? I just want to get through high school. Let's not get carried away."

Dad laughed, then nodded. "Thank God." He gave me a quick kiss on the head, then turned back to his sauce. "I just about had a coronary saying that."

Mom laughed in the living room and Dad smiled. Mom always found it funny when Dad referenced his silent heart. He'd had a coronary years ago, and it hadn't had anything to do with the idea of me getting married. Dad didn't like going into specifics about it, but he'd told us that a hunter had forced his conversion. And that right there was a huge reason why we lied. Vampires weren't universally loved; some people wanted us all dead. Hunting us to extinction was one of the world's most accepted forms of genocide, even if our existence was mythical to most humans.

I knew the reason. I knew the stakes. It still sucked, though.

Pulling my teeth back up, I grabbed the handle on the pot brimming with blood. Stepping over to a coffee carafe waiting nearby, I carefully poured the yummy treat inside. We could drink blood cold, but our family preferred it hot. Especially the undead among us. Mom and Dad didn't generate their own heat. They didn't need it anymore, but they both enjoyed the feeling of being warm, so they gravitated toward any source of heat they could find. Kind of like lizards.

"I know it's important to lie, Dad. I just hate *always* having to do it." When my pot was nearly empty, I looked up at him. "And I'm still not really sure what to call you? The last time Arianna was here, I almost messed up and called you Dad."

Dad frowned as he grabbed the pot of noodles. Stepping over to the sink, he poured the water and noodles into a strainer and said, "Well, I'm your grandfather's wife's brother, who is helping out your mother by staying here with the three of you … only your mom is gone a lot visiting her boyfriend, so my wife and I end up watching you and Julian most nights …"

I raised an eyebrow, just like he did sometimes. "And in simple terms, that makes you my … ?"

He paused while he thought of an easier way to say all that. "I'm your … That would make you and me … We'd be …" Frowning, he shook his head. "Just call me Teren."

With a sigh, I said, "And that's weird for me to say."

Setting the empty pot in the sink, Dad walked over to me. Squatting to look me in the eye, he put a hand on my shoulder. "I know, Nika. I realize that aspects of our lies are strange to talk about, and I realize that you don't want to have to lie at all, but it's for the safety of our family ... and our family's security comes first. Always." Straightening, he added, "And besides, it's only as odd as it is because the two of you were so young when we moved here, and we've been here for a while now. Once we move on, the lie will be simpler. I promise." Our family didn't stay in one place for too long—ten to fifteen years max. We'd moved here when I was five years old, so our max time was quickly approaching.

Dad took my empty pot of blood from me and gave me a comforting smile. "Now, why don't you and Julian set the table. Dinner is just about done."

After dinner, the four of us went for a walk around the neighborhood. It was a ritual we'd started when Julian and I were about ten. Mom said it was for the fresh air, but I think she really just wanted us to have something to do together each night. Something more interactive than all of us staring at a TV for hours. I didn't mind. Salt Lake was beautiful, and we almost always found something interesting on our walks. With our eagle eyes and ears, we could pick out things most humans missed. I once saw a rabbit chasing a cat through the slats in a neighbor's backyard fence. Brave rabbit. I hoped it won.

Mom and Dad held hands while they walked in front of Julian and me. Dad stroked Mom's thumb the entire time. Julian watched the mutual affection impassively, but there was a wistful happiness inside him. His feelings were full of pride and contentment, just like mine. If children learned by watching their parents, then ours were shining examples of how to keep love alive. Ironic, since they were technically dead.

I'd heard some of my peers talk about their parents before—about the distance and coldness between them, about how they never wanted to get married if that was how they were destined to end up. Even though I couldn't talk about it, my parents were the opposite of their experience. It made me want to talk about them even more. I wanted to give my friends hope by using Mom and Dad as positive examples of what marriage could be. But, to the outside world, Teren and Emma were just a fresh, young couple who had only been married for a few years. And, in the lie, they weren't really related to me anyway.

I stopped watching Mom and Dad after a couple of blocks, and focused instead on the land around me. Even though I'd been born in California, and returned there a few times a year to visit my aunt, Salt Lake was my home. I was going to miss it when we had to leave in a couple years. Everyone had agreed that we would stay until Julian and I were done with high school, then the entire group would pack up and head to wherever the two of us decided to go to college. We liked to stay together. Safety in numbers, my dad often said.

Looking around, I thought Salt Lake was the perfect place for a bunch of partial vampires. The city itself was just as mythical and contradictory as we were. According to our geography teacher, this entire area used to be covered by a prehistoric lake. Portions of the city were located on what used to be former beaches, and that was really weird to think about. The city was almost entirely surrounded by mountains—dry and brown rolling ones in the forefront, soaring white monoliths in the background—but it was near-arid here, more like a desert at times. It was just like us, seemingly one thing on the outside, but something else entirely on the inside.

Even the city's tourism slogan seemed aimed at our family. Whenever I saw the signs, I chuckled. *Visit Salt Lake. Different by Nature.* It was so very true for us. We were about as different as you could get—a fluke of nature. Even to full vampires we were a bit of a mystery. A breed of our own, that was what Gabriel called us. It made fitting in anywhere challenging.

Our path eventually led us to a very familiar house. To our neighbors, this was the place where our "mother" spent all her free time when she wasn't with us, but in actuality, this was where Starla and Jacen lived. It was a two-story place in a style Starla called "modern." I supposed it was. With harsh angles, black accents, and huge glass panels that would probably take a non-super-speedy human hours to clean, it stuck out next to the more traditional homes around it. Starla liked that a lot. Even though our nature demanded a little privacy, part of Starla craved the limelight. Having hot clothes, a contemporary home, a sporty car, and, in the eyes of the neighborhood, a much younger boyfriend, was how she stuck out.

The lights were on as we walked by, and Dad glanced over at the house. We couldn't feel Starla and Jacen, since they weren't blood related to us, but we could hear them laughing. Clearing his throat, Dad said, "Good evening, Starla, Jacen."

Starla instantly appeared in one of the windows upstairs. She was wearing a short robe that barely covered her rear. A strange mixture of desire and revulsion swept through Julian as he stared at the woman who was genuinely old enough to be our mother. Julian immediately snapped his gaze to me, and his mood shifted to embarrassment. A flush highlighted his cheeks, and we both stared straight ahead. Yeah, sometimes feeling what someone else was feeling was beyond mortifying. For both parties.

"Evening, vamp boy, vamp family."

Mom frowned as she looked up at the scantily-clad woman. "Maybe you should consider getting some curtains for all those windows, Starla?" She looked back at Julian, who was studiously ignoring Starla. "There *are* innocents about."

Starla laughed and raised a blood-red wine glass in her hand. "If I can still make the young men blush, then I'm not going to stop strutting my stuff." Her other hand slinked down to untie her robe. It slid open to reveal an underwear set that looked just as pricey as the rest of her. Even I had to admit that she looked good. She put women half her age to shame.

Mom made a disgusted noise and slapped her hand over Julian's eyes, even though he hadn't been looking. Dad tugged on Mom's other hand, signaling that it was time to move on. Then Starla was harshly jerked out of view, and Jacen stepped into her place. He was shirtless, just wearing lounge pants. My eyes widened this time. He looked good, too. I felt an emotion similar to what Julian had gone through earlier—attraction mixed with disgust. Pulling Mom's hand from his eyes, Julian tossed a smirk my way; his amusement flooded into me.

"Sorry about that," Jacen murmured, running a hand through his shaggy, blond hair.

Starla popped up beside him, muttering, "Knock it off, Jace!" but he held her back with one toned arm, firmly keeping her from going back on display.

Shaking his head, Dad murmured, "We'll let you ... get back to your evening."

He started leading us away when Jacen said, "Hey, sorry Starla was late again today with the kids. I told her to leave earlier, but she ... dawdled."

Pausing, Dad looked up at Jacen. "She was late?" He looked back at Julian and me. "Is that why it's been taking you guys so long to get home from school?" I shrugged and nodded. Dad could feel our locations shifting from place to place. He must have assumed *we* were the slow pokes. But Starla being late was typical. From the window I heard her mutter, "Tattletale," to Jacen.

Smiling, I said to Dad, "You could let us get a car of our own? Then you wouldn't have to worry about it."

Dad frowned at me, then said, "I'll call you tomorrow, Starla. So we can discuss this when you're not busy."

Jacen and Starla disappeared as the four of us continued our walk. While we couldn't see them anymore, we could still hear them—there was a lot of giggling going on. Mom and Dad picked up the pace a bit.

At the halfway point along our circular route, we came across a long moving van parked in the driveway of a modest, one-level townhouse. Julian and I stepped into the street to walk around it. Dad paused and looked for the homeowners. I knew the look on Dad's face and wanted to groan, but didn't. Dad was going to offer to help, and if the new owners took him up on it, we'd all be expected to help too … and then we'd be here for the next several hours. I was all for lending a hand, but I'd already mapped out my evening, and it included cranking out my English paper and talking to Arianna for an hour before bed, not lugging around various boxes of other people's junk.

"Hello?" Dad asked. Mom snuggled into his side as she stopped with him.

The back of the moving van was wide open, and a person came out from behind some large boxes and jumped down onto the street with Julian and me. I audibly gasped, and not because I was surprised. Everyone in my family looked at me, and I felt my cheeks flame red-hot. I couldn't help it. A boy—no, a *man*—was standing on the road beside me, and he was the most incredibly good-looking man I'd ever seen. Well, who I wasn't related to anyway.

Oddly, he sort of looked like the men in my family, but that was probably because his hair was jet-black. His eyes were a dark, piercing brown, though, the kind of eyes that trapped you and never let you go. A part of me *wanted* to be trapped by them.

Running a hand along an attractive amount of light stubble on his jaw, he looked us over. My heartbeat skyrocketed when his eyes passed over mine. Maybe it was my imagination, but they seemed to linger on me a moment before moving to my parents.

The gorgeous man's gaze settled on Dad. "Yeah?" His confused expression was adorable.

Dad gestured to the truck. "I see you're moving in. Can we lend you a hand?"

He paused as he thought about Dad's offer. I couldn't tell how old he was. He seemed younger than my dad appeared, but older than me. I fervently hoped that he wasn't *so* much older than me that he found my age undesirable. I chewed on my lip while he answered Dad's question. "That would be great, thank you."

I inwardly did a happy dance over the fact that we'd be staying here for the next several hours. And, fortunately for me, there were enough street lamps nearby that my parents' glowing eyes wouldn't be a factor once the sun fully set; no one would notice the faint phosphorescence that was a dead-giveaway of our race. It was meant to subdue prey, and was only really visible in pitch-blackness. It was a side effect of vampirism that my brother and I didn't share, thankfully.

The boy looked back at me, and I tried to give him a calm, grown-up smile, so he wouldn't think I was just a giddy, sixteen-year-old girl. My heart was still unnaturally fast though, and knowing that every member of my family could hear it only tripled my embarrassment; I knew that Julian found my struggle to rein in my hormones hilarious. But I didn't care, because tall, dark, and handsome smiled back at me ... and it was *amazing*.

Just when it seemed that he was about to speak directly to me, the front door of his new home opened. We all twisted to look as an older version of the boy stepped out of the house. His hair and jaw line were speckled with gray, and he was clearly related to the boy who was accelerating my heart. With similar dark and piercing eyes, the older man gave us a onceover. "Something going on, son?"

"Hey, Dad, these guys were just passing by. Offered to help."

The older man stepped to the back of the truck and leaned against it. Mom and Dad moved closer to Julian and me as the boy's father appraised us all. Mom lifted a hand to indicate the truck when she reached my side. "We'd love to lend a hand. We're pretty strong."

I bit my lip to hide my grin. Yeah, we were definitely strong. The older man gave us a polite smile, then walked over to clasp his son on the shoulder. "Thank you for the kind offer, but I think we can handle it. We're pretty strong too."

The man's son smiled and looked right at me. My heart was pounding in my ears as butterflies danced in my stomach. Wow, he was attractive. The man watched his son closely for a second, then added, "Besides, taking care of one's own mess is good for the soul. Builds character."

The boy looked over at his dad and frowned, but didn't say anything. My father cleared his throat, then started herding our group around the truck and back onto the sidewalk. "Well, I certainly understand that," he said. Dad nodded back at the men as we started walking away. "Good luck, and welcome to the neighborhood. Maybe we'll see you around?"

The older man nodded, his hand still clasping his son's shoulder; he was still staring at his dad, frowning. My disappointment that we were leaving was so great that my feet felt encased in cement. With each plodding step I took away from the good-looking stranger, my spirit sank. Julian poked me in the ribs, but I ignored him and his never-ending amusement. If I had to tolerate his over-the-moon feelings for Raquel, then he could put up with my impromptu passion for the neighbor.

Just as we reached the corner that would take the dark-haired boy from my sight, I turned my head to get one last look at him. Surprisingly, he was watching me leave. Even more surprisingly, he had a small smile on his lips. I wasn't sure if the smile was specifically for me, or if he'd just been touched by my family's offer, but my body didn't care. My heart thudded against my ribcage, and I couldn't slow it down. And I didn't want to. The surging pulse invigorated me in a way I hadn't ever felt before. I felt ... alive. Wholly and truly alive.

As I reluctantly pulled my gaze from the hot boy down the block, I met eyes with Dad. Frowning at me, he murmured, "Maybe we should find a new route for our walk. Shake things up a bit."

I rolled my eyes at him. *No way, Dad. This route is just fine.*

The attractive neighbor stayed in my head for the rest of the night. Thinking about him made lying about my family a little easier, and I finished writing my English paper by imagining that I was having a conversation with him, telling him the things that I could tell him, none of which was the truth. If I told him the truth, he would be moved out by morning.

I almost told Arianna all about him when she called me later that night. I didn't though. It wasn't that I didn't *want* to tell her—I was actually dying to describe him to her in graphic detail—but it wasn't something that I wanted to talk about around my super-hearing family, and since my parents' room was the only "quiet" room in the house, any conversation about the super-cute neighbor would have been very public.

As I crawled into bed, I did my best to ignore the memory of those dark, piercing eyes. Between yawns, I heard my brother sleepily mutter, "Night, Nick."

Thinking about his eventful day, I firmly pushed those beautiful eyes into the recesses of my memory. Feeling Julian's contentment as he settled into bed, I murmured back, "Night, Julie."

Dad's voice drifted down the hall to us as he stepped into his room, where Mom was already climbing into bed. "Good night, kids."

Mom echoed Dad's sentiment, then giggled and whispered, "Close the door, Mr. Adams. Your secretary would like a word with you in private."

Dad chuckled and then, mercifully, the door closed. Julian groaned from his room. "God, they're so embarrassing."

"Yeah," I sighed. As I closed my eyes, the darkness of the night wrapped itself around me, comforting me. Within the blackness, a pair of even darker irises grew inside my mind's eye; they seared my soul.

I AWOKE THE next morning feeling groggy. The deepest, most restful part of sleep had been elusive, hiding from me just when I'd been about to find it. I'd tossed and turned for hours, drifting in the fog of being half-awake and mostly asleep. If I'd gotten into the coffee habit like some of my friends, I'm sure I would have woken up yearning for a cup. As it was, all I really wanted was a glass of cold water, and maybe some cucumbers for the bags under my eyes.

Mom and Julian were still in their rooms, but Dad was downstairs so I shuffled down to see him. He was in the living room, watching the sun rise when I entered. He looked contemplative, so I stopped to watch him. Not looking back at me, he quietly said, "Good morning, Nika."

Stepping up beside him, I peered up into his face. His light eyes were flicking over the beauty of the morning, absorbing it. "Morning, Dad. You okay?"

With a peaceful smile on his face, he looked down at me. "Of course." Slinging his arm over my shoulders, he tilted his head. "Why wouldn't I be?"

I examined his face for a moment, then shrugged. "I don't know, you just seemed ... thoughtful."

He smiled wider and raised a perfectly arched brow. "Thoughtful doesn't always mean there's a problem." I twisted my lip at him, and he chuckled. Returning his gaze to the window glowing gold with early morning light, he sighed. "I was just thinking about Great-Gran ... and all of the other purebloods ... they don't get to enjoy moments like this." When his eyes returned to mine, they were soft with sympathy. "Sometimes it's easy to forget just how good we have it ... all the benefits, few of the setbacks. I just like to take a minute now and again to appreciate the things that can so easily be taken for granted."

"Like sunrises?" I asked.

Dad kissed my head, squeezing me tighter. "Like sunrises."

I wrapped my arms around Dad's waist and watched the colors of the world blossom into life with him. Everything was crystal clear to my eyes; I could even pinpoint the microscopic flaws in the glass. I preferred it like that, though. There was beauty in imperfection, it was all in how you looked at it.

After a quiet moment, Dad asked, "Are you all right?"

"Yeah, just tired. Didn't sleep well."

I yawned after my statement, and Dad chuckled. "Thinking about that boy down the street?"

Pulling back, I cringed as I looked up at him. "Dad ..."

He held up his hands and shook his head. "I know, I know ... you don't want to talk about it." He paused, then added, "But ... if you ever did ..."

Smiling, I leaned up to kiss his cheek. "I know ... you're here for me."

I felt Mom's presence entering the room, and Dad and I twisted to look at her. Her long, brown hair was up in a high ponytail, and she was dressed in casual knit pants and a yoga top. Although her body didn't need it, Mom still liked to work out on occasion. That familiar look of peace washed over her as she approached her husband, her sire. "Sorry, am I interrupting a bonding moment?"

Dad dropped his arm from me to reach out for her. "Yes, but that's all right. I enjoy your interruptions."

Mom leaned up and gave him a soft kiss. "Since it's early, I thought I'd get in a quick class before we headed out to the ranch." While Dad kept his features schooled as he nodded at her, his eyes roved over her figure. I turned my head to give them a little more privacy. The sound of another light kiss filled the air, and Mom let out a low giggle. I rolled my eyes, not even daring to look at the two love birds.

Just as I was about to remind them that I was standing right beside them, Mom tapped my shoulder. "Want to come with me, Nika?"

I glanced between the two of them, then shrugged. "Sure ... why not." Besides the fact that Mom's yoga class was great exercise—it made my arms shake, and considering my strength, that was saying something—maybe we would drive past the neighbor's house ... and maybe he'd gotten up bright and early to continue unpacking the truck ... and maybe he'd smile at me again.

CHAPTER FOUR

Julian

I HEARD MOM and Nika leave, felt Dad loitering around downstairs, but it was way too early to get up so I drifted back to sleep. When I woke up again, Mom and Nika were coming through the front door, laughing and complaining that their legs were going to be sore for the next three days.

Stretching and yawning, I decided to go join the living … and the dead.

When I got there, Nika was sitting at the kitchen table, a third of the way through her cereal. There was an odd sort of excitement inside her, a feeling that had been there ever since she'd spotted that guy moving in down the road. It was a little shocking, but my sister was finally developing a crush. While it made me happy that I would no longer be the only one of us having embarrassing feelings that made me curse our bond, I wasn't looking forward to my sister's mood turning all ooey-gooey, lovey-dovey.

Well, if I knew my sister—and I did—the crush wouldn't last long. Nika was pretty sharp, and even if she did have a romantic buried deep inside her, she was more practical than passionate. She wouldn't let herself fall for a guy who wasn't *exactly* right for her. My sister had always had this ability to see the truth of a situation and adjust her feelings accordingly. Unlike me, she would never pine for someone who wasn't available.

My mood sank some as I sat beside Nika. Sensing the emotional shift, she lifted her eyebrow in question. Ignoring her curiosity, I forcefully shook Raquel out of my thoughts, and said good morning to everyone. Mom promptly placed a bowl of food in front of me, then ruffled my hair like I was still three-years-old. Smiling at her, I murmured, "Thanks," and dug in.

Leaning against the counter, Mom returned to her conversation with Dad, something technical about the herd at the ranch. Tuning them out, I glanced at Nika. Her warm brown eyes were locked on Mom and Dad, intently listening to the conversation about ringworm and foot rot. As I looked back at our parents, I realized another reason why Nika's blossoming feelings were surprising. Nika wanted what Mom and Dad had—that intense, loving, unshakable connection that sometimes embarrassed the crap out of me. Nika wanted it so much that she tended to put every guy she saw on a set of scales—Dad on one end, the aforementioned schmuck on the other. Predictably, every teenager she'd ever come across had failed her internal test.

Sometimes I feared that they always would, that Nika would be alone forever because no one would ever be able to reach the pedestal she'd put Dad on. But then I remembered we were young. Mom and Dad had found each other late in life—God, they'd been just a few years shy of thirty!—so there was hope for Nika. And me too, if I could ever stop wanting to be with Raquel.

An hour later, we were on the road to our typical weekend destination—Adams Ranch. It was a spot that my sister and I still loved going to, even after all these years, even with our parents. While most kids our age were trying to avoid their family, we enjoyed being with ours. And the ranch was special, a place where we could be ourselves, unafraid of who might be watching. True, there were some ranch hands about, so we always had to be aware of them, but for the most part, they stayed clear of the main house.

Peter Alton, a guy who seemed more ancient than Gabriel, led the crew and kept the hired hands in line. He'd been with our family since before Nika and I were born. Dad said he'd married him and Mom, and had been around since Dad was young. While no one in the family spoke of it, we all knew that Peter knew our secret. He had to. He'd been around us for decades, and there was no way he could have missed the fact that only Grandpa Jack seemed to age. But Peter was loyal to our family, and we trusted him with our lives. Literally.

The ranch wasn't too far away from the heart of the city, but it felt like stepping into another universe. Dad entered a code near the gate, and the massive iron doors began to creak open. The family name was spelled out in large, ornate iron letters along the top of the gate. The middle A was split in half as the doors pulled inward—AD on one side, MS on the other.

I always felt a sense of obligation when I drove through those letters. Nika's name would change when she got married, and as the youngest man in the family, it was up to me to carry on the name. Not that my supernaturally long-lived Dad was going anywhere, but the weight of that responsibility was still on me. I'd confessed that to Dad once, and he'd told me not to worry about it. He'd said the family name had changed several times since Halina had started the ranch, back when she'd been human. In fact, Dad's first name was a tribute to one of those past surnames—Teren was Imogen's last name.

We followed the driveway until we reached a wide loop in front of the house, like our own private roundabout. In the center of the circle was a fountain with a giant statue of a woman crying. There was a smaller fountain like this one in the entryway of the ranch in California. We hadn't lived there since I was five, but we usually checked on the old homestead when we were in town.

Dad swung around the circular drive to get to the garage, and I glanced at the front of the house as we passed it. It seemed more like a private boarding school than a home for just a handful of people. It had been made from deep-red brick, which reminded me of the *Three Little Pigs*—no wolf would be able to blow this sucker down. At the highest points, it rose to four stories. Not many knew it, but it went almost as far underground. Several tall, slim chimneys soared from the home to touch the sky. The roof they rested upon seemed equally eager to touch the clouds, with high, pointed arches everywhere. All of it made the home seem overly extravagant, a place that was beautiful to look at, but you didn't dare touch anything. But, much like us, that was a façade. It was warm and welcoming here ... it was home.

THE NEXT GENERATION

Dad drove his Prius through a circular building that connected the house to the garage. Well, it was more of a covered breezeway than a building, but it matched the style of the home so well, it seemed like you were about to drive right through the dining room or something. We all got out of Dad's car before he turned and backed it into the garage. Even though we weren't that far from the city, under an hour by car, even less on our vampire feet, the air here seemed fresher.

The back of the house was no less grand than the front, but the backyard was where all the fun things were. There was a ton of stuff to do here—play basketball, tennis, or go for a swim in the pool inside one of the outbuildings. The pastures around the house stretched back as far as a human eye could see. My sister and I used to play a supernaturally difficult game of croquet in those fields when we were younger. We'd honed our abilities by making shots from one fenced yard to another. We'd also gotten a severe talking to whenever we'd accidentally nicked a cow in the process.

Dad zipped out of the garage and joined us as we headed for the back of the house. Nika opened a door and stepped inside, into the main living room. Gabriel was already turned in our direction when we entered, since he'd heard us coming. The ancient vampire smiled and nodded his dirty-blond head. "Good morning, Nika, Julian ..." he glanced behind us to our parents, "Teren, Emma." Standing in a bright patch of sunshine, he tilted his head to the windows. "Beautiful day, isn't it?"

Gabriel was at the same sun-tolerance level as Alanna, but he'd had the windows here vampire-proofed, so the family could be comfortable during the day. Well, everyone but Halina. Gabriel still couldn't get the formula strong enough to help her. He was getting closer, or so he said, but he hadn't perfected it for his pureblood girlfriend yet.

Dad waved at Gabriel. "Good to see you. The last few times we've been up, you've been away."

Gabriel frowned. A shaft of light caught his eyes, and the dark jade lightened into a sea green color. "Yes. Jordan was having an ... issue ... at the Los Angeles nest." He smiled, a little smugly for a guy his age. "It's been taken care of though."

Mom and Dad looked at each other, and a silent conversation passed between them. Nika bunched her brows, and I felt the curiosity rising in her, too. What exactly had he taken care of?

Putting his arm around Mom's shoulders, Dad asked, "Anything we need to worry about?"

Calm, and seemingly unperturbed by anything, Gabriel smiled widely and shook his head. "No."

Alanna and Imogen buzzed into the room then, their appearances so fast, they almost seemed to materialize from thin air. But my eyes had seen them blurring—Imogen from the dark cherry staircase in the corner of the room, Alanna from the archway leading to the kitchen. Alanna came up to me, while Imogen wrapped her chilly arms around my sister.

"Good morning, sweethearts," they both cooed.

"Morning, Grandma," Nika and I said at nearly the same time.

Pulling back from me, Alanna glanced at the injury near my eye. It was healing nicely, but it was obvious that I'd been cut recently. She didn't say anything, though, just smiled and moved over to hug Nika.

After everyone had hugged and welcomed us, Mom turned to Alanna. "Where's my mom?"

Smiling warmly at her daughter-in-law, Alanna pointed outside. "She's helping Jack in the pasture."

Grinning, Mom looked out the wide windows that offered a sweeping view of the fields. "She is? With what?" Mom said, laughing in amusement.

"Well, Jack is fixing a fence. Linda volunteered to be his assistant."

Dad frowned and twisted to his mom. "I told him to wait until I got here."

Alanna shrugged and sighed. "You know how he is, dear. If he *can* do it himself... he will."

Shaking his head, Dad muttered, "Well, he's going to 'help' himself into an early grave if he doesn't take it easy every once in a while."

Alanna bit her lip. Staring at her, she seemed to be the same age as Dad. Her youthful face was smooth and flawless, and the board-straight hair running down her back was thick and just as dark as mine. But Dad's comment reminded me just how old she really was, and just how old Grandpa Jack was. A very human Grandpa Jack.

Imogen placed a hand on her daughter's shoulder. She seemed just as young as Alanna in her face, but her "style" gave her age away. Dark hair piled atop her head in an intricate bun, Imogen typically dressed like an old-fashioned schoolmarm, while Alanna preferred the more casual, rancher look: jeans and a button-up shirt.

At seeing the look of sympathy on Imogen's face and the look of grief on Alanna's, Dad swallowed and shook his head. "Sorry, Mom ... Gran. I just ... worry about him." Dad looked back at Mom. "Linda too."

Mom rubbed Dad's back as his eyes grew shiny. A bubble of sadness crept into me from Nika, and I subconsciously reached out my hand for hers. I felt the same way—everyone in the room did. Grandpa Jack and Grandma Linda were human, and were going to stay human until the very end of their natural lives. That was the sucky part of living forever; you lost people along the way.

Reaching her hand up to touch his face, Mom softly said, "I worry too, Teren, but ... it's not today." She gave him a soft kiss on the cheek. "Today ... as Gabriel so wonderfully put it ... is a beautiful day."

Dad nodded and Alanna sniffed, then smiled. Cheerily, she looked at all of us and asked, "Anybody hungry?"

Nika giggled, and feeling her melancholy slip away, I relaxed the hold on her hand. We all said no, but Alanna looked like she was going to make us something anyway. Shaking his head, Dad told her, "No, really, Mom. I'm gonna go help Dad. Thank you, though."

He turned to leave, but Gabriel held up his hand. "Hold on, before everyone disperses, I think someone would like to come up and say hello."

His gaze drifted to the floor, to where Halina was sleeping. Only ... she wasn't sleeping. Now that I was paying attention to her, I could feel her minutely moving, like she was pacing. From below the earth, I heard a disgruntled voice murmur, "Hello."

"You're still awake, Grandma?" I asked, confused as to why she was burning the midnight oil. In her world anyway.

"Yeah ..." was her mumbled response.

She didn't seem happy that she wasn't sleeping, and I had to wonder why she was still up. Gabriel strode to the middle of the room and looked down at where she was beneath us. Chuckling, he tilted his head at the floor. "This was your idea, love. You wanted to surprise them. Don't tell me that you're now ... afraid?"

Halina's form immediately shifted positions. There was a secret door beside the cherry staircase that Imogen had used earlier. The door was disguised as a large bookcase, but it swung inward on heavy hinges to reveal the hallway to the rooms underground. Halina was right at the edge of that thick door. My heart started thudding. She couldn't come out here during daylight hours; she'd fry to a crisp.

"I am afraid of nothing ... love."

There was a fair amount of venom in her voice, but Gabriel easily kept the peaceful smile on his face. Alanna and Imogen clasped hands, looking nervous. Mom and Dad looked at each other, then Gabriel. "Can she come out here?" Dad asked. "Did you ... did you fix the flaw in the glass?"

Dad looked really nervous about all of this. If Gabriel had gotten just one tiny thing wrong ... Halina would be seriously hurt. She could even die from the exposure. I wasn't sure how quickly it took a vampire to burst into flames, since I'd never seen it, but I didn't want to find out.

Nika clenched my hand as we waited for Gabriel's response. "I had a breakthrough, and I believe it will be strong enough for her ... with limited exposure, of course."

Halina harrumphed. "Yes, and it's the words 'believe' and 'limited' that concern me. You still haven't told me how long?"

Gabriel twisted in the direction of her voice. "I'm not sure ... but I'm positive that you'll be comfortable for at least twenty minutes. Perhaps longer."

"You were also positive about the vaccine for silver that you gave me. I itched for two weeks straight!"

Gabriel twisted his lip. "I did apologize for my miscalculation." Shaking his head, he cleared his expression. "But that was a different matter. I am confident that *this* will work."

The room fell silent as everyone considered the ramifications of him *miscalculating* on this one. She wouldn't come out of it a little itchy.

The bookcase silently pulled inward. When there was just enough space for a person to squeeze through, it stopped moving. We all held our breaths, waiting for Halina to pop her head out. Well, everyone but Gabriel was frozen in anticipation. He was breathing as normally as if he were alive, beaming with confidence as he watched the hole in the wall.

From the empty space, I heard, in Russian, *"I am not afraid of anything, damn it."*

Just when I thought she was going to spend all day in that dark hallway, her hand came out to touch the living room wall. A foot shortly erupted from the darkness, then another one. Inch by inch, she cleared the recess. No direct light was reaching her from where she stood, but she cringed anyway, averting her eyes, waiting for the pain that normally would have stopped her in her tracks. Gabriel walked over and took her hand. Gently, he urged her forward.

Concern and astonishment clear on his face, Dad stepped forward too. I couldn't tell if he was going to encourage this, or put a stop to it. Mom seemed unsure as well, but she grabbed his hand, halting him. Dad looked back at her, but stopped moving.

Nika's heart was pounding as hard as mine as we watched Gabriel escort Halina into a bright patch of sunlight ... the first sunlight she'd seen in over a century. She hesitated at the edge of the light, pulling against Gabriel's hand. Then she inhaled, lifted her chin, and stormed into the disastrous ring of rays to meet her fate head-on.

Dad dropped Mom's hand at that point, ready to surge forward and rescue Halina if needed, but Halina ... was fine.

We all stared at her wide-eyed as she lifted her hands to examine the light and shadow playing across her flesh. "Oh my God," she whispered. Lifting her head, she looked up at Gabriel beside her. "You did it." Blood-red tears formed in her eyes and trailed down her cheeks. The tears shimmered in the bright rays. I marveled at seeing my grandmother in natural lighting. While still unnaturally pale, the undead woman glowed with life in the sun. "You really did it," she repeated.

Gabriel gave her a warm smile, nodding. "Only for short periods of time, yes, but it *will* work for you." Cupping her cheek, his face filled with a tender emotion that was rare to see on him. "I will find a way for you to walk *in* the sun one day. I promise."

Halina giggled like a little girl, then threw her arms around Gabriel. Nika started crying as she watched the newly-freed vampire frolic in the sunshine. Glancing over Nika's shoulder, I saw that Mom was crying too; even Dad had tears in his eyes. Awed by Gabriel's mind and Halina's courage, I watched in silence as Halina spun in circles on the daylight-filled carpet, her long, black hair wild and free.

Finally, Imogen walked up to the pair, her pale face still in shock. "Mother? Do you feel all right?"

Halina twisted around to her daughter, then scooped her into her arms. "I feel incredible!" Sighing, she rested her head on Imogen's. In Russian, she whispered, *"This is how I wish I could have raised you ... bathed in sunlight. You deserved to have that childhood. I'm so sorry I could not give it to you."*

Imogen shook her head, and answered Halina in her native tongue. *"It wasn't your fault. It wasn't ever your fault, Mother."*

Halina nodded, and the pair hugged. Then everyone was hugging the pureblood vampire who, good or bad, had created us all. After a few minutes of joyful wonderment, Dad gave Halina one last hug and blurred away to go help Grandpa Jack with the fence. Nika and Mom went with him, to say hello to Grandma Linda. I stayed behind, wanting to speak to Halina before she had to hide away for the rest of the day.

Alanna scuffed up my hair, gave me a chilly kiss on the cheek, then blurred away to the kitchen to finish cooking lunch. I smelled bacon in the air, and bread ... and fresh blood, probably from the same pig that had supplied the bacon. If anything, our family never let any part of an animal go to waste.

Gabriel and Imogen stayed behind with Halina. Gabriel watched her intently, looking for any sign of distress, but there didn't seem to be any yet. Imogen watched her with a face full of joy. Halina was grinning more than I'd ever seen her as she examined different body parts in the sunshine. She was wearing an exceptionally tight, short skirt, and was watching how shadows formed across the curvature of her thighs when I approached her.

"Grandma?"

She immediately spun to me. A dark section of hair whipped around her face, and she grabbed a piece and smelled it. Inhaling, she murmured, "Maybe it's my imagination, but I swear I can smell the light on me." Dropping her hair, she giggled again. "It's glorious."

I smiled and nodded, happy for her, even though my thoughts had drifted somewhere else since seeing her. Halina had certain abilities that none of us had, and ... even though Dad had said no, I wanted her to use some of those abilities to help my situation—to help Raquel.

Noticing my expression, Halina stopped laughing and tilted her head. "What is it, Julian? You seem pensive. More so than usual."

With a sigh, I sat on a nearby couch. Seeing that it was draped in sunlight, Halina sat down next to me with a wide smile on her face. She was like a kid again, experiencing the warmth of the sun after an eon without it.

I couldn't even imagine the joy she must be feeling right now. It made me feel a little guilty over what I was about to ask her.

"I wanted to know ... Um ... Well, if I had a problem at school, could you help me fix it?"

Her pale eyes, eyes that matched mine, narrowed as she searched my face. "Does someone suspect something?"

Her face was all business as she asked, and I was instantly reminded of Halina's role in our family. While Nika played at being my protector, Halina was the real bodyguard when it came to our safety. She'd wipe the minds of the entire city, if necessary, to keep us safe.

I immediately shook my head. "No, no it's nothing like that." Feeling a little stupid, I mumbled, "I got into a fight with this guy at school yesterday ..."

Halina immediately relaxed, pulling her legs up on the long couch so that every inch of them was touched by the sun. "Oh." She crooked a grin at me. "Did you win?"

I heard Imogen sit down, and I knew she was listening to the conversation. Alanna was probably listening too, but neither woman commented about me fighting. I supposed they would when I was finished with Halina. I really hadn't planned on telling them all, but I needed Halina's help, and the truth was the only way I was going to get it.

Gabriel impassively stared at us while I answered Halina's question—he was far more concerned with her health than my teenage drama. "Well, Nika kind of made it a draw ... I guess." Remembering my rage, I bit out, "But I wanted to rip him apart, Grandma ... my teeth even dropped."

That immediately got Halina's attention. She straightened from her lounging position and furrowed her brow. If I'd dropped fang in front of a handful of gossiping teenagers, she'd have some serious cleanup work to do. Shaking my head, I quickly added, "No one saw ... my mouth was closed."

Halina relaxed again. She glanced over at her daughter, also in a bright patch of sunlight, then back to me. "You are a vampire, Julian. Diluted or not, your emotions are more ... profound than a human's." Raising a corner of her lip, she added, "But don't resent them for their limitations, for they are ... only human."

I smiled at her comment, then sighed, remembering what I wanted to ask her. "We were fighting over this ... girl." I swallowed after saying it out loud, and looked down. I felt my cheeks heat and immediately felt concern from Nika; I instantly tried to level out my embarrassment so she wouldn't blur back in here. I'd really rather have this conversation on my own.

When Halina didn't say anything, I peeked up at her. She only raised an eyebrow in question and waited for me to further explain. Biting my lip, I whispered, "I've got a thing for his girlfriend." Her smile widened, amused. Feeling my cheeks heat even more, I quickly added, "And he treats her like shit!"

"Julian!" Imogen and Alanna scolded at the same time. Halina chuckled, and Gabriel finally cracked a smile.

Wondering why I'd even started this humiliating conversation, I began to talk faster. "She deserves better, but for some reason she won't leave the jerk on her own. You could make her though. You could make her tell the creep to take a flying leap! Hell, you could even make that happen!"

My heart started beating harder with my impassioned words. I was breathing heavier, too, as anger and embarrassment swirled within me. I could feel Nika start to come toward me, then stop. Her concern was still there, but she'd changed her mind about running to my rescue. I was glad for it.

While I worked on breathing in and out slowly, trying to control myself, Halina coolly raised an eyebrow. "You're right ... I could."

Realizing what I'd just said, what I'd just told her to do, I swallowed and averted my eyes. Jerk or not, I didn't want Russell dead. Just ... gone. As I sorted through my shifting feelings, Halina calmly gave me an answer. "No, Julian. I will not trance him ... or her."

Leaning over my hands and knees, I exhaled long and slow. I'd expected that from her—really, I had—but it was still crushing. To be so close to an easy solution ... and then to find it was completely out of reach ... sucked. "You could make her life better," I whispered.

Halina snorted, and I looked back at her. Closing her eyes, she laid her head back, enjoying the rays of light on her face. "If I went through my nights giving better lives to miserable humans ..." she cracked an eye and looked over at me, "I'd starve to death." I frowned at her comment and she sat up straight. "They reap what they sow, Julian. It's not up to me to change that."

"But he's bad for her ..."

Smiling, Halina shook her head. "There are many things that are dangerous to humans—cigarettes, drugs, alcohol, driving, donuts ... vampires—" she glanced over to the wide windows filled with light, " ... the sun." Sighing, she returned her eyes to mine and shrugged. "Even the air she breathes every day is suspect. The very world she lives in is toxic to her, Julian. What's a crappy boyfriend compared to all that?"

I started to object, and she raised a hand to stop me. "Yes, I could make her leave her boyfriend ..." I smiled, and Halina shook her head. "But that doesn't mean she will go to you, and it doesn't mean she wouldn't find another creep to fall in love with. And before you ask ... no, I won't make her fall for you. I won't force a child to be a mindless automaton, living a life I have chosen for her. Not even for you, Grandson."

Lowering my head, I was instantly reminded of Dad's very similar conversation. I didn't want Halina to force Raquel to like me, and as much as I hated to admit it, Halina was right. Just getting Raquel away from Russell wouldn't solve the problem. She would probably just find another guy to treat her like dirt. For whatever reason, Raquel wanted that; otherwise, she would have left Russell ages ago. And I could never, ever be that kind of a jerk to her.

Lifting my jaw, Halina's face was sympathetic as she eyed me. Then she flinched and started rubbing her arm. From across the room, Gabriel's gaze narrowed as he watched his patient. "How are you feeling, my dear?"

Halina shrugged as she glanced at the sun-drenched windows. She started to say, "Fine," but then cringed and turned away from the bright light. Gabriel blurred to her side in an instant.

Reaching down, he scooped her up like a child. "It's time to go, love."

She kicked, squirming to get away. "No, just a little longer ..." Her eyes, red with unshed tears, looked over Gabriel's shoulder, to the wall of windows bathing her in warmth, and in pain. "Please, Gabriel ... it's been so long."

Imogen rushed to her mother's side while I stood beside Gabriel, trying to block as much direct light from Halina as I could. Imogen frowned in concern. "It's hurting you, Mother. You should go back downstairs." Halina hissed in a quick, pain-filled breath, her arms and legs retreating from sight so that Gabriel had to hold her like a ball.

Kissing her forehead, Gabriel murmured, "I am sorry, Halina, but the glass is only a temporary patch. I have not yet found a permanent solution to the problem, and you need to go, before your discomfort turns deadly." His face full of concern now, he blurred her back to the entrance of her underground lair. Before disappearing, he paused and let Halina take one last look at the sun she'd missed for so long. A sun she painted over and over on her canvases downstairs.

Smiling, even though her face clearly showed an escalating amount of pain, Halina leaned her head on Gabriel's shoulder. My heart broke for her as I watched a bloody tear run down her cheek. Then Gabriel dashed away with her. Not sure whether I should feel happy or sad, I put an arm around Imogen. Her smile was just as conflicted as she wrapped her arm around my waist and kissed my head.

From downstairs, deep below the earth, we both heard Halina tell Gabriel, "I saw the sun today for the first time in more decades than I care to count. You have given me a gift beyond compare." She let out a low, husky laugh as she added, "But I will try my very best to repay it ..."

Knowing exactly what she meant, I felt a wave of embarrassment begin to swell. Just as I was letting go of Imogen to go help Dad with the fence, Alanna swept back into the room. Lips twisted into a frown, she shook her head. "Don't leave just yet, Julian." She motioned to a plush chair. "We should have a talk about your fighting. Sit ... please."

With a sigh, I sat down. I knew I shouldn't have brought that up. Oh, well. This was bound to happen this weekend anyway ... might as well get it over with.

CHAPTER FIVE

Nika

I LOVED COMING out to the ranch with Mom, Dad, and Julian. I loved it so much that time seemed to fly by whenever I walked through the front doors. It seemed like only a split-second passed between helping Dad and Grandpa with the fence and packing up my things to leave.

Sighing, I slung my backpack over my shoulder. From the opulent room next to mine, I heard Julian respond to my sad sigh. "It's not like we won't be back, Nick." There was a definite smile in his voice, and a heap of humor in his mood. He knew as well as I did that we came here almost every weekend.

I took one last look at all the fine things speckled throughout my room, the physical, financial investments that the family had made, and then I walked over to Julian's room. His space was no less magnificent: a four-poster bed in a rich, deep mahogany, a matching night stand, dresser, and wardrobe closet, all adorned with an assortment of pillar candles and vases of fresh hydrangeas. Magnificent, red draperies, arranged to perfection, framed a wide bay window that took up almost an entire wall.

Watching Julian zip his backpack shut, I said with a frown, "I know. It's just ... nice here."

He peeked up at me, his light eyes reflecting a sudden spark of curiosity. Even without Julian saying it, I knew why he was silently questioning my comment. Yes, the ranch was nice, but our spread back home was equally luxurious. But luxury wasn't what I'd meant.

Clarifying, I told him, "It's nice to not have to hide, to not have to be so careful all the time." I blurred over to Julian, to punctuate my point. His only reaction to my sudden appearance in front of him was a sympathetic nod.

Heading downstairs together, we ran into Grandma Linda on the wide, elaborate staircase that dropped down to the first floor. Grandma had a bit of a hunch to her back, as age had tightened up her body, and she took her time going down the dozens and dozens of lacquered steps. Julian and I rushed to her side, each escorting her with a supportive arm under hers. Truly, either one of us could have scooped her up and carried her down, but Grandma was just like Mom and Aunt Ashley, and wanted to do as much as she could on her own. Come to think of it, aside from vampirism, the Taylor side of our family was just like the Adams side.

Patting my arm, Grandma tilted her neck to peek up at us. "Thank you, children."

It made me smile that she still saw us as little kids, zipping around the house when she was trying to get us to focus on our math assignment. "You're welcome, Grandma." Grandma's hair was the shiniest silver now, and she wore it in a bob that hung right at ear length, so she could conveniently tuck it away. I tucked a loose piece for her, and she smiled.

Mom, Dad, and the others met us in the living room. Mom hugged her mother, telling her to stop playing at being a cowgirl and start taking it easy. Grandma replied, "I'm in the last half of my life. Now's not the time to hold back." Mom had tears in her eyes as she nodded and hugged her again. I tried not to think about what that meant.

Grandpa Jack cleared his throat, then gave his son a hug. Dad patted his back, then told him, "I'm only a phone call away if you need help with anything, Dad." Then he smirked. "And I can get here really fast if I need to."

Grandpa chuckled and nodded. His hair was just as silver as Grandma's now, and as I watched my parents say goodbye to their parents, the elderly couple almost seemed like the husband and wife who ran this place. But as soon as the two of them disengaged from Mom and Dad, Grandpa was surrounded by Alanna's cool embrace, and the look of love, adoration, and contentment that passed between them was unmistakable. They were the couple who were going to be by each other's side until the very end. Even if the end never came for one of them.

Shaking the dark thoughts out of my head, I said goodbye to everyone. I hugged Halina last. Smiling at me, then at Julian, she told us, "Enjoy your schooling, children, but ... be careful of your surroundings. Be mindful of how many lives you come into contact with. When we leave this place, I'll need to blur you out of their memories."

Julian immediately frowned. I could feel the disappointment growing in him, and I knew exactly who he was thinking about. "All of them, Grandma?"

Her mouth in a firm line, Halina nodded. She glanced over Julian's shoulder at our father. "It is better ... for everyone ... if the memory is taken as quickly as possible." Her eyes flicked back to Julian, then me. "I know you care for people here, but we cannot risk them seeing you, or us, later in life. Not with our appearances never changing."

Julian lifted his chin. "That's if we decide to not take Gabriel's shot and become undead vampires. What if we do take it? What if we keep taking it? What if we decide to age like Starla? What if we decide to stay human? Or ... stay as human as we can."

Feeling his determination made me snap my head to stare at him. He was serious about this. My jaw dropped as I considered the future he'd just mapped out. If Julian decided to live a completely human life ... then he would die ... just like humans did. A hollowness filled my heart at the thought of living for eternity without him. He was my best friend. No, he was more than that. We almost shared a soul we were so close. And I didn't want to take the shot. I didn't want to age unnaturally. I wanted to be with my family for as long as I could, and that meant I had to die and become an undead vampire. So I could be like them ... so *Julian* and I could be like them. Anger flew up my spine. It mixed with shock and sadness, then transformed into loneliness. He couldn't do that to me. To *us*.

Mom stepped forward. "Julian, you don't mean that. You don't understand what you're saying."

Twisting his head to her, he dropped his eyes for a second, then raised them to hers. "Yes, I do, Mom. I completely understand what I'm saying." Feeling the tension in the room, and the well of confusion coming from me, Julian looked around with a conflicted expression on his face. Sighing, he turned back to Halina. "I don't know if that's what I want. I just ... wanted to ask the question." He looked around the room again. "Is it wrong to ask?"

Dad stepped forward and put a hand on his shoulder. "It's perfectly fine to ask, Julian." Grabbing Julian's other shoulder, Dad twisted him so he was squarely facing him. "I know exactly what you're feeling right now. I felt it too. And yes, you have options available to you that weren't available to me. And yes, if I'd had them, I might have considered what you're considering ... but then I wouldn't have what I have now." He shook his head, his eyes intense. "You have time ... a lot of time. You don't know where your life is going to go from here, so don't make that choice yet. Keep your options open." Dad sighed, then kissed Julian's head. "I promise you, son ... it will get easier to let them go."

Julian dropped his head, sadness washing over him so fast it stole my breath. I clasped his hand, silently begging him not to choose a life that left me without him.

It was painfully quiet when we were finally in the car driving home. The radio was off, and no one was speaking. The only soundtrack to the moment was the heartbeats coming from the backseat and the hum of the tires on the road. Everyone looked out the windows, lost in their own thoughts. And even though I couldn't hear those thoughts, I was sure they were all centered around Julian and his out-of-the-blue question about keeping his mortality.

Staring out the windshield, I couldn't help but notice the symbolism before me. The headlights lit the road, but only for so far. After that, the world was dark and empty, full of possibility and uncertainty—much like the paths of our own lives. While Mom and Dad had gotten through the bends and curves of their unknown road, and were now traveling down a long, straight highway, our paths were still too twisted and tangled to know which way they'd turn out.

After another moment of the silence, Julian whispered, "I won't do it. I won't take the shot. I'll be an undead vampire."

Mom sighed and bowed her head. Looking up, she locked gazes with Dad, and I saw a lifetime of love pass between them in their communicative gaze. It made me proud to be a part of them. It made me ache for a connection that intense.

Shaking her head, Mom turned around to face Julian directly behind her. Smiling, tears in her eyes, she put a hand on his knee. "You're saying that to make us happy, but you can't know yet what you will or won't do." Mom paused, then lifted her chin. "We will support whatever decision you make, Julian, and we will love you every day."

She turned around then, but not before I saw the tear roll down her cheek. I couldn't stop myself from glaring at Julian, couldn't help being irritated that he was hurting our parents because he had some stupid crush on some insipid teenage girl. Julian ignored my anger and stared out the side window.

When we got home, Mom was still upset, even though she tried to act like she wasn't. I could tell from the way Dad urged her to go upstairs that he wanted to have a private conversation. I was also sure that Mom would cry once they were alone. Dad gave me a quick kiss on the head, then sighed and gave Julian an extra-long hug. Glancing between the two of us, he shook his dark head. "Don't stay up too late. You have school tomorrow."

Once Dad disappeared into his room, and Julian and I were alone in the hallway, I turned to him and slapped his arm as hard as I could. And considering I was a vampire, the hit was exceptional. The resounding smack was satisfying, as was his cry of pain. It was well worth the backlash of feeling the pain I'd just caused.

"Jesus, Nick, what the hell?"

Hands on my hips, I spat back, "What was that about, Julian? Are you really considering dying to be with a girl who doesn't want to be with you?"

Julian immediately straightened, his jaw tightening. "No, I was considering living a normal life, and normal lives include dying." Folding his arms over his chest, he raised an eyebrow. "Don't tell me that you've never thought about it, because I know that you, the one who is so tired of hiding and lying, has thought about not having to do it anymore."

My jaw trembled as I shook my head. Sure, I'd thought about it. I was a sixteen-year-old girl who wanted to be just like all the other sixteen-year-old girls. How could I not think about it? "Not ever having to lie … The price you'd have to pay for that is too high, Julian. The only way you could live your life without ever lying … is to leave the nest. To leave the family." My eyes filled as I stared at him, my momentary anger slipping back into pain. He couldn't leave. He just couldn't. "You'd have to live without us. We'd have to live without you."

Julian sighed as he watched long tears streak down my skin. Waves of sympathy rolled off him, and shaking his head, he pulled me in for a warm hug. "It was just a split-second thought, Nick." He rubbed my back, just like Dad did when we were upset. "I'm not going anywhere."

I nodded into his shoulder, hearing his heartbeat, alive and strong beneath me. He held me until he felt my emotions leveling, then he pushed me back. Crooking a smile in the way that made Arianna sigh, he said, "You didn't have to go all Mom-zilla on me."

I laughed as I shoved him away from me. It was a long-standing joke between the two of us that Mom sort of loved to wail on Dad when she got upset. She'd never hit Dad as hard as I'd just hit Julian, and Dad usually laughed and took her attacks without complaint, but there had been a lot of smacking throughout my childhood. When I'd finally called Mom out on it a few years ago, she'd been extremely embarrassed and had made an effort to restrain herself. At least, she had when she was in front of us.

"You didn't need to upset everybody by bringing it up, Julie."

Julian looked down, shaking his head. "Yeah, I know." His pale eyes peeked up at me, apologetic. "It just ... slipped out before I could stop it."

Nodding, I rubbed the spot on his arm where I'd brutalized him, then shuffled off to bed.

I WAS THE last one to wake up Monday morning; I could feel and hear everyone else downstairs. Rolling onto my side, I collided with Spike and reconsidered. The old pup was still asleep as he lay beside me. I gently stroked his graying fur, careful not to wake him. He used to come out to the ranch with us all the time, but we'd started leaving him at home recently. Halina had jokingly told us that we should keep bringing him since he was slower and easier for her to catch now. Well, I thought she was kidding. She wouldn't really nibble on our dog. We watched him very closely whenever he was there, though, just in case.

I gave him a soft kiss, listening to his heavy, wheezing breath, then popped out of bed and got ready for my day. Downstairs, I could hear Julian having a quiet conversation with our parents. He was apologizing, again, for upsetting them yesterday. They were telling him not to worry about it, that he had every right to decide how he wanted to live his life.

Sighing, I shook my head and made my way to the bathroom. I was halfway there when I heard Mom stop mid-sentence and say, "Good morning, Nika."

I yawned. "Good mor ... ning ..."

Dad and Julian chuckled at my answer, and I shook my head again. Normal families waited until they actually *saw* each other to talk to one other, right? My family had a lot of closed-doors conversations.

And as I turned on the water to the shower, those conversations resumed. Dad switched from Julian's comment yesterday to Julian's fighting Friday. "If he comes up to you again, just walk away, okay? There's too much at stake for you to start something with a human."

Julian sighed, his mood resigned. "Yeah, I know."

Dad added, "And please, try to stay away from his girlfriend. I know it's hard, but if she's with *him*, then she shouldn't be with you."

Julian didn't say anything to Dad's comment, but I did. Under my breath, I murmured, "Amen to that."

Julian didn't hear my barely-there speech with the noise from the water—our vampire ears just weren't enhanced enough to pick up the slight sound amongst the noise. Dad heard me just fine, though. "Nika," he warned.

"Sorry." I rolled my eyes as I washed my hair. Yeah, most families didn't have conversations in the shower, I was sure.

By the time I joined my family downstairs, it was nearly time to go. Mom shoved a piece of toast at me, telling me to, "Eat something," while she sipped on her blood cocktail. I grudgingly took the toast, even though I really wanted a glass of what she had, instead of a hard piece of bread in my dry mouth.

Mom's brown eyes watched me as she tipped back her drink. After swallowing it, she examined how much was left in the glass, then handed it to me. My spirits brightened instantly as her chilly hand pressed the warm cup into mine. "Here, I'm full, you can have it."

As Mom wiped her mouth, I tipped the glass back. My fangs dropped as soon as the tangy goodness hit my tongue. It was fresh from the ranch, a new batch that we'd brought back with us, and it was incredible. I might not need it like my mom and dad, but I thoroughly enjoyed it when I got it.

Having downed it too fast, I burped up an air bubble when I was done. Julian smirked at me. "Nice, Nick. Real ladylike."

Fangs still extended, I gave him a quick "bite me" hiss. Playing along, Julian dropped his fangs and growled at me. He'd been working on perfecting that deep, throaty growl that Dad had, the kind that made the hairs on the back of your neck stand up. He was getting pretty good at it, too, and a shiver went through me. Feeling a little out of my league, I pulled my fangs back up. Julian immediately started laughing.

"Stop it, you two, we need to get going," Mom scolded, zipping upstairs to get the rest of her stuff.

Dad, casually sipping on his blood, watched her leave, then looked over at Julian. Baring his fangs in a terrifying, threatening way, Dad rumbled a low growl that vibrated deep inside my chest. It made my tiny hiss and Julian's little rumble pale in comparison. I had to rub my arm to calm the goosebumps that popped up. Dad winked at us when he was done. "That's how you do it, son."

Mom blurred back into the room and almost smacked Dad's arm before stopping herself. "Quit teaching them bad manners." She twisted back to me as Dad smiled and slid his arm around her waist. "You guys ready?"

Shoving the toast into my mouth, I nodded. Julian stood up and looped his backpack over his shoulder. While his mood was mainly amused, thanks to Dad's little display, he was also suffering from a mild case of nerves. Whether that was about seeing Russell at school or about seeing Raquel, I had no idea. I rubbed his back sympathetically either way.

We all piled into Dad's car, and he dropped us off at Starla's house so she could take us to school and he could continue on to work with Mom. Starla opened the door wearing lounge pants and an almost see-through tank top. A part of me wanted to cover Julian's eyes ... and Dad's. His gaze was staying firmly focused on her face though. "So, you'll pick them up on time today ... like we talked about?"

Starla shrugged as she stretched, not seeming to care too much about what she and Dad had talked about over the weekend. "Sure thing, V.B."

Dad shook his head at Starla's nickname for him, then turned to us. "Have a good day at school, kids." He kissed my head. "Good luck on your homework, Nika." Waving at Julian, he headed back to the car to Mom. She was leaning through the open window, watching him jog toward her. Dad slowed as he approached her, then ducked his head through the window to give her a quick kiss. Mom was giggling as he trotted around to the driver's side.

Starla groaned as she opened the front door for us to come inside. "God, those two are still sickeningly sappy." Glancing back at my brother and me, she murmured, "I hope the two of you don't end up like them. I might have to stake myself."

Julian looked over at me and rolled his eyes as Starla turned away from us. Striding into the living room, her walk sultry, Starla plopped down on the couch. Jacen walked into the room as she sat down. Glass of blood in hand, he looked between his girlfriend and us. Remembering that I saw him shirtless a few days ago made my face heat. Feeling my embarrassment, Julian grinned and looked away. Damn bond.

"Uh, Starla, sweetheart ... aren't you forgetting something?" Jacen turned to Starla, who was examining her nails on the couch.

She peeked up at him, flicked her eyes down his body, then smirked. "No, I'm pretty sure I took care of that this morning."

If an undead vampire could still blush, I was sure Jacen would have turned bright red. Instead, he immediately looked away from her and took a quick sip of blood. Starla chuckled, while Julian and I glanced at each other.

Jacen was a lot more reserved than Starla, and her risqué comments usually made him seem mortified. But as he peeked back at her with the corner of his eye, I wondered if he actually enjoyed her provocative talk. I tried not to think too hard about it, since these two were sort of family to me.

Swallowing his drink, Jacen glanced at us. "Shouldn't you be getting them to school?" Fangs extended, he looked back at Starla. "They'll be tardy again."

Starla rested her spiky hair back on the couch and sighed. While she seemed liked she'd just gotten out of bed, her hair and makeup were flawless. Of course, she hated not looking her best, so she'd probably slept that way. "They'll be fine. I need to work on this hang nail."

She resumed working on her nails, and Julian and I both dropped our bags to the floor. Procrastinating was nothing new when it came to Starla. Jacen set down his glass and walked up behind her. It really seemed like Jacen was Starla's brother. They looked so much alike, or had, at least, when Starla was a lot younger. But Jacen wasn't related to her, and was, in fact, quite older than her, and his power and influence were clear when he approached her and put his hands on her shoulders. Leaning down, he whispered, "Gabriel wouldn't want you to make them wait."

Starla glared up at him, annoyed. Jacen shrugged, and she sighed and stood up. "Fine," she muttered, "I guess the nail problem can wait until I get back. I wouldn't want to disappoint Father." She strode over to us, snatching her keys from a table in the entryway. "You guys ready?" She didn't even wait for our response before opening the door and heading outside.

Used to Starla's behavior, Julian and I immediately picked up our bags and followed her. Starla did have moments of warmth, but, much like Halina, they were few and far between. Nobody was about to tell either woman that they were similar in that regard though; they hated being compared to one another.

Jacen waved as we left. "Have fun at school, guys."

Starla took us down side streets to get to school, so we ended up not driving past the hot neighbor's house. It made me a little sad; I was dying to catch another glimpse of him. We'd driven past his house on the way home from the ranch last night, but we hadn't seen anyone, and the moving truck had been gone. I had to believe he and his dad were busy putting everything they owned away. Moving sucked. Maybe he would venture outside when he was done unpacking, though, and then I'd get another peek at him. One good thing about the weather here—it stayed decent well into the fall. That left a lot of time in the next few weeks for outdoor activities. And he'd seemed like the athletic type at first glance. He had a lean enough body anyway.

I started to smile, thinking about that trim physique, imagining the tight lines that he surely had. I got carried away, thinking about those deep, dark eyes, and had to adjust how I was sitting. Julian, sitting behind me in the back seat, cleared his throat, his mood annoyed. He frowned at me at the same time I frowned at him, and, shaking my head, I tried to clear my mind ... and my emotions. I should be more careful with my thoughts. They stirred feelings that I didn't want to share with Julian, especially since I knew how awkward it was to feel those same feelings coming from him when he fantasized about Raquel. And I shouldn't be fantasizing about a man who was a stranger anyway. That wasn't like me.

Starla pulled up to the front of our school, weaving her way in-between a couple of busses that were letting kids out. Mom and Dad had talked about us taking the bus, but we had begged them to not make us get on one; we'd rather walk. No kids our age used the bus system. Not if they could help it.

Revving her engine, Starla glanced over at me, then back at Julian. "All right, we're here ... and right on time." A few kids in the yard looked over at Starla and her flashy car, and some of the guys tossed playful smiles at the hot, older blonde who was playing our mom. Ugh.

"Thanks," I mumbled, getting out of the car; Julian was a step behind me. Arianna appeared from somewhere inside the crowd and waggled her fingers at me ... or at Julian, I really wasn't sure.

Looking through the glass at Starla, Arianna smiled and gave her a wave. "Hi, Mrs. Adams."

Starla gave her a half-grin and a tepid wave. "It's *Ms*. Adams," she murmured, a little sullenly.

Once our doors were closed, Starla stepped on the gas and took off. A couple of kids had to back up to not get run over by her. Arianna stepped to my side, frowning. "Your mom is always in such a hurry ..."

Sighing, I looked back at my best friend. "It's the plight of being a single mom." Julian snorted, then sniffed to cover it.

Arianna's eyes immediately locked onto him. "Hey, Julian. Feeling better?" Her wide eyes drank in my brother as she pointed to the mostly healed line on his face, the last residual evidence of his fight on Friday.

I was 100 percent certain that if Julian leaned over and decided to lock lips with Arianna right now, she'd let him. But, of course, Julian didn't see Arianna that way, so he only shrugged as he looked over her shoulder, searching for Raquel. "Yeah, I'm fine ... thanks."

I knew the second Julian spotted Raquel. Not only did his heartbeat triple, but his emotions swirled all over the place—happy, excited, sad, wistful. The flood gave me a bit of a stomachache and I pushed him away from me. Sometimes distance helped ... a little. Julian looked back at me, understanding. "Sorry," he murmured, embarrassment now joining the mix.

I shook my head while Arianna asked, "Sorry for what?"

Pushing Julian farther away from us, I told him, "Just go ... even out. Please."

He sighed, then nodded and trotted off in the opposite direction of Raquel. I was glad for that; he really needed to keep his distance from the unavailable woman.

"Why did you send him away?" Arianna asked. "I was just about to make my move," she added, playfully wriggling her eyebrows.

Her statement made me grin. Arianna had never openly made a move on Julian ... just flirted with him at every opportunity. Not knowing how else to explain the weird exchange that had just happened, I told her, "Sorry, I just need some space from him." I rolled my eyes and looped my arm around hers. "It was a *long* weekend."

Arianna laughed at my comment, like she understood sibling rivalry. I felt guilty for saying it though. I didn't like making it seem as if Julian was an annoyance I wanted away from, but the real situation was too complicated to explain, and would be hurtful to Arianna. It was kinder to stay quiet and let her think she had a shot with Julian, because, who knows, maybe his obsession would stop one day and he would see Arianna in a different light. It would be pretty awesome if they ended up together—my two best friends. But with how Julian was feeling right now, that wish was a long-shot.

I unintentionally kept tabs on Julian throughout my day. I tried to respect his privacy, but whenever there was a spike in his emotions, I catalogued it. For the most part, his day was pretty mellow, but there was an edge of sadness to him. I figured he was watching Raquel and Russell from a distance, like usual, and he was trying really hard to not interfere. I gave him as much sympathy and encouragement as I could whenever his mood shifted to the low side.

Thinking about my emotive brother made me laugh out loud during a discussion in health class, when someone made the comment that boys were completely void of feelings. Several girls turned to stare at my outburst, and Arianna giggled as the teacher shushed me, but I couldn't help it. I might only be attached to *one* teenage boy, so maybe I couldn't speak for the entire gender, but I wanted to assure the sullen girl in my class that boys felt just as much turmoil as girls. They were just better at ignoring it. Usually.

After English class, where I turned in my paper with a huge smile on my face, since my B.S. family story pretty much kicked ass, I trudged out to the football field to wait for my "mother" with Arianna. This time, Julian met up with us right away. I cringed when I noticed that his best friend had tagged along.

Long and lanky, Trey was sort of an odd friend for Julian. He was outgoing and flirtatious where Julian was ... quieter. By the way Trey amused Julian, though, I figured that was part of the reason they were bonded. Opposites attracted, even in friendships.

Trey also liked to indulge in ... all natural herbs. On a near-daily basis, he had a faint pot odor about him. Nothing normal humans would probably pick up on, but we sure did. My parents didn't like that at all, but Julian defended him, saying pot wasn't as bad as other drugs kids our age did, and Trey's home life kind of sucked, so pot was how he dealt with it. But Julian's most effective argument was the fact that Trey's overabundant marijuana usage had made him dull enough that he probably wouldn't notice if we "slipped up" and said or did something we shouldn't around him. Mom and Dad had semi-okayed the friendship with Trey, but they were watchful of Julian. I'd caught mom sniffing his dirty laundry on more than one occasion. Gross.

"Ladies." Trey plopped down on the grass, wedging his way inbetween Arianna and me, and tossed his arms around us both. Arianna rolled her eyes, but giggled too.

"Trey ... Julian ..." Arianna's face was turned toward Trey as she spoke, but her eyes were locked on my brother as he walked around behind us. Ignoring her stares, Julian sat down by me.

Rolling my shoulders to dislodge Trey's arm from my body, I looked over at the man now glued to my side. "There's an entire football field to sit on. Why are you bruising my hip?"

Trey laughed. "Because you two have the most beautiful hips in town." He leaned into me until his face was about an inch away; the smell coming off him nearly gave me a buzz. "Why wouldn't I want to get stuck between them?"

Arianna scoffed and pushed Trey's shoulder away. Julian groaned and tossed some grass at his friend. "Man, that's my sister you're talking about."

I took a more proactive approach to Trey's comment. I yanked on his shirt with one hand and shoved on his back with the other—forcing him away from us. I used just a tiny bit of my extra strength and he rolled pretty far down the embankment. Julian stared at me wide-eyed, alarm streaking through him. I'd made it look as natural as possible, but it was still an impressive feat for a girl my size to physically remove a boy Trey's size.

Luckily for us, Trey was a natural clown and Arianna assumed that he'd done it on purpose. She laughed at Trey as he caught himself. "Dork." Trey seemed a little caught off guard, but since we were on a slope, he didn't appear to put too much thought into how I'd done that. He laughed just as much as Arianna.

Julian relaxed as he glanced between the two amused—and not suspicious—humans. He frowned at me, though, and I could see the disapproval in his eyes as much as I could feel it. Lifting one shoulder in apology, I murmured, "Sorry, used a little too much oomph."

Julian sniggered at my comment, shaking his head. "You could say that again," he whispered, under the humans' hearing.

As Trey rejoined us, adjusting his stocking cap so that it covered most of his chin-length hair, a horn honked. We all turned to look at Starla's shiny sports car waiting for us, surprisingly right on time. Trey whistled. "Damn, that car is just as hot as your mom, Julian."

Standing, Julian smacked his friend's arm. "First my sister, now my mom?"

Trey blinked at Julian's expression. "What? Your family's hot." Arianna giggled, her eyes drifting over Julian's face.

Standing up, I grabbed Julian's elbow. "Come on, we gotta go. It's library day."

Waving to our friends, we jogged over to Starla's car. Pulling down her bug-like sunglasses, Starla looked us over as we hopped in the car. "Make sure you tell Papa Adams that I was on time today."

Closing my door, I grinned ear-to-ear at her. "Library please."

Starla popped her glasses back up, then snapped a bubble with her gum. "Sure, it's your afternoon to waste."

Starla sped over to the city library, dropping me off before zipping home with Julian. I spent every Monday afternoon there, checking out new books, returning old ones. Sure, I had amassed an obscene amount of electronic books on my tablet, but there was something about bound books— the slight smell of dust, the crinkle of the page as it turned, the yellowing of the paper as it aged, the stains, spills and tears, each one with a story that was completely aside from the book's story. Sometimes I found that examining used books was nearly as interesting as reading them.

And really, there was no better place, besides the ranch, to spend an afternoon. The Salt Lake City library was a work of art, as glorious on the outside as it was on the inside. It was six stories of angled glass, holding over a half-million books, more if you considered the stores of electronic books that you could download. There was a curving wall that embraced the huge plaza outside. You could walk up that huge ramp to a garden on the rooftop—such an incredible sight, such an amazing view. And with shops and cafes on the ground level, and reading galleries above, the library was more a small city than just a place to go and read books. It was one of my favorite places.

Inhaling the scent of thousands of pages of aged paper, I slowly meandered through the tall shelves, wondering what I was in the mood for today. Knowledge? Romance? Fantasy? Murder? I could have it all if I wanted, and how many times in life could a person have it all? That limitless feeling gave me an odd sense of empowerment as I walked through the shelves.

Thinking of Julian and his latest episode, I made my way over to the self-help section and browsed through the hundreds of titles available. It was a little alarming how many books had been written on how to live a better life. Being human wasn't easy. And being a human who was part vampire was even less easy. Unfortunately, there weren't any books on that subject. There were, however, a few that I thought might help Julian deal with his fears better. That was, if I could ever get him to read a book that didn't include pictures.

Wondering if the topic was appropriate for him, I picked up a book on how to deal with abandonment. I was examining the beautiful swan on the cover when I felt and heard a person behind me. I tensed, feeling my personal space being compromised, right as the person spoke. "Interesting choice. Were you abandoned?"

Turning, I prepared to tell the stranger intruding on my solitude to mind their own business. Then I faced said stranger and all words left me. It was the super-hot neighbor boy who'd moved in last week … the one who had been filling my mind during my quiet moments.

"What?" I mumbled, speech an overwhelming prospect now that the real-life version of him was superseding my fantasy version … in a good way. My memory hadn't quite captured the depth of his brown eyes, the exact shade of his dark hair, the rough stubble that made him seem way too old for me.

Smiling, he pointed at the book in my hands. "The book ... is it for you?"

Feeling heat flush my cheeks, I shoved the book back on the shelf. "No, my brother ..." I immediately shut my mouth. I couldn't tell a complete stranger that my brother was abducted as a child and still had panic attacks about it. "No, I was just looking."

Seeing my obvious embarrassment, the boy backed up, hands raised. "Sorry, I didn't mean to intrude ... that was really rude. It's just ... it's one of my favorites, and I highly recommend it ..." he raised one corner of his lip and my heart sped up a little, "if you were doing more than looking."

His eyes never leaving mine, he reached up on the shelf and grabbed the book that I'd haphazardly replaced. Still silent, he handed it back to me. "Thank you," I whispered, cognizant of the stillness in the air between us.

"Do you remember me?" he asked, stepping toward me again.

Hell yes, I remember you. Furrowing my brows, I shook my head and hoped my cheeks weren't bright red. "I'm not sure. You look kind of familiar, but ... ?" I bit my lip as my heart thudded in my chest.

The boy looked down, then back up at me. The darkness of his eyes instantly captured me. I wanted to swoon ... and I wasn't even entirely positive what "swooning" meant. "I met you last week, sort of, when your family offered to help move my family in." He smiled, and a small sigh escaped me. God, he was gorgeous. I immediately coughed a little to cover it.

Smiling wider, he extended his hand. "Hunter."

I blinked and backed up a step. "Excuse me?"

He frowned at my reaction and lowered his hand. "My name ... is Hunter."

My cheeks felt on fire as embarrassment coursed through me. In my family, "hunter" had an entirely different meaning than someone's name. Stepping back up to him, I reached for his lowered hand. "Oh, sorry ... mine's Nika."

CHAPTER SIX

Nika

I WAS TRYING not to stare at Hunter. He was so intriguing, though, I couldn't stop myself from watching his every action, big or small. As we walked toward checkout, his low voice tingled my alert ears and my curious eyes strayed to his body. There was a sleekness to the way he moved, a power and grace that awkward teenage boys didn't have. There was a similar confidence in his smile as he made small talk with me. Also, unlike boys my age, he appeared to know exactly who he was, and had accepted himself ages ago. Not that he seemed to be conceited, thinking he was the be-all and end-all or anything. No, he was just comfortable with himself.

Maybe I was coming to a snap judgment about his ego, but I didn't think so. Just the fact that he'd recommended a very personal book about recovery without any trace of embarrassment made me believe in his maturity. Regardless of his actual age, Hunter had left boyhood behind a while ago.

Realizing I couldn't fantasize about the neighbor any more than Julian could fantasize about Raquel, and for a lot of the same reasons—I'd probably shake Hunter's confident swagger right to the floor if I dropped fang in front of him—made a wistful sigh escape me. *This couldn't happen.*

Tilting his head, Hunter paused in the middle of his story. "I'm sorry. I'm boring you, aren't I?" Again, he didn't seem embarrassed—just curious and courteous.

Smiling, I shook my head. "No, I actually think you're right. Dogs are far superior pets than cats." I didn't mention that I felt that way because cats had proven to be too skittish to handle being around vampires. I still hadn't successfully held one.

Placing his stack of books on the counter, Hunter gestured with his dark head to the title that had started our little conversation: *Where the Red Fern Grows*. When I'd noticed him carrying it, I'd confessed that it was my mother's favorite book. He'd gone on to tell me that he'd wanted a dog ever since reading it, but he moved around so much with his dad that he'd never been able to have one. I'd had to tell him about Spike after that, and he'd spent the last several minutes talking about the virtues of man's best friend.

"Yeah, there's nothing on this Earth more loyal than a dog." He paused, his eyes losing focus as he thought about something. "Except family," he whispered.

My smile was huge as I silently agreed with him. His eyes flicked over my face, drinking me in, and my heart thudded painfully. I was light as air as he stared at me. So light, I was sure I was going to float away at any moment. It was the most wonderful feeling I'd ever had, and more than anything right now, I wanted to touch him, and I wanted him to touch me.

He took a step closer to me as I placed my stack of books beside his. Not thinking about what I was doing, I brushed my thigh against his hand swinging freely at his side. Most humans wouldn't have caught it, but I felt his thumb intentionally stroke my leg. I thought I might pass out.

"Card?"

A gruff voice swung Hunter's and my attention around. A woman with a tighter-than-tight bun was giving us a blank stare, hand extended. "Library card?" she repeated.

Hunter gave her a warm smile, then reached into his back pocket for his wallet. Not quite as warm, I frowned at the woman disrupting my moment, then dug into my school bag for my card.

Stepping out of the doors of the library into the main walkway of the massive building, I glanced over at the quiet reading areas above the shops and cafes. Normally, I'd grab my new books, buy some hot chocolate, and head up to one of the plush chairs along the solid glass wall. From there, I had a spectacular view of the city on one side of me, and floors and floors of books on the other side. Pretty much heaven. I wasn't sure if Hunter wanted to sit and read right now, though, and since I wasn't ready to say goodbye to him yet, I was willing to forgo my usual routine for this one, special Monday afternoon.

Hunter's dark eyes were sweeping over the architecture of the place, and he let out a low whistle. "This is sure impressive."

I looked back at the wall in front of us, trying to see it from the perspective of a new visitor. Hunter was right; it was a sight to see. Mainly made from glass, all the different shop entrances were identical. Thick columns separated the entrances, rising to the roof. With the way the columns intersected with the floors of each level, the entire wall sort of reminded me of a giant checkerboard. And that was just the one wall. The levels behind us had curving stairways that led to the floors above, each level holding more specific and rare books. As a result, the upper levels were a lot quieter than the lower levels. I hung out up there sometimes, just to get some silence. Well, as much silence as a super-hearing vampire could get in a place like this. I was used to the buzz, though, and tuned it out when Hunter spoke to me again.

"Want to take a walk outside with me? I want to check out the water wall."

I nodded, both eager to show him my city's beauties and spend a little more time with him. Hunter looked up as we passed underneath the main piece of art in the library's indoor plaza. It was a mobile consisting of thousands of metal books suspended at different levels. The books were all in various stages of being open, and they resembled a swarm of butterflies. Amazing. Hunter whistled again, and it made me smile that he seemed to appreciate how beautiful the world could be. Boys my age tended to overlook it.

As we approached the glass doors leading outside, I began to wonder again about his age. If he was too old ... well, I should probably just say goodbye right now. Dad would never let me hang out with someone Dad's age. Or the age he appeared to be anyway.

Walking into the sun-lit plaza, I smiled up at Hunter. "So ... you're new here. Are you going to be enrolling in school soon?" I held my breath, hoping that was a subtle enough way to ask him his age. I hated that it sort of pointed out my age, but ... I had to know.

Hunter tilted his head back, smiling as the sun warmed him. It was sweet, watching him enjoy the little things; it made my stomach flutter. Glancing over at me, he asked, "Do you mean high school?" I nodded, biting my lip. Straightening his head, Hunter frowned. "No, Dad homeschooled me. I graduated ... a while ago."

As we approached a reflecting pool in front of the glass wall of the library, we stopped. A slight downward turn still on his lips, Hunter quietly asked, "Are you still in high school?"

I wanted to deny it, since I didn't feel like a high schooler, but it was a fact I couldn't ignore. And I hated lying anyway. It was no way to start a relationship ... not that Hunter and I were starting one. But while there were some things I *had* to lie about, to protect myself and my family, my age wasn't one of them. "Yeah ..." I inhaled a big breath, then told him, "I'm sixteen ... I'll be seventeen in June."

Hunter's eyes flicked up as he did some math in his head. After a second, his smile returned, along with his captivating eyes. "Well, I'm twenty ... so we're only four years apart. If I were still a senior, you'd be a freshman. That's not so bad."

I couldn't keep back the smile at the way he'd phrased our age difference. It didn't seem so unreasonable that way. Besides, I'd be done with high school in another year. Then it wouldn't matter at all. Of course, then I would be moving away ...

Shaking my head to clear those thoughts, I pointed over to the waterfall he'd wanted to see. "Come on ... the wall's over here." I extended my hand for him to take, my heart beating so hard I thought for sure even his human ears could hear it. Hunter glanced at my hand, smiled wider, then took it.

The warmth of his skin on mine was unlike anything I'd ever experienced before. I'd held hands with boys a time or two before, but none of those instances compared to this. The last boy I'd held hands with had been suffering from a severe case of nerves—I'd smelled it—and his hands had been really clammy. I'd wanted to instantly pull away and scrub my palm dry on my clothes, but out of politeness, I'd resisted. Hunter, though ... his confidence extended to his skin; he was warm, dry and soft. I wanted to stroke his hand with my thumb, but I didn't want to be too forward, so I forcefully halted a completely different instinct.

We stepped in front of the wall he'd wanted to see, hands still clasped together. I felt like I should release him since we were here, but he didn't let go, so I didn't either. Feeling a joy racing through me that I'd never felt before, I slyly observed Hunter while he watched the never-ending supply of water cascade down the granite wall of steps.

"It's incredible. And so relaxing. I could listen to this sound all day long."

I smiled up at him, loving the fact that he could be so open with a person he didn't even know. It made him seem vulnerable and fearless, all at the same time. "Me too," I whispered, stepping into his side. "This is one of my favorite places in the city."

His fingers tightened in my hand as he looked down at me. There was something in his eyes as we locked gazes. Interest? Peace? Appreciation? I wasn't sure, but it made me feel ... giddy. In the back of my mind, I felt Julian's curiosity, and I was sure he would ask me about my mood later, but I didn't care. Julian could endure it for now. There was no way was I squelching this feeling for him.

Hunter shook his head a little, like he was shaking himself out of a trance, then he returned his gaze to the water. Thinking of something he'd said earlier, I told him, "I was home-schooled for a long time too. Up until my freshman year."

Hunter looked back at me and smiled. "Sucks a little, doesn't it?"

Laughing, I nodded. "It had its moments." Thinking back to my years of solitude on the ranch with my family, I sighed. "It had its great moments too, though."

Hunter eyed me for a moment, then nodded. His gaze floated up to my hair, and his expression reminded me of the way Halina had watched the sunlight bounce across her skin this weekend; he just seemed to be savoring the vision of me surrounded in prisms of light. "This is my favorite time of day," he whispered, his eyes returning to mine.

Nerves tingled my stomach. The way he was unflinchingly looking at me, like he was seeing everything about me ... it was more than I was used to outside of my family. Giggling to offset the intensity, I looked up at the sky and estimated the time. "4:15?"

Hunter laughed at my comment. "Well, maybe not this *exact* time, but afternoons in general. When the world is at its brightest." He shrugged. "Everything seems so full of promise during the day."

Tilting my head, I raised an eyebrow. "Sweaty tourists complaining about the heat makes you think of ... promise?" He gave me a grin that nearly melted me. I was about to add onto my comment when I felt something. Or rather, I felt some*one*.

Frowning, I looked over my shoulder. "Speaking of 4:15 ..." Feeling my mom and dad nearly to the library, I sighed as I looked back at Hunter. "I have to go. My...Teren ... is going to be here soon."

Hunter's eyes shifted over my shoulder, to where I'd just been looking. He twisted his lips. "Teren?" His eyes returned to mine. "Your boyfriend?"

My eyes went wide, and I laughed out loud. I immediately stifled it. I might not feel like a teenager, but I could sometimes act like one ... and I didn't want to act young in front of Hunter. "No, no, definitely not." Running a hand through my hair, I thought about what to call him. Dad had never really narrowed down the right verbiage for me. "Teren's the guy who asked to help you and your dad move. He takes care of me and my brother when my mom's away. He's ... sort of family."

Having to halfway lie to Hunter made some of my high fade, but his corresponding grin perked it right back up. "Ah, I remember him. So, how are you 'sort of' family?"

I cringed. "It's one of those complicated, through-marriage things."

Hunter nodded. "Gotcha. Well, I guess all that really matters is the 'not boyfriend' part." He squeezed, then released my hand; I had to stop myself from reaching for his fingers again. "I should get going too. I'm on my bike today, and it's a bit of a ride back home from here."

He indicated behind himself, and I glanced over at a bicycle stand next to the library—the metal piece of art was literally the words "bike rack." A lone bike, which must have been Hunter's, was parked in the "b." Dad would at least approve of Hunter's vehicle choice, if not his age.

Hunter's voice brought my attention back to him. "It was nice to meet you, Nika." His eyes flicked around the plaza. "Thanks for showing me around."

I could feel my cheeks heating as I smiled. "I didn't really show you very much."

He raised an eyebrow. "Maybe we can meet again then. How about Friday?"

I nodded. "It's a date."

I held my breath after I said it. I hadn't meant to call it a date, but if he was willing, I was willing. Hunter dropped his eyes to the stone beneath our feet. "I'd like that, Nika." His eyes lifted to mine. "Very much."

My heart fluttering wildly, I could only give him a stupid wave before trotting off to where I could feel my father stopped and waiting for me. Dad would honk soon if I didn't start moving toward him. And if I still didn't move, he'd come get me. I really didn't want him to see me making plans with Hunter. Only four years apart or not, Dad would immediately put a stop to me ever seeing him again.

I hopped into the back seat of Dad's car with a huge smile on my face. Mom and Dad both glanced at me. As Dad slowly drove away, Mom commented on my mood. "You're awfully chipper. Good day today?"

Mellowing my smile, I did my best to appear like today was just any average Monday. And for the most part, it had been. "Aren't I usually chipper?"

Mom grinned, turning back around to face Dad; subconsciously, their hands met and clasped together. It instantly reminded me of holding Hunter's hand, and a tiny bit of my smile returned. "Extra chipper then," Mom added, gazing at Dad.

Dad smiled as he glanced over at her. Watching them look at each other was like watching dialogue in a movie with the sound off; things were being said, I just couldn't hear it. There was so much depth to their silent conversations. And yes, most of it was ooey-gooey, just like Starla had complained about, but it was rare in this day and age, and there was something to be said for romanticism. Or maybe I was just having a sappy moment after my little encounter at the library. Whatever the reason, my parents' mutual affection made my smile widen. "Nope, just a normal day."

When we got to our Bavarian mini-palace in the 'burbs, Mom received a phone call from Aunt Ashley and went upstairs to talk to her. I yelled a "love you, miss you, Auntie," into the phone as Mom skipped up the stairs. Aunt Ash still lived in California with her husband. We'd visited her just a handful of weeks ago, during summer break, but I still missed her. Julian matched my sentiment, then started heading up the stairs, probably to put away his backpack since Mom had scolded him about it last week. I heard Mom laugh into the phone then call back, "Ash misses you guys, too."

As Mom and Ashley settled into a conversation, Mom sighing as she sat on her bed, Dad twisted to face me. "I think I lost my helper for the evening." Smiling, he raised a dark brow at me. "Want to fill in for your mom? Help me make dinner?"

I nodded at Dad, still on a small high from my boy-next-door encounter. Removing my backpack from my shoulder, I told him, "Sure. I'll go put this away and be right back."

As I was turning, Dad slowly said, "I'm making chicken. Do you want to do it?"

Inhaling, I twisted back to Dad. I knew exactly what he meant by that. Dad bought live chickens, kept them in a coop in the backyard. When Dad said he was "making chicken," he meant from scratch—from being alive and well, to plucking and cooking. I was used to it, though; he'd done this my entire life. But Dad usually did the killing, draining them dry in a matter of seconds. Julian and I had never actually killed anything. We'd never even bitten a living animal. The blood we drank was poured into containers for us, and it felt different drinking it that way. Not quite so animal.

I bit my lip, thinking about what it would feel like to take the life of a creature, even a stupid creature like a chicken. The vampire in me drooled at the idea of fresh, from-the-vein blood, but I was more human than vampire ... and I just couldn't do it.

Shaking my head, I frowned. "No, I don't want to do that." Feeling bad that I couldn't live up to the non-human side of my nature, I dropped my eyes from his. "Sorry."

Dad blurred in front of me, lifting my chin. "Hey, you don't have to be sorry for that ... ever. Respecting life is honorable, Nika." He smiled at me, lifting my mood with his acceptance. "I'm proud of you, no matter what side of yourself you embrace, okay?"

While I nodded, Dad added, "Besides, your mom won't do it either."

From upstairs we both heard, "That's because it's disgusting!"

Dad rolled his eyes, then walked to the slider that led out back. "I'll meet you in the kitchen when the chicken's ready to be cooked."

Exhaling in relief, I nodded again and turned to go put my stuff away. Mom was laughing with Ashley over the chicken conversation when Julian popped his head into my room. Leaning against my door frame, his face was as amused and intrigued as his mood. "So ... good time at the library. You find a really, really, *really* good book or something?"

He chuckled a little as I scowled at him. "We really need to nip this bond in the butt," I muttered, glad that Mom was so busy with Ashley that she wasn't paying attention.

Julian grimaced as he sat on my bed. "Preaching to the choir, sis. Preaching to the choir." Leaning back on his hands, he searched my face with curious eyes. "So, what did happen to you?"

Listening closely to Mom, I whispered, "I ran into the neighbor boy from down the street." Sitting beside Julian, I opened my heart to the feelings that had been surging around me all afternoon.

Julian closed his eyes for a second as my emotions pummeled him, then he shook his head. "The guy with the five o'clock shadow? Nika ... is he even our age?"

I shrugged, not wanting to talk about this with Mom nearby ... or Dad. He was in the backyard, and preoccupied in his own way, but he could still hear us. "Close enough." For my parents' benefit, I added, "He just pointed out some really good books for me. Gave me some helpful advice, then let me show him around the library." Glancing through the wall to Mom's room, I added, "You know how much I love exploring that place."

Julian frowned, seeing right through my misleading comments. "Yeah, I know ... I felt it."

Putting my hand on his arm, I mouthed, "Later."

Julian nodded, understanding, but he was concerned, and I was sure it was the "close enough" comment that had him on edge. Well, that and the swarm of feelings I'd let flow from me just now. They were still coursing through me; just thinking about my afternoon had me elated. Julian sighed as he stood up.

"We should ask Gabriel again about our bond. There's got to be a way to block it." His face was solemn, and I felt the same reluctance that he felt. As annoying as our connection was at times, we'd had this bond since birth. Severing it would be ... hard. But continuing to keep it as we grew and matured would be hard too. There were feelings that we were each beginning to have that were *really* private. And ... sex ... God, I couldn't even think about sharing that moment with Julian connected to me. I'd rather stay a virgin my entire life.

I nodded, my face equally solemn. "I know. It's time."

Julian lowered his head, a small amount of sadness sweeping over him. I felt it too, the loss, and gave him a swift hug. "We'll just have to stay close the old-fashioned way, Julie."

He grinned at me as we pulled apart. His mood lifting, he let out a dramatic sigh. "Yeah, and besides, with our luck … there won't be a way to block it."

I laughed, then groaned. God, I really didn't want us to be connected through *everything* in our lives. Julian laughed at my reaction, completely understanding me, like he always did. Arm around my shoulder, he walked with me back downstairs.

Dad was just entering the kitchen when we got there. He had a small smile on his face as he went about plucking the chicken. Mom was right … it was disgusting. Julian stayed to help him, but I headed to the living room to wait out the gross part. I'd help when the chicken no longer looked like it had just been walking around the back yard. I might have grown up around this kind of stuff, both here and at the ranch, but I didn't necessarily like being an active part of it. It made me feel a little weak at times that I didn't want to do it. My grandmothers could butcher a cow in seconds without being bothered in the slightest by the carnage. But me? I just couldn't handle it.

Mom joined me in the living room once her conversation with Ashley was over. Sitting down beside me, she exhaled and relaxed back onto the white cushions. She twisted her lip as she listened to Dad and Julian working. "You know, I've seen him do it a hundred times, but it's still too disgusting to watch." Looking over at me, her frown deepened. "You'd think I'd be numb to it by now."

I chuckled at her. "I was sort of thinking the same thing."

Mom grinned and slung her arm around me. I shivered as I nestled into her chilly side. "Well, aren't we two peas in a pod."

Dad chuckled in the kitchen while Julian muttered, "Wusses."

Before I could object to Julian's comment, Mom looked at the solid wall that separated the living room and the kitchen. Clearly talking to Dad in the next room, she told him, "Ashley said Ben wants to come up soon. You're supposed to call him." I brightened at Mom's comment. I loved

THE NEXT GENERATION

Ben. He was one of Dad's best friends, and even though we weren't blood relatives, he felt like family, and all of us were very close ... even though his wife and child had no idea what we really were.

Dad blurred into the room, his hands full of feathers. Mom and I grimaced at the exact same time. Dad ignored our reaction in his sudden excitement. "Really? I didn't think he'd be able to come up this soon."

He looked over at the handset next to Mom on the couch, then started heading to it, like he was going to call Ben right now. Mom put her hand over the phone, frowning as she pointed at Dad's feathery-fingers. "I don't think so, chicken-plucker. Maybe after you've cleaned up?"

Dad's face was torn between amusement and annoyance. Seeing his expression, Mom smiled and murmured, "Besides, Ash said he went out to dinner with Tracey. They'll be gone for hours."

Dad blinked, his expression relaxing. "They're back together?"

Mom looked down. Shaking her head, she sighed, "I don't know. I think they're working on things."

Mom peeked up at Dad as Julian walked into the room. A layer of melancholy fell around everyone as we all absorbed Ben and Tracey's marital troubles. From the little I'd overheard when we'd all been down there several weeks ago, Tracey had finally gotten fed up with Ben's habitual lying.

The fact that Ben was lying to cover up the existence of vampires cut a little close to home for us. In his desire to help our family, and his own, Ben had become the human liaison with Gabriel's old nest in Los Angeles and the growing number of vampires taking up residence in San Francisco. With Gabriel and Jordon's help, Ben was implementing "rules" that any vampire living inside the city had to obey. Rumor had it that Ben was also "taking care of" any vampire who chose to not follow his rules. Ben was sort of the guardian of my birth city. Pretty cool. And, not that I'd mention it out loud, since Ben was practically family, but he was super-hot to boot.

But even if Ben was helping humans and vampires live in harmony with each other, my parents felt a huge amount of guilt over his muddled relationship. They felt responsible for showing him that our kind was real, for pulling back the curtain, so to speak. In fact, they felt so bad about the dissolution of his marriage that I'd heard them discussing finally wiping Tracey ... and Ben ... so they could have a fresh start. They'd already been blurring Tracey's mind whenever we visited her, smudging the details of

Mom and Dad's youthful appearance in her brain. But Halina couldn't run down and "alter" Tracey whenever she suspected something odd about Ben and his role as enforcer and peacekeeper. A full wipe was a more permanent solution, one they were reluctant to make.

Mom's eyes watered, and she looked away. Dad sighed and looked at the floor. "Emma ... we should ..."

"We'll talk about it later, Teren."

I felt Julian's uncertainty as he stepped next to Dad. I understood, I felt it too. I wanted to help, but it was an odd situation without any real answers. Having one foot in our world and one foot in the "real" world, it was a fine line for anyone to walk.

Clearing his throat, Julian tried to lighten the mood. "So, uh, is Ben going to bring ... her?"

A laugh escaped me as Mom and Dad looked over at Julian. He frowned, genuinely unhappy. It only made me laugh harder. Dad smiled, already appearing lighter as he examined his son. "What? It's cute, Julian."

Crossing his arms over his chest, Julian didn't seem as amused as everyone else. I felt the slight smile in his mood though, the relief that he'd made Mom and Dad somewhat happier. "It's annoying, Dad. And a little creepy."

Mom tightened her arm around me as she told Julian, "It's just a crush, Julian. All little girls get them. She'll grow out of it."

Julian sighed, shaking his head. I eased back on my laughter, feeling his annoyance, but I couldn't help my glee at his predicament. Ben and Tracey had a daughter named Olivia, and Liv adored Julian. No, adored wasn't quite the right word. Liv thought the sun rose and set by Julian's command, thought the stars twinkled in his presence, thought he was the greatest human being ever put upon this Earth. Basically, she worshipped the ground Julian walked on. She might only be eleven years old, but she was already certain that she'd be marrying Julian one day. In fact, they were going to have five kids; she'd told me that during our last visit.

Mom and Dad laughed at the look on Julian's face, their momentary heartbreak lifted. Dad nodded back at the kitchen. "Come on, let's finish up. We'll discuss ways you can thwart her advances." Dad laughed harder as Julian's frown turned into a scowl. Before Dad turned to leave, he blurred over to Mom and me. "Em?"

Mom wiped her eyes and looked up at him. Grinning like a little kid, Dad extended his hands full of feathers ... then blew the white mess all over us. Mom and I screamed in surprise and disgust. Needless to say, Mom lost her self-control and shot to her feet to whack Dad on the shoulder a couple of times before he blurred back into the kitchen.

After he was gone, Mom stared down at herself. She was covered in little white tufts. Then she looked over at me, equally covered. She started laughing as she plucked a couple of tiny feathers from her hair. "Jackass," she muttered.

I DIDN'T GET a chance to tell Julian about my day until after Mom and Dad retired for the evening. Kissing us goodnight, they walked to their bedroom hand-in-hand. Right before Mom closed their door, I heard her tell Dad, "You have something to say for yourself for that little feather incident?"

Moments before the door clicked shut, Dad's husky voice answered her. "I have plenty to say ..."

Mercifully, the door sealed a second later, and Julian and I weren't subjected to any more of our parents' flirting. Julian blurred into my room through our joint bathroom. "So ... spill. What really happened this afternoon?"

I smiled, Hunter's eyes filling my brain. "It was pretty much what I told you happened." Sighing, I laid back on my bed. "But it was so much more than that, Julie." Glancing over at him, I shrugged. "I felt something. Sparks. Something the guys around here just don't give me."

Julian grimaced and nodded. "That much of it, I got."

Sighing, I sat up. "Sorry."

Julian rolled his eyes. "I suppose it's payback for all the times you've had to endure ..." He sighed, stopping himself from talking about *her* for the zillionth time. "Well, are you two going to start seeing each other? Do I need to prepare for ... anything?"

Knowing what he was referring to, I frowned. How were we going to have intimate relationships with other people, and not share it with each other? Well, I guess that question would have to wait. Nothing like that was going to happen with Hunter and me. Not anytime soon anyway. We'd only just met.

"No, nothing like that." I shrugged. "We might meet up at the library once or twice a week, that's all." Julian raised an eyebrow, like he didn't believe me. Feeling my own mix of excitement, wonder, and nerves ... I didn't believe me either. Putting my hand on Julian's arm, I added, "But you can't tell Mom and Dad about us."

Julian blinked. "There's an 'us' now?" Narrowing his eyes, he asked, "Why?"

I glanced at the wall separating us from our parents. Luckily, the soundproofing worked both ways. "You were right about his age." I looked back at Julian. "Mom and Dad wouldn't approve." Dad especially. He wouldn't be thrilled about his baby girl dating a boy who was no longer in his teens.

"How old is he, Nick? Can he vote?" I nodded and Julian immediately asked, "Can he drink ... legally?"

Biting my lip, I whispered, "Almost ..."

"Nika?" The way he said my name clearly implied that he thought I was being an idiot.

Irritated, I shook my head and spat out, "Hey, at least he's single!"

Julian stood up, anger and sadness sweeping through him. Remorse and grief welled in me as I stood and put my hand on his arm again. I hadn't meant to justify my crush by belittling Julian's. That wasn't fair, or nice. Julian's temper cooled, but he still wouldn't look at me. "Sorry."

It was unnecessary to say it, since Julian could feel it, but he finally looked at me. "Just be careful, Nick," he said, his mood settling. "Don't turn into an absentminded schoolgirl on me now."

Lifting a lip, I muttered, "I wouldn't dream of it."

CHAPTER SEVEN

Julian

IT WAS OFFICIAL ... my sister had turned into an idiot. Well, I supposed that wasn't a fair assessment. And Lord knows I wasn't one to talk about being foolish, but her heart was spouting rainbows and moonbeams for a guy she'd talked to *one* time. At least my feelings for Raquel had built over time—I hadn't just looked at her once and known that I'd do anything to be with her. I wasn't quite sure if that was where Nika's head was, but her heart was screaming, *"Take me, I'm yours."* It was a nightmare for me.

But at the same time, a part of me was happy for her. She was right when she'd said that no other guy had made her feel that way before. I knew that for a fact. And I *did* want my sister to feel the joy I felt when I thought about ... things. But this guy? I wasn't so sure. Maybe it was my big brother protectiveness kicking in, but there was something unsettling about him. Something I didn't quite trust. Then again, I'd never talked to him, so what did I know. Besides the fact that he was almost old enough to buy us beer. Hmmm, well, I supposed Trey would be stoked about that.

Nika was a ball of excited energy as Starla took us to school a few days later. I was pretty sure it wasn't the upcoming hours of tedium that were making her giddy either. When her eyes flashed over to where neighbor-boy lived, I figured he was the reason for her mood. She'd been exceptionally upbeat all week, but nothing like this. She must be planning to see him again today. Great. Well, at least it wouldn't be at school, since he was too old to be there. I'd have a few hours reprieve before the gushing started.

When we screeched to a stop in the school parking lot, Nika leaned forward in the back seat to tell Starla, "I'm going to the library again after school today."

Ah, the library ... that would explain Nika's gaiety. I tried to contain my concern as Starla shrugged and popped a bubble with her apple-flavored gum. "Sure thing, kid." By the way she said it, Starla clearly didn't see why Nika would want to waste her time with a bunch of books. If Starla realized that Nika's "library" had just turned into the equivalent of a romantic candlelit restaurant, she might have appreciated it more. And she might have felt the same protectiveness I was feeling. Or maybe not. Starla was a bit ambivalent about the whole parenting thing.

Hopping out of Starla's car, Nika and I watched in silence as our "mom" peeled away as fast as she possibly could. Once the super-hearing woman was gone, Nika twisted to face me. "Stop worrying, I'll be fine."

With those words, she walked past me, to where Arianna was waving at us. I noticed Arianna's grin widen when her hazel eyes locked onto mine. I frowned at Nika's comment, and Arianna's smile faltered a little. Not wanting Arianna to think I was upset with her, but not wanting to smile and encourage her either, I hurried to catch up to Nika. "I'm not sure you should meet this guy alone. Maybe I'll come with you."

Nika stopped in her tracks, irritation prickling through her like thorns across her skin. "I'm sixteen. I don't need a chaperone."

Crossing my arms over my chest, I blanketed her thorny annoyance with my levelheaded concern. "Really? Should I call Dad and ask him his opinion on the matter?"

Nika shook her head and resumed walking. "You wouldn't do that to me, Julian, so don't even try that empty threat."

I grabbed her arm, stopping her. "You're being careless, Nika, and that's not like you." She locked eyes with me; hers were begging me to let her go see this guy who had finally sparked her interest. Sighing, I released her arm. "Just ... We have to be more cautious than most people, Nick. You know that."

"It's a public place, Julian. Lots of people, lots of activity. I'll be as safe as any other girl there." Looking down, she added. "And you'll know the instant I'm not."

I wanted to expound on that comment, but Arianna popped up right beside us. Trey was a step or two behind her. "You two look sullen. Everything okay?"

Nika's mood immediately surged with excitement. The rush from her made goosebumps spring up and down my arms. Grabbing Arianna, Nika exclaimed, "I have a date after school!"

Arianna was naturally euphoric for Nika. She screamed in excitement, and I had to close my eyes it hurt so much; super hearing wasn't a blessing around teenage girls. Trey, looking a little dazed, slung an arm around Nika. "No, no I don't think so," he said.

Grimacing, Nika shrugged off his arm. Smiling that Trey agreed with me, I murmured, "Yeah, I don't think so either."

Arianna glanced at me, interest in her eyes, and I shifted my attention back to Trey; his gaze was slightly unfocused as he nodded at my sister. "Yeah, you have to date me first, Little Adams."

Nika gave him a look that was priceless. As much as she tolerated my friendship with Trey, the idea of dating him repulsed her. He was sort of the epitome of everything she *wasn't* looking for in a boyfriend.

Arianna ignored Trey's comment and focused on mine. "Why don't you approve, Julian?"

Looking over at her, I debated what to say. Her eyes held an intelligent inquisitiveness that Trey's often lacked, and I knew she wouldn't accept a nothing answer. Deciding it was all right for her to know at least one of my concerns, I shrugged and adjusted the backpack on my shoulder. "He's too old. Almost old enough to buy her beer."

Trey immediately changed his opinion. Slapping her shoulder, he grinned ear-to-ear. "Never mind, Little A. Date away, date away."

I rolled my eyes, while Arianna looked back at Nika with eyes the size of saucers. "Really?" She smiled, intrigued. "Do tell."

The two of them giggled as they walked away arm-in-arm. Arianna glanced back at me once, then focused her attention on Nika, who was telling her all the things that made her date fabulous, despite his age ... or maybe because of it.

I lifted my hands in defeat. "Am I the only one who sees this as a bad thing?"

Slinging his arm over my shoulder, Trey scrunched his face like he was deep in thought, then he nodded. "Yes."

I looked over at him, shaking my head and feeling a little dizzy from the smell emanating from him. It cleared my head, though, and I let my concern over my sister's love life shift to the back of my mind. That was when my own love life hit me full force—Raquel passed right in front of me.

She was gorgeous in the early morning light. Her dark hair had subtle, auburn undertones that shimmered in the sun. Her skin was smooth and even, highlighted with rosy blush and shadow in shades of brown that emphasized how incredibly beautiful her dark eyes were. She was perfect. "Hey, Raquel. How are you?"

She started, like she'd been so lost in thought, she hadn't even noticed me standing there. That hurt a little; I always noticed her.

Stopping in front of me, she nervously looked around. "Oh … hey, Julian. I'm fine...I'm great. How are you?"

I didn't buy her statement for a second. Ignoring her question, I said, "Can we talk for a minute? Really talk?"

My heart raced as she bit her lip. By the way her eyes roved over my face, I could tell she wanted to say yes, that she wanted to talk to me, but she was clearly nervous about Russell finding us again. Knowing his schedule by heart, I knew we had some time before the lazy asshole showed his face on campus. Stepping closer to her, I begged her to talk to me. "Please, he won't be here for another ten minutes … and I just want five."

Raquel nodded, then leaned in closer. "Russell is on a rampage after … No one can see us." Looking around, to see who might be watching, she whispered, "I'll be in the storage closet on the first floor." She glanced at Trey beside me, but he was on my side, and wouldn't say anything to Russell. After giving me a quick smile, she hurried off to the main building as fast as she could.

Exhaling in a long, controlled way to slow down my surging heart, I twisted to face Trey. He was grinning at me. "Nice. Five minutes ain't a whole lot of time, bro. You sure you can pull that off?"

Ignoring his innuendo, I ran my hand back through my hair. "Holy crap ... What the hell am I going to say to her?"

Trey shrugged. "I don't know. What do girls like to hear?" He thought for a second while my nerves spiked. Feeling Nika's curiosity, I tried to calm myself down. I didn't need her coming back to check on me. I just needed her to leave me be for the next five minutes, so I could be alone ... in a storage closet ... with Raquel. Holy crap.

Thinking of something, Trey brightened. "Tell her you like her shoes."

"What?"

Trey pointed to my shoes, like he was unsure if I knew what he was talking about. "Her shoes, man. Girls love getting complimented on their shoes."

I shook my head. "What? Why?" You could buy shoes almost anywhere. It wasn't like her shoes were something specific to her. It seemed ridiculous to comment on something that a dozen other girls at this school also had.

Knowing I was running out of precious time, I didn't let Trey explain. His explanations could be a little out there anyway. Sprinting across the lawn, I heard him shout, "Good luck, dude!"

Right, luck. Crap. What the hell was I doing?

Before I knew it, I was opening the door to the storage closet. I felt really stupid as I glanced up and down the hall to see if anyone was looking, but I could hear Raquel sighing and pacing on the other side of the door. That trumped everything else. Seeing that the coast was clear, I blurred the door open and zipped inside. It was faster than I should have moved at school, but I had to get to her. Luckily Raquel's back was turned and she didn't see me. She heard me, though. With a start, she twisted to face me. Her heartbeat was heavy in the quiet air; it matched my own.

After a moment of staring at each other, her heart quieted. Mine sped up. "You wanted to talk to me?" she whispered.

I stepped closer to her. The room was only lit by the hallway light that was filtering in through the slats along the lower half of the door. Soft, indirect light caressed Raquel's body, highlighting her features. Mixed with the stillness in the air, it energized me ... made me speechless.

"Julian? What did you want to talk about?" she repeated, her voice soft.

Taking a step toward me, her hand brushed my leg. I glanced down at where we were connected, then found my voice. Looking back up at her, I whispered, "You're too good for him, Raquel. You should leave him."

"Julian ..." With a sad sigh, she shifted her weight between her feet. "I know you don't like him, I get it, but he's not ... He's not always ... Sometimes he's sweet; you just don't see it."

"You're right," I softly told her. "I only see the guy who yells at you all the time, who picked a fight with me because I tried to defend you. If he's sweet, then I *definitely* haven't seen it," I said, shaking my head.

Her eyes filled with moisture as she intently peered at me. "I never asked you to defend me." She stepped closer, until her body touched mine. "While it was incredibly kind of you ... I don't need you to fight for me, Julian. I'm fine."

I held my breath. Feeling the curves of her pressed against me, ignited me in ways I wasn't sure I wanted to be ignited. Not if she wasn't mine. Dad was right; I should have kept my distance. Instead, I cupped her cheek, brushing aside a tear that had escaped. "You're not fine, though. You're not even happy."

Leaning into her, I murmured, "Why are you with him, Raquel? Why are you willing to sacrifice your happiness for his? How is that fair to you?"

She pulled away, her eyes clearly pained by my questions. "You're only seeing the bad parts, Julian." Biting her lip, she looked around the small, dark space we were in. "I should ... I should go. We shouldn't be in here ... together. Russell wouldn't like this ..."

Grabbing her other cheek, I held her directly in front of me. My body blazed with compassion for this wounded creature before me. If I could heal her ... help her ... it would be worth the pain of never having her. "I care about you, Raquel, and that means I want to see you happy. He makes you miserable, and it kills me to watch your spirit die a little more each day. You're my friend ... *more* than my friend, and I like you too much to stay quiet about it." My voice hitched on me. I couldn't believe I was telling her these things. Usually dark, enclosed spaces were too terrifying for me to even be inside, but somehow, being in this space with her, I didn't feel claustrophobic. I felt ... free. I felt brave. I could tell her anything.

Confusion swept her features, tightened her face. "More than my friend?" she whispered.

Leaning my head against hers, my breath fast, my heart thudding, I murmured, "Yes ... I will always be your friend, but if you want me to be more, I'd ... I would ..."

"Julian ... I ... I don't know. Maybe ..."

Her breath washed over me, and I shuddered. I wasn't sure how much longer we had, but I never wanted this moment to end. Life was perfect right now. My fingers were on her soft, tear-stained skin, our bodies were close together. I felt her warmth, her heat, and I heard her heart soaring as fast as mine. We were one, in sync, and, for the first time ever, I felt like she was reciprocating my feelings.

Without internally debating it, without even thinking about it, I moved my head so that my mouth hovered over hers. I hesitated a moment, waiting for her to pull away. When she didn't, I pressed our lips together. Her soft mouth on mine weakened my knees. It was so much better than I'd ever imagined. And what made it even more amazing as I moved my lips over hers ... she moved hers too. She was kissing me back.

I was sure my heart was going to break through my ribcage and explode all around the room as her lips moved with mine. I could feel Nika's curiosity shift to concern, could feel her presence start to move toward me, but I ignored it, ignored her. I didn't even care if she busted us. I wasn't going to stop this moment for her, for anyone. I was never going to stop this moment.

Unfortunately, Raquel wasn't quite as untroubled as I was. Pushing me back, she breathlessly muttered, "No ... I can't do this."

My heart shattered as she stepped around me. "Raquel, wait ..."

Hand on the doorknob, she shook her head. "I'm sorry, Julian, I can't. I know you don't understand why, but I'm ... I'm in love with Russell ... and I can't do this."

Before I could object, she opened the door, then closed it behind her. I blinked, blinded by the sudden light followed by the sudden darkness. As that darkness became my entire world, I sank to the floor. The bell signaling that school was starting trilled in the air, but I barely heard it. My jaw trembled as Raquel's last words mixed with the residual feeling of her lips on mine. She loved *him*? Even with how he treated her? God ... why? I'd treat her so much better. She'd have a different world with me. Why didn't she want that? Why didn't she want me?

As my thoughts swirled darker and darker, the tightness of the room closed in on me. What was once a sanctuary with Raquel beside me turned into something sinister with her gone. A cruel chuckle emerged from the back of my brain, the furthest recesses of my memory. A disturbing laugh that had been followed by a heavy metallic thud, as a car trunk had closed around me. I'd been sealed in darkness ... sealed in terror. The remembered feeling crawled over my skin, and I began to shake.

"Nika ..." I whispered, hating to call for her, but too terrified to move.

She was there instantly, opening the storage closet door ... bathing me in light again.

I looked up at her, grateful, ashamed, frozen in fear. She immediately dropped to her knees, cupping my cheeks, examining me. She didn't ask if I was all right; she already knew I wasn't. She knew exactly what was wrong with me—had felt this terror before. She knew I couldn't get out of it on my own, not with how deeply I was entrenched in it. She knew I needed her right now.

Nika looked behind her, to see if anyone could see us, then she put her arms around me and physically yanked me from my self-imposed prison. I cried out in agony as Nika's force sprawled us into the middle of the empty hallway. It wasn't physical pain that pierced me, though. It was remembered pain, remembered terror. I curled into a ball, still shaking. This was bad. Raquel's stake to the heart had mixed with my fear ... I couldn't snap out of it.

Luckily, Nika was there to shove me out of it. At first, she shook my shoulders. When that didn't do much, my breathing still ragged and fast, she took the more aggressive approach.

She slapped me.

The force startled me so much, I blinked and finally focused on her. She grimaced, looking apologetic. "Sorry ... getting you out of the room didn't help as much as I thought it would."

I nodded, sitting up. The fear that had been jacking up my body was dissipating now that I'd been knocked back into the present. I held onto every real thing around me—the coldness of the floor, the sting in my cheek, Nika's concern. Everything about *this* moment pushed back the lingering panic attack, shriveling it to nothing.

"Thank you," I whispered, standing. Nika stood with me, still studying me. Embarrassment coursing through me, I looked back at the closet that had started the whole incident. "We should go. We're late."

As I started walking away, Nika called out, "Julian ..."

I knew what she wanted to talk about ... and I just couldn't yet. It was too fresh. The joy with Raquel, the heartbreak, the terror. I couldn't talk about it yet. Nika would have to be happy with examining my mood swing for now. The words would have to come later.

Looking back at her, I shook my head. "Not now ... please?"

Sighing, she nodded. "I love you, Julie."

I nodded in return. "Love you too, Nick."

I'D LIKE TO say that my day improved when I got home, but I'd forgotten about something. Okay, maybe I hadn't forgotten. Maybe I'd pushed it to the back of my mind. Ben and his daughter were in town this weekend for a visit. Ben was cool, but his daughter ... she redefined the word clingy.

"Julian!"

Thin, reed-like arms instantly cinched around my waist. If I hadn't known otherwise, I'd have assumed that the girl who had me in a death grip had blurred to the door to attack me. But Olivia was human. A speedy human, but human, nonetheless.

"Liv." I patted the top of her head, much like I patted Spike's. She reacted in the exact same way. Giggling, she buried her blonde head into my chest. I looked up at the sound of someone chuckling.

"Hey, Julian. She's been waiting all afternoon to see you."

Ben was watching us from the kitchen entryway, a steaming mug of coffee in his hand. He was solid for a man in his mid-forties, still fit and muscular. And while his hair was streaked with blond highlights, it was also streaked with gray. Ben had seen a lot of action, in the supernatural sense, and faint scar lines were visible to me, even from the distance between us. Even still, he was what my sister referred to as hot. She said he was aging well. I took her word for it.

Ben took a sip of his coffee, grinning at his daughter manhandling me. Frowning, I discreetly tried to push her away. Smiling wider, Ben shook his head. "Liv, leave the poor man alone. You'll crush him."

The young girl finally pulled back. Switching her assault to just my arm, she beamed up at me. My smile felt weird, forced, as I glanced into the open, loving, and honest gray eyes locked onto mine. Being idolized so blatantly was surreal.

As we walked as one into the living room, Ben stepped forward to join us. "Sorry, we're a bit early. Teren said we could come by anytime today, so we hopped the first flight out." Looking around the house, Ben asked, "Where's Nika?"

I sighed as I removed my backpack and sat on the couch. Liv sat at the same time I did, like we were synchronized swimmers rehearsing on dry land. Feeling Nika's joy getting stronger and stronger, I cringed. "She's ... at the library." *With our too-old neighbor who better not hurt her, or I'll be blurring through the streets of Salt Lake to get to her.*

Ben looked confused by my strange reaction, and I relaxed my face into blankness. "How are things?" I asked, mainly to stop him from asking questions.

Sighing, he sat on the couch. "Busy," he murmured, staring into his coffee cup. "Really busy." Snapping out of whatever mood he was in, Ben smiled and relaxed back on the cushions. "Which is why I'm glad we're here. No better place to rest than at the ranch with the Adamses."

As Liv cuddled into my side, I concentrated on the tightness around Ben's eyes. He was lying, but that was to be expected with Liv in the room. He probably wouldn't tell me what was really going on anyway. He'd save that conversation for Dad. It wasn't fair. I was sixteen—practically a man—it was time for me to be let in on the secret conversations. Maybe I could help?

Realizing that I hadn't even been able to help myself get out of a storage closet today, I let go of the ridiculous idea that I could be a superhero like the guys in the comic books littering the floor of my room. Like my dad. Heroes didn't have panic attacks in small spaces. Nope, no hero I had ever read about seized up as the walls closed in. That was when the real heroes got stronger.

"You okay there, Julian?"

Ben's voice freed me from my pity party, and I forced myself to smile. "Yeah ... I'm fine." And really, I was. Now that the shock of my attack was over, I could linger on the one pleasant aspect of today. Before my heart had been torn in two, I'd had my first kiss ... and it had been glorious.

Ben and I made small talk while we waited for the rest of my family to get home. Well, we tried to make small talk. It was hard to get a word in edgewise when Liv started in with her endless jabber. When I finally felt my parents leaving the heart of the city, heading for home, I was surprised to feel that Nika wasn't with them. As soon as I felt their presence leaving hers behind, alarm shot through me. What the hell? They were leaving her to wander the city with a stranger who was probably only interested in getting in her pants? Why would they do that? Wow, this had to be their first major parental fail. Well, in recent years anyway.

I shot up off the couch, staring back at the city they were rapidly leaving behind. Liv was dislodged from my body at my unexpected movement, and Ben rose to his feet, instantly on alert. "What is it?" he asked, his voice all business.

Frowning, I turned to face him. I couldn't explain what was troubling me for two reasons. One, Liv wouldn't understand how I knew my parents had abandoned their daughter, and two ... I didn't want to blow the whistle on Nika. Even though I objected to what she was doing, there was a sibling code of conduct that we followed, and it included not ratting each other out.

Smoothing my features, I pointed to the backpack at my feet. "I just remembered that I have some homework to do ... and I'll get in trouble if it's not done before my parents get home."

Ben narrowed his eyes, clearly not buying my crap. Liv sighed forlornly and clutched my arm. "Don't leave me, Julian."

I tried to brush her off, but it was Ben who made her stop. "Let him go, Olivia."

Not able to look Ben straight in the face, I quickly darted out of the room. Once hidden in my bedroom, I started pacing. "What are you doing, Nika?" I muttered, glad that, for once, no one could hear me.

I was still upstairs, pondering my sister's absence, examining her boisterous mood for any sign of trouble, when my parents walked through the front door. I heard them greet Ben and Olivia and decided to confront them on the whereabouts of my twin.

Remembering at the last minute to walk at normal speed, for Liv's sake, I strolled into the living room. Mom was giving Liv a hug while Dad was enclosing Ben in a one-armed greeting. The two friends were physically very different now, since Ben looked the age my dad actually was. But with their huge smiles and playful teasing as Dad commented on Ben's frosted tips, you'd think they were both my age.

Dad turned from his friend when I stepped into the room. Keeping an even expression, I asked, "Where's Nika?"

Dad grunted as Liv left Mom's arms to tackle him. If Liv had a second crush, it was my father. Understandable, since the two of us were so similar. Scooping Liv into a hug, Dad smiled and shrugged, not at all worried about the possibility of his little girl being deflowered tonight. "Arianna showed up at the library and asked if Nika could go to a movie with her."

I blinked. "You agreed to that?"

A small laugh escaped Dad as he told me, "You guys are sixteen now. You can go out with your friends from time to time."

As Dad released Olivia, I asked him, "And how's she getting there? How's she getting home? Who else is going to be there?" I knew I shouldn't have asked any of those questions, not if I wanted to keep Nika's secret date a secret, but really, my parents were being duped ... and these were questions they should have asked Nika before letting her prance all over the city.

Dad tilted his head as he looked at me. Mom and Ben stopped their quiet conversation and looked at me too. I smiled in the most nonchalant way I could. Mom frowned. "Nika and Arianna are going with a group of friends. Arianna's mother is going to drop them off and bring Nika home when the movie is over. You seem concerned, Julian ... why?"

Glancing between my parents and Ben, all of them now way more curious than I wanted them to be, I nervously spat out the first thing that popped into my head. "Well, I want to go too. Maybe they can pick me up?"

Olivia immediately chimed in. "If he's going, I want to go too!" She leaned around my dad to ask Ben, "Can I?"

Ben cocked an eyebrow at her. "Can you hang out with a group of teenagers on a Friday night, unsupervised? No."

Olivia pouted, but didn't ask again. I looked over at Mom. "So, can I go?"

Mom shrugged. "I guess, although ..." She seemed unsure how to phrase what she wanted to say. After another moment of debate, she told me, "Sometimes a girl needs to be around other girls ... without her big brother."

I frowned, but couldn't argue with her logic. Not without tattling on Nika. I was pretty certain Arianna was covering for Nika, so she could spend some more time with the neighbor boy, and tonight was about as far from a "girls' night" as you could get. I wasn't sure, though, so I didn't object. Instead, I said what any boy my age would say. "Can I go to Trey's then?"

Dad sighed. He wasn't a big fan of Trey, but so long as I didn't partake in Trey's vices, Dad was okay with us hanging out. Mom and Dad locked gazes for a couple moments, having some silent conversation, then Dad finally said, "That's fine, Julian. Don't be late though. We're heading to the ranch in the morning."

I nodded at him, then dashed upstairs to get my stuff and call Trey. I could hear Olivia complaining as I grabbed my coat. *Sorry, Liv, but a brother's gotta do, what a brother's gotta do.*

CHAPTER EIGHT

Nika

I COULD *NOT* believe the situation I was in, and I wanted to kill Arianna for putting me in it. I wanted to give her a big ol' kiss, too. Thanks to her showing up at the library and fast-talking my dad into a girls' night, I was now on my way to my first official date … ever. And even though I'd spent the last couple of hours with Hunter, I was nervous.

Arianna smiled at me encouragingly as she flipped through the blouses in her closet. "You seem nervous … are you? Didn't you just spend the afternoon alone with Hunter?" Stopping on a low-cut blouse that my mother would never let me leave the house wearing, Arianna turned to face me and exclaimed, "And, wow, Nika, Hunter is hot. I approve." She winked at me, then tossed the blouse at my face.

I caught it easily, my fingers sliding along the silky fabric. Before I could respond to Arianna's comment, she started in on another one. One she'd mentioned before … several times, actually. One that made me cringe internally. "And that Teren guy … no matter how many times I see him, I just can't get over how attractive he is." A dreamy expression lit up her face as she flopped onto her bed. "He's so sexy, with that black hair and blue eyes … just how I picture Julian looking in a few years."

As Arianna lost herself in a fantasy involving my father ... ugh ... I closed my eyes and suppressed a shudder. Quickly reopening them, I smacked her thigh. "Stop that! He's family, and I really don't need to watch you mentally undressing him." God, I definitely didn't need to see that. "You drooling over Julian is bad enough."

Arianna scowled as she sat up. "For the millionth time, I do *not* drool." She lifted her chin, her calm smile returning. "And besides, Teren is only related to you through marriage, right? So, he's not technically family. Genetically, I mean. It's totally okay for you to ... think about him."

I bit my lip. Yes, in the lie, Dad was my grandfather's wife's brother ... not a blood relation to me. "I've known him forever, though, and he feels like family ... so it's gross."

Arianna flipped to her stomach and indicated the blouse she wanted me to put on. "I suppose that's true. But your family and your extended family is super-hot, so you'll just have to give me a pass when it comes to appreciating them. I'll try to keep my comments to myself, though, if that helps." She smiled as she tapped her feet together.

I sighed, but grudgingly agreed to let her have her fantasies about my dad and my brother. So long as I didn't have to hear about them, I supposed it was fine.

Once I was changed into the clingy top Arianna was letting me borrow, I smiled and did a twirl in the mirror. I'd have to change back into my regular shirt before I went home, but, I had to admit, it looked good on me. Arianna grinned as she popped up beside me. "Eat your heart out, Hunter," she murmured.

We were both giggling as we finished getting ready. Our cover story to Dad involved Arianna coming along, so she was actually going to come along. That was okay with me; I felt a little better about doing this with her there. It felt like less of a lie. I hated deceiving my parents, and I never would have if Arianna hadn't started the ball rolling. But when I'd felt Mom and Dad approaching, I'd physically ached to stay with Hunter. Arianna had tossed out a possibility to prolong our evening, and I'd jumped all over it. And really, it wasn't entirely a lie. We'd told Mom and Dad we were going to see a movie with friends ... and we were. I hadn't known Hunter long, but I considered him a friend.

Once Arianna and I were both ready to go, we headed to the living room to find her parents. That was when I felt something that made me frown. Arianna noticed my expression. Maybe thinking I was still nervous, she put her arm around my shoulder. "Hey, it will be fine, Nika. And I'll be a few rows back, cheering you on." I forced a smile as I thanked her for the support.

It wasn't nerves killing my buzz, though. No, it was a presence moving toward me. A presence that should have been spending the night at home. Julian. Julian knew exactly what I was up to, and he had a very disapproving demeanor about him. I'd been ignoring his mood for a while now, since he had nothing to worry about, but that hadn't hampered his concern, and now he was on his way to me. When we met up, he was either going to watch me like a hawk all night, or try and take me home. Either way, he was going to put a damper on my date.

"Damn it," I muttered.

"Hmmm?"

I shook my head at Arianna, slapping on a giddy grin. I couldn't tell her that she'd be seeing Julian sooner than she thought. Oh well, at least it would improve *her* night to have Julian trailing along. It would almost be like we were double-dating, like Arianna had always wanted.

When Arianna's mom dropped us off in front of the theater, Julian was already there, just around the corner. Either I'd taken longer to get ready than I'd realized, or he'd taken some supernatural shortcuts. That last one better not be the case. Julian knew better than to risk exposure over something as stupid as wanting to crash my date.

Butterflies tickled my insides as I waved goodbye to Arianna's mom. If Julian was here, Hunter was probably here too. He was meeting us inside. Even though it hadn't been that long since we'd parted, I couldn't wait to see him again.

Arianna and I locked elbows as we headed to the main doors. I felt Julian approaching but ignored it. I had to. Normal girls didn't "feel" their brother lurking.

"Nika?" a familiar voice behind me said.

I wanted to roll my eyes at the surprise in Julian's voice. If you didn't know what I knew, you'd assume by the questioning way he'd said my name that he was shocked to run into me. Twisting around, I muttered, "Julian." My tone was flat, not surprised in the least. I probably should have acted surprised, but I was more irritated than anything else.

While he looked appropriately startled, Julian's pale eyes were defiant, and his mood was as prickly as my own. He hadn't been happy when he'd realized that I wasn't going home with Mom and Dad. He'd been ... alarmed, which was ridiculous. I was perfectly safe. As he stared at me now, he was a blended mixture of relief, worry, disapproval, and maybe just a bit of embarrassment. He hadn't wanted to come, but duty had left him no other choice. I sighed and relaxed my mood. I couldn't blame him for his protectiveness; I was the exact same way with him, after all.

Julian's emotions lightened as he felt mine evening out. A tiny smile cracked his lips and he nodded, just enough for me to see.

Of course, all that silent conversing happened in just a few microseconds. Arianna broke the moment by squealing, "Julian? What a small freaking world!"

I shook my head, my grin uncontainable. Yeah, right ... serendipity, that was why Julian was here. Someone I *was* surprised to see stepped up to Julian from the street. Trey. Looking over at Julian, he muttered, "Dude ... you're fast." Trey had a skateboard tucked under his arm, just like Julian, but Trey, for obvious reasons, hadn't been able to keep pace with my brother.

Arianna had broken away from me in her excitement at seeing Julian here. If Trey hadn't shown up, I was pretty sure she would have grabbed Julian's arm and pulled him tight, but with Trey here, she stopped herself. Tucking some light brown hair behind her ears, the electric neon sign above us highlighting her natural blonde undertones, Arianna said, "Hey Trey. What are you guys doing here?"

Trey blinked and stared up at the marquee covered in movie titles. "We're gonna catch the new zombie flick."

I exhaled in relief. Good. They were seeing a different movie. No way was I going to see zombies getting their heads blown off on a first date. Second ... maybe. Julian tilted his head, studying my expression and my feelings. He looked up at the reader board, then told Trey, "Actually, I wanted to see the new rom-com."

I didn't react to his movie choice, but my mood dropped. The new romantic comedy was what we were going to see. Julian smirked, amusement that he'd guessed right filling him. I loved my brother, but just then, I wanted to go Mom-zilla on him.

Arianna squealed again and finally latched onto Julian's arm. "That's what we're seeing." Batting her eyes at Julian, she murmured, "You can sit by me if you like."

Julian was instantly uncomfortable, and I crooked a grin at him. Served him right. Trey shrugged, not really caring what they saw, and the four of us headed through the doors for my "group" date. I spotted Hunter instantly. He was leaning against the edge of the ticket counter, one foot causally crossed over the other. He hadn't had time to go home and change, so he was still wearing the same black shirt hanging over faded blue jeans. His five o'clock shadow was visible to me, even from the door. Arianna was right ... he was hot, and my heart skipped a beat.

Julian made a derisive snorting sound, and I twisted around to glare at him. Under my breath, I snipped, "Be nice to Hunter or I will shave off your eyebrows while you're sleeping."

Julian blinked at my threat, then furrowed his, for the moment, still intact brows. "Wait, his name is Hunter? Really?"

Julian asked that at normal volume, and everyone twisted to look at him. My brother blushed as he looked between Arianna and Trey. Neither of them had heard my comment to Julian. To them, it looked like Julian had glanced at Hunter and then magically come up with his name.

Arianna looked a little confused by Julian's strange, but profound, outburst. Trey was impressed. "Dude, did you just pull that out of your ass?" He glanced at me. "Is that his name?"

I nodded absently, hoping Arianna didn't think too much about my brother's pronouncement. Trey looked back at Julian and exclaimed, "Oh my God, you're a freaking psychic!" Putting both hands on Julian's shoulders, he seriously asked him, "Okay, when am I finally gonna get laid?"

Arianna and I made the exact same disgusted noise and left the two boys to discuss Trey's virginity. Hunter noticed my approach and straightened. A glorious smile brightened his face, and I sighed again, my nerves evaporating. Arianna, beside me, asked, "How did Julian know that?"

Glancing at her curious face, I responded, "I told him on the way in ... you just didn't hear me."

Arianna looked thoughtful, but didn't say anything more about it. Hunter gave my entourage a once-over, then settled his gaze on me. My enhanced vision caught the slight widening of his dark eyes as he glossed over the seductive top I'd changed into. Respectfully raising his vision to my eyes, he asked, "Are you sure about this? I don't want you to get in trouble or anything."

I'd reluctantly parted ways with Hunter inside the library when I'd felt my dad approaching to pick me up. After Arianna had secured permission from my "guardian" for me to go to the movies—Dad even going so far as to call my fake-mom to get the official okay—I'd gone back into the library to tell Hunter the good news. I'd been so nervous that he wouldn't want to go on an official date with me. It was kind of forward, really, for me to plan a night out without even asking him. Well, okay, it was forward of Arianna, since the whole thing had been her idea, but I'd gone along with it. He hadn't minded though. Smiling ear-to-ear, he'd said he'd love to spend the evening with me.

"It's okay, I won't get in trouble."

Julian stepped up to my side at that point. He was so close to me that he was a little in front of me; I had to take a step back to not get stepped on. He was emanating protectiveness, both internally and externally. I almost expected him to ask Hunter, "What are your intentions with my sister?" Luckily for him, he didn't.

Sticking out his hand, he crisply said, "I'm Nika's brother, Julian."

Hunter nodded as he took Julian's hand. "Right, I remember you from the street. Hunter. Hunter Evans."

As the two men had a silent stare-down while they shook hands, Trey popped up on the other side of me. He looked around the lobby in a secretive way, like he was conducting a drug deal and didn't want the authorities to bust him. In a whisper, he asked Hunter, "Hey ... when exactly do you turn twenty-one?"

While Hunter looked unsure how to answer that, I shoved Trey away from me. "Knock it off, Trey. He's not old enough to buy you beer, and he wouldn't if he was."

Trey pouted. "What about wine coolers? Those are practically Kool-Aid."

Arianna shook her head at him. "You need help. You know that, right?"

Shrugging, Trey murmured, "I'm getting some munchies ... anybody want anything?"

He left before any of us even answered him. Hunter blinked, then returned his attention to me. Extending his hand, his voice soft, he asked, "Would you like something?"

I grabbed his hand, tender and warm, and shook my head. No, everything I wanted was right here. A glow of happiness wrapped around me as Hunter walked us over to the ticket line. I felt Julian's mixed state as he got in line with Arianna. He was both happy and worried for me, and he definitely didn't trust my date. I exhaled in frustration over the fact that I had a chaperone—I really hadn't wanted one tonight—but then I let it go. Roles reversed, I'd be right behind Julian, watching his every move too.

A few minutes later, Hunter and I were seated in the dark theater, close together, but separated by the arm rest. I suddenly wished this theater had armrests that lifted, so holding hands wasn't quite so awkward. Julian was two rows behind us, smashed in-between Arianna and Trey. Arianna had insisted on that seating arrangement, since she was convinced Trey would cop a feel during the movie. Or perhaps she was hoping my brother would.

As the previews began, Hunter and I made small talk. He asked what my favorite food was. I gave him my human response, since I couldn't exactly tell him that a steaming cup of blood was right up there with the best deep dish pizza in town. I also couldn't tell him that I could hear his blood surging through his body, and while I would never, ever bite him … the sound was alluring, the bulging vein in his neck enticing. It just added to the attraction of him. But he would never know that.

I laughed at a joke he made, painstakingly aware of just how close his head was to mine. While we weren't as close as I would have preferred, we were a lot closer than we'd been at the library. I'd never been kissed before … not really. Not a man to a woman kiss, anyway, and just imagining his lips lowering to touch mine sent my heart into overdrive. I felt incredible, beautiful, and desirable as Hunter stroked my thumb with his while he talked to me.

Julian sighed as the movie started, and I could feel how uncomfortable he was. I couldn't help it though. I couldn't stop the feelings surging through me, and I didn't want to. Julian had felt something similar earlier today, when he'd been with Raquel in that closet, so I knew he understood. He understood and I understood. It sucked, but bonded feelings was the hand we'd been dealt.

THE NEXT GENERATION

Sometime during the movie, I laid my head on Hunter's shoulder. It brought his heartbeat closer to my ear and I reveled in the sound, in the closeness I felt. He tilted his head to rest it on mine, and I thought I could die happy right then and there. Then a spike of something went through me. Hatred. Anger. Betrayal. Pain.

Dislodging Hunter, I jerked my head around to look at Julian. Hunter whispered, "What is it?" But in my concern, I ignored him.

Julian wasn't looking at me, but over and to the left of me. I leaned past Hunter to see what had my brother frazzled. When I spotted the problem, I really wasn't surprised. Raquel and Russell were here, voraciously making out in the front row. My heart broke for Julian as I twisted to look back at him. He met my eyes this time. His face stony, he shot to his feet. Irritating everyone around him, he waded past the sea of knees to get to the aisle. He stormed out of the theater shortly after, Arianna following in his wake. Trey blinked, but stayed put.

I was torn. My instinct was to go to Julian—to help him, protect him, comfort him. Sitting idly by, while he was hurting, felt wrong. But, leaving the serenity of my date was about the last thing I wanted to do right now.

"Nika?" Hunter asked, his thumb running a circle over my skin.

Sighing, I looked back at him. "I have to go, I'm sorry."

Hunter frowned, but nodded. "I'll come with you."

Smiling, I nodded and let him help me up. I was sure Julian wouldn't appreciate all the attention he was about to get, but well, I needed to be with Julian, and I wanted to be with Hunter, so my brother was just going to have to deal with the company.

Julian was outside with Arianna when we got to the lobby. Twisting to Hunter, I cringed. "Would you mind staying here while I talk to him?"

Surprising me, Hunter smiled. "I think it's pretty amazing of you to put everything on hold to help your brother. Like I said before, family is everything."

He gently pushed me forward, then tucked his fingers into his back pocket while he waited for me to return to him. The smile on his face was full of pride and admiration, and I felt a little invincible as I headed out the doors to see Julian. The feeling left me as Julian's mood darkened at my approach.

"I'm fine, Nika."

Arianna was holding his hand; hers was white, he was squeezing back so hard. His face was tight, his eyes heavy with emotion, an emotion that was searing me with its intenseness. As the glass door closed, separating us from the lobby, I countered, "I know you're not, Julian."

His eyes hardened when they met mine, then his grief broke to the surface and he completely fell apart. Face desolate, he whimpered, "Nick ... she kissed me. She said she might like me. She said ... maybe ... And now she's making out with *him*, and it's like none of that ever happened. What does that mean?"

Right at that second, I'd never wanted to drain someone of all their blood more in my life. Arianna apparently felt the same. Hugging Julian tight, her eyes shot daggers into the movie theater, where Raquel and Russell were probably still going at it. By the steel look in my friend's expression, I surmised that Julian had filled her in on his unrequited feelings for Raquel. She was hurt and pissed.

Feeling horrible for the misleading situation my brother was stuck in, I wrapped my arms around him. He groaned at the sudden female attention, and pushing us both back, he muttered, "I'm fine, really. I just need some air."

As if on cue, a light breeze swirled around us. A hint of blood was in the cool air, something no human would ever notice. Julian and I both inhaled. The scent was incredible, akin to smelling a BBQ down the street. Lips in a hard line, Julian locked gazes with me. "I'm gonna go hunt down something to eat."

By the fire in his belly and the look in his eye, I wasn't quite sure what he meant by that. I knew Julian would never stalk a human, but, he might go after an animal ... might let the beast take over so he could block out the pain. Absently, I wondered if he'd blur to the ranch, hunt one of our cows. Our grandparents would certainly let him. Halina would probably even join him. Of course, if he traveled away from the city, it would alarm my parents. They wouldn't be happy if he went that far without their permission.

I didn't have to ask for clarification, though, since Arianna said, "I'm coming with you." Julian looked about to protest, but Arianna stubbornly shook her head. "You shouldn't be alone right now, Julian."

Seeing that he wasn't going to be able to shake her, Julian finally conceded. "Fine ... let's just get out of here."

I gave Julian a final hug, whispering, "Talk to me later, okay?"

He nodded, then told me to tell Trey he'd call him later. I waved after the pair as they started walking away. Julian was slumped over. Not happy, not sad, just … numb. Arianna was the exact opposite. She locked her hands around Julian's arm and looked back at me with an *'Oh my God!'* face. I wanted to tell her not to get her hopes up. Julian was emotionally wiped. Him agreeing to her tagging along wasn't the romantic connection she was hoping for, he just didn't have the energy to tell her no.

Shaking my head, I turned around to find Hunter holding the door open for me. Pointing up the street, to where I could feel Julian retreating from me, he asked, "The kid gonna be okay?"

I smirked at his comment as I passed by him. "That *kid* is my twin, and, yeah …" I glanced back outside as Hunter let the door shut, " … I think he'll be fine."

Hunter grabbed my hand eagerly, like he'd missed holding me for the few minutes we'd been apart. My heartbeat sped up as his dark eyes sparkled at me. "Twin, huh? So, do you guys have some psychic connection, some special twin-bond?"

I unintentionally laughed. God, did we ever. "Ah, I guess … maybe … if you believe in that sort of thing."

Beneath what he thought I was capable of hearing, Hunter said, "I've seen crazier."

We went back to our movie hand-in-hand. Getting back into our original seats, I noticed that Trey hadn't moved much; he was still blankly staring at the screen, possibly not even seeing it. Raquel and Russell hadn't changed much either, still attached at the mouth, much to the dismay of the people sitting around them.

I pressed into Hunter as much as I could with that divider between us. When his arm draped over my shoulders, I sighed just as dreamily as the actress in the film we were watching. If it weren't for the flickering of pain coming from Julian, this moment would have been perfect. I tried to block out Julian, but his emotions were soaring. A bit of guilt seeped into me that I was so high while he was so low, but by the end of the movie, Julian's mood had improved. A trickle of amusement flashed through him from time to time, and I hoped whatever Arianna was doing to distract him kept working. I didn't want my brother to be in pain. Not over Raquel.

Once the credits were rolling, I waited in my seat until Russell and Raquel separated and left the theater. They hadn't even watched the movie. What a waste. Russell could have saved himself some cash and mauled her in the backseat of his car. For Julian's sake, I really wished he had.

I glared at them as they walked by. Hunter twisted to see who my baleful stare was directed toward. Turning back to me, he asked, "Those two have something to do with your brother?"

Immediately, I realized that all the drama that had played out here tonight was very high school-ish. I didn't want to remind Hunter of my age, so I smiled and changed the subject. "Do you want to go for a short walk with me? I'd like to show you something."

His smile charming, Hunter nodded. "I'd love to."

He stood, then held out his hand to help me up. I hid a smile at his manners. That was another thing Dad would approve of. Trey was just exiting his row when we got there. He looked confused as he held his skateboard in one hand, and Julian's abandoned board in the other. "Where is ... everybody?"

Keeping my face straight, I told him, "Julian and Arianna left halfway through the movie. Why don't you call him and have them come back, so we can get a ride home from Arianna's mom?"

Trey nodded, baffled, and juggled the boards around so he could dig into his pocket for his phone. I glanced back at Hunter, apologetic, and rolled my eyes at Trey. Tucking a loose strand of hair behind my ear, Hunter's face shifted into embarrassment. "I really should be the one giving you a ride home. I sort of feel like a bad date for making you ride with a friend's mom."

I shook my head, swinging his hand as we continued up the aisle. "That's okay, this actually works out well anyway." Especially considering that my dad would be ticked if Hunter dropped me off instead of Arianna.

Hunter's face darkened. "Yeah, it still feels ungentlemanly though." A small smile lightened his features. "But, then again, I hadn't planned on going out, and I only have my bike. I doubt you'd want a ride home on the handlebars." As I was laughing, he added, "And I have to run an errand with my dad on the other side of town anyway, so yeah, I guess you're right, this works ... for tonight," he amended.

We stepped out into the night air, and I peeked up at the pitch-black sky highlighted by a moon shining so brightly, you'd swear the chunk of rock emitted its own light. Peeking over at Hunter, who was also appreciating the clear, moonlit night, my curiosity got the better of me. "You and your dad are running an errand in the middle of the night? What are you doing?"

If my eyesight wasn't as good as it was, I probably would have missed it. Hunter's eyes tightened, his teeth gritted, but when he looked over at me, his face was perfectly relaxed. "It's a family thing." I nodded, accepting, but not understanding. My family did weird things at night too.

Knowing I didn't have much time left to spend with him, and really wanting to show him something before Arianna's mom showed up, I put his family errand aside and tugged on our laced fingers so he'd follow me. The night was much cooler than the day had been, but I was still comfortably warm in my jacket, even with only a slinky, satiny top underneath. The air was fresh, the faint hint of blood in it gone now. Whatever creature had been wounded earlier was either downwind or had been carried off.

Putting the circle of life out of my mind, I concentrated on the man beside me. It still surprised me some that he'd agreed to see me tonight. I was young and inexperienced. He was mature. Why he'd spend time with someone who still had a curfew was beyond me, but I was grateful, regardless.

Not too far from the theater was the place I wanted to show him. Salt Lake City had parks and fountains everywhere. It really was a beautiful place to live. Since Hunter had just moved here, I thought he might appreciate a tiny bit of sightseeing, and since he'd enjoyed the water wall at the library, I thought he might like one of my favorite fountains.

Holding his hand tight, I pulled him into a plaza highlighted with bright spotlights. His face was peaceful as he took in the quiet beauty around him. I led us to what appeared to be a solid wall jutting out of the cement, but as we got closer to it, it was clear that it wasn't a wall at all. A never-ending cascade of water was spilling out of the top of the wall, creating a perfect, liquid curtain.

Smiling, Hunter dropped my hand and stepped around to the opposite side of the fountain. Through the wall of water, I could see the hazy outline of his body. Reaching a hand to the curtain, he murmured, "Wow, this is incredible."

His finger poked through the sheet of water, disrupting the perfect flow as it split around him. I reached my hand out, threading my fingers with his as the water surged around us. I clearly recalled being here with Julian years ago and doing something similar. Of course, Julian had yanked on my hand and pulled me through the cascade of water, instantly drenching me. As Hunter and I locked gazes through the chilly fountain, I was certain he wouldn't do that to me.

Fingers still locked, we moved to the edge of the fountain, our bodies creating a wave of disruption as we went. When we got to the end, we let each other go, and I didn't even care that my hand was red and stinging with the cold. As Hunter walked back around to me, his face lit from above by the moon, and below by the spotlights nearby, I only cared about the look in his eye.

Walking up close, he reached for my wet hand with his. "Thank you for sharing this with me." He leaned in closer, until our bodies were touching. The sound of the rushing fountain next to us was suddenly nothing compared to the pounding in my chest; I barely even heard it. "Thank you for spending time with me tonight. I really enjoyed it."

He lowered his head, and all I could think was, *Oh my God ... is he going to kiss me?* Somehow, I managed to tell him, "I really enjoyed it too."

"Good." His head tilted toward mine, so that our lips were a hairsbreadth apart. I stiffened, unable to move, dying for him to touch me. He didn't get any closer, though. He held his body against mine, his mouth tantalizingly close. Even though I'd never kissed a boy, I knew I was about three seconds away from attacking him if he didn't do something right now.

Finally, he whispered, "May I ... ?"

He didn't finish his question ... I didn't let him. "Yes," I answered, closing the gap between us.

As his lips moved over mine, I was struck with how soft and gentle it was. His fingers came up to caress my cheek, and I had to forcibly tell my knees to not buckle. It was difficult though; I suddenly felt like taffy. After an eternity of our tender melding, he finally pulled away. Not ready to let him go, I stretched up on my tiptoes to find his lips again. He chuckled as our blissful moment continued. I couldn't contain my smile anymore as we gave each other soft pecks of affection.

After a moment, he finally pushed me back again. I frowned, still not wanting to stop. Stroking my cheek with his thumb, he shook his head. "I'd love to stay here with you, Nika, but you need to go find your brother and your friends." I wanted to tell him that I knew exactly where my brother was—that he was pacing back and forth in front of the movie theater—but I didn't.

Sighing, I nodded. As I cupped my hand over his on my cheek, he added, "I need to go meet with my dad now anyway. Tomorrow?"

I started to brighten at the prospect of seeing him again in twenty-four hours, but then my face fell. "No, I can't. I'll be gone all weekend."

Hunter's face fell, too, which made me really, really happy. "Oh, okay. Monday?"

I was nodding before he even finished his question. "Definitely." Before he could stop me, I leaned up for another kiss. I just couldn't get enough now. He chuckled again, but readily kissed me back. The sensation was so overwhelming, I had to remind myself over and over to concentrate on keeping my fangs up.

CHAPTER NINE

Nika

HUNTER AND I walked back to the movie theater holding hands. As I already knew, Julian was there, waiting with Arianna and Trey. Arianna's eyes were aglow as she watched me reappear with Hunter. I could tell she was dying to ask me if anything had happened. Hopefully, she'd wait until we were alone. Julian's eyes were narrowed as he stared at Hunter. He already knew exactly what had happened. Or could correctly guess anyway, having felt my bliss, excitement, contentment …

Trey was sitting on his skateboard on the curb, skipping rocks across the street. He glanced up when he saw me. "Oh, hey. Where'd you guys go?"

Ignoring him, I turned to Hunter. "You should probably go before Arianna's mom gets here. She doesn't know this was really a date."

Hunter frowned. "I should meet your parents, so we don't have to hide."

Stepping into him, I shook my head. "It's just my mom … and she won't let me see you." Grinning, I whispered, "You're too old."

Hunter gave me an incredulous look. "You make me sound like a dirty old man."

Under his breath Julian muttered, "If the shoe fits …"

I threw Julian a glare, and pulled Hunter to the side of the building where the bike rack was holding his BMX in place. "It's just for right now. When the time is right … I'll tell my mom, and we'll be out in the open." I grabbed his other hand and peeked around for witnesses. My friends were watching us. So much for privacy. Ignoring them, I locked gazes with Hunter. "Until then, it will be our little secret."

Hunter grinned at me, then indicated my spying friends with his head. "And theirs?"

I pursed my lips, wishing we were back at the water curtain. Hunter chuckled at my expression, then lowered his lips to mine. I suddenly didn't care where we were. I heard Arianna giggle, Trey whistle, and my brother sigh, but their presence didn't matter to me any more than our location did. All that mattered was the perfect way Hunter and I fit together. Kissing was definitely one of my new favorite things.

Julian's voice broke the moment for me. He hissed, "Nick," and I knew that meant he'd spotted Arianna's mom. I broke off from Hunter and backed away from him. When I returned to the street, Arianna giggled and wrapped her arms around me. I forcefully made myself turn my back on Hunter, pretend I didn't know him. As a minivan pulled up to the curb, I risked a glance though. Bike in hand, Hunter was watching me, smiling. The confidence he exuded was crystal clear, even from the space between us.

As the side door on the van automatically opened, Hunter lifted his thumb to his ear, his pinky finger to his mouth, miming a phone. His face clearly asked, *"Can I call you?"*

I thought about it for a second. We'd exchanged numbers this afternoon, and the thought of talking to him this weekend made leaving him that much easier. I'd have to sneak off to have a real conversation, but that was all right. The ranch was a big place … and I could run really fast. I nodded at him, then quickly turned back to the parent who was dutifully picking us up from an innocent night at the movies.

Arianna cracked open the passenger door and asked, "Mom, can we give Trey and Julian a ride, so they don't have to board back home?"

Trey held up his skateboard, pointing at it, so Arianna's mom would know what her daughter was talking about. I was pretty sure she knew what a "board" was. As her eyes scanned Trey and my brother, Julian gave her a small wave. "Hey, Mrs. Bennett."

Smiling, Arianna's mom waved our group into the van. "Sure, why not. Trey, your place isn't too far, and I'm already going to Nika and Julian's house. How was the movie?"

Arianna told her mom that it was great, even though she'd only seen half of it. I smiled, watching the mother and daughter. Arianna's mom was one of those really involved PTA moms who volunteered for just about every activity under the sun. As a result, she knew things about nearly every kid in class, including where most of them lived. She was the type of mom my mother wanted to be, but couldn't. My real parents had to take a backseat to Starla in these matters, since she was our "stage" mom. The wife of my grandfather's wife's brother showing up to fundraiser committees would be ... strange. That didn't stop my mom from learning as much as she could about our lives and our friends, though. She stayed as involved as possible.

We all scrambled into the car. I peeked out the window as the door closed, but Hunter was gone. Sighing, I leaned back in my seat, disappointed that my impromptu date was over. Even though he didn't approve of Hunter, Julian patted my arm in sympathy. Remembering how horrible his night had been, I put my hand over his for a second. We didn't speak, but we didn't need to. His emotions told me that he was hurting, but not as badly as before, and he knew I was sorry for his pain, but glad he was feeling better.

Trey's stop was first. Grabbing his board, he pointed a finger at Arianna's mom. "Thanks, Mrs. B." As the door rolled open, he backed up to it. Faking like he was taking several shotgun blasts to the chest, Trey dramatically fell out of the van. He tried to catch himself, but missed and landed on his ass on the cement driveway. His skateboard clattered to the street and started rolling away. Scowling, Trey rubbed his injury while Julian chuckled at him.

"Idiot," Arianna murmured.

Trey popped up and bowed as the van door closed. Julian waved at his friend while we pulled away. Once Trey was gone, I found where I'd stashed my T-shirt under the seat and discretely changed back into it. Mrs. Bennett was humming to herself as she drove along, and didn't seem to notice I was removing clothing. Julian was staring out the side window, lost in thought. When I was done, I leaned forward and tapped Arianna's elbow resting on the door. She glanced back, and I subtly handed her the silky blouse, mouthing, "Thank you." Hunter had definitely appreciated the alluring outfit.

Moments later, Mrs. Bennett was dropping Julian and me off at home. The lights were on and my parents were still awake; I could feel them in the living room. Dad got up and started moving toward the front door right as the minivan's door started sliding open on its motorized hinges.

Julian and I thanked Arianna's mom simultaneously, which made her smile and comment on the wondrous nature of twins. I stopped myself from smirking at her as I stepped from the vehicle. People always commented on our twin connection when we did anything at the same time. A joint teacher we'd had last year had almost had an embolism when we'd sneezed together.

"Bye, Arianna." A huge grin bursting out of me, I gushed, "Thank you ... for going to the movies with me."

Leaning out her open window, Arianna giggled conspiratorially. "Yeah, it was fun. We'll have to do it again sometime." She winked at me, then directed her gaze to Julian. Instantly, her face sobered. "Remember what I said, Julian. She's not worth it."

Her gaze as she stared at Julian was so full of longing it broke my heart. I wanted to slap my brother over the head and scream at him, *You idiot! Look at what's right in front of you!*

Julian shoved his hands in his pockets and averted his eyes. His mood was both embarrassed and speculative. As the van door started closing, Julian finally met Arianna's eyes. "Thank you for talking to me tonight, Arianna. I really appreciate it."

The smile he gave her was small, but you'd think he'd just professed his undying love for her by the corresponding grin on her face. "Anytime, Julian. Anytime." The door shut completely and Arianna closed her window and waved at us while the car backed out. When they were gone, I looked over at my brother.

Without returning my gaze, he told me, "Don't say it," and started heading for the door that Dad was opening. Knowing Julian had more to scold me about than I did him, I kept my mouth shut. I couldn't make Julian like my best friend anyway.

Dad was frowning as we stepped up to him. Well, he was frowning at Julian. "What happened to giving your sister a girls' night?"

A flash of guilt shot up my spine. Julian peeked at me as he stepped around Dad to get inside. "We got bored."

I knew it was more than that, though, and I kept my head down as I stepped around Dad, too. A chilly hand on my shoulder stopped me and I froze, terrified. Did Dad know that I'd really been out with a boy? That I'd had my first kiss tonight? Could he ... smell Hunter on me? My heart started to pick up, and I willed everything in my body to slow down the telltale organ. Being alive was so inconvenient at times.

Dad was studying my body's reaction as he asked, "Did you have fun?"

I nodded as I forced a smile. "Yep." Hoping to dissuade his suspicion, I leaned up and kissed his frozen cheek. His face instantly lightened and relaxed. "Thanks for letting me go, Dad."

"Sure."

He was smiling as he closed the door and guilt poured into me. I hated omitting details from him, but he would flip out if he found out about Hunter. And ... I was starting to really like Hunter. When Mom walked into the room, I decided I would come clean about him when things between us got more serious. Right now, it was casual, so it didn't really matter. As my guilt began to lift, Julian raised an eyebrow in question. I ignored it, since I couldn't answer him anyway.

Mom kissed Julian's cheek, and I saw my brother shiver a little. She smirked at him, then asked, "Enjoy the movie?"

Julian looked away, but smiled. Regardless of how his night had ended, he was still happy that he'd gone. That he had, in his eyes, protected me. As Mom gave me a hug, Ben walked into the room. Grinning ear-to-ear, I let go of Mom and rushed over to him. Tossing my arms around his neck, I gave him as hard of a hug as his body could handle. "Uncle Ben! I'm glad you're here."

Ben chuckled and hugged me back. "I missed you too, kiddo." His breath sounded a little strained, and I eased up on my grip. Even though I'd seen Ben over the summer, it felt like an eternity. In my excitement to hang out with Hunter tonight, I'd completely forgotten he was coming to Salt Lake; I instantly felt bad. "I'm sorry I went out. I forgot you were in town."

Laughing, Ben released me. "Nika, I don't expect you to pass up on time with your friends to hang out with an old man."

His words oddly reminded me of Hunter's, and my chest swelled with a warm, languid emotion as I thought of his dark, piercing eyes. I gave myself exactly three seconds to wonder what Hunter was doing at this precise moment in time, then I shoved him from my mind for the night. Playfully, I tossed out, "You're not old, Uncle Ben."

Ben's blue eyes sparkled as he looked back at me. He was older, sure, but definitely not "old." His face would still attract most girls, and I was sure Arianna would have a few colorful adjectives if she saw him. I was also sure she'd find a way to officially become a part of my "hot" family after that.

"Well, thank you, Nika. That's the nicest thing I've been told in a while." His face fell a little, and hushed conversations about his marital woes popped into my head. Disengaging from him, I hoped that Tracey wizened up to just how amazing her husband was. He was number two in my book, right below my dad.

"Is Liv here?"

Ben smiled and pointed upstairs, to where I could hear someone sleeping in one of the spare rooms. Julian sighed.

Julian and I were urged to go to bed after that, since we were leaving for the ranch bright and early in the morning. Mom and Dad stayed downstairs with Ben. They talked long into the night and I tried to stay up to listen, but sleep harkened, and I obeyed its call.

WE PILED INTO Mom and Dad's cars in the morning, since we wouldn't all fit in one. Somehow, Julian managed to get stuck in Mom's sunshine-yellow Volkswagen Beetle with Olivia. As Ben and I hopped into Dad's Prius, I couldn't help but laugh at my brother. His expression was comically put-out when Olivia settled herself right beside him in the back seat.

I didn't think Julian realized it, but he had a lot of dating options. If only he could wean himself off Raquel. Not that Liv was really an option for him, since she was way too young. Although, the age difference between Olivia and Julian wasn't much greater than the age difference between Hunter and me. A fact I tried not to think too much about. But still, girls fell for my brother all the time. He had the good looks and the pensive, brooding demeanor to go with them. And, on top of that, he was a hopeless romantic, more so than me even. A deadly combination.

I heard Liv squeal in delight when we arrived at the ranch. Mom and Julian were cringing as Mom's car pulled up beside Dad's. A young girl's scream was twice as loud in the confines of a small vehicle, especially to a vampire. Dad chuckled and looked over at a clueless Ben. "Your daughter wants to see some horses."

Ben looked over at Olivia, who was incessantly chatting away to Julian. Julian was nodding, and opening his mouth to speak, but Liv wasn't letting him get a word in edgewise. Amused, Ben returned his eyes to Dad. "Guess I'm going to have to break her heart about that one, since you guys don't use horses. I know I've told her that before. She must have been too young the last time we were here." He smirked as he added, "Horses are too tasty for Halina to leave alone."

Dad grinned and looked back at me. "You can train animals, but you just can't train a vampire."

From beneath the house, I could just make out a tired voice responding with, "I heard that."

Dad and I glanced over to where Halina's underground rooms were and chuckled. Ben followed our gaze, then asked, "Is she still awake?"

Dad nodded as he popped open his door. "Yep, for a little bit." His smile radiant, he told Ben, "You gotta see this. You're not gonna believe it."

Ben's expression was naturally curious.

Minutes later, our group was in the sunlight-protected living room, hugging the vampiric and non-vampiric members of my family. Liv was in seventh heaven, jabbering nonstop as she bounced between all the new people in her midst. Granted, as Ben had mentioned, Olivia had met everyone here before, but it was so long ago to her young mind, it was as if it had never happened. Youth was sort of a natural mind-wipe.

Ben was shaking hands with Gabriel when Halina opened her hideyhole and strolled into the room streaming with natural light. Ben's mouth dropped to the floor. He kept glancing from the windows to Halina, and back again. Then he snapped his gaze to Gabriel. Face ashen, he whispered, "What did you do?" As comfortable as Ben was around vampires, he didn't seem thrilled at the idea of them suddenly being able to roam freely during the day. I supposed that would make his stewardship of San Francisco all the more challenging if he had to be on his toes with full vampires twenty-four-seven.

Slinking up to Ben, Halina ran a hand seductively down his arm. Gabriel's only reaction to her flirtation was to raise an eyebrow, then his face went neutral again. He was well-aware of Halina's provocative nature.

Answering for Gabriel, Halina purred, "Relax, it's temporary." She sighed and leaned against Gabriel's arm. "Fifteen minutes a day is about all I get." Smiling up at the love of her life, she added, "But what a glorious fifteen minutes it is."

As Ben was shaking his head, still dumbstruck by the implications of Gabriel's latest invention, Olivia broke the short span of silence. "Why do you live in a wall?"

Halina's cool gaze floated down to the one person in the room who had no idea just how spectacular this was. "Because I'm awesome," she snipped. Julian snorted at hearing Halina say a word that was really out of place for someone her age, not that Olivia would know that. Not missing a beat, Halina asked Olivia, "Why do you never shut up?"

Mom, Dad, and Ben frowned, but none of them commented on the vampire's blunt question. Gabriel cracked a smile, amused. Grandpa Jack and Alanna looked at each other while Julian and I tried to hold our laughter. Halina often asked the questions we all wanted to ask, but out of politeness, couldn't. Halina didn't really give a rat's ass about etiquette.

As Liv blinked in surprise at the direct question, Imogen scolded her mother. "Halina ..."

Halina glanced up at the daughter who was really more of a best friend to her. "What? It's a valid question."

We all hung out with Halina in the living room for her fifteen minutes. Olivia seemed curious about why Halina had a time limit with us, but, out of politeness—or fear—she didn't ask. I could tell when Halina's free time was ending. She started flinching and pulling down her super-short dress, like she was trying to stretch the tiny piece of fabric so that it covered the long, lean thighs she was showing. Not too long after that she was twisting away from pools of light, finding darker areas in the sunny room to sit. Recognizing the signs of her body starting to reject whatever temporary shield he'd put up, Gabriel scooped up Halina and forcibly started to return her to her hideout. She clung to him in pain, but stubbornly asked for more time. He didn't give it to her, and moments later the pair were deep below the earth, where Halina was safe from the toxic sunlight.

As soon as Halina was gone, Olivia turned to her dad and rapid-fire asked, "What's wrong with her? Is she sick? Is she dying?" She paused a fraction of a second, then added, "Is she a vampire?"

The room was suddenly very quiet as everyone turned to look at her. Ben broke the silence with laughter. He scuffed up her hair as he jokingly told her, "You need to stop reading those scary stories. I've told you before, vampires aren't real." Pointing to where Halina had disappeared, Ben explained, "She has a rare sun allergy. It's deadly to her, except in this room. Here she's safe ... if only for a little while."

Olivia's normally sparkling face saddened as she looked at Halina's secret door. "Oh ... that's sad. I can't imagine never being in the sunshine." Ben put an arm around her while I shared her sentiments. I couldn't imagine it either ... and if I'd been born a few generations back, it would have been my fate. Looking up at her dad, Liv added, "Is that why she never does any fun stuff with us back home?"

Ben nodded. Halina went with us on our family trips, so she could blur Tracey's memory. She was only needed when we got there, so she could ease the shock of my family's youth, and when we left, so she could blur the memory of my family's features. It wasn't the ideal way Halina liked to do things—she'd much rather wipe a person clean—but it worked for now. She did the same sort of mental cleansing with Aunt Ashley's husband, Christian. When Halina wasn't needed on those trips, she left us and did her own thing. Since arrivals and departures always happened at night, Olivia had never been told about Halina's condition.

While Ben was explaining Halina's allergy to Olivia in greater detail, Gabriel popped back into the room. Face grim, the aged vampire stepped up to Ben. "I'm glad you're here. We might have a problem."

Ben turned away from his daughter and looked up at the emerald eyes regarding him. His face instantly shifted from devoted father to fierce warrior. It was an expression I'd seen on him before, when he'd been called away for work while we'd been visiting in California. Understanding Gabriel's vague statement, he asked, "The same problem as L.A.?"

Gabriel nodded, crossing his arms over his chest. "So it seems. I'm not sure yet, but ... there was another incident."

"What do you mean by incident?" I immediately asked.

THE NEXT GENERATION

Julian's voice overlapped mine. "What problem in L.A.?"

We were both ignored.

Ben hung his head, then ran a hand through his hair. My father broke apart from his conversation with Grandpa and Alanna. As he walked toward the pair, Ben looked up at Gabriel again. "Damn ... I guess I'm staying a while."

Olivia's eyes grew about ten sizes larger as she locked her sights on my brother. "We're staying!" She latched her arms around her father. "How long, Daddy? Are we staying here or at Julian's? Can I go to school here? Will Mom be coming up? Are we going to move here?"

Ben sighed and looked down at her. He seemed lost as to what question to answer first. Seeing a need for a distraction, Imogen, Alanna, and Grandma Linda bustled Liv out of the room with promises of freshly baked chocolate chip cookies. It was a tactic that had always worked on Julian and me when we were younger. Not anymore though. A steel resolve built up in Julian and mixed with his curiosity. My mood was similar.

My father was just as confused and curious as we were. He held that curiosity until Olivia was safely preoccupied, then he flicked his gaze between Ben and Gabriel. "What's going on?" he asked, then he settled his gaze on Gabriel. "I thought you said the thing in Los Angles was taken care of. I thought you said it was no big deal?"

Gabriel coolly returned his gaze. "I believed it was. Now, I think otherwise." He said it completely flat, void of emotion. Gabriel could be that way at times. Mom said it was his age. Things just didn't rile him up anymore. Not very often anyway. It made me wonder if we'd all be that aloof ... eventually.

Dad wasn't so aloof. Face hard, he looked back at Ben. "I think I need to be filled in now."

Standing, Ben nodded. "We should go somewhere private."

I immediately stood up, irritated. "We should know, too. We're almost adults." Lifting my chin, I straightened my back. "We can handle it."

Julian came over to stand beside me. "Yeah, if something is going on, we should be informed."

Frowning, Mom walked over to our expanding circle. She didn't say a word, just placed her hand on Dad's arm. He glanced at her, then back to us. "No, you're not adults yet. Some things you just don't need to be burdened with."

Floored, I blurted out, "That's bullshit!"

"Nika!" Mom reprimanded, her matching brown eyes fiery.

Embarrassed, and a little livid, I sputtered, "If there's some danger in the city, shouldn't we know what it is?"

Twisting to me, Dad put his hands on my shoulders. "No, you should trust that your family will protect you. The only thing a sixteen-year-old should have to worry about ... is school. And please ... don't swear."

He patted my shoulder while I burned holes into him with my eyes. Ignoring my stare, he turned to Gabriel. "Maybe we could discuss this in your lab?"

Gabriel looked over at me then Julian. As he nodded to my father, he studied our reactions. I could tell that he was analyzing us, probably wondering if we were both angry, or if it was only me, and Julian was feeling my anger. I wanted to snap at him, tell him that we were mutually upset, but I didn't. I might snap at my father from time to time, but Gabriel ... well, no one really talked back to him.

As the group disappeared into the hallway that led downstairs, Grandpa Jack stepped between Julian and me. Putting a hand on each of our shoulders, he sagely told us, "I know it can be hard, but sometimes it's best to stay away from the vampire drama. For as long as you can anyway." Grandpa's face was lined and worn, but his eyes were peaceful and full of love for his family. Chuckling a little, he added, "Besides, all that stress will turn you gray."

I glanced up at his silver hair. Feeling some of the tension in my body easing, I allowed a short laugh to escape. Julian's mood leveled as well, as Grandpa led us into the kitchen to help with the cookie-making. By the banging and laughing emanating from that room, it was clear that my grandmothers had decided to turn a relatively small event into a full-on production.

Coated in a light dusting of flour, Olivia was over the moon. Chuckling at her, Julian took a seat at the table with Grandpa. The two of them drifted into a conversation about fishing. It was a pastime all the men in my family enjoyed. As I walked over to help Grandma Linda "sort" the chocolate chips, I tried to ignore the quietness in the rest of the house. Gabriel's lab was soundproof, and whatever problems were being discussed were beyond my ears.

It was quite a while later before they all reappeared again. I looked at my parents expectantly as they joined us in the kitchen, but all they said was, "How are the cookies?" I discretely watched them all afternoon, but there was no hint of worry or stress in their mannerisms. Gabriel didn't rejoin our party, but that wasn't too unusual. He preferred to sleep during the day so he could stay up with Halina all night.

It was early evening when I got a surprise that I should have been expecting. The last rays of the sun were bathing the sky in a fiery display of color, with burnt orange swirled with light yellow and deep crimson. Julian and I had been playing croquet with Olivia, and even though it was my turn, I paused to absorb the sun's beauty. I knew that sunsets were based in science, but it was hard to witness such an extraordinary sight and not see something completely beyond science—something magical and unexplainable ... much like my family and me.

Julian and Olivia were taking in the sight as well when my phone buzzed in my pocket. Tearing my eyes away from the horizon, I glanced at the screen. Hunter. My heartbeat started to thud as I stared at his name. Julian snapped his head to me, and I muttered, "I gotta go," as I casually walked behind the building that housed the pool. Once I was away from Olivia's watchful eye, I blurred out to a field that was beyond my family's hearing.

Taking a deep, calming breath, I answered the phone. "Hello?"

"Hey, Nika ... it's Hunter."

The grin on my face was so large I was glad Hunter—and my family—weren't there to witness it. Trying to hide the adrenaline rushing through me, I told him, "Oh, hey, what's up?"

Mentally cursing myself for sounding like a carrot-munching rabbit, I shut my eyes and waited for his answer. "I was just ... thinking about you. What are you up to?"

Leaning against a fence nearby, my eyes roved over the piles of presents the cattle had left behind. "Just trying to avoid stepping in anything nasty."

"Huh?"

Laughing, I added, "I'm at my family's cattle ranch ... in one of the pastures."

There was a long pause on Hunter's end, then, "There were a dozen possible answers that I thought you might give me. That was not one of them." He chuckled, then asked, "A ranch? I've never been to a ranch. Sounds like fun."

I glanced around at the peaceful acres around me, the dark shapes of cows winding down for the evening. "It is. It's one of the best places on Earth."

"That's nice that you have that ... anchor. My life is a little more chaotic."

Grabbing a lock of my hair, I twirled it around my finger while I pictured Hunter's dark eyes. "Because you move around so much?"

A tired sigh escaped him. "Yeah. Don't get me wrong, all the new places and people are exciting, but ... a part of me would like to feel ..."

"Home?" I whispered.

I could hear his smile through the phone. "Yeah, exactly. I'd like to feel like I have a home." He inhaled, then added, "But Dad's job requires him to move around, and we only have each other, so, I go where he goes."

My heart sank as I thought of Hunter packing up and leaving one day. I understood the importance of family though. I was bound to mine for eternity. "Oh ... what does your dad do?"

"Ah ..." He thought for a moment, then said, "He's an independent contractor ... so he goes where the work is."

Knowing how volatile the economy could be, I cringed as I asked, "Are you guys going to be staying here long?" A spike of nerves rushed up my spine as I wondered if it was forward of me to ask him that question.

Again, I could hear his happiness through his words. "I hope so, Nika. I really hope so." I bit my lip to contain my squeal, but I couldn't contain my smile. While I resisted doing a little happy dance by the cow patties, Hunter added, "I know we've just met, but I already really like you ... and I'd like to keep getting to know you."

"I like you, too," I gushed. Clearing my throat, I tried to sound more adult. "I'd like that, too."

Hunter sighed. "I don't want to have to sneak around to see you, though. Maybe I should come over and talk to your mom?"

My back went ramrod straight as I looked back at the ranch house. I could feel my family stirring, but so far, they were giving me my privacy. I tried to picture my dad meeting his baby girl's "date." It was hard to envision that meeting going well. "I don't think so, Hunter. Not yet anyway," I quickly added, so he wouldn't be discouraged.

He still sounded disheartened though. "Well, maybe you could have dinner at my house some night? Meet my dad? I don't like hiding anything from him. In fact ... he already knows about you."

I blinked as I turned to look back at the horizon. "Oh ..." A little guilt seeped into me. Hunter was being open and honest while I was being sneaky. I hated it, I really did, but I knew my family would put an end to this blossoming romance if they knew about it. They'd all say I was too young, and Hunter was too old. Wondering what his dad thought, I timidly asked, "What did he say?"

"He told me you were young, and I needed to be careful with you." Embarrassment flashed through me at all the many things that sentence hinted at. It was quickly replaced by ... curiosity, and maybe a little bit of ... longing. In my silence, Hunter added, "He'd also like to meet you, which is why I think dinner at my place sounds like a great idea. What do you think?"

I wanted to instantly say yes, of course, but I had to consider the homing device that was an inbred part of me. I not only had to fib to get out of the house, I had to fib about where my location would be pinging me all night long. That complicated matters. And it added more lies to the lies I already hated telling. But ... to be invited into Hunter's home, to meet his family, to see how he lived everyday ... it was an irresistible draw. "I think it sounds great ... someday."

"Well, I hope it's someday soon."

A presence from the house started zooming toward me. Tensing, I quickly told Hunter, "I have to go. Talk to you later?"

"Yeah, okay, sure." He said that reluctantly, like he didn't want to hang up yet, but I had to, since a conversation with him was not something I wanted a family member overhearing.

As I slid the phone back into my pocket, Halina phased to a stop right in front of me. It was only then that I noticed that the sun had sunken completely, and the ranch was bathed in blackness. The whites of her eyes glowed with a phosphorescence that lit her face in a terrifying and awesome way. "Who's the boy?" she asked.

Surprise and worry flashed through me. She *had* heard my private conversation. Some of it at least. Enough to hear Hunter's voice on the other line. But how much had she heard? As casually as I could muster, I told her, "My lab partner at school." I actually did have a male lab partner in chemistry, so it wasn't a complete and total lie.

Halina regarded my face with her haunting eyes, and I felt the hypnotic peace of her gaze slowing my heartbeat, calming me down. That was the purpose of a vampire's blazing eyes—to help subdue their prey into submission. While it was a neat trick, I was grateful I didn't have to worry about that particular vampiric trait. My eyes were as lackluster in the darkness as any human's.

Finally, Halina gave me a secretive smile. "He cute?"

I wanted to gush and tell her that he was insanely hot, but I didn't want to pique her already peaked curiosity. I was just happy she'd bought my answer. "He's all right, I guess."

Shaking her head at my lukewarm reply, she pointed to the house with her thumb. "Dinner's ready."

I breathed a sigh of relief that this wasn't going to become an inquisition, then I blurred back to the house with Halina.

CHAPTER TEN

Julian

IT WAS A hard weekend for me. I spent the bulk of it avoiding Olivia while Nika ducked out of the house every so often to take phone calls from her sort-of boyfriend. But that wasn't what made it difficult. It was my mind replaying my romantic moment with Raquel, and then instantly remembering her heated moment with Russell in the theater. It stung. I stung.

It wasn't as if I'd never seen them together before. I had. But I'd only witnessed light pecks and hand holding. What had been happening in that movie theater was a full-on precursor to sex. I was positive that if they hadn't been doing it already, they were now. It killed me. Especially when I thought about her lips on mine … the way she'd looked at me, begged me with her eyes to save her, confessed she might have feelings for me …

I knew I had to let her go, had to move on, I just didn't know how. I'd liked her for so long that everyone else paled in comparison now. Somehow, I'd turned her into my ideal woman. Nika wanted me to move on with Arianna. I'd even briefly considered it while she'd stayed with me at a diner on that fateful night, eating my fries and trying to make me smile. She was very … sweet, and easy to talk to. But while Arianna was cute and nice, she didn't make my chest ache; she wasn't the one I fantasized about.

Late Sunday night, after Ben shepherded his exhausted daughter to sleep, and Mom and Dad closed their soundproof door, Nika stepped into my room. I looked up at her approach. My sister was beautiful, with thick, wavy brown hair and eyes that were a warm, welcoming shade of brown. Even though she was frowning at me, I saw happiness in the curves of her features. She was falling for this Hunter guy, and while I wasn't sure about him, I was at least thankful that he'd brightened Nika's outlook on life, and love. Now, if only mine could be lifted.

She sat next to me on the bed, her gaze drifting over my face. I slapped on a smile and her frown deepened. I couldn't fake out my sister. "So much has been going on, we haven't had a chance to talk about what happened at school yet. Do you want to?"

I averted my eyes. "There isn't much to say, Nick."

She put her hand over my folded ones. "You were frozen in that closet, Julian. You haven't completely frozen up like that in ... a long time."

I tried to look at her, but I couldn't, and my gaze drifted to our fingers instead. "I don't know what happened. I was fine ... then I wasn't. It was just a closet. It's so stupid that I was scared of a freaking closet."

Nika squeezed my hands under hers. "It wasn't stupid, Julian, and it wasn't just a closet ... you know that. You were back there again, weren't you?"

Shame swelled in me as I finally met her eyes. "I was three years old, Nika. Why can't I let it go?" My face darkened, along with my mood. "I'm a vampire. Vampires aren't scared of anything. I should be stronger."

Her gaze softened as she studied me. "You're sixteen. You're a kid."

I couldn't stop my smirk. "So are you."

She started to smile, then her face fell. "I get scared, too, Julian. It terrifies me that I could lose you again." She tossed her head back and forth. "I *can't* lose you again."

I looked away, no longer able to handle seeing the emotion as well as feeling it. "You won't," I whispered.

Nika sighed, then changed the topic. "Do you want to talk about Raquel?"

While Nika's spirits evened, mine plummeted. "Nothing much to say there either. She's with Russell. She loves ..." my voice hitched, " ... Russell."

Nika was silent as her hand shifted to my back. Her emotions expressed it for her, but she said it anyway. "I'm sorry, Julie."

I nodded at her. "I know, Nick."

Her face turned impish. "You know, you could always date—"

I shoved her shoulder away from me, knowing exactly what she was going to say. "Stop trying to play matchmaker." I laughed as I shook my head. "I'm not going to date your best friend."

Giggling, Nika indicated the guest room. "Actually, I was going to say Olivia."

I made a move to grab her, to put her in a headlock and give her a wet willy or something, but she blurred away from me. "Bitch," I joked.

Retreating to our mutual bathroom, she tossed out, "Just saying," before disappearing into her room.

I was smiling and rolling my eyes at her as I laid down on my bed. I felt lighter though. "Thanks, Nick."

"Anytime, Julie."

ONCE WE GOT back to school, I avoided Raquel. She'd made her choice, obviously, and trying to have a heartfelt conversation with her again wasn't going to do me any good. Sure, in her confusion, she might kiss me again, but that was all it would be—a stolen kiss in a closet—and I wanted more. Why set myself up for pain like that?

I managed to make it through the rest of September that way, most of October too. I kept my head down when they were near and shifted my focus to my friends and schoolwork. I might have started flirting a little with Arianna, but it was just to ease the heartache, and it was never anything serious, no more than how Arianna often flirted with me. I'd toss my arm over her shoulders when Raquel walked by. I'd lean in close to tell her something when Raquel was watching us across the cafeteria. It irritated Nika, and I hoped it wasn't leading Arianna on, but seeing the flash of jealousy in Raquel's eyes was almost addicting. It made my long days of watching her with Russell ... bearable.

I was waiting for Starla after school one afternoon with Nika, Trey, and Arianna, when Raquel's jealousy finally seemed to get the better of her. Arianna and I were sitting on the steps leading to the library, the long overhang of the building protecting us from the rain that had started. Arianna was sitting on the step right behind me, her legs on either side of me as I leaned back into her body. My head was resting on her stomach and she was trailing her fingers through my hair in a repetitive pattern that was surprisingly peaceful. I knew the way we were sitting was couple-like, but when she'd pulled me into her, I hadn't been able to resist. Nika was upset; I could feel the disapproval coming off her in waves.

My sister had asked me several times to stop flirting with her friend. She'd tell me, "If you don't like her, don't encourage her." But the thing was ... I did like Arianna. Maybe not in *that* way, not in the way I liked Raquel, but I enjoyed being around her. We'd had a lot of quiet conversations since she'd helped me get through my torment at the movie theater, and I found myself looking forward to talking to her. And if I was honest, I looked forward to flirting with her too. It felt really ... nice. Although, I supposed that was a habit I needed to break. Before Arianna got hurt.

Just as I was thinking that I should move away from Arianna, Raquel walked by. She did a double take when she noticed the way we were sitting on the steps, and a flash of something dark and vindictive spiked in me. *How does it feel?* I initially wanted to push the bitter feeling back, but it was better than pain, so I welcomed it instead, and stayed where I was on Arianna's lap. She sighed with contentment while Raquel seemed torn.

Surprising me, Raquel stopped and stepped under the overhang with my group. Looking at the students lingering nearby, she muttered, "Hey, Julian."

Staying where I was, I watched her every move. "Hey, Raquel."

Arianna, maybe feeling a little possessive, rested her hand on my chest. I thought to remove it, but the look of dismay on Raquel's perfect face lifted my heart, gave me a burst of painful hope. Was she upset at the idea of me having moved on? Did that mean she still cared about me? Still considered me ... a maybe?

Arianna's heart started increasing as she stroked her fingers over my chest. I knew I should stop her, move away from her, but with Raquel openly staring at me, I couldn't move; I could barely breathe. I hadn't said more than two words to Raquel since the closet incident, and this was the longest we'd looked at each other in a long time. Nika wasn't happy about Raquel being here, about the swarm of feelings resurfacing in my chest, but for now she was holding her tongue. I didn't know how much longer that would last.

Raquel pointed at Arianna and me. "Are you guys going to the Halloween party at Derrick's tonight?"

Adrenaline shot through me. She was asking about my plans? She hadn't done that since before Russell and I had gotten into it at the beginning of the year. Even though I was euphoric, I acted like it was no big deal. "Probably not. You?"

Raquel shrugged and tucked a dark lock of her hair behind her ear. It revealed a long, shapely neck that both sides of my nature longed for. "Yeah ... Russell wants to go."

She frowned after she said it, and I resisted every instinct I had to comfort her, to tell her that she could do better than Russell, to tell her that Arianna and I were just friends ... to tell her that I still wanted her. But being distant from her was drawing her closer, so I didn't say anything that was in my heart. Knowing she was waiting for some shred of hope that I would be there, I told her, "I'm sure you guys will have a good time." Not wanting to sound callus, I smiled and added, "Actually, I hope you have a great time."

She nodded at me, eyeing Arianna uneasily. "Thank you. I guess I should go. I hope ... I hope you change your mind and come."

She spun on her heel and walked away, seemingly flustered and embarrassed. Confusion welled in me as I watched her leave. *I hope you change your mind and come?* She *wanted* me to go to the party. Was she changing her mind about Russell? About me? About *us*?

I tried to sit up, but Arianna's grip on me tightened. Just as I was beginning to think that maybe I'd already misled Arianna, Nika snapped, "Mom's here, Julian." Her voice was as prickly as her mood.

I glanced over at her narrowed eyes, then turned to see Starla's car pulling into the lot. Arianna sighed as she let me go. Hopping up, I grabbed my bag. I wasn't sure what to do with Arianna now, since we'd somehow shifted our flirting into something more than casual; I hadn't meant to. Most of the time, I just followed her lead. Bouncing to her feet, Arianna said, "Are you sure you don't want to go to that party tonight? I think it could be fun." She gave me a small smile that was almost shy. It was ... kind of adorable.

Confusion tore through me as I looked at her; had she always been this pretty, or had she done something to herself in the last several weeks? New haircut? Different makeup? "I don't ... I don't know," I told her. I'm not really a party person ... or a costume person."

Nika muttered, "Or an honest person."

None of the humans heard my sister, but I glared at her anyway. Starla honked her horn at us, and Arianna sighed again, then gave me a radiant smile. "Have a good weekend, Julian, and call me, if you need to talk about ... anything. I'm here for you." She turned her smile to my sister. "I'll talk to you later, Nika."

She bounded away, nearly skipping; her kind words left a warmth hovering over my chest. *I'm here for you.* I'd never heard anyone but my family say that to me.

Just as I was about to head off to my "mom's" car, Trey grabbed my arm. His face oddly serious, he said, "You were joking, right? You *are* going to that party tonight, aren't you? It's gonna be huge, Julian."

I glanced over at the direction Raquel had taken, and again, confusion roiled within me. Should I let her comment go? *I hope you change your mind and come.* With a sigh, I finally told him, "Yeah, I'll be there."

He smacked my shoulder in approval as Nika stormed off, ticked now. I sighed, said goodbye to Trey, and followed her. Catching up, I asked, "Why are you mad?"

She spun in the rain to face me. "You've been flirting with Arianna for weeks. I think in the beginning, it was just to get a rise out of Raquel, but now ... I feel how happy you are when you're around her, Julian. And maybe it was stupid of me, but I thought you were actually starting to like her. But with the way you got all confused and hopeful when Raquel invited you to that party ... well, it's obvious that nothing has changed. It's still all about Raquel. And now you're blowing off Arianna to be with her? You got Arianna's hopes up, just like I asked you not to, and now you're dumping her, like some jackass, lamo ... guy! Is that who you want to be, Julian?" she asked.

Her biting tone got under my skin; it also struck a nerve. She might have a point, not that I was going to concede that while she was snapping at me. "A guy? Yeah, I would like to be a guy, because, if you hadn't noticed, I *am* a guy!"

Starla honked her horn again as Nika stood still as stone in the rain. Beads of it collected in her hair. Maybe it was my imagination, but I could almost hear the drops sizzling in her anger. "Don't be a *guy* ... be a man. If you don't want to be with Arianna, then leave her alone. She deserves better."

She spun again, leaving me standing alone in the rain. Shame pelted me as I watched Nika slam Starla's door shut. She was right. I liked Arianna, in the friendly sort of way, and she did deserve better—she deserved someone amazing, like she was. Someone who thought the sun rose and set with her. I would tell her. The next time I saw her, I would sit her down and be brutally honest with her. I liked her as a friend, but that was it ... so the flirting needed to stop. I didn't want to hurt her like Raquel had so often hurt me.

Head down, I trailed after my sister. Starla spun out of the lot before I even got my door closed all the way. She immediately took Nika to the library, since she spent every day after school there on her still-secret dates with Hunter. As Nika exited the car, I muttered, "I'm sorry, Nick. I'll tell her I don't see her that way. I'll leave her alone."

Nika paused. Face still stony, anger washing up and down her body, she nodded stiffly, then slammed the door shut. I sighed, and Starla chuckled as she pulled away. "Score one for Nika ... she owned your ass back there." She popped a bubble with her gum, her gaze locked on mine in the rearview mirror. "Serves you right for being a prick."

Closing my eyes, I leaned my head back on the seat and wished I could magically teleport like so many vampires in the movies could. That would be a much handier super power than excessively good hearing.

Starla took me home next, and seeing Ben's rental car in the drive made me sigh. If he was there, then Liv was there too, and I felt like I'd been fawned over enough for one day. Thanking Starla for her parental duties, I opened the front door and stepped inside. By the response, you'd think I was a soldier returning from the war.

"Julian!"

Liv's arms cinched around me, and I struggled to breathe. For such a young girl, she was exceptionally strong. Coughing, I removed my bag from my shoulder and held it out. "Hey, Liv, you want to give me a hand and run my bag to my room?"

She brightened and nodded her head so hard I thought she might give herself whiplash. "Sure thing, Julian." She had my bag halfway up the steps before I could even tell her thank you. I peeked over to the living room, to see if Ben would scold me for using his daughter like that, but Ben wasn't in there. Tuning in, I heard him talking to someone in the kitchen.

"I'm at Teren's now. When he gets home, we'll go check it out. Like I said, I'm not as good at spotting these as you, but better safe than sorry."

Curious, I tiptoed into the room. Ben was frowning, cell phone to his ear, while he hunched over the kitchen table. There was an open laptop, but I couldn't see the screen from where I was. The table was covered in newspapers; they all seemed to be opened to the classifieds section. Ben's finger traced lines over the black print as the person on the other line spoke to him. "What about the one I showed you last night? Were you able to follow up on it?"

Ben sighed, closing his eyes. "We were too late. I cleaned up the best I could, but—"

A floorboard creaked under my weight, and I stopped moving. Even though he was human, Ben heard me and stopped explaining. The voice on the other end heard me too. "Is someone there, Ben? Is it Teren?"

Straightening, Ben locked gazes with me. "No ... Julian."

"Ah, I see. I'll let you deal with that then."

The line disconnected, and Ben set his phone down. Wondering how to explain to the adult before me that I was spying, I slapped on a smile. "Hey, Ben. You, uh ... looking for a job?"

Ben gave me a business-like smile. "Something like that. I didn't hear you come in." He snapped the laptop shut.

Shrugging, I walked over to the table and examined the slew of papers; a handful of the classifieds were circled in red. "Sorry, I was just hungry ... wanted to get something to eat but didn't want to bug you."

Ben nodded and started cleaning up the newspapers as I tried to read the details of some. They seemed like random *Help Wanted* listings. Maybe he really was looking for a job. He'd been here a while, helping Gabriel with his super-secret L.A. type problem. A problem that none of the adults would discuss around any of us kids.

Wondering if he'd slip up while he was preoccupied with cleaning, I asked, "Was that Gabriel on the phone?" Ben stopped collecting papers and glanced at me. "It sounded like him," I added.

Shaking his head, Ben quickly swept away the rest of the mess. "Your hearing never ceases to amaze me." Folding the papers into a more manageable pile, he met my eye. "Yeah, that was Gabriel."

Determined to get some answers, I crossed my arms over my chest. "And what did he want? What exactly did he show you last night, and what did you have to 'clean up'?"

Ben stared at me a moment, weighing me. Then he flashed a smile that made the women melt, or so I'd been told. "Don't worry about it, kid. Your dad and I have it under control."

"Didn't sound like it. It sounded like you were too late. It sounded like you needed help." I snatched the pile of papers from him, lightning fast. "What are these about?"

Ben blinked, then snatched the papers back from me. "I know you want to help, Julian, you and Nika both, but your parents have asked for you two to not be involved ... and I have to respect that." Running a hand through his highlights, he let out a weary exhale. "I'm sorry, I can't tell you anything."

He tucked the newspapers under some books on the counter, hiding the last of the "Services Needed" postings. He gave me a blank look that all adults give children when they aren't going to budge on something. It irritated me. I wasn't a kid anymore, and I didn't need to be sheltered.

I felt Nika's buoyant mood start to shift toward curiosity as Ben and I stared each other down. The mounting tension in the room was only broken by Olivia, who burst around the corner and attached herself to my body. "I put your bag away, Julian!" Her cheeks were rosy as her bright face searched mine like I had all the answers to life's most important questions. "Can I do anything else for you?"

Ben raised an eyebrow. Not tearing his gaze from me, he asked his daughter, "You're doing chores for him?"

I cringed as Liv twisted to face her dad. "Just little ones."

Ben put a hand on her shoulder. "You don't have to do that." He shifted to cup her cheek. "I'm going to take you to the airport in the morning, so you can go visit your mom for a while. Why don't you go get your stuff together?"

Liv frowned and looked back at me. "I don't want to go."

Ben sighed and pulled her in for a hug. "I don't want you to go either, sweetheart, but Mom misses you, and you've missed too much school." His eyes were moist when he pulled away from her. Tucking a golden lock of hair behind her ear, he told her, "But if I'm not done here soon, I'll have Mom send you back for a visit, okay?"

While Ben had been staying here with us, he and Tracey had been shuffling Olivia back and forth. It was hard on her, to be shuttled around, flown from one parent to the other. But Ben got antsy when she was away from him for too long. I'd heard him tell Dad that not everyone in San Francisco appreciated his services. He was worried that some ticked off vampire would harm his daughter ... or his wife. Even though Ben was devoted to my family, even though he'd left mixed-vampire bodyguards behind to watch over his loved ones, being here was a struggle for him. I could see the weariness all over his features. One more reason he should let my sister and me help. All hands on deck.

Olivia nodded sadly before trudging out of the room. Standing, Ben faced me. "She adores you, Julian. Please don't make her do things for you." With those words, he grabbed the laptop, books, and papers, and left me alone in the kitchen.

Nice. I'd been reprimanded for using two girls today. Well, wasn't I turning into a full-fledged dick. Pretty soon, I'd be cornering guys in the locker room and roughing up my girlfriend. No. No, I'd never do that.

Before too long, my parents came back home with Nika. She was bubbly, having spent a good chunk of her afternoon with Hunter. My parents were still in the dark about that. They just assumed that Nika had a love of books that bordered on obsession. During dinner, Nika brought up our spat after school. "Hey, sorry to snap at you earlier."

Mom and Dad were in a conversation with Ben, both of them pretending to eat the bits of food on their plate, since Olivia was seated to my left, watching everything. Undead vampires couldn't eat human food anymore. I wasn't sure what would happen if they did, but Mom had hinted once that it wasn't pretty.

"It's okay, you were right," I told her.

She smiled brighter. Like most girls, Nika loved hearing that she was right. Glancing at Mom and Dad, she asked, "So, are you still ... ?"

She didn't finish her question since our parents were in earshot, but I knew what she was referring to—she wanted to know if I was still going to go to that Halloween party with Trey. Honestly, I'd put it from my mind once I'd gotten home, but, now that she mentioned it ... "Yeah, yeah I think so."

Nika pushed some chicken around her plate, not too thrilled by my answer. She didn't say anything more though. She couldn't really. If she outed that I was going to sneak off to some underage drinking party, then I might out her secret boyfriend. And even though Nika and Hunter were taking things slowly, usually only meeting at the library during the week, their friendship was not something Nika wanted to share just yet.

After dinner, Dad and Ben left the house to look into whatever it was Ben had found in the classifieds. Mom seemed worried as she stared out the front windows, playing with the heart locket around her neck. The gold locket opened to reveal baby pictures of Nika and me, along with tiny pictures of Mom and Dad. Dad had given it to Mom when she was pregnant with us; she wore it almost every single day.

I played a board game in the dining room with Olivia while I waited; Nika gabbed with Arianna in her bedroom. I wasn't quite sure how to sneak out of the house with two supernatural parents. It wasn't just their hearing that I had to watch out for. No, the blood bond was the real problem. I had an internal GPS spouting my location to them twenty-four-seven. There *was* a way to turn it off—that was what had happened to me when I was younger—but I didn't know what the drug was that I'd been dosed with. All I remembered about it was that it had made me sick to my stomach ... and it had burned. I'd felt on fire as the shot had moved through my veins.

I pushed the memory of that horror away as Olivia took three of my checker pieces. I didn't need to have a panic attack right now. And besides, shutting off the bond wasn't an option either. Sure, I'd be able to ditch my parents, but if I suddenly dropped out of their senses, they'd call in everybody to find me. The whole family would be on alert. That level of stress wasn't my goal tonight. *No* stress was my goal tonight. No stress ... and seeing Raquel.

I looked up at Mom in the window when I felt Dad's location start to firmly head toward home. Sighing, Mom rested her head against the glass and murmured, "Thank you." I wasn't sure if she was thanking Dad, or thanking fate.

Her face was a picture of peace when he finally walked back into the house. Dad's face was the same. They instantly locked onto each other, like they'd been apart for years, not hours. They were kissing and whispering words of affection while Ben scooted around them, unfazed. He was used to their passionate homecomings. We all were. It was their special bond that fueled the reaction. Well, that and a giant helping of love and respect. But the bond drove them to want to be together, gave them each a euphoric feeling when they met up. I couldn't imagine what having a connection like that must feel like, although, I did get a tiny buzz whenever Raquel was near me. Arianna, too, in a way.

As Ben walked over to his daughter, he mumbled under his breath, "I'm so glad that bond has tapered off over the years. I really don't want to ever find you guys going at it in my car again."

I snorted. Ben's eyes locked on mine and he paled, like he'd again forgotten that I could hear him just as well as my parents. Mom pulled away from Dad, her mouth wide open. "Ben!" She indicated me with her hand. I bit my lip to stop myself from laughing; Dad couldn't stop himself. Nika continued chattering to Arianna upstairs. Preoccupied with her own conversation, she didn't seem to have overheard Ben's comment.

Olivia looked confused by everyone's strange reactions. "What's going on?"

Ben quickly changed the topic. "Time for bed, kiddo."

He hustled her upstairs. Mom and Dad kissed me goodnight, then headed up to their room. By the look on Mom's face, I could tell that she was dying to know what Ben and Dad had discovered. I also knew that the pair wouldn't talk about it until they were behind their soundproof door. This worked well for me on the hearing front, but made it trickier too. With the door closed, I wouldn't be able to tell when they were asleep. They could stay up all night talking. If I tried to sneak out of the house and they were awake, I'd have hell to pay.

Trudging up to my room, I thought maybe I'd have to skip the party after all. Nika was off the phone with Arianna when I entered my room. She was sitting on her bed, waiting. I didn't know if she was waiting to talk to me, or waiting for my parents to fall asleep. Realizing that between my parents and my watch-guard sister, I was thoroughly stuck at home, I slipped into the bathroom, brushed my teeth, and got ready for bed. Nika watched me without comment. When I was done, I closed my door to the bathroom, effectively blocking her out. "Goodnight, Nick."

"Are you staying home then?" she asked.

Flopping onto my bed, I took off my shoes with my toes. I could feel the pulsing enclosure of my family's presence imprisoning me. I'd so wanted to see Raquel tonight ... I just had no way to leave. "Looks like it ..."

"That's probably for the best, Julian. Raquel may act interested at times, but she's—"

I cut off her well-intentioned speech. "I'm tired, Nika. I just want to go to sleep."

Nika murmured okay, then was silent. Sighing, I closed my eyes and tried to forget that—right now—Raquel was at a party with Russell ... and she might be looking for me. My phone buzzed, but I ignored it. It was just Trey, asking where the hell I was. He'd forget about me soon enough, once he found some illegal substances to indulge in. I just couldn't handle telling him that I couldn't make it. It was too disappointing.

Two hours later, I was still wide awake. Staring at the light fixture in the center of the room, I debated abandoning sleep all together and going downstairs to watch some TV. Then I wondered if maybe I could sneak out after all. Sitting up, I glanced at the clock. It was late, but not too late. A bunch of partying teenagers could still be going strong. Looking over to the closed bathroom door separating my room from Nika's, I murmured, "Nick? You awake?"

Silence met my ear. Well, mainly silence. I could pick out the light breathing sounds of Ben, Olivia, and my sister. I could also hear their slow, steady heartbeats. They all seemed to be asleep. My parents, though, that was a gamble. If I cracked their door to check, they could wake up. If I just left, and they were still awake, I wouldn't get very far, and I'd be in a massive amount of trouble.

Grabbing my shoes, I decided to take the risk of leaving. If they were up, and I got in trouble, then ... so be it, I got in trouble. If they weren't up, and I got to see Raquel all decked out in her Halloween costume, well, that was worth a little scolding.

I grabbed my jacket off the floor before quietly closing my bedroom door. Careful to not wake up my sister, I tiptoed downstairs. A floorboard creaked near the front door and I froze. No sounds in the house changed, and I tried to still my rapidly beating heart, tried to smooth the adrenaline running through me. Being loud wasn't the only thing that could wake up my sister. If my emotions were strong enough, that might wake her up too. Taking long, slow, deep breaths, I opened the front door and stepped through it.

This was where my parents would question me if they were still awake. Leaving the house would certainly stoke their curiosity. Walking as nonchalantly as I could, I grabbed my skateboard resting at the edge of the flower garden near the porch. Nothing so far. They must be asleep. Terrified and thrilled, I set down the board and skated off. I started counting in my head. I was sure I wouldn't get to twenty before someone started shouting. When I made it to fifty, I started relaxing.

My grin huge, I used a bit of my inhuman strength to propel the board as quickly as I could. I also grabbed the phone from my jacket pocket and texted Trey. *'I'll be at the party in fifteen.'*

His response was a little slow. *'Dude, I thought you were already here?'*

Shaking my head at him, I dug in a little harder. No, not yet ... but soon.

Derrick's house was pretty far from mine, on the edge of the city. The night was frigid as I strode up the dusty drive. Kids were milling about outside, though, too entertained to mind the nip in the air. Everyone was dressed in some type of Halloween costume. Wearing jeans and a T-shirt, I stood out, but I didn't care. I wasn't here to win a costume contest. Hopefully, I'd be winning Raquel's heart away from Russell. That was my goal tonight.

I left my board on the brown lawn, near a prickly bush that had seen better days. Derrick's place was on a couple of acres, and was secluded enough that no one would probably call the cops on a bunch of rowdy kids. His parents were constantly gone on business trips, which made his place the ideal weekend party spot. I'd never actually been here before, but I'd heard some pretty crazy stories.

You would think that teenage drinking and partying would be almost non-existent in a city that was so centralized around a religion that frowned on any mind-altering substances, but, that wasn't the case tonight. Plastic cups filled with toxic-smelling liquid were everywhere around me as I stepped into the two-story party central.

A zombie and a mummy were hanging out by the front door. They both checked me out, then ignored me. I wondered how I was going to find Trey as I walked through the swarm of partiers. He found me though. I was trying to politely squeeze through a couple of barely clad genies when he barged into me. Slamming me from behind, he made me bump into the girls. One of them smacked me when I accidentally brushed her chest. Trey started laughing uncontrollably as they walked away in a huff.

"Thanks, man," I muttered.

He wiped his bloodshot eyes. "That was priceless, Adams."

I could tell from Trey's appearance—and his smell—that he'd been here a while and he was clearly feeling no pain. Knowing he'd know where my girl was hiding, I leaned in so he could hear me above the din of the crowd and music. "You seen Raquel?"

Trey looked confused for a second, then nodded. He was dressed as a court jester, and the bells on his hat jingled as he indicated upstairs. "She went up there."

My heart dropped as I glanced at the stairs leading to the second floor ... where the bedrooms were. "She alone?"

Trey's hand on my shoulder swung my attention back to him. "Let it go, man." He held up a joint. "Smoke this and you'll forget all about her."

I shook my head and started wading through witches and warlocks to get to the stairs. Trey followed close behind. "Julian, you don't want to go up there."

Furious and in pain, I ignored him. I didn't know what I'd been expecting. Raquel had told me she was coming here with Russell. There had just been something in the way she'd asked me to change my mind and come, something in her voice when she'd seen me with Arianna. I thought ... I thought coming here tonight might change everything for us. Trudging up the stairs, I wasn't sure what I was going to do once I got to the top.

People around me were laughing, talking, drinking, and there seemed to be a line to get into the bedrooms ... the make-out rooms. And more, I supposed, but I couldn't think about that. Thinking about Raquel and Russell going at it might make me throw up. I tried to weasel my way to the front of the line, but a football player grabbed my shoulder and pushed me back.

"Wait your turn, douche!"

Glaring at him, I imagined pushing him so hard he flew all the way to the back wall. Even though he was bigger than me, I knew I could do it. And it wasn't helping my anger any that I could clearly hear moaning and groaning coming from each of the three closed rooms. I could even hear a bed squeaking in the far one. Not seeing Raquel in the hall, I had to imagine that she was in one of the bedrooms.

Trey pulled on my shoulder when I didn't back down from the jock in front of me. "Dude, ease up."

I couldn't. I was too hurt to ease up. Raquel was miserable with Russell, but she wouldn't leave him. She'd shown me her vulnerable side ... she'd kissed me. But it hadn't changed her mind, and now ... She could be having sex with him. The couple crying out so loudly that the kids in the hall were chuckling at them could be Raquel and Russell. I had to grab my stomach it hurt so much.

I was just about to physically remove the man blocking my path when I heard something that stopped my heart. In the bedroom closest to me, a soft voice said, "No, Russell, I don't want to go that far."

I held my breath. It wasn't Raquel that was screaming, "Yes," and about to finish in the far room. She *was* with Russell, but they were just kissing. Funny how that was comforting to me now. My hand balled into a fist while I waited for Russell's response. If he tried to force her ... I would end him.

"What? Don't give me this shit, Raquel. You get me all worked up ... again ... and then you turn me down ... again? I'm not taking this crap anymore." I heard clothes being adjusted, bodies shifting.

In a panicked voice, I heard Raquel tell him, "Don't be mad. I will ... just not like this ... not at a party."

"Whatever," he muttered.

My body was searing with anger when he opened the door. Also dressed as a football player, Russell made a show of zipping up his pants as he exited the room. The kids in the hall cheered, clapping him on the back. The verbal couple hit their peak just then, adding to the joyous sounds. I clenched my stomach harder.

Trey pulled on my arm. "Let's go, man."

I was the only one who knew nothing had happened in that room. As Russell passed, I couldn't help but tell him, "Better luck next time."

Russell glanced at me, but didn't react to my comment. He gave me a derisive sniff, stumbled, and headed down the stairs. I figured he was drunk, and had missed my diss. He probably hadn't even gotten a full look at me, otherwise he might have started something. The jerk who had been blocking my path to the bedrooms finally darted into a free room with his cheerleader in tow, and I took the opportunity to sneak ahead of an oblivious couple making out in the hallway. Trey raised his arms in a questioning gesture, and I gave him a quick smile before I headed into the bedroom that Raquel was still in.

Raquel and Russell had been in the master bedroom by the size of the bed and the contemporary décor. Raquel was sitting on the edge of the mattress, looking forlorn, when I closed the door. Hearing me, she looked up. "Russell?" Her face fell a little. "Oh ... hey, Julian. You decided to come to the party after all, huh?" Wiping under her eyes, she asked, "Arianna here?"

As I sat beside her on the bed, I tried to block out the image of Russell zipping up his pants. I also tried to ignore the fact that they'd been rolling around on this bed only moments ago. Raquel was dressed as a fairy. Her hair had been elaborately curled and pinned, but some of the dark strands had fallen loose. Her eyes were masked in pastel makeup; some of it was smudged. Her outfit was disheveled, slightly out of place in some areas. She was absentmindedly fingering a set of wings in her hands. "You shouldn't be in here," she whispered.

Seeing the pain on her face, I shoved aside my heartache, replacing it with concern. "Are you okay? Did he ... hurt you?"

She glanced up at me, her eyes wet. "No, we didn't do anything. I told him no." She frowned as she searched my face. "I don't know why I'm telling you that."

My heart skipped a beat. "Raquel ... I ..."

She stood up, cutting me off. "I should go find Russell ..."

Standing, I grabbed her hand. "Don't ... stay here with me."

She stepped closer to me, but her eyes darted around the room, over the bed. "Julian, I ..."

Intimate sounds from the other rooms seeped into my head. They didn't make me sick this time ... they made me want her even more. I felt the warmth and desire for her growing as we stood there, staring at each other. Knowing Nika was asleep, and for once my feelings were my own, I embraced them. I opened myself up to them. Pulling her closer, I cupped her cheek. "You deserve better, Raquel. You should have seen his face when he left this room, like you were an object he'd won." I shook my head. "I'd never treat you like an object." I leaned in, and my body pressed along the length of hers. "I ... I think I love you," I whispered. It felt so true after I said it, but at the same time ... incomplete. The possibility of growth was there, and I wanted to explore it with her. I *wanted* to love her.

"Oh ... Julian. Sometimes I think ... I could love you too. Maybe ..."

She pressed her lips to mine then, and I thought I might die from the burst of joy exploding through me. I kissed her as softly and tenderly as I could, trying to show her that I could be different than Russell. Kind in a way he wasn't. Raquel returned every soft kiss, even sought my lips when I pulled back a little. She was changing her mind about us, I was sure of it.

Feeling bolder, I cupped her other cheek, drawing her in. Her lips parted, and I ducked my tongue inside. She made a noise that sent a chill straight through me. I couldn't believe I'd caused that erotic sound to come from her, and I really couldn't believe it when her hands slid up my chest and snaked around my neck. Our mouths moved together in an increasingly passionate tempo, and before I knew it, I had her pressed against the bed. She folded, sitting down and laying back on it. I hovered over her, our mouths still locked as one. Then our bodies met. I was ready for her, ready for more. I rocked against her and she cried out again. I couldn't believe it.

Full of so much love and passion I thought I'd go crazy; I broke apart from her lips. Dragging my mouth down the neck that I longed for, I told her, "We'd be great together, Raquel ... perfect."

Her body wrapped around mine, and I pressed into her again. I thought I might explode if I did that too many times. It felt so good though, I couldn't stop. Her hips met mine, her breath as fast as my own. Then her body stiffened. She clutched my shoulder, and hissed, "Oh God, Julian ... yes."

I watched the euphoria on her face, watched her gasp and close her eyes. Was she ... ? I wanted to experience it with her, but I didn't want to push her, and she'd already told Russell she didn't want to go that far at a party. Pulling back, I watched my beautiful fairy exploding. When her face relaxed, the entire moment changed. She closed her eyes, then she hitched a sob. Alarmed, I moved away from her. "Raquel, what is it?"

Her hands flew to her face. "Oh, God ... I shouldn't be doing this."

She rose from the bed, tears down her cheeks now. My earlier bliss evaporated at the devastation on her face, and I tenderly grabbed her hand. "Please don't shut down on me again. Don't turn your back on us. You like me, I know you do, and we could be amazing, Raquel."

She looked at me, her face torn. "But I'm in love with Russell, Julian … I'm sorry." Biting her lip, she added, "And you're with Arianna, you shouldn't be in love with me."

Standing, I shook my head. "No, Arianna and I are just friends." I cupped her cheeks. "You can't really love him. You wouldn't keep kissing me if you loved him." I pointed at the bed. "*That* wouldn't have happened, if you loved him."

Twin tears rolled down her cheeks as she pulled her arm free. "I'm sorry … I have to go."

With that, she turned and left. Another couple barreled into the room once she was gone, and I was quickly pushed out. My face was blank as Trey walked up to me. I felt numb inside. No, I felt dead. For the second time, she'd pulled me in, then pushed me away. For Russell.

Looking me over, Trey held his joint out to me. "Want to smoke now?"

I glanced down at the drugs, then back to the bedroom where Raquel had broken my heart. Again. The hole in my chest was worse than any stake wound would have been. Needing a break from pain and suffering, I twisted back to Trey. "Yeah … give it to me."

Smiling, he did.

CHAPTER ELEVEN

Nika

I WAS HAVING a nightmare. It was a nightmare I hadn't had in a while. It was one of those that jerked me into reality, made me question what was real and what wasn't when I woke up. It was an especially terrifying dream for me, because it was based in reality. It was about Julian … about his abduction.

I woke up with a start, clutching my sheets to my chest. My heart raced as I exhaled heavy breaths. In the dream, Julian was missing, our blood bond gone. All I'd been able to sense was his fear, his fear mixed with my own. It was awful.

Tears were in my eyes as I laid in my bed, begging my body to return to normal. "Julie?" I whispered, terrified my dream was real.

When he didn't answer me, I slowly began to realize that he wasn't at home. Through the bond, I could feel him miles away from here. Alarmed, I sprang to my feet and burst through our mutual bathroom. Flying into his bedroom, I looked around for any sign of foul play. Since his room was always a disaster, it was impossible to tell what had happened here.

Trying to control the panic rising in me, I focused on what he was feeling. Was he hurt? Scared? No … he wasn't. As I paid more attention to him, I felt his … euphoria. It was strange though, not like normal joy. It was almost like he was obliviously happy—giddy. He felt light and airy, but in an unnatural way. Just tapping into his emotions was giving me a buzz. I giggled a little as his elation settled over me. And that was when it hit me.

"Oh my God, Julian … you're wasted." My head snapped to the direction my derelict brother was. "You went to that freaking party and now you're wasted!" I hissed that as quietly as I could, but it really didn't matter, since my super-hearing parents were behind soundproof doors.

Sensing that Ben and Olivia were deep in REM sleep, I quickly changed and headed downstairs. No way was I going to let Julian stay out all night drunk or stoned. Who knew what kind of trouble he could get into. Knowing I was going to get in just as much trouble as Julian if I got caught, I grabbed my dad's keys from his jacket hanging by the front door. I felt like every jingle the keys made when they touched each other was going to wake up somebody, but I wanted to get to Julian fast. Well, fast and discreet. I could run to him in the blink of an eye, but a human could see me if they caught the right angle. Since Julian wasn't in pain or in trouble, it wasn't worth the risk. And showing up at a party in a car was easier to explain than saying I was out in the middle of the night on foot.

I opened my dad's Pruis as stealthily as I could. Grateful for once that it wasn't a noisy muscle car, I started the engine. The whine was slight, but I didn't hear or feel any rustling in the house. Exhaling the breath I'd been holding, I backed out of the drive and sped my way to Julian.

The house where he was partying was in a secluded area just outside of the city. It was the farthest house away in our school district, just on the edge of being too far. The gravel driveway was long and twisted, with an open gate at the beginning. For a moment, it reminded me of the ranch.

Checking in with those vampires, I made a note of where the rest of the family was. So far, nobody had started heading toward Julian and me. If any relatives back at the ranch were curious over why our locations had started moving, they weren't doing anything about it. Of course, we were far enough away from the ranch that they wouldn't really be able to tell that we'd left the house; I doubted they could even tell we were gone. All I could feel from them was a vague sense that they were east of me. We'd have to be much closer for the bond to get more specific.

There were so many cars in the driveway that I had to park far from the house. Even though it was chilly and late, kids were ambling about. They were all dressed up in some sort of costume, and I instantly felt out of place as I stepped from the vehicle. Sensing my brother in the heart of the two-story home, I headed that way.

Zombies coated in latex and fake blood were everywhere; it was definitely the "in" costume this year. As I walked through the wide-open front door, it almost looked like the house was under some sort of paranormal siege. But, if it was, then it was the happiest siege in all of history. Smiles, laughter, dancing, and kissing couples were everywhere I turned. Plastic cups were in almost every set of hands and from the smell wafting out of the cups, I was sure it wasn't lemonade.

I felt my brother off to the left of the house, so I pushed my way through the crowd to get over there. I was stopped by several kids from school who wanted to chat with me. Most of them seemed surprised to see me; I generally wasn't the partying type. None of them knew where my brother was when I asked. I knew exactly where to find him, but for appearances, I had to ask around. When I made it to the kitchen, I got a little lost. My brother was below the kitchen, but I had no idea how to get down there.

Derrick, the senior who lived here, was chatting with a slutty nurse by the refrigerator. He was dressed as an Egyptian Pharaoh; the two outfits clashed like crazy. If the nurse was his girlfriend, they really should have coordinated better. Stepping up to him, I tapped his bare bicep. He glanced at me, then turned back to the inebriated nurse hanging on his every word.

"Derrick?" I asked, tapping him a little harder.

Obviously not wanting to be interrupted, he glared at me. "Yeah?"

"You got a basement?"

He pointed to a door that was slightly ajar. Now that I was paying attention to it, I could smell the pungent odor of pot coming from that direction. Cursing my idiot brother, I darted for the door. Derrick called out after me, "Don't burn anything down there."

The smell of weed and incense was stronger with every step I took. The basement was dark; the only lights in the room were black lights. It made my teeth gleam and my white shirt glow. I was sure my eyes glowed a little too ... a weaker version of the rest of my family's eyes. The room I stepped into was a den/pantry. Shelves of food lined the wall, most of them jarred or canned. A couple of couches were in the center of the room, a large TV next to them. I could easily picture Derrick and his family coming down here to play board games or watch a movie. When the room wasn't full of kids getting high, of course.

A thin layer of smoke hung in the air as pipes were passed back and forth. My brother was sitting on a couch with Trey, laughing as they shared a bright white cigarette-like joint. Julian seemed completely oblivious to the fact that I was here. Even in his current state, he had to know I was; our bond was intact, even if his mind wasn't. All I felt from him was joy though, a joy that made me want to giggle, dance, and sing. I kept a firm hold on my sobriety as I stepped up to him.

"Julian, it's time to go," I stated in my most authoritative voice.

Twisting to look at me, he took a long drag off the joint he was holding. I tried to rein in my anger as I watched him inhale it, hold it, then slowly exhale it. "Hey, Nika, when did you get here?"

He started laughing as he handed the pot to Trey. I was concentrating on not reacting to the drug's effect on Julian's emotions when I noticed it. The black lights made his teeth shine in the darkness ... and his canines were much longer than they should have been—about as long as our teeth could go. He had his fangs completely extended.

I gasped and grabbed his face. "Julian! Stop it!"

I tried to close his mouth but a spike of irritation flashed through Julian's giddy state and he hissed at me, then growled. It was the low, intense growl that our dad had taught him in the kitchen. It made the hairs on the back of my neck stand up. The potheads in the room didn't react to it, but Trey did.

"Dude! That was fantastic!" He took a hit from his joint. "I take it back ... your costume's not lame. Well, no, being a vampire is still lame, dude ... but the growl is cool."

My eyes snapped to Trey's. "His costume?"

Trey was dressed as a joker or jester; his hat had little bells on it that chimed when he moved. As he nodded, his glazed eyes locked onto Julian's teeth. "Yeah. The outfit sucks though ... you really should have a cape ... maybe some blood running out of your mouth." He reached over and touched one of Julian's fangs. My eyes were as wide as they could go. "But your teeth are so real they're freaky. Where'd you buy those anyway?"

Crap. This inspection of Julian's teeth needed to end right now. High or not, Trey might piece some things together if it went on for too long. Using strength that was unnatural for me to have, I pulled Julian to his feet. He was irritated at being manhandled, but then a laidback smile crept over his features. His high flooded me, and I closed my eyes. It was hard to separate his feelings from mine while his body was being herbally enhanced. I chuckled, then my eyes flew open. "You're making me high!" I hissed under my breath.

Julian laughed. "Really? That's ... awesome."

I shoved his shoulder, feeling a little unsteady on my feet. "No, it's not ... it's weird." I brought my fingers to my head; the lighter Julian felt, the lighter I was starting to feel. It was disorienting, to say the least. "Come on, we have to go. Mom and Dad will kill you if they figure out where you are."

Julian shrugged, then trudged along behind me. Trey popped up beside us. I blinked at him, feeling sluggish. The residual pot in the air wasn't helping me fight off my brother's lackadaisical mood. "Where are you going?" I asked him.

"With you. I need a ride home." He grabbed a skateboard off the floor, like that was his only other option, and he really didn't want to take it.

I sighed, then wondered if I should even drive in this state. Like the blood bond, our emotive bond was stronger the closer we were to each other. Now that my high brother was right beside me, I was feeling no pain too. But, I reminded myself, those emotions and feelings weren't mine. I was fine. I was sober. And I could shove Julian's feelings to the back of my brain if necessary. Even still, I giggled when he giggled.

Julian was all smiles and hugs as we exited the house. I had to pull him away from about four different people that he wanted to chat with like they were long-lost friends. I prayed he didn't run into Raquel. I'd never get him home if he spotted her.

Luckily, we didn't run into her. We did, however, run into my best friend.

Arianna stopped short when she came across us in the entryway. She looked like she was leaving. Pulling my brother behind me, my mouth dropped open when I saw her. "Arianna? I thought you said you weren't going to the party?"

Arianna's eyes were wide as she took me in. "Hey, Nika! I wasn't going to but ..." Her voice trailed off as she noticed that I was pulling my brother behind me. "Julian? I didn't know you were here."

My brother, in his everything-is-right-in-the-world mood, squirmed away from me and latched onto Arianna. He lifted her a foot in the air. "Arianna!" he exclaimed, squeezing her tight. Arianna, dressed as an adorable, yet sexy, piece of candy corn, giggled and wrapped her arms around him. I sighed. I'd rather have him run into Raquel right now than Arianna.

With a sigh, Julian set her down. He didn't release her, though, and his arms were still cinched around her waist. "I'm glad you're here. It's been kind of a shitty night, and I need my friend to talk to ..." He blinked, then shook his head like something had surprised him. "You're really pretty. Do you know that?"

Arianna's cheeks filled with color, and her eyes softened with warmth as she gazed at him. Feeling that a "moment" was about to happen, I tapped on Julian's shoulder. "We have to go, Julie. Like, now."

Julian blinked at me, then complied and let her go. Arianna's heart was racing as she reluctantly stepped away from him, and I was sure she would chide me about my "timing" later. I was doing her a favor though; Julian wasn't in his right mind.

When it was clear that Julian wasn't going to go anywhere voluntarily, I grabbed his hand and pulled him forward. The sudden movement made him giggle, and, still high through him, damn if I didn't giggle too. Julian clutched Arianna's hand at the last minute, pulling her with us, and Trey loped after us all, the bells on his costume jingling in a merry way that matched Julian's mood.

Arianna walked close by my brother's side as we headed into the frigid night. "You a vampire, Julian? I like your teeth."

With a mental groan, I twisted back to glare at him; he should know better than to show his teeth, even if he was passing it off as a costume. Smiling broadly, he still had his fangs out for the entire world to see. Thankfully, no one thought anything of it, but still, he shouldn't be exposing himself like this. Julian winked at Arianna, laughing as he answered her. "It's lame, I know, but it was the easiest costume I could come up with."

Snuggling into his side, Arianna murmured, "It's sexy."

She said it in a low, sultry voice that I probably wasn't supposed to hear, but I did, and I stopped in my tracks. Julian and Arianna, oblivious to the world around them, crashed right into me. Julian thought it was funny while Arianna looked embarrassed. I divided the two inappropriately flirty friends, letting go of Julian and looping my arm around Arianna.

She was reluctant to leave my brother, casting long, wistful glances behind us as I pulled her forward. Once she thought she was out of Julian's ear shot, she said, "Did you hear him, Nika? He thinks I'm pretty. I think he might finally be interested." She was ear-to-ear smiles.

With a sad sigh, I shook my head. "He's totally high, Arianna. I wouldn't put much stock in anything he says or does right now."

Arianna frowned as she peeked back at him. "Yeah … but even still, he could be getting over her. He could like me …" Her voice was so hopeful, it broke my heart, and I didn't have it in me to burst her bubble. I knew what Julian felt when he was around her, and yes, he liked her, enjoyed her company, found her appealing … but even with all that, his heart was somewhere else.

Not able to say that to her, and not wanting her to get hurt by his inhibitions, I kept the two of them apart while we walked to the car. With Trey and Julian stumbling and laughing, pausing for fifteen minutes to find Julian's skateboard somewhere on the lawn, it took forever to get there. Embarrassingly, I stumbled a few times too. Arianna caught me, asking if I was all right. I told her I was fine and hoped that I was.

When we got to the car, I told Julian to get into the back seat, hoping a little space would help with my osmosis-high. Trey hopped in the front seat right as Arianna turned to me. "Can I get a ride home? Sarah dropped me off earlier."

I paused before answering her. If I said yes, she and Julian were going to be backseat buddies the entire ride home. I couldn't leave her stranded though. "Um … sure."

Julian crooked a grin while Arianna darted around to the other side of the car. He reached down to open his door to the backseat, and I grabbed his arm. Leaning in, I whispered, "Please leave her alone, like you promised?"

He blinked at me, then made some strange gesture with his face that was both a "Sure" and a "Whatever, leave me the hell alone."

"Nika?" Julian and I both turned as a voice in the night said, "Is that you?"

Surprise overrode my buzz as Hunter strode toward us. I was again taken aback by how sultry he was in the moonlight. His hair was even darker, his eyes deeper and more penetrating. Even the rough stubble along his jaw was sexier than in the daylight. I bit my lip as his lean body stopped right in front of me.

"Hunter? What are you doing here?"

I reached up to hug him as I said it, and he held me tight, kissing my cheek. We'd been keeping things pretty mellow as we were slowly getting to know each other, but I melted into his side, euphoric at being close to him again. Or maybe that was just a side effect of being next to Julian. Either way, I leaned up to give Hunter a soft kiss. He returned it, speaking through the small breaks in our pecks. "Well … Dad and I … were in the area … heard the noise … thought we'd make sure everything … was okay. He's scoping out the other side."

Giggling, I pulled away. "How very civic minded of you. You're not going to call the cops, are you?"

Hunter's dark eyes swept over the kids partying on the lawn. "For underage drinking? Nah. If no one's being hurt than—"

He cut off as his eyes locked onto Julian. Maybe it was my imagination, but Hunter's face seemed to drain of all its color. He seemed ghostly white in the light of the moon. He didn't say anything, just kept staring at Julian. As Hunter tensed and started to reach behind himself, my brother blinked, then looked annoyed. "What? You want me to leave so you can make out with my sister?"

Julian frowned, the move looking a little strange around his fangs. Then he started giggling and fell back against the car. Hunter was by his side in a flash, helping him stand up. Hunter seemed both alarmed and confused as he helped Julian straighten. He kept searching his features, touching his hands, then he put his palm against Julian's head, like he was taking his temperature. My heart started to race as I wondered if Hunter suspected that Julian's fangs were more than a prop.

But then, as suddenly as he'd seemed worried … Hunter was fine. Shaking his head, he asked Julian, "You all right, man?"

Julian looked a little offended at being fondled by my boyfriend. Worried that he'd say or do something stupid, I opened Julian's door and shoved him and his skateboard onto the seat. Quickly closing his door, I stood in front of it, blocking Hunter's view. He stared through me, like he was looking at Julian through my body. "Your brother's costume is pretty realistic."

I giggled. "How do you know? Seen many vampires?" I wanted to slap my hand over my mouth after I said it. Damn Julian and his stupid high. Hunter raised an eyebrow at me, and, needing to distract him, I looped my arms around his neck and pulled him into me. I found his lips as fast as I could. My stall tactic seemed to work, and he melted into my embrace. Julian's drug-enhanced euphoria took me over, and I let it. I poured my joyous mood into my moment with Hunter.

He pressed me into the car, his hands running up my back, and my elation turned into desire. Oddly, I felt Julian's mood shift into the same sort of desire. I couldn't worry about it, and I was too buzzed to be concerned by it. Hunter flicked his tongue into my mouth, and I groaned as I wrapped my leg around his. I suddenly wanted to stay at this party, maybe find a quiet room upstairs to explore this burgeoning passion with Hunter. My mind started hazing, and I couldn't recall why I'd even started distracting him in the first place.

Hunter pulled away from me after a moment. "Nika?" he panted. His eyes searched mine. I couldn't quite keep mine focused on him. "You seem …" He frowned. "Are you drunk?"

I shook my head and worked harder at blocking out Julian's soaring mood. "Nope, I'm completely sober." Closing my eyes, I inhaled a deep breath. The fresh air helped clear Julian out of my system a little. "But my brother isn't, so I should get him home."

Hunter's eyes stared through me, like he was looking at Julian again. Concern was on his face when he refocused on me. "Are you going to be able to get him home okay? Do you want me to follow you?"

Appreciating the offer, and wishing I could take him up on it, I pushed Hunter back and stepped away from the car. "No, I got it. Thank you." I gave him a warm smile, then looked back at my idiotic brother. All I could see was the back of Julian's head as he voraciously made out with Arianna. "Goddamn it," I snapped, banging on the window.

Trey startled, but Julian and Arianna completely ignored me. Giving Hunter an apologetic smile, I told him, "I have to break this up … and I really should get him home."

Hunter nodded, then reached out to stroke my cheek. He had rings on every one of his fingers that were connected by thin chains over his palm that attached to a bracelet around his wrist. It was an odd piece of jewelry, something I couldn't recall ever seeing on him. In fact, try as I might, I couldn't remember him *ever* wearing jewelry, at least, not on his hands. As the cool metal brushed my skin, Hunter's smile widened. Grasping my cheek, he gave me a quick kiss on the forehead and said, "You've been avoiding coming over for dinner. No more excuses. How about Monday night?"

Seeing that Julian was starting to lay Arianna down on the seat, I quickly nodded at Hunter. "Okay, yeah, sounds good." I wasn't sure how I'd swing that with my parents, but one hurdle at a time.

Hunter nodded, backing up as he watched me run around to the other side of the car. Opening the rear door, I shoved Julian off Arianna and pulled her out of the vehicle. Her candy corn hat was askew and her hazel eyes were dazed. "Will you drive?" I asked, tossing her the keys. Before she could object, I ducked into the backseat with Julian and closed the door.

Arianna gaped at me, then got into the driver's seat. I smacked Julian's thigh. Hard. "You told me you'd leave her alone!" I hissed as Arianna started the car.

Julian jerked his thumb out the window, to where Hunter was still studying us. "You turned me on!" he hissed back.

Luckily the radio kicked on, so neither Trey nor Arianna heard that. I felt my face searing with heat as embarrassment and disgust waged war within me. Julian's mood stayed level, and I momentarily wished for a little more of his herbal retreat—anything to dull the mortification.

Julian turned to look out the window at Hunter as Arianna backed up the car. My boyfriend waved, the metal on his hand flashing in the headlights. Now that I was paying attention, his other hand was similarly adorned. Shaking his head, I heard him mutter, "Smooth, Hunter ... way to freak out over a set of fake teeth." He was shaking his head and chuckling to himself as the car pulled away.

Having heard him as well, a more-sober Julian whispered, "What did he mean by that?"

The earlier look of panic on Hunter's face instantly registered with me, and below human hearing, I told Julian, "He knows vampires are real."

Julian's eyes flashed to mine. Fear sliced through his buzz, and he pulled his teeth back into place. "What?"

I glanced at Arianna and Trey as we pulled onto the road, but they weren't paying any attention to us. Well, Trey wasn't. Arianna was glancing at Julian every once in a while, but I was certain she hadn't seen his teeth changing size. "We'll talk about it later," I murmured. Twisting back to him, I snapped, "When you're not stoned!"

Julian sighed, then leaned his head against the glass.

Arianna drove to her house first. She was practically radiating joy when she got out of the car. "He kissed me, Nika!" she beamed, glancing at Julian in the back seat. I could feel guilt and remorse streaming from my brother, and I tried to curb my annoyance. It wasn't entirely his fault.

"Remember what I said, Arianna ... he's wasted."

She nodded like she understood, but from the way she nearly skipped to the door, I knew that fact was currently lost on her. All she cared about at the moment was that he'd kissed her. She was going to get hurt by this ... and I was partly to blame. Damn it.

I drove Trey to his place while Julian started nodding off in the back seat. By the time I was parked in Trey's driveway, Julian was stretched out in the back of the car, snoring away. While I wasn't looking forward to dragging his sleeping butt to his room, I was grateful that he was unconscious; my mind was clearing with Julian passed out. It made it easier to concentrate on driving.

Trey yawned as he muttered goodbye to me, then he started to get out of the car. I grabbed his arm. "Hey, don't give my brother drugs anymore."

Smirking, Trey shook his bell-covered head. "I didn't force him, Nika. And after the night he had with Raquel, he needed it."

I let Trey go; Julian had mentioned to Arianna that he'd had a bad night, I just hadn't had time to ask him why. "What happened?"

Trey shrugged. "Well, I don't know for sure ... but I think they had a pretty spectacular make-out session." My mouth fell open in surprise, and Trey added, "Then she ditched him and left the party with Russell. He was pretty torn up about it, so I calmed him down."

"Oh ..." My heart broke for Julian as I pictured the torment he'd been dealing with while I'd been sleeping. I must have been seriously out of it to not have been awoken by Julian's twisting emotions. I couldn't help but feel a little guilty that I hadn't been there for him. I glanced at my brother asleep in the back seat, then back to Trey's bloodshot eyes. "Thank you for watching over him."

He gave me a medicated smile. "Anytime, Nika. He's my family too."

Trey's comment made me want to cringe, but I held my smile. Trey may be family now, but as soon as we left Salt Lake … he wouldn't remember anything about Julian, or me, or our hot mom. Halina would make sure of that.

Trey waved goodbye to me and wandered off to his house, skateboard in tow. Sighing, I headed back home with Julian. It was nearly morning. I couldn't tell if our parents were moving around yet, but I hoped they were still sound asleep. I sped back to the house as quickly as I dared. Getting pulled over right now would suck. As it was, I had no idea how I was going to hide the smell wafting from Julian. Even if we did get away with this, his stench would be a dead giveaway to my super-smelling family. He'd have to shower and do a load of laundry before they woke up.

Not meaning to, I drove past Hunter's house. There were a couple of ways to get into our neighborhood; sometimes my family took the route that went by Hunter's place, sometimes they didn't. My heart always spiked whenever they did … and that was probably why Dad didn't often drive that way. As I rolled by it now, my heart again shifted, but to concern this time. I wasn't sure how it was possible, but for a split second there, Hunter had known what Julian was—what he *really* was. Odd, since all he'd seen were Julian's teeth. But that one, small glimpse had been enough to make him believe the fangs were real. He'd dropped the ridiculous notion before we'd parted ways, but … he'd believed it for a few minutes … and that was concerning.

As slowly as the car would go, I pulled into our driveway. Heart pounding, I shut off the car and waited. From what I could tell, all was quiet in the house. My parents were still locked away in their room, their presence unmoving. No creaks or moans or traces of light suggested that Ben or Olivia were awake. Exhaling, I tried to calm my heart as I stepped out of the car. We might actually get away with this.

Opening the rear door, I tossed Julian's board onto its normal resting place near the lawn. Then I yanked him from the car. It took supernatural strength to do it, but I finally got him to his feet. Propped up on me, he semi-woke up. "We home?"

"Yes," I crinkled my nose, "and you stink."

Julian smelled himself as I maneuvered us to the front door. "I do not ..."

I opened the door as quietly as I could. Thankfully, my dad hated squeaking doors and kept them well lubricated. Sometimes super hearing worked in my favor. Still fighting off the need for sleep, Julian yawned and leaned on me as I trudged us up the stairs. Great, I was going to have to tuck him in, or at least throw him down. I tiptoed past the room Ben was staying in, not wanting him to wake up. I didn't need to worry though—he was already awake.

Cracking the door right as we walked by, he murmured, "Need a hand?"

My heart spiked as I gasped in surprise. Julian startled, hissing at Ben with his fangs extended. Ben raised a pale eyebrow while Julian slapped a hand over his mouth. "Sorry," he mumbled into his palm ... then he started laughing.

I chastised my idiotic brother in my head while Ben turned his curious eyes to mine. "Is he drunk?"

Pulling Julian toward his door, hoping against all hope that my parents weren't awake too, although I wasn't sure if that mattered now since Ben had caught us red-handed, I shook my head. "No, not ... drunk."

Not deterred by my movement, Ben followed us into Julian's room. Even though I could have carried Julian with no problems, Ben decided to help me, and ducked his shoulder under my brother's. He cringed. "Whoa ... no, he's high, isn't he?"

I sighed. Thanks to the pot-laced room my brother had been baking in for who knows how long, the smell was unmistakable, even to a human's nose. Being vague, I only told Ben, "I'm not really sure."

I'd wanted to get Julian showered and cleaned up, or at least changed into clean clothes, but Julian took one look at his bed, and, giggling, he broke away from us to flop on top of it. Realizing we were pretty much screwed anyway, I left him alone. He was already snoring when Ben pulled me back into the hallway.

Arms crossed over his chest, Ben stared me down. Even dressed in loose pajama pants, he could be imposing. "You want to tell me what happened tonight?" His blue eyes glanced up at my parents' door. "How'd you get out of here without them knowing?"

I looked behind me. "They're asleep." I twisted back to Ben. "We don't notice the bond when we're asleep."

Curious, Ben asked, "But what about the others? Halina must be awake?"

I nodded. "Yeah, probably, but she's too far away to tell that Julian and I moved. To her, it would have felt like we were still at home."

I hoped that would satisfy Ben and he would forget about his original question, but, no such luck. "And why did you leave?"

Suddenly feeling very tired, and a lot more sober now since Julian was sleeping it off, I yawned. "Julian snuck out to … meet a girl. I followed him when I realized he was gone."

Ben's eyes widened as he looked over at Julian's closed door. "Julian has a girlfriend? I didn't know that."

I bit my lip in shame, knowing Julian wasn't the one with a secret love interest. "No, the girl he likes is seeing someone else. It's sort of … drama."

Ben smiled and looked back at me. His eyes were suddenly laced with sadness. "Love usually is."

Feeling bad for his relationship troubles, I gave him a sympathetic smile. He patted my shoulder then indicated my parents' door. "I'll have to tell them about this. I'm sorry."

My heart dropped a little, but really, I'd never expected to get away with any of this. My only real dilemma was Hunter. Did I tell my parents about him noticing Julian's teeth? If I mentioned Hunter, then I'd have to mention what he was to me. And my parents weren't going to like that I had an undercover relationship blossoming. They'd put a stop to it for sure. They'd probably erase *me* from his memory, as well as Julian's fangs.

I swallowed and nodded, dread locking up my voice. No, I couldn't tell any of them about Hunter … not yet. And besides, I didn't know if there was even a problem with Hunter. He'd seemed convinced that he'd made a mistake and Julian was a human wearing a realistic costume. He hadn't seemed alarmed or scared of me or my family. He hadn't seemed worried or freaked out. He'd even made plans to have dinner with me—a dinner I had no idea how I was going to go to. But even if something had convinced Hunter that Julian was 100 percent human, I knew one thing for sure now … I would have to be very careful from here on out with my boyfriend. For whatever reason, an active imagination or a past experience, he *knew* about vampires. And that made him a threat. A threat I was beginning to fall in love with.

And here I thought Julian was being an idiot.

CHAPTER TWELVE

Nika

MUCH TO MY surprise, my parents went easy on me after Ben told them what had happened. Dad said that running out of the house to make sure Julian was safe was a noble thing to do. In fact, the only thing they were disappointed at me for, was the fact that I didn't wake them up so we could all leave together to "rescue" Julian. But with a sad, reminiscent smile, Dad confessed that he'd been a teenager once too, and even though he didn't have any brothers or sisters, he understood not wanting to get someone in trouble.

So, I got away with my part of the crime with not much more than an hour-long talk behind closed doors. Julian, however, was not so lucky. His punishment lasted all weekend.

First, Dad made him go with Ben and Olivia to the airport. He had to hold Liv's bright pink carry-on bag. While I was sipping hot cocoa out at the ranch, Julian was knee deep in Olivia's preteen tears, some for having to leave her father, most for having to leave Julian. I felt his discomfort the entire time.

When Ben finally brought Julian out to the ranch, he had a few brief minutes of hope that he'd get to do something fun. That ended when Dad forced him to do health inspections of the entire herd with Peter and the crew. Julian was sullen, annoyed, but he didn't complain as he threw on extra warm clothes and extra high boots. I could feel Julian's remorse as he headed out to the pastures, but I wasn't sure if Julian was feeling bad about getting high, or bad about what he'd done to Arianna. I hoped it was a little of both.

By Sunday night, everyone in the ranch had made Julian do some gross or menial task for them. Alanna had made him help with butchering dinner; his part had been to clean up the unusable remains. Imogen had made him rewind every roll of yarn that had partially untangled, which seemed like all of them. Gabriel had made him measure out and bottle vials of the miraculous shots that kept mixed vampires alive indefinitely; there were hundreds of them. After inspections, Grandpa had made him help repair some barbwire fencing with the ranch hands—meaning, he had to do it without using his enhanced abilities. Grandma Linda had made him help her finish our childhood scrapbooks, and she hadn't even started on them yet. And Halina had supervised as she'd made him clean out every gutter on every building ... in the middle of the night.

Julian was sound asleep on the drive home. I figured he'd think twice before touching pot again.

Julian had bags under his eyes Monday morning. He kind of looked like he'd spent the entire weekend on a bender, not working hard for our family. Starla commented on it while Dad was dropping us off at her place before school.

"Whoa, what the hell happened to you, Julian? You look like you played chicken with a semi-truck ... and lost."

Julian yawned as he brushed past her. Smirking, Dad answered for him. "He indulged a little on Friday night, so he had some extra ... chores ... this weekend."

Starla's face turned to disgust. "At that smelly, crappy ranch?" Dad's face darkened at her comment, but Starla twisted to watch Julian flop onto her couch and missed his expression. Julian curled into a ball like he was going to take a nap. I ducked by Starla as she murmured, "Poor kid."

Dad looked over at Julian and shrugged; he was still upset about the whole thing, more so the drugs than the sneaking out. "Yeah, well, he's still being punished so he'll need to be picked up immediately after school."

Seeing an opportunity, I piped up, "Hey, Dad, a friend asked if I could come over after school and stay for dinner. Is that okay?"

Dad paused his frowning at Julian to glance at me. "Which friend?"

I tried every mental trick I knew of to keep my heart as slow and steady as possible. My nerves spiked, though, and Julian cracked an eye open. His sullen mood was curious now, and I figured he hadn't heard me making plans with Hunter on Friday night; he'd been pretty preoccupied at the time. And he'd been so busy being punished this weekend that we hadn't had a chance to talk about Hunter, about what had happened, about what Hunter knew about our race. Tonight would be my first chance to try and figure out why Hunter believed what he did, but it meant I had to lie to my father, and I really hated doing that.

I shrugged. "My partner for a project at school. We need to work on … an assignment."

Dad nodded. The academic part of my lie appealed to him. "Yeah, okay. Just don't stay out too late."

"I won't, and you don't have to worry about picking me up after school. I'll get a ride with my friend. They live right around the corner from our house." I purposely didn't mention if my partner was male or female. As Dad nodded again, I grinned and sat next to Julian on the couch. Julian asked me a million questions with his eyes, but thankfully, he didn't verbalize any of them.

Running a hand through his jet-black hair, Dad returned his attention to Starla. "Okay. Don't worry about Nika … but …" his light eyes flicked over to Julian, " … he shouldn't be alone during his punishment. Maybe you could bring him back here and stay with him until I get home?"

That got Julian's attention. "Dad," he whined.

Dad shot him a cool glance that shut off any further objection. Starla snorted. "Geez, V.B., didn't you ever get a little wasted as a kid? He looks beat, why don't you cut him some slack?"

Dad gave her a dry look. "When you have kids of your own, Starla, you'll understand."

She snorted again right as Jacen walked into the room. "Oh, hell no. You couldn't pay me to have kids. Why do you think I'm with a sterile man?" She jerked her thumb at Jacen. He blinked and promptly left the room.

Closing his eyes, Dad shook his head. "Well, now that that's settled." Opening his eyes, he waved at us on the couch. "Have a good day, kids." He pointed at Julian. "I'll see you right after work." A crooked grin lightened his face. "I have a couple of projects for you."

Julian groaned and dropped his head back onto the couch. After Dad left, he whimpered, "Just kill me, Nika. Run a stake through me and kill me."

He gave me pleading eyes but mine hardened. "You'll get no sympathy from me. Especially after what you did to Arianna."

Sighing, he lifted his head. "I'm sorry about that, Nick. I don't know what came over me ..."

I felt his mood shift to confusion and regret, and a little something else. Interest maybe? Knowing I was partly at fault for what happened that night softened my temper. Julian still needed to make this right though. "You need to tell *her* you're sorry, not me. She thinks it meant something, Julian."

Julian nodded as he stared at his hands in his lap. "I will." He peeked up at me. "I will today."

His face darkened along with his mood. Even his bright blue eyes seemed a little duller. Of course, that was probably more from exhaustion than anything else. He wasn't looking forward to returning to school though. I wasn't sure if that was because of Raquel or Arianna. How my quiet, brooding brother had managed to weasel his way into a love triangle, or, square, to be more accurate, I'd never know. But now he was sort of stuck there. Then again, I was secretly dating an older man who knew vampires existed. I hadn't seen that one coming either.

My nerves picked up as Starla drove us to school. I was feeding off Julian's anxiety, using his energy to fuel my own. It happened on occasion, when we were both feeling the same thing. Julian eyed me, curious again, but he didn't ask anything in front of the pseudo-parent we were with.

Starla had a question for me, though. As Julian and I stepped out of her metallic sports car, she pulled her bug-like sunglasses to the edge of her nose. "So, Nika, where are you *really* going after school?"

I was sure all the color drained from my cheeks, but I kept my face stone-still. Meeting her eye, so she'd believe me, I told Starla the same thing I'd told my dad, "I'm going to a friend's house, to work on a project, just like I said."

Starla was amused, and unconvinced. "Sure thing, kid." Pushing her glasses back up her nose, she revved the engine of her car. Some kids nearby twisted around to look, but Starla ignored them. "Whatever you're doing that you don't want Papa Adams to know about is your business, but …" she indicated my body with her finger, " … *you* be in charge of your protection. Don't rely on the man to do it. Their sensibilities seem to fly out the window when it comes to sex." She smirked and punched the gas; the partially open passenger's side door slammed shut as she squealed around a corner.

Julian turned to me as I gaped at the location Starla's car had been just seconds before. Did she really say that to me? "Oh my God, is she right?" Julian's eyes were wide when I looked over at him. "Are you having sex today? Because I can't handle that, Nick. I'm not ready!"

He looked so worried about the prospect of having to "feel" that through me that a tiny bubble of nervous laughter escaped me. "No, Julian. I'm not … doing that today." I shook my head and turned toward the school. Hopefully my cheeks weren't too red, although, it was a little nippy out, so it probably wouldn't be too odd if they were.

Julian grabbed my shoulder, stopping me. "But you *are* doing something you don't want our parents to know about, aren't you?" He crossed his arms over his chest, and his expression clearly said that he knew where I was really going, and he didn't think it was a good idea. His mood was radiating protectiveness. Damn, he was going to haul me home with him, kicking and screaming if need be, if he thought I was going to be in any sort of danger.

"You don't need to worry. I'll be fine at Hunter's house."

Julian frowned and looked back at where Starla had disappeared. "Nika … you shouldn't …" He didn't have a stronger argument and let his words die. His face when he turned back to me was pleading for me to reconsider my love interest. "At least wait until I can come with you?"

I smiled. "You want to hang out in my boyfriend's room with me? That might get weird for you."

My brief amusement passed as true concern about Hunter filled me. Looking around, I lowered my voice. Kids were just starting to trickle in, most of them scurrying to the warmth of the buildings, not loitering around outside like us. "Do you remember running into Hunter Friday night?" By the blankness on my brother's face, I could tell he barely remembered Friday night. Sighing, I filled in the gaps for him. "He saw your fangs, and somehow, for a minute there, he recognized them as real. He changed his mind before we left, but still … he knows vampires are real."

Julian grabbed my arm, cinching it tight. He wasn't about to let me go now. "We need to call Grandma. We need to wipe him … now!" His pale, frantic eyes searched mine. "Do *not* go over there alone, Nika!"

I cringed in pain, and Julian relaxed his grip on me. His panic was ramping up my nerves, but I tried to ease his worry with pure confidence. "He's not a threat to me. He … he loves me." Julian blinked, surprise flooding through him. Seeing a question coming that I didn't want to answer, something along the lines of, "How do you know? Did he say it?" I quickly added onto my statement. "And he doesn't suspect us. We're clear in his eyes. But he knows the myths are true, and I need to know why."

Still holding my arm tight, Julian clenched his jaw. "I don't like this."

Prying his fingers off my bicep, I nodded. "I know, but he's important to me, and I'm not going to wipe him on a whim."

Julian shook his head. "He believes in our kind, Nika. That's not a whim. He's dangerous …"

My eyes stung as I considered Julian's words and feelings. They were in line with my own. I knew this had been a foolish flirtation from the very beginning. Now it was moving past foolish, into the realm of insanity. Concealment was our family motto, and we'd erased minds for much less than what Hunter knew. Hell, we would erase everyone when we left this city, just to be on the safe side. But I couldn't wipe Hunter. Not yet, not when our romance was just beginning. I cared too much to just cut him loose like that.

Problem was, I didn't know what Hunter knew, what he believed in, or where his beliefs came from. Was he just a fan of myth and mythology, of pop culture? Or did he know a vampire? Had he had a run-in with one? Was he scared, or merely curious? Could he accept me … if I told him the truth? Did he know about mixed vampires? The common "Hollywood" vampire wasn't the same as my family. We were an offshoot of them, and most humans had never heard of "living" vampires. That worked to our benefit, made it easier to hide in plain sight. But … if Hunter *did* know, if he believed in mixed vampires as well as pureblood vampires, well, that could be a problem if he had certain prejudices.

My voice full of determination, I told Julian, "I like him. I *really* like him. And if there's a chance that we could work ... that we could be together honestly, then I need to try. I can't erase him without trying." Clutching Julian's arm, I begged, "Just let me have a chance with him, Julie ... please?"

Julian sighed, and I felt the remorse and regret surging through him. I was in this spot because *he'd* gotten wasted at a party and let his fangs slip. Responsible didn't even begin to cover how he felt about it. If this went badly, he'd never forgive himself.

His voice wavered when he answered me, and I felt his concern shift to fear. "You have to promise me that you'll be careful. That, if you need to, if he turns into a threat ... you'll run. You'll run as fast as you can."

Nodding, I threw my arms around him. "I'll be fine. I'll be perfectly safe. I promise."

Someone walked up behind me, and I felt Julian stiffen. Letting go of him, I turned to see Arianna watching us. Her green-speckled brown eyes were hopeful as she stared at Julian. Knowing her as well as I did, I could see that she was in her favorite sweater, a light green shade that complemented her eyes. Her shoulder-length hair had a slight curl to it, curls that had probably taken her a half hour to perfect. Her lips shimmered with a light sheen of peach lip gloss and her lids and cheeks were brushed with color. She'd primped for my brother ... and he was about to break her heart. It killed me, and for the millionth time, I wished I could make my brother permanently stop liking Raquel.

A nervous energy trickled out of Arianna as she lifted her hand in a small wave. "Hey, guys."

Her eyes briefly flicked to mine before shifting back to Julian. My brother was embarrassed, contrite, and his smile to Arianna was brief. "Hey," he murmured, a puff of warm air escaping his lips.

Arianna shivered and nodded her head at the main building. "Guys heading to class? It's chilly out here."

Julian nodded and started walking. He walked right past Arianna without looking at her. I could tell by his mood that he was incredibly nervous around her. He probably had no idea what to say. To Arianna, though, it looked like he'd just brushed her off. Her face fell as Julian trudged away from us, head down and hands in his pockets.

"Did I say something ... wrong?" Arianna looked over at me, crestfallen.

Directing as much anger as I could into my bond with Julian, I told Arianna, "No, he wants to talk to you alone. He's going to stop where he is and wait for you."

Arianna looked doubtful at my pronouncement, but I hadn't said it for her benefit. It had been a direct order to Julian. I watched as he shook his head in irritation, but then he stopped where he was on the lawn, waiting for Arianna. Her expression immediately brightened. "Oh, guess you were right." She giggled. "You guys really do have a psychic twin thing going on."

I rolled my eyes. *Yeah, don't I know it.* As Arianna bounded away from me to get to Julian, I told him, "Go easy on her ... please?"

Julian glanced back at me and discretely nodded. When Arianna caught up to him, she latched onto his arm. "Walk me to class while we talk?" she asked, a spring in her step. It broke my heart that she thought she had a chance with Julian. Well, she'd know by the time they got to her class that she didn't. Not meaning to eavesdrop, but needing to get to class myself, I followed several yards behind them.

Julian's reluctant mood seeped into me as he gently separated from Arianna. I could see her confusion as Julian began the process of stomping her romantic fantasy to pieces. "Hey, uh, we should talk about Friday ..."

Arianna looked around, then leaned into him. "It was amazing, Julian. You're a very talented kisser. Even with those fake fangs." As Julian looked back at me, embarrassed, Arianna latched onto his arm again and murmured, "I'd like to try it again sometime without the pointy accoutrements. I think you nicked me a few times."

Julian snapped his gaze back to her. "I did? I'm so sorry." Opening the front door to the main building, he sighed. "Actually, that's what I wanted to talk to you about. There won't be a next time, Arianna."

I stopped walking as I watched the heavy door close on Arianna and my brother. With the distance and the noise of the students around them, I couldn't solidly hear their conversation. It was as much privacy as I could give them. Even still, as I watched through the glass, some of their words filtered out to me.

Adjusting his backpack, my brother was the epitome of shame and regret. I heard the words, "sorry" and "friend" and "Raquel." Arianna's face was pale white as she listened slack-jawed. Then splotches of heat filled her cheeks and I heard, "you kissed me," and "freaking jerk!" Shaking his head, Julian started to tell her something else, but she turned around and stormed off. Sighing, I continued my way into the building.

Julian was still by the doors, staring after Arianna while the kids in the hallway stared at him. His emotions were high, and conflicted. That conversation had hurt him more than he'd expected, and I put a hand on his back in sympathy. "I'll talk to her, Julian. Maybe I can smooth things over?"

He looked back at me, his tired eyes moist. "I don't want her mad at me, Nick. I don't ... want to hurt her. I ... I like Arianna." He looked even more confused after he said that.

Patting my sullen brother on the shoulder, I headed toward Arianna. Luckily, she and I had the same first period. I could get to work on calming her down immediately. Or try to anyway.

Arianna was sitting at her desk, arms crossed over her chest when I approached her. Her cheeks were still red, and her eyes were glistening. I didn't need an empathic bond to know she was hurting. She'd put her heart out there, and, unintentionally or not, Julian had smashed it to pieces.

"Hey," I said, sitting beside her. "How are you ... doing?"

When she looked over at me, the tears building in her eyes fell to her cheeks. "He still wants her ... After everything, he still likes *her* ..." Her voice hitched, and I heard a sob coming. I immediately wrapped my arms around her, then asked the teacher if we could be excused. Arianna needed to release her grief, and she couldn't really do that in the middle of class.

It took most of class for her to calm down. When it was time to part ways, she gave me a crushing hug. "Thank you, Nika. I needed to let that out." When she let me go, she seemed stronger. And harder. "Don't take this the wrong way, but I kind of hate your brother at the moment."

"Understandable," I said with a sigh. I'd already told her that Julian had been high that night, and not thinking straight. I'd already told her that he felt really bad about letting their flirtations go too far. And I'd already told her that he cherished their friendship. Arianna understood all that, and I knew she'd forgive Julian in time, but for right now, for the sake of her sanity, she needed to be pissed at him.

Letting go of Julian and Arianna's woes, I started focusing on my own. I was excited to see Hunter, I always was whenever we met up, but I was nervous about it too. A lot more nervous than I'd ever been before. I wasn't just sneaking around behind my family's back to date an older boy anymore. No, now I was sneaking around behind their backs to date a guy who knew vampires were real. That put an entirely different twist on things. But then, maybe I was making too big a deal out of this. Maybe Hunter knowing was a good thing. After all, I'd always wanted to share my secret with the man I loved. I'd always wanted the open and honest relationship Mom and Dad had, and if Hunter and I were seriously going to have a future together ... he'd have to know about me eventually. Maybe I'd just confess to him tonight? See how he handled it?

Waiting for my brother at lunch, I texted Hunter and let him know that I was free to hang out after school if he wanted to come pick me up ... in a car, not on his bike. My phone buzzed in my hand as Julian dropped onto the bench beside me. Groaning, he let his head sink to the table.

"How'd your class with Arianna go?" I asked.

He peeked an eye up at me. "We have gym together, Nika. We played dodgeball today."

I bit my lip to not laugh. I'd been feeling aches and pains from Julian ever since his second period. Granted, with our abilities, Julian could have easily caught and deflected any ball Arianna might have chucked his way, but that wasn't how we were hardwired. Concealment, deception. Julian would have let the balls hit him on purpose, would have missed catches he could have made with his eyes closed. He would have lofted balls to other kids when he could have driven them straight through the walls. It was how we'd been taught to blend in, and it was instinct now that we'd done it so often.

Picturing Arianna slinging heavy ball after heavy ball at him finally made laughter escape me. Julian wasn't as amused as I was and closed his eyes as he rested on the table. That was when someone approached who startled us both. Arianna calmly sat down across the table from us. She gave me a bright smile, completely ignoring Julian. "Hey, Nika."

My mouth was wide open as I watched her pour some dressing onto her salad. I hadn't expected to see her at the same table with my brother for a long time. Julian lifted his head when he heard her speak. His mouth was wide open too. Between the two of us, we probably looked mentally challenged.

Trey plopped down beside Arianna before Julian and I could change our expressions. He jerked his thumb at us while twisting to Arianna. "What's up with them?" Trey seemed oblivious to the miracle of Arianna and my brother sitting at the same table. Then again, Trey looked a little glazed, so it was quite possible that he'd imbibed a bit before school. Or maybe even during school.

Arianna shrugged, her voice and face light and bright. "No idea." Her smile perky, she took a bite of her salad.

That was when my brother found his voice. "We ... cool, Arianna?" I could tell from the hope blossoming inside Julian that he thought Arianna had worked out all her aggression during dodgeball, and they could slip back into their old friendship now. I wasn't so sure.

Arianna smiled as she finally looked over and acknowledged him. "No, not even a little."

Julian's mouth twisted into a frown. "I said I was sorry. I didn't mean for ... that to happen between us ..."

Arianna returned her attention to her salad. "I heard you the first time, Julian. And I'm sorry you're still stuck on someone who doesn't want you, but I've decided I'm not going to make the same mistake. You don't want to be with me, then fine, your loss." She peeked at him from the corner of her eyes. "But that doesn't mean we're going to be 'buddies' again, like nothing happened. I'm not going to be your sounding board every time she hurts you, not after you've hurt me. I'm here for Nika. *She's* my friend."

She shoved her fork into her mouth while Julian gaped at her. Trey looked confused. Leaning over, he asked Julian, "What the hell did you do to her, man?"

I gave Arianna a prideful smile at clearly and concisely speaking her mind. Hopefully Julian thought twice in the future about getting carried away in the moment, and hurting someone in the process—even if he *was* being influenced by my soaring feelings and mood-enhancing substances. A part of me wanted to explain my portion of the evening to Arianna, but I couldn't. She wouldn't understand.

When silence resumed around the table, I read my message from Hunter. *'Great! See you after school.'* My heart sped up as I pictured his dark, piercing eyes and confident smile. Yeah, maybe I *could* tell him. Maybe I could start our relationship off by being completely honest with him. I wanted that, more than anything. Especially now, since I was lying so much to so many people—Hunter, my friends, Mom and Dad. Julian was the only one I wasn't lying to. If it weren't for him, I think I'd go insane with all the lies I wrapped around me.

Julian and Arianna kept up their tense peace for the rest of the day, meaning Arianna continued to ignore his very existence. It bothered Julian, filled him with longing and regret, like he hadn't realized how much her friendship had meant until it was gone.

He was watching Arianna talk to Trey on the football field when I met up with him after school. "If you start to like her *now* after you've misled her and hurt her ... I might have to stake you," I playfully told him, trying to lighten his pensive mood.

He gave me a small, unamused smile when he looked over at me. "I don't like her like that. But I did like being friends with her." Sighing, he looked back to Arianna laughing in a shaft of sunlight. "I already miss her, and it's only been one afternoon."

"Well, you can't play with people's emotions forever, Julian, and you knew she liked you. You knew you had to be careful, and you weren't."

Knowing that Julian had been too worked up to eat at lunch, I reached into my bag and handed him an apple. Grabbing it, Julian looked down and nodded. That was when fate decided to shove love in Julian's face. Russell and Raquel walked by hand-in-hand. Sensing her, hearing her, or maybe even smelling her, Julian's eyes shot up. Russell noticed, and he shot Julian a victorious glare. Hate welled in my brother and his left hand squeezed around my apple, bruising it, while his right hand curled into a fist. I put a calming palm on his shoulder, just in case he decided to fight for Raquel's heart right then and there. Raquel glanced over at Julian, gave him a small, apologetic grimace, then quickly averted her eyes. Remembering that Julian and Raquel had ... done stuff ... Friday night, I squeezed his shoulder in sympathy.

The patchy cloud cover overhead thinned and bright sunlight fell on my brother. I took that as a positive omen, that maybe eventually good fortune would swing his way, but my brother hung his head, utterly defeated by the women in his life. I wasn't sure what to say to him, so I said nothing, and watched Russell escort—or shove, depending on how you viewed it—Raquel to his car.

That was when I noticed a set of eyes watching Julian and me, and I did a double take. Hunter was leaning against a dingy green truck across the street from the school. He had his arms crossed over his chest as he leaned against the door. When he noticed that I was watching him, he lifted his fingers in a wave; they were bare, no jewelry at all. The smile that accompanied that small gesture sent my heart into overdrive. Julian lifted his head at hearing it.

"What?" he muttered.

Delight and nerves surged through me, and I knew my grin was huge. "Hunter's here."

Julian's eyes followed my gaze. He wasn't nearly as delighted as I was. "Great, another person who probably hates my guts. Or would anyway, if he knew I routinely drank cow's blood."

Frowning, I looked back at my morose brother. "Stop being such a pessimist. Besides, we don't know how he feels about us. That's one of the things I want to find out." I smiled again, hopeful. "He could be really receptive to the idea."

Julian's eyes, paler in the sunlight, narrowed at me in disapproval. "This is a horrible plan, Nick. The worst one you've ever had, I'd say. We shouldn't take any chances with this. We should call Grandma."

Sighing, I let my gaze drift back to Hunter; he was still intently watching my brother and me. "I'll be fine, Julie. Don't worry about me. Just ... have fun with Dad."

Julian smirked at me before he turned and walked away. Whatever Dad had planned for Julian tonight, odds were good it wasn't going to be fun. Shaking his head, Julian took a bite of his apple and trotted off to the football field to wait for Starla with Arianna and Trey. I thought Arianna would stick to her normal routine and hang out with Julian until Starla showed up, even if she did refuse to look at him, but when she noticed that I wasn't heading her way with him, she immediately said goodbye to Trey and turned to walk home. Julian paused and raised his hands in the air, incredulity stinging him. I sort of agreed with him, I sort of agreed with her. Being stuck between the two made me reconsider my earlier desire to have my brother date my best friend. I'd constantly be the monkey in the middle.

Turning my attention back to Hunter, I noticed him studiously watching my brother. I had no idea what he was thinking, but a soft smile was on his face and he seemed to be chuckling to himself. Knowing I needed to get away from here before Starla showed up—she'd tell Dad for sure if she saw who my "friend" really was—I darted across the street.

All smiles, Hunter straightened at my approach. I wanted to give him a hug, but didn't dare do it with so many eyes about, so I clung to the strap of my backpack to resist the urge. With a swagger that made my eyes wander to his backside, Hunter walked with me to the other side of the vehicle. He even opened the door for me; I'd only ever seen my dad do that. "Your chariot," he murmured, bowing a little.

Laughing, I hopped inside. Even though the truck was dingy on the outside, it gleamed on the inside. The scent of vinyl cleaner hit my nose, and I wondered if Hunter had spiffed it up this morning, just for me. "Thank you, sir," I teased as he closed the door.

As Hunter walked around, I shifted my gaze to Julian on the football field. He was watching me and my sharp vision caught him rolling his eyes. He'd heard that comment, and he thought Hunter was being cheesy. I thought he was sweet, and I cocked an eyebrow in defiance. Julian wisely turned away.

When Hunter slipped into the truck, his smell overpowered the car cleaner ... and he smelled so much better. I wanted to snuggle into his side in the wide bench seat, but I had to be careful still, since Starla's eyes were even sharper than mine, and I didn't know when she was going to show up. Turning the ignition, Hunter told me, "So, I get you all afternoon *and* all night?" He crooked a grin. "What will I do with you?"

I bit my lip and thought of a couple of things we could try ... But then I remembered what I needed to find out tonight, and the difficult choices I was tossing around. I either told Hunter the truth about Julian and me, and hoped he was fine with it, or I firmly convinced him that vampires were fairy tales and he was crazy for believing in them. Or, worst-case scenario, I called Halina and had her wipe Hunter. I still wasn't sure what path to take. A lot depended on Hunter's views, and that was what I wanted to suss out tonight. But when I studied Hunter's expression as he drove us away from school, I began to wonder if any of it was even necessary. He didn't seem worried or suspicious at all now. Maybe I should just let the whole thing slide.

No, I couldn't. Not with my family's safety on the line. This was bigger than just the two of us.

Wondering if I should broach the subject now, I cleared my throat and played with the zipper on my jacket. Hunter glanced at me as he drove back to our neighborhood. "You okay? You seem nervous." He fully looked at me. "I was just teasing about what we could do. I'm okay with … whatever you're okay with, Nika."

I felt my cheeks flush with heat as I considered his words. We'd kissed, several times, but it had all been innocent. Passionate, but innocent. Tucking my hair behind my ears, I told him, "No, I'm not nervous, I just …" He'd turned back to the road, and I paused my thought to examine the sculpture of his face. So handsome, but there was an edge there too. Something slightly dangerous. Or maybe I was just imagining it.

Clearing my throat, I shifted my focus and said, "When I saw you Friday night, you seemed freaked out by my brother for a second. Why?"

Hunter looked uncomfortable as he scratched his stubble and flicked quick glances at me. It was odd to see apprehension on him, since he usually oozed confidence. "Uh, no … I wasn't freaked out, I just …" He pursed his lips as he thought of what to say. Studying him, I wished I could read his emotions like I could read Julian's. It would be nice to know what he was feeling … and if he still suspected anything.

His expression switched to a laugh, and he shook his head. "I thought something for a second, but I was way off. It was stupid, and I don't know why it even crossed my mind …" He bit his lip as his sentence trailed off.

Curious if he would tell me, I asked, "What do you mean? What did you think?"

Pulling onto a side street, Hunter deflected my question. "Doesn't matter. I was wrong. And I'll admit I was wrong." He grinned like he was handing me a victory I hadn't asked for.

Distracted by his smile, I let the conversation drop. There was no easy way to ask him if he believed in vampires anyway. It wasn't something I could spout at him without sounding a little crazy, and if I'd misinterpreted his shock Friday night, I didn't want him to think I was completely unhinged. And it was entirely possible that I *had* misjudged his reaction. It was plausible that he'd just been surprised to see my brother high. Maybe he'd had a problem with drugs in his past, and seeing Julian like that had brought back some old feelings. I didn't know Hunter well enough to know for sure. All the more reason to spend the evening with him.

CHAPTER THIRTEEN

Nika

WE PULLED UP to Hunter's place not too much later, and seeing the modest dwelling made me smile. It was a typical one-story rambler with slightly overgrown hedges and a huge crack in the walkway. The shutters were slightly askew and a little faded. It seemed worn around the edges. One thing, however, *was* new since the last time I'd driven past the home.

Smirking, I looked over at Hunter. "Your house is pink."

Hunter's gaze turned toward me as he sighed. "Yeah, the landlord decided it needed a coat. He calls it salmon, but you're right … it's pink."

There was a cute expression of sullenness on Hunter's face. Both Hunter and his father were a little on the … macho side. The idea of them retiring for the night in a home that resembled a pale sunset was too much to resist. I started laughing.

Hunter frowned, then shifted it to a smile. He silenced me with his lips, and I was a little breathless when he pulled away. "Want to come in? My dad's gone, so we've got the place to ourselves for a while."

I nodded, excited and nervous at the prospect of being alone with him. Sure, we'd been alone before, but nothing like this, nothing quite so intimate. So far, our alone moments had been in public—meeting up at the library for an hour or so before my dad showed up, going out to a packed theater to watch a movie, or heading to a bustling restaurant to grab a quick bite.

Having actual dates with Hunter was tricky, since I had to pretend that I was hanging out with Arianna, and that usually meant I had to be dropped off or picked up. There was a lot of deception involved in dating Hunter. I hated that it had to be that way; Hunter did too.

As I walked through his front door, he turned to me. "If we're going to be getting any closer, Nika, I really should meet your mom." Walking around behind me, he started removing my jacket. A shiver went down my shoulders when his fingertips grazed me.

"You will ..." I wasn't sure how to tell him that it would be so much easier for me if he didn't ever meet her. Starla would be fine with us dating. Hell, she'd probably encourage me to do whatever I wanted to do with him. But my parents, my actual parents, would want to meet him too. And they wouldn't be nearly as open to the idea of their daughter with an older man. "Someday," I sighed. *When I'm eighteen.*

Hunter hung my jacket on a coat rack by the front door. He removed his as well, and my eyes lingered on the tight muscles I could see working beneath his thin shirt. "Well, I'd feel better about dating you if we could do it in the open." He turned back to me, a crooked smile on his lips. "I feel like I'm doing something sinister whenever I hang out with my girlfriend."

Euphoria burst through me, and the questions I knew I needed to ask him slipped to the back of my mind as that word he'd said tumbled through my brain—*girlfriend.* "Really?" I started to giggle, then stopped myself. I didn't want to act too young around him.

Walking over to me, Hunter nodded. "Yes, I feel very sneaky around you."

A small laugh trickled out as I placed my hands on his chest. "No, I meant the girlfriend part."

His grin matched mine, then he lowered his lips to mine. "What else would you be to me, Nika?"

I found it hard to concentrate while his soft lips were playing over mine. "Um, well ... okay ... I guess you can meet my mom."

I stiffened with surprise after I realized what I'd just said. Pulling back, Hunter smiled. "Now it's my turn to say it. Really?"

His dark eyes searched mine as he waited for me to confirm my unthinking pronouncement. I wanted to take it back, but staring into his deep, soul-filled eyes, I couldn't. Hunter had wanted to be honest from the very beginning. I'd been so worried about him hiding secret knowledge from me, but I was the one who was holding secret knowledge ... from my family. And I hated the knot of tension that cropped up whenever I had to lie. I hated having to bite my tongue when I wanted to tell Dad about how great Hunter was. And I hated that I had to hide the smile that wanted to break out on my face whenever I thought about him. I didn't know how I'd do it, or what they would say, but I knew I needed to come clean. My parents needed to know about Hunter. Especially if there was a small chance that Hunter believed in our kind.

Meeting his gaze as calmly as I could, I told him, "Yes, really."

Hunter's lean body relaxed in my arms, and he seemed really content with the fact that the secrecy would soon be over. He'd be less content once he finally came face to face with my dad. Or my grandfather's wife's brother who was living with us to help our mother, since that was how Dad would be introduced to Hunter.

"Good," he murmured, bringing his lips back to mine. "Then we can stop sneaking around, and I can take you out on a proper date."

I smirked under his lips. "If my da—" Tension tightened my body as I quickly caught my near slip-up. I couldn't say dad around Hunter. Feeling my rigidness, Hunter pulled back to look at me. As I'd been taught, I seamlessly smiled and covered my ass. "If my mom doesn't ground me for life, that is."

Hunter frowned as his eyes searched mine. I wasn't sure if he'd caught the correction, or if he was just unhappy with my statement. Either way, his frown turned around a second later. "I'm sure she'll be okay with us, once she gets to know me." He smiled wider. "I'm very likeable."

I kissed him in agreement; he was *very* likeable. To me anyway. My brother was still on the fence about the whole situation. Even more so now, since I'd spilled to him that Hunter was possibly aware of supernatural beings. As I kissed Hunter, I could feel my brother's nerves. I sent calming vibes in his direction, but it wasn't helping much. Julian was worried about me, and probably would be until I returned home.

Squeezing my hand tight, Hunter led me on a tour of his place. The house they rented wasn't huge, so the tour didn't take very long. Stopping in the hallway before a thin, dark brown door, Hunter said, "This is my room," and pushed the door inward.

Having only ever been inside one boy's bedroom—my messy brother's bedroom—I was surprised when I looked around Hunter's space. I'd been expecting to see chaos similar to Julian's, or possibly a haphazard attempt to clean a once-trashed room. But Hunter's room was neat, tidy. I think it would pass a military inspection. Every book on his bookshelf was perfectly lined up. His bed was crisply made with deep blue sheets, the pillows perfectly arranged. A small desk was next to his bed—the only thing on it was a closed laptop. All his dresser drawers were closed, and as I peeked into his closet, the rest of his clothes were hung neatly on hangers. And not a single one of his shirts was slipping off the hanger, slowly descending to the floor.

The rest of the house had been just as immaculate, and I'd assumed Hunter's dad had been the reason. Now I thought differently. Turning back to where I was watching him in the doorway, I muttered, "You're a neat freak."

Amused, Hunter walked into the room and grabbed my hand. "I wouldn't say I'm a freak ... but I do like things orderly."

I shook my head as I sat on his bed. "You and my brother would *not* get along well.

He didn't have a response to that, just kept his dark eyes glued on mine. It was unnerving to be watched so intently. It made my heart race. Julian's emotions spiked along with mine, and a flash of irritation went through me. Damn bond. I couldn't even get nervous about sitting on a bed with my boyfriend without Julian getting concerned about my safety. I was fine. I was safe. Just ... nervous.

Hunter spotted my shifting emotions. "Are you okay? Is this too much for you?" He indicated his bed with his hand.

Sighing, I pushed Julian to the furthest recesses of my brain. He would just have to trust that I'd let him know if I were in danger. I put my hand over Hunter's, reveling in the warmth radiating from his skin. "This must be weird ... dating someone so much younger than you."

Hunter's hand came up, his fingers threading through my hair. "Not weird, just ... different."

My heart was thudding as his fingers brushed my cheek. I wasn't sure what I wanted to happen as my eyes drifted over every inch of his exposed skin. "Different ... how?"

Leaning in, he placed his lips along the vein in my neck. I tilted my head, allowing him access. Hunter's maneuver appealed to me for more than one reason; I had to suppress a growl from the vampiric part of me, and I had to concentrate extra hard to keep my teeth firmly pulled up.

"I have to be careful to not go too fast with you," he whispered into my skin. Electricity shot up my spine as his nose ran up my neck. "Like right now, for instance. I want to lay you back on my bed, taste your skin, but ... I don't want to push you into anything."

My eyes rolled back, and I grabbed him, yanking him down on top of me as I fell back to his sheets. Careful not to hurt him with my revved-up strength, I pulled his mouth to mine. "You're not ..." was all I got out before our lips connected.

He shifted his body so our hips lined up, and a whimper escaped my lips, dissolving into his mouth. I'd never kissed a boy like this, lying down, his body tangled with mine, the sensitive bits all lined up where they needed to be. It activated some animalistic part of me, and not the vampire part. No, it was far more primal than that creature. It was an almost overwhelming desire to be taken by a strong, confident, virile man. To be claimed. Consequences, ages, races—everything got shoved to the corner as the beast within raged to get out.

By the speed of Hunter's heart and breath, I could tell he was losing the battle against his own primal needs too. A small section of my head acknowledged my brother's disgust and mortification, but the more the beast wanted out, the easier it was to push Julian back.

As Hunter returned his mouth to my neck, his tongue finally darted out to taste my skin, while his hands ran up my hips. The way our bodies intertwined, the way his lips moved over my skin, the way his hands felt every inch of me ... This was fate, I was sure. This was the boy I was supposed to love. This was my "Happily Ever After," if such a thing existed. And right at this moment, I knew that a part of my heart was being removed from me and placed into him, and I would never get it back. I would never have my heart completely to myself after this. He would always carry a piece of it from this day forward. I just hoped he was kind with it.

Letting out an erotic sound I didn't know I was capable of making, I closed my eyes and moved my hips against his. A low rumble met my ear, and Hunter firmly pressed his hips against mine. I gasped and cried out at the same time. I could feel how much he wanted me, how ready he was to do more than kiss. Knowing that I made him feel that way made my brain fuzzy. I felt like I was under some kind of wonderful drug in his arms, a drug far more powerful than experiencing Julian's high. Desire shot through every part of me, and I clutched at Hunter, silently begging him to press his body into me again.

He didn't.

Shifting to my side, he sat up on an elbow. He was breathing harder as he looked down at me; I was nearly panting. "Wait, Nika ..."

My hands slid up his chest as I shook my head. "I'm okay, you don't have to stop." Fire was burning through me, and I just wanted him to lie on top of me again.

I laced my fingers around his neck and pulled, but he stubbornly resisted. "No ... I think we should stop."

Swallowing, I tried to get some semblance of control back. "Why? We're just making out. Can't we make out?"

Leaning away from me, Hunter cocked an eyebrow. "I don't know about you ... but that was a little more intense than just making out for me." Leaning in, he kissed my cheek. "I was about three seconds away from ripping your clothes off."

I stopped breathing as I pictured him doing just that. He chuckled as he looked down at my face. "Stop looking so hopelessly adorable, or I might have to change my mind."

Exhaling—shivers of want, need, and lust leaving my body—I sat up. Reason began to return as I sat cross-legged on his bed. Making out with an older man did present some problems. Especially an older man who obviously wasn't a virgin. I might be content to kiss for hours, but he would want more. And with how lost I'd been in the baser instincts ... I might want more too. And I just wasn't ready to go there yet. I wanted to be in love my first time. And while I adored Hunter, I wasn't sure if I was fully in love with him yet. There were still too many unknowns between us.

While I found myself respecting him for knowing his limits, and putting the brakes on our hot moment before it tipped into something too intense to stop, I couldn't resist teasing him a little. "Maybe I want you to change your mind?"

Smiling, Hunter looked down at his bed, then back up at me. "You're going to be a problem for me ... I can tell."

Grinning, I slung my arms around his neck, and he pulled me into his lap. I could tell he still wanted me, but he didn't try to restart the fire we'd had. He merely held me in his arms. My respect for him grew even more as I lost myself in his dark eyes. "You're right, Hunter. I'm not ready to go there yet." Running my fingers through his hair, I added, "Thank you for not letting me put myself in that position."

Nestling into his lap, I laid my head on his shoulder. He sighed beneath me, his hand running a circle over my back. "Well, before you start to think too highly of me, you should probably know ... I'm still picturing your bare skin laid across my bed."

Still feeling his readiness, I chuckled. "Yeah, I know. I can tell."

Hunter adjusted his position beneath me, pushing me a little farther down his legs. "Well, that's embarrassing."

I stopped his hands from trying to move me and stared him in the eye. "No, it's sweet. No one's ever ... wanted me like that before."

Holding very still, Hunter cupped my face. "That you know of," he whispered. "I'm sure you've made more than a few of the boys at your school ... uncomfortable."

My eyes widened. "God, I hope not."

Laughing, Hunter brought his lips to mine. "We'll wait until you're older, Nika. Until you're ready."

I nodded and laid back down on his shoulder. Sadness swept over me. When I was older, I'd be leaving—off to college, and new adventures. And even if I wasn't scheduled to leave Salt Lake, with how often Hunter and his dad moved around, he could be going first. Although, Hunter was old enough to make his own decisions. Maybe he would stay if his dad got called away. Maybe he would stay here with me. Maybe he'd even leave here with me. Maybe.

Wondering how long I'd get to keep him, I murmured, "Where does your dad work again?"

Hunter's arm around me tightened. "He's ... independent. Why?"

Sighing, I looked up at him. "I was just wondering if he'd get called away to another job before I got ... older."

Hunter inhaled as he closed his eyes. If I didn't know any better, I'd say he was smelling me. "Like I said ... you're going to be a problem, aren't you?" He cracked open an eye; the desire in his gaze was palpable.

I grinned at him and shrugged. It was sort of empowering to know that I could bring a powerful man to his knees with just a hint of innuendo. I didn't want to abuse that power, though. That was how girls got cocky. Or cruel. But it was definitely an ego boost to feel that way.

As things simmered down between Hunter and me, I felt Julian's tension relax. He hadn't been thrilled about the wash of euphoria running through me, and it wasn't only because it had been so uncomfortable for him to feel it. No, he didn't trust Hunter, and his distrust reminded me that I had things to discuss with my boyfriend—things that didn't have anything to do with sex.

Sliding off his lap, I took a moment to glance around his spotless room. There was nothing alarming in it—just a typical room. Well, maybe it was a little sparse on decorations, but Hunter did travel a lot. Walking over to his nightstand, I picked up a picture of Hunter when he was younger, maybe Olivia's age. A girl had her arms laced around Hunter's neck in the picture; her eyes were as dark and piercing as his as she beamed into the camera. She looked to be just a few years older than him in the picture, maybe the age I was now.

Hunter's eyes were fixated on the photo in my hands as I twisted to him. "Who's the girl?"

Lifting his eyes to mine, he told me, "My sister."

Looking back at the picture, I noted all the similarities that marked them as siblings. "Oh, you didn't tell me you had a sister. She doesn't travel around with you and your dad? Did she settle down somewhere?"

"No ... she's here."

Hunter sniffed, and I looked back at him. I'd never seen a girl around Hunter and his dad. They were an all-boys club as far as I could tell. But by the solemn look on Hunter's face, I started to think that maybe I shouldn't have asked. Curiosity propelling me forward, I set the picture down and walked over to him.

"Where is she?"

Hunter stood and left the room without answering me. Feeling melancholy stirring in his wake, I followed him. As we walked, I started running through a list of bad things that might have happened to his sister: insanity, dementia, disfigurement. I even considered vampirism ... maybe that was how he knew of our kind, if he did, in fact, know. I expected him to go to a closed bedroom door, or maybe to stairs that led to a basement level or a secret attic, but he didn't. He went back to the living room.

Pointing to an inconspicuous container on the mantel of the fireplace, he said, "She's right there."

His eyes were downcast as he pointed, and a knot of sadness sealed my throat as I instantly understood. She wasn't deranged or handicapped. She wasn't hidden away from society, and she hadn't been turned into a vampire. She was dead. Dead-dead.

"She would have been twenty-five this year. Maybe getting married. Maybe starting a family. I could have been an uncle by now ... if things had been different."

Stepping closer to the mantel, I could see that the container I'd originally thought was an empty vase wasn't a vase at all. It was an urn with small handles on either side. It was smooth, speckled granite, with just a hint of pink mixed into the black and gray. If its reason for being wasn't so tragic, I'd have thought it was beautiful. "What happened?" I whispered, turning back to him.

"She died." By the flatness in his voice, I knew that was all he wanted to say on the subject.

Even though I wasn't bonded with him, it was easy for me to feel his pain. I couldn't imagine losing my pesky, brooding brother. Just the thought tightened my stomach, and I sent loving feelings Julian's way—feelings he'd probably misinterpret, since I *was* with my boyfriend.

A thought hit me as I walked over to Hunter. Maybe he believed in my kind because he'd run into one before. Maybe he'd had a run-in that hadn't ended well for his family, for his sister. Becoming a vampire didn't turn a good person evil or anything, but, just like humans, some vampires liked to kill. And with the added element of feeding, those vampires killed often ... and usually in cold and cruel ways, or so I'd heard. As Dad had told Ben when they'd been discussing it, human or vampire, some people were just messed up.

Lacing my arms around Hunter's neck, I peeked up into his face. "Did something hurt her?"

Hunter regarded me with a bemused expression. "She got sick ... didn't make it." Pushing my shoulders back a little, his eyes turned guarded. "What did you mean by some ... *thing*?"

My mouth dropped open as I considered that maybe I should have approached my question in a different way. I probably should have asked him if some*one* had hurt her. Hunter was bright enough that he'd caught the word choice and he was definitely curious. That again made me wonder what he knew.

Nerves locked up my throat. Whether I liked him or not, vampirism was such a taboo topic for me, that it was hard to open up about it. "I just meant ... a *thing* ... like ... an accident or a bullet ... or an animal ... or something."

Hunter looked away, back to his sister's urn behind me. "Oh ... no ... she just ... got sick ..." His brows drew together while he thought about his sister's death.

I cupped his cheek, bringing his eyes back to mine. His expression was a mixture of pain and pride. Hunter, like me, regarded family above all else, but this wound was still fresh for him, and I felt bad for bringing it up. "I'm sorry. I shouldn't have asked about her. I didn't mean to make you sad."

A small smile lightened his features. "Don't be, I like thinking about her." His eyes got a faraway look as his smile widened. "She was the bravest person I've ever known. And so strong ..." His eyes returned to mine. "You would have loved her."

Smiling, I dropped my head. "Do you think she would have liked me?"

Hunter squeezed me tight. "Of course." Leaning in, he whispered in my ear, "She loved whatever I loved."

Eyes widening, I peeked up at him. *Did he ... just say he loved me?* Speechless, I could only stare at his amused face. Before my throat loosened up enough to talk, the front door burst open and Hunter's gruff father stormed through it.

"Hunter, you here? I got something for you to check out ..." Stepping into the room, he instantly spotted Hunter and I holding each other next to the fireplace and stopped talking. "Oh, I see you're ... busy."

Hunter eyed the bundle of newspapers under his dad's arm, then nodded his head at me. "Dad, this is my girlfriend, Nika Adams. Nika, my dad, Connor."

A silent conversation passed between the two men, then Connor smiled at me. "That's right, you were coming over for dinner tonight, weren't ya?" He scruffed up his hair with his hand, then extended it to me. "Nice to finally meet you, Nika. Hunter talks about you nonstop."

Hunter rolled his eyes. "Dad ..."

Connor threw his son a grin as he shook my hand. When we separated, Hunter pointed to the stuff under his dad's arm. "I'll look at that after dinner. Speaking of ... we should figure out what the heck we're gonna eat."

Connor laughed. His face, while gruff and grim, was light and breezy as he joked around with his son. The bond between them was undeniable. Connor looped his arm around Hunter, pulling him away from me. "You stay right there, Nika. Let us bachelors try and make a decent meal for you."

Hunter laughed as he trailed his fingers down my arm while Connor pulled him away. "We'll just be a minute or two. Don't get scared and run off, okay?"

Giggling at the two bachelors, I drew an X over my heart and promised to stay put. I sat on the couch while the boys scurried off to the kitchen to try and impress me, and I tried very hard not to listen to their conversation, but, being who I was, it was hard for me not to hear things. As cupboards opened and pots banged together, I heard Connor say, "She seems nice."

Smiling as I examined a framed photo of a duck in flight on the far wall, I heard Hunter reply, "I told you she was."

A harrumph came from Connor. "What have you told her?"

My smile evaporated as Connor's words sunk in. What had he told me about what? Even though I didn't need to look, I stared at the entrance to the kitchen, listening as intently as my vampiric ears could.

Hunter sighed. His response was quiet, but my sharp hearing still caught it. "Nothing, Dad, I'm not an idiot."

"You're dating a child. Your intelligence is still in question."

I bristled at Connor's words. So did Hunter. "I'm dating an innocent girl who makes me happy. Don't I get a shred of ... normalcy?"

Just as I was wondering what the heck that was supposed to mean, Connor let out a weary exhale. "Just be careful, Hunter. If you like her ... if you really like her ... then be careful. You know what happens to innocent girls around us."

"I know. I remember ..."

My heart started beating faster as I contemplated all the various ways that sentence could be interpreted. I didn't know what any of that conversation had meant, but it all sounded bad. Standing, I wondered again just who I was dating. Really, aside from the fact that he had amazing eyes and a heart-stopping smile, I didn't know anything about him. I knew he moved around a lot. I knew he didn't have a job, but kept busy by helping his dad as an independent ... something. I *now* knew that he had a sister who'd gotten ill and passed away. And I knew he might think vampires were real. That was about it. And that wasn't a lot to go on.

But Hunter had never seemed dangerous to me. Sure, an edge of danger was around him, but it had more to do with his confidence and the way he moved—like a predator. But I'd never once felt like his prey. Around me, he'd always been a gentleman, reminding me to take things slow, telling me that he wanted an open and honest relationship. The two different images were confusing, to say the least.

My heart surging in my chest, I considered leaving. I could zip away and be safe at home in an instant, with Hunter and his dad none the wiser. As they shifted their conversation to a debate between steak and spaghetti for dinner, my eyes swept over the room, searching for a reason to stay, hunting for a reason to leave.

You know what happens to innocent girls around us.

With Connor's words in my brain, my eyes locked onto Hunter's sister's urn. Stepping closer to it, I murmured, "Do they mean you? What are they talking about?" I felt a little moronic asking a dead girl's ashes a question, but with my heart racing and my nerves spiking, I needed an answer somewhere.

And that was when I got one ... sort of.

Examining the smooth polish of the granite container, I noticed that the front of it wasn't quite as smooth as the rest. It was clever, it was subtle, but to my eyes, it was plain as day, especially now that I was paying such close attention. Two upside down triangles were etched into the top of the stone, near the rim. Their long points ended halfway down the urn, with small circles falling off the points. Staring at it, I knew, without a doubt, that the image was meant to represent vampire fangs ... dripping with blood.

I didn't know what it all meant, but it was enough to scare the shit out of me. I wanted to go home. I wanted my family. I wanted to run, but fear froze my body solid.

I was startled from my stare down with the etched fangs when a body popped up beside me. I jumped a foot in the air when Hunter touched my shoulder. "Nika? I've been calling your name. We need you to break the tie on what to have for dinner." Examining my expression, Hunter slowly asked, "Are you okay? What were you doing in here?"

I stifled a scream with my hand as I stepped away from him. His face turned both puzzled and alarmed as he reached out for me. I wasn't sure what to do, wasn't sure how I'd gotten myself into this situation. And to make it worse, I wasn't even sure if I was in danger or not ... but I'd never wanted to hiss at a person more in my life. Caution tempering my animal instinct, I shifted my hand to warn him away from me. "Why are there bloody fangs on your sister's urn, and what happens to innocent girls around you?"

My voice warbled as it came out, but that was nothing compared to the look of shock on Hunter's face. "You heard ... ?" His eyes drifted to his sister's urn, then snapped back to mine. "How did you recognize what those were? We made them abstract for a reason."

Stepping closer to me, he grabbed my arm. I flinched and clenched my jaw to stop myself from baring my fangs at him. Leaning into me, his eyes and voice intent, he whispered, "What do you know, Nika?"

It was childish, it showed my age, but my only response was to glare and ask, "What do *you* know, Hunter?"

Hunter searched my face, then sighed. Glancing into the kitchen, he whispered, "I know that there are things on this Earth that look like people, that act like people, but they aren't really people. I know you're going to think I'm crazy ... but ..." he eyed his sister's urn, then he pulled his gaze back to mine, " ... some monsters are real, Nika."

Fear traveled up and down my body in waves. Still shaking, I raised my chin. I'd wanted to know what he knew, but I'd never expected it to happen quite like this. I thought I'd confess what I was to him and he'd take me in his arms and love me anyway ... like Mom had with Dad. But by the steel in his eyes and the cold way he'd said *monster*, I was certain he didn't have a romantic view of my species, if we were indeed the monster in question. And I was pretty positive we were.

Wishing I could teleport, turn into fog, or melt into the floor, I quietly asked, "What monsters?"

Hunter eyed me like he was gauging whether to be honest with me. After a moment, he let go of me and crossed his arms over his chest. He stood a little taller, and the air of danger around him returned. I wanted him to smile. I wanted him to tell me he was joking. I wanted him to relax his stance and tell me with stars in his eyes that he loved me no matter what. But he didn't. Instead, he confirmed what I'd been afraid of him confirming.

"Vampires, Nika. Vampires are real." He walked over to his sister's urn and opened a hidden drawer in the base. Turning back to me, he held up a silver stake. "And so long as they exist, we're all in danger."

Knowing I shouldn't, I bolted for the door.

CHAPTER FOURTEEN

Julian

"JULIAN? YOU GOT something on your mind?"

I stopped pacing the entryway and looked back at Dad watching me from the living room. Keeping my smile light and breezy, even though my insides were a mess, I told him, "Just restless." Wondering if he'd agree to a request, since I *was* on probation, I immediately asked, "Can I go for a run?"

He narrowed his eyes, and I added, "A human run … just to still my head."

And my emotions. They were spinning faster and faster as I felt Nika's nerves increasing. I'd been keeping track of her emotions ever since Hunter had picked her up from school. Earlier this afternoon she'd been running in the normal gambit of excitement and nervousness that was typical when she was around him. At one point her mood had changed to a passion so intense my stomach had roiled, but I'd managed to push it to the back of my head as I'd started on the to-do list Dad had left for me. It was amazing how washing dozens of windows could distract my mind from my sister's raging hormones.

Thankfully, Nika's desire had simmered down. I didn't want to think about what that meant, but I knew my sister well enough to know she hadn't slept with Hunter. Made out, most definitely ... but I was pretty sure she hadn't gone all the way with him. I hoped not at least. There was just something about the guy I didn't trust. And that was why I was starting to panic as I aimlessly loitered around our front door.

Sometime in the last twenty minutes or so, Nika's natural nervousness had shifted into genuine concern. A concern that was ratcheting higher and higher as Dad mulled over my question. Feeling her anxiety sharpen, I held very still so as not to alarm my father. But if Nika's emotions leapt any higher, I was going to get her, grounded or not.

Examining me closely, Dad said, "Dinner's soon. Can you wait until after?"

My nerves made me boisterous, and I bounced on my feet. "I'll be back before then. I just ... need to move."

Dad smirked. "Well, I can find things for you to do, if you're that energetic."

"Teren ..." Ben lifted an eyebrow and glanced at the stack of papers he wouldn't ever let me see.

Dad followed his friend's gaze then looked back up at me. "Yeah, all right ... just be home before dinner." He grinned. "Your mom's cooking."

He started to chuckle, and Mom tossed out, "Bite your tongue, Mr. Adams. There is nothing wrong with my cooking."

His sky-blue eyes still locked on mine, Dad answered, "Yes, dear."

I waved some feeble goodbye to my family, and then fled into the darkening night. I would have loved to stay and chat with Ben and Dad, maybe try to eavesdrop on whatever secret they were always discussing, but I had to get to Nika. In the last five seconds, her nerves had shot to full-fledged panic. Even though I knew Dad would be irritated at me for running so fast, I shotgun-blasted away from the house. Getting to Nika was all I cared about. I was a mere streak, a blur of motion, a trick of the eye, as I locked onto my sister's location and sped to Hunter's home. Whatever he was doing to terrify her, was going to stop. Right now.

From inside the modest house, I heard Hunter saying, "Wait, Nika ..." My fangs dropped as I zipped up his front steps and tore open his door.

Nika was right there, and I grabbed her, pulling her behind me. A low growl escaped my throat as I protectively crouched low in front of her. She immediately tugged on my arm. "No, Julian. No exposure."

I stopped my rumble and slipped my fangs up, caution overriding my fear. Hunter stopped as he saw me in the doorway. Luckily, he'd been so focused on Nika, he hadn't noticed my teeth. But as his girlfriend was securely behind me, he couldn't help but notice me now. "Julian? What are you doing here?"

Slowly backing Nika away from him, I shrugged. "Mom changed her mind. She wants Nika to come home. Now."

Hunter nodded, and slid something silver into his back pocket. His face fell as he looked at Nika. I could feel my sister shaking, but her mood was leveling now that I was with her. Looking back into his house, Hunter bit his lip, grabbed Nika's coat from a rack by the door, then came outside with us. Hunter closed the door behind himself while I backed Nika up another foot, forcing her down the front porch steps.

His face confused, Hunter locked eyes with Nika as he handed me her jacket. "Can I call you, Nika? I think ... I think we should talk about this."

I had no idea what they needed to discuss, but Nika stiffened and clutched my arm. Her voice was shaky when she spoke. "I should go. I don't want to make my mom mad."

Hunter reached out for her, but I shielded her body with my own. Whatever this was about, Hunter had just lost the right to touch my sister. I'd rip a hole in his throat before I let him hurt her. Nika tugged on my arm again as Hunter implored, "I'm not crazy, Nika. Please, I didn't want to freak you out. I just ..." He sighed, lifting his hands into the air. "I like you, and I wanted to be honest with you. But I'm not crazy ... or dangerous. You don't need to be scared of me."

Hunter looked like a man on the verge of desperation, and Nika stopped pulling on me. Her mood slowly trickled from fear to sympathy. Seeing her pause, Hunter again reiterated, "I'm not crazy. Vampires are real, Nika. I've seen them."

Puzzle pieces started clicking into place, and Nika's earlier fear started washing into me. He did know. He really did know about us. God, what the hell did we do now? As Hunter took a step forward, I put my hand up to stop him. His face turned frustrated as he glared at me. "I'm not gonna hurt her, Julian. I just want to talk to her. Would you mind giving me a minute to talk to my girlfriend?"

"She doesn't want to talk to you right now. She said she wants to go home." My voice was surprisingly calm, considering the icy terror that was flashing through me.

It didn't get any better when Hunter showed me what was in his back pocket. A stake. He actually had a freaking stake in his pocket! A silver one, no less. I wanted to hiss, but instead, I shoved Nika down the rest of the steps, away from the threat before us. Hunter furrowed his brows as he followed us down to the sidewalk. "What the hell is wrong with you two?"

I flashed my eyes up to his and did what I did every day of my life—I pretended I was a normal, human boy. "Dude, you're talking about vampires and holding a weapon in my face, and you're asking what the matter is with *us*? You sure about that not being crazy bit, Hunter?"

Hunter glanced at his stake, then tossed it to me. "Here, you take it then." I caught it without even looking at it. Hunter flicked his eyes between Nika and me. "I wasn't threatening you. I was just making a point. Don't walk away thinking I'm crazy, Nika. That's all I ask." He slumped over as he focused on my sister. "If you're going to leave me, don't do it for that reason. Because I'm not crazy, and I'm not dangerous, and I would never hurt you. I promise."

He shrugged, looking lost. "I don't hurt anyone. I *help* people. I've dedicated my entire life to helping people ... people just like you and your brother."

I relaxed a little as I realized that Hunter might know about pure vampires, but he didn't know what *we* were; he didn't know about mixed vampires. He was talking as if we were all on the same team: humans against the vampires. As if it were that simple. I wanted to scoff at his naivety.

Nika's feelings softened, and she stepped out from behind me. "I don't think you're crazy, but what you're doing ... it isn't right."

Even while Hunter looked happy that Nika didn't think he was looney, he seemed upset by her response. "Not right? How is protecting good people from soulless, bloodsucking nightmares not right? I can't think of anything *more* right."

Nika and I both closed our eyes at his description of our race. A shiver went through Nika that matched my own. "Vampires aren't necessarily evil," she whispered. I shot her a glance, reminding her to shut the hell up, but Hunter ignored my reaction.

His face disbelieving, Hunter told Nika, "Don't tell me you believe the current craze running through pop culture—that vampires are warm and loving romantics who only want to find their eternal soul mates? Don't tell me you believe that the little inconvenient part about them draining people dry is an endearing character flaw?"

Nika raised her chin, and stupidly began defending our kind when she should have been redirecting the conversation. "No, I'm not saying that either. All I'm saying is that no race is entirely good or entirely bad. You're generalizing. You're oversimplifying." She eyed him up and down. "You're committing genocide."

Hunter's mouth dropped wide open. "Oh my God. You're freaked out because I'm destroying them ... not because you doubt they exist." His eyes widened as he began to understand. "So, you must know a vampire. You're *protecting* a vampire." He shook his head. "How could you protect one? How could you betray your own people?"

Confusion and pain rang through Nika. I understood. *Our* people ... were both races. Choosing a side wasn't possible for us. We loved both equally. Tears in her eyes, Nika told him, "I didn't say that either. I just know that nothing is cut and dry, nothing is black and white. There are always shades of gray ... always."

Hunter crossed his arms over his chest. "Not with me. Not after everything I've seen." Glowering at my sister, he added, "And if you actually knew a vampire—a real one, not a fantasy from a book—then you'd understand. I'm doing the world a service."

My sister stared at him, crestfallen. Her heart and soul were shattering; I could feel it. It tore me, but her safety was more important than her relationship problems. I started to pull her away from him, but Hunter stopped me.

"Before you run off ... can I have my stake back?" He held out his hand as he avoided meeting my sniffling sister's eyes.

Pushing Nika toward home, I shook my head. "No. No way, man."

Hunter narrowed his eyes at me but didn't try to physically restrain me. As we walked away from him, he called out, "I'll find out who you're protecting, Nika. I'll find out, and my dad and I will take care of it. Because that's what we do—we take care of them. They're not people, Nika!"

Turning from him, she muttered, "Yes, *we* are."

She locked gazes with me as we both heard Hunter's front door slam shut. "We need to tell Mom and Dad now, Nika." I lifted the stake in my hands for emphasis.

She nodded. "I know." Her heart cracked as she slipped on her jacket.

At a human pace, Nika and I ran back home. Dad opened the front door as we approached the porch. He was confused and concerned to see Nika with me. He'd felt her nearby, same as I had, but he'd assumed she was safe and sound, having dinner with her friend from school. If only studying had been what my sister had been up to recently.

Without pausing, Nika and I jogged into the house. Our expressions must have alarmed the remaining adults—Ben and Mom swarmed into the entryway. Mom eyed us from head to toe as Nika and I clasped hands, drawing strength from each other.

"What's going on?" Mom asked, looking between Dad and us, like somehow Dad had all the answers.

He didn't though. I did.

"I think we might have a problem ..."

Bringing my free hand up, I unfurled my fingers from the object that was so reviled in my family. The silver shaft gleamed in the bright lights of our home, throwing prisms of light around the group huddled around it. Mom gasped and backed up a step. Ben clenched his jaw, his face darkening. Dad let out a low rumble that sent a shiver down my spine.

Dad's light eyes snapped up to mine. "Where did you get that?"

I was about to answer him when Nika sniffed and hung her head. "He took it ... from my boyfriend." Her emotions were blazing with pain. It made me ache to be so close to her, but I wasn't about to pull away. Releasing her hand, I threw my arm around her shoulder, pulling her pain in tight.

"Boyfriend?"

Mom and Dad both said that at the same time, and Nika raised her eyes to them. Embarrassment and guilt washed over her, but she met their gazes as steadily as she could. "I've been seeing Hunter Evans for the last month or so. He's our ..." She looked back at the front door, staring through the heavy wood like she wished she could see through it. "He's our neighbor."

"You're seeing ... the neighbor boy?" Dad's entire body went rigid with tension. As calmly as he could, he asked Nika, "And what was he doing with a stake, Nika? Was he messing around, or does he know vampires exist?"

Shaking, Nika nodded and whispered, "He knows."

Dad exhaled a quick breath that did nothing to ease the tightness in his body. "And is he ... okay ... with us?" He nodded his dark head at the hated stake in my palm. "Or does he want to plunge that through our hearts?"

Nika met his eyes, torn. Even though she was scared and shocked and hurt ... she still cared for Hunter, deeply. She knew as much as I did that what she said right now was going to determine Hunter's fate. Even though I wanted to answer Dad, I bit my tongue. This needed to come from my sister.

A tear dropped to her cheek as she stared at our father. "Dad ... please ... don't hurt him."

Dad closed his eyes, his fears confirmed. Ben snapped to attention. "You have a hunter in your neighborhood, Teren. I'll call Halina."

He twisted away from us as he dug into his pocket for his phone. Nika sprang into action, grabbing Ben's arm with her super-human strength. "Wait! No, please ... don't call her yet."

Mom pried Nika off Ben. "Nika ... honey ..."

Ben glanced at our family, his mouth in a hard line, then he walked into the living room, phone in hand. He was calling our grandmother seconds later. Nika started to panic. Gripping Mom's arms, she shook her head and tried to speak over the knot in her throat. "No, please, Mom. She'll kill him."

Mom tried to pull Nika into a comforting hug, her worried eyes flashing to Dad's. Nika saw the exchange and broke away from Mom. She started pleading again, but with Dad this time. Tears were streaming down her cheeks as she flung her arms around him. "Please, Daddy ... please. She won't wipe him, she'll kill him. You know she will."

Dad closed his eyes and swallowed. "Nika ... she has to know."

His tone did nothing to calm my sister's panic attack. Her pain sent ripples through me, and my eyes misted over as I watched her begin to lose it. I couldn't imagine being in her place right now. I couldn't imagine condemning someone I loved to death. It tore me just to think about it. And Nika was right. Halina would never let Hunter and his dad live. Not if they were actively exterminating our kind. And with the rigid look on Hunter's face when he'd talked about "saving" humanity from the soulless, bloodsucking nightmares ... I had to believe that the stake in my palm had been used a time or two. I immediately dropped it.

As it clanged to the floor, Nika started to sob. She pulled at Dad's shirt as he tried to soothingly pat her back. "Please, Daddy ... don't let her hurt him. Please ... Let's just leave ... go back to California."

Dad shook his head, tears in his eyes now too. "I'm sorry, Nika. We can't just ignore this."

Ben was conversing with Halina on the phone. Well, sort of. All he said was, "We need you here." The line disconnected, and we all felt Halina's position shift toward us—fast. She'd be here in minutes.

Nika looked over at Ben, then back to Dad. Her face was as pale as our undead grandmother's. "Please, Daddy. Hunter doesn't know. He doesn't know about our family." She pointed over to Julian. "We're not in danger. He thinks we're human."

Dad looked over at me, and I nodded. From all I'd seen, that was true. He didn't suspect us ... for now. "He thinks we're normal, but ..." I eyed my sister nervously, " ... he thinks Nika is protecting a vampire, and he wants to know who." I averted my eyes from my sister as she twisted to glare at me. I'd had to say it though. Now wasn't the time for half-truths.

Nika's wide eyes went back to Dad as she tried again. "Please don't let her kill him. I ... I love him, Daddy."

Dad sighed and hung his head. "She has to know, Nika. She has to know ... everything." He looked back up at her. "I'm sorry, sweetheart."

Nika tore away from Dad. Zipping upstairs, she slammed her door shut. I flinched as I heard wood breaking. As her sobs filled the sudden silence, Dad looked over at Mom. She walked up to him and nodded. "You're doing the right thing, Teren." She looked over at Ben walking back to us and nodded at him. "Halina has to know about this."

Ben nodded back, his face all business. Casting Dad a meaningful glance, he added, "This might have something to do with our problem, Teren. We'll have to talk to Gabriel."

Dad bit his lip and shook his head. "How did I miss this?" he muttered.

Mom patted his chest as she leaned into his side. "Because, like I keep telling you, you're not omnipotent."

Dad gave her a half-smile and started chuckling. I crossed my arms over my chest as irritation flared in me. Nika had just confessed something hard and heartbreaking, and here they were, referencing a secret they still wouldn't talk to us about. A secret they thought might be connected to Hunter and his dad ... somehow.

Fueling my fire with Nika's pain, I snarled, "I think it's only fair if Nika and I know about this 'problem' now. Especially since Nika's boyfriend is probably going to die because of it."

My words and tone stopped Dad's laughter. It stopped Nika's tears too, as she paused in her grief to listen. The adults in the room turned to stare at me, and I straightened, trying to look equally as adult as they were. "What's going on?" I asked.

Dad looked down at the ground as he debated with himself. Nika left her room. Stopping at the bottom of the stairs, her eyes bloodshot, she whispered, "Did Hunter do something bad?"

Dad looked up at her, his face softening. "I don't know, Nika. I don't know if he has anything to do with this."

I raised my chin. "With what?"

Dad looked between the two of us, then over to Mom and Ben. Ben frowned, but Mom nodded. Dad returned his gaze to mine. "Did I ever tell you how Gabriel's old nest gets blood? Human blood?"

My eyes widened. I hadn't realized that Gabriel's old nest drank human blood. I slowly shook my head. Nika walked into the room, equally silent, and grabbed my hand. Dad sighed and nodded. "Yeah, I didn't think I'd ever mentioned it." He contemplated a moment, then told us, "They don't kill humans, but there are some who prefer small sips of people to draining an animal. To find humans willing to give up a pint or two ..." he swallowed, pausing, " ... they place ads in the classifieds."

I immediately thought over the stacks of papers Ben had been going through, the hours he'd spent on his laptop. "Are vampires placing ads *here*?"

Ben nodded. "Yes. It's a simple enough way for vampires to find feeders."

Nika stepped forward, shaking her head. "I don't understand what any of this has to do with Hunter."

As we felt Halina almost at our door, Dad said, "Some hunters have caught on to this little trick. They're answering the ads." Dad looked between the two of us, his expression as even as he could make it. "They pretend they want to be fed on. They even let the vampire take a bite." His eyes got a faraway look. "Then their partner stakes the vampire while he or she is distracted." He shook his head. "The vampire doesn't even realize he's in danger, until it's too late."

Nika stepped up to Dad, her eyes sad and soulful. "You think Hunter is answering ads? Killing vampires?"

"Possibly ..." He stroked her cheek, then pulled her in for a hug.

Ben stepped forward. "We've been looking through the ads, trying to spot any that might be from a vampire ... so we can warn them ... but they're tricky to spot. Vamps use puns and word-play to find feeders." He sighed. "It'd be so much easier if they just asked for a neck to bite."

I was about to ask to see some of the ads they were looking through when Halina arrived at the house. Everyone but Ben turned to look at the door seconds before she opened it. Long, dark hair streaming behind her, she was the picture of confidence as she strode into the room. Even though fall was in full effect, and it was nippy in the evenings, Halina was still dressed like she was heading to a party, or a club—her dress was short, tight, and as black as her pile of loose hair.

The four-inch heels of her thigh-high boots clicked on the floor of the entryway as she sauntered into our circle. "You rang?"

While Halina appeared to be just a year or two older than Nika and me, she wasn't. She was the oldest person in the house. Well, for a few seconds anyway. Gabriel stepped into the house after Halina. The truly ancient vampire gave us a brief nod of greeting as he closed the front door that Halina had left open for him. Stepping up to his girlfriend, he seemed the exact opposite of her—sandy blond hair, jade green eyes, and a modest wardrobe that would have passed for a casual Sunday brunch attire at any country club across America.

His youthful face curious, he turned to my father. "What is it, Teren?"

Dad ran a hand through his hair, then pointed at the silver stake resting on the ground where I'd dropped it. "We might have an issue."

Halina followed his gaze. When she spotted the object near Dad's foot, she hissed and backed up a step. I understood the reaction. Even as only a partial vampire, I wanted to get away from the cursed object.

Her head snapped up to Dad's, her pale eyes fiery. "Where did this come from?"

Gabriel beside her bent down to pick up the stake. He stopped when he noticed it was pure silver. He didn't have as much of an allergic reaction to silver as a pureblood vampire, but as a second-generation vampire, it was still an uncomfortable sensation for him. Alanna said it was like a never-ending bee sting.

Seeing his dilemma, Dad reached down and picked it up. It didn't affect him anymore than it affected us. One of the perks of having diluted blood. He held it up to Halina, who hissed at it again. "Nika met a boy who has an ... unhealthy interest in vampires."

Halina snapped her head around to Nika. "A hunter?" Her fangs dropped as her lips curled into a sneer. Even for me, who genuinely loved and cared for her, the sight was unnerving. "It's been a while since I've hunted a hunter. Where is he?" she growled.

Nika stepped forward, her face pale and her heart beating fast. Grabbing Halina's forearms, her tone came out with a touch of command to it. "You can't hurt him."

Halina narrowed her eyes at Nika as she jerked her arms away. She wasn't used to being talked to in that tone of voice. I had to believe she didn't much care for it either. "Actually, dear, I can."

Nika's voice softened as her eyes moistened. Through our bond, I felt her struggle to wrangle her emotions, to remain calm and impassive, but she was wildly swinging from panic, to fear, to anger. It made me nauseous. "I know you can, but please ... don't."

Crossing her arms over her chest, Halina stared Nika down. "Why on Earth wouldn't I?"

Nika looked around, feeling small and alone in a room of adults who didn't understand her. Silently, I grabbed her hand. She was never alone, not with me here. She clutched me tight. "Because I care about him. Because ... I think I'm in love with him."

Mom frowned as she reached out for her daughter. "Honey, you haven't known him long enough to know—"

Nika whipped her brown head to Mom's, cutting her off. "How long did it take you to know with Dad?"

Standing right next to each other, the similarities between mother and daughter were unmistakable. Especially when Mom's face softened into a love-filled expression as she glanced back at Dad. Nika's face looked the same when she talked about loving Hunter. "I think a part of me knew that first day," Mom whispered.

Nika grabbed Mom's hand. "Then you understand." Her eyes went back to Halina's, imploring. "Wipe him, wipe his father ... but don't hurt him, don't kill him." Her voice warbled on the end of her sentence.

Halina twisted her lips, clearly not liking the complication to her simple remedy. Sighing, she muttered, "Fine, I'll let the little murderer live ... just for you." She raised her eyebrows. "Now where would I find him?"

Her face finally relaxing, Nika nodded in the direction of our neighbor's home. "Hunter and his dad live just a few blocks away."

Halina blinked. "Wait, your vampire hunter boyfriend is named ... *Hunter?*" Her lip curled into an amused smile. "And you didn't find that the least bit suspicious?"

Nika frowned as Halina turned to Dad. "We failed somewhere, Teren." Chuckling, Halina spun on her booted heel. "Now one of you come show me where he lives."

Nika immediately released herself from Mom and started to follow Halina as she made her way to the door. Dad grabbed Nika's arm, stopping her. "And where do you think you're going?"

Eyes wide, Nika shook her head; determination bubbled up as her top emotion, just edging past fear and relief. "If she's going to raid my boyfriend's house, I'm going with her."

Halina paused at the door and looked back. "I said I wouldn't kill him."

Nika raised her chin, her eyes still locked on Dad's. "I'm going with her."

Dad raised his chin, his eyes equally determined. "You're too emotional about this, Nika. If something goes wrong ..." He shook his head. "I'm not letting you be a part of this. It's too dangerous."

Nika's face flushed with color as her temper rose to the surface. Feeling that maybe I could subdue a father-daughter battle of wills, I stepped forward. "I'll go instead."

Nika had been about to speak. She stopped and stared over at me. Dad did too. He shook his head. "Julian ... we're not talking about teenagers with overactive imaginations. We're talking about hunters ... *vampire* hunters ... who might be expecting a visitor tonight, since they believe Nika is protecting someone." He shook his head. "It's too dangerous, son."

Nika brushed past Dad, again heading for the door. Dad blurred in front of her, stopping her. Palms pushing his chest, Nika snapped, "Either he goes or I go, Dad!"

Looking anxious and irritated, Halina crossed her arms over her chest and started tapping her foot. She obviously wanted to get this over with. Gabriel waited patiently beside her for the outcome on what family member would be accompanying them; he didn't seem to care which one of us it was. Dad looked between Nika and me, clearly not wanting either of us to go. Seeing that I was calmer than my sister, on the surface at least, Dad finally pointed at me.

"Okay, Julian, you can go."

"Teren! No!"

Dad looked back at Mom after her outburst. Shaking his head, he told her. "It's fine, Emma. I'll go, too, make sure he's safe." He pointed at Nika. "You and Ben stay here with her." His pale eyes narrowed as he looked over at a glowering Nika. "Make sure she stays put."

Ben nodded at Dad's command, although, he looked like he wanted to go too. Mom didn't seem happy with the idea, but grudgingly nodded as well. Blurring to me, she gave me a swift hug, then kissed my cheek. "Stay with your father. And ... stay safe."

I swallowed and nodded, wondering why the hell I'd just agreed to this. Leaving me, Mom blurred over to Dad. Cupping his cheek, she murmured, "You be safe too. I can't ... I can't lose ..." She swallowed, not able to finish her statement.

Dad smiled as he removed her hand from his face. "I'll be fine, Em. I promise."

Tears in her eyes, Mom nodded. From the door, I heard Halina tell Gabriel, "Their faith in our abilities is inspiring, isn't it? Should we say our goodbyes now, love, in case we're staked in the next twenty minutes?"

Gabriel chuckled, and I looked over at him. Bowing, he grabbed Halina's hand and kissed it. "Should I die tonight, know that your presence warmed my cold heart."

Halina gave him a seductive smile as she cozied up to his side. "You warmed me as well."

Dad cleared his throat. "Okay, let's just go and get this over with."

One by one, our hunting party exited the house. Still wondering what I was doing, I left last. Gratitude flowing from her, Nika whispered, "Make sure they don't hurt Hunter, and …" Turning, I locked gazes with my sister. A tear fell from her eye, splashing onto her cheek. "Stay safe, Julie."

Nodding at her, I closed the door.

CHAPTER FIFTEEN

Julian

THE BLUR TO Hunter's house took ten seconds at most. I spent all ten of those seconds wishing things were different. My sister had never been one to settle. She'd found unacceptable faults with every guy she'd ever been introduced to; Grandma Linda called her an old soul. She hadn't been content with lazy, video-game-playing teenagers. She'd wanted more, and she'd found it in Hunter.

And now, she was going to lose him.

Halina would never let Hunter remember Nika. She'd wipe him clean, just to be on the safe side. She'd probably send him and his father packing, too. By morning, the man who made Nika grin brighter than I'd ever seen would be on the other side of the country. I think that was the real reason Nika had wanted to go with Halina. Well, one of the reasons—she definitely wanted to make sure Halina didn't drain her boyfriend—but she also wanted to say goodbye. It broke my heart that she wasn't going to get that moment.

Halina was faster than us all, and I felt her presence stop at the edge of Hunter's neighbor's yard. Dad was with her when I got there, pointing out Hunter's house. Slowing beside them, I glanced around the dark yards.

Standing next to a bushy tree, still clinging to most of its golden leaves, we were protected from most of the neighbors' views. Odds were good that no one had seen us materialize out of thin air.

Listening, I could hear that most of the neighbors were absorbed in blaring television shows. The neighbor in the yard we were standing in was watching one of my favorite crime shows. I'd much rather be home watching it right now than skulking around a stranger's yard, preparing to obliterate the memory of a couple of armed and dangerous vampire hunters. Hell, I'd rather be back at school, watching Russell and Raquel make out than be doing this. Okay, maybe not.

Crouching, Halina began to make her way over to Hunter's place. Lights were on, but I couldn't hear any sounds from inside. She crept around to the secluded backyard, her bright, phosphorescent eyes leading the way. Gabriel was a pace behind her, his glowing eyes sweeping the yard for threats. Dad stayed back by me, protecting me as promised.

What we were doing started ringing a warning bell in my head, and the darkness around me started closing in. My vision narrowed, and Halina and Gabriel's glow-in-the-dark eyes dimmed to pinpoints. My breath increased, my heart following. I tried to control the panic attack forming—my family needed me, I couldn't afford to break down—but lifelong fears were hard to push back.

The pitch-black yard started to feel just like the tiny, cramped trunk that I'd spent endless hours in when I was younger. Rationally, I knew it didn't make any sense, we were in the wide-open outdoors, after all, but my mind was using my nerves to play tricks on me. I wanted to help my sister more than anything, but at the moment, I wasn't sure if I could even keep walking.

I felt Nika's concern rise higher as my anxiety shifted to fear. Just when I started shaking and my knees felt like buckling, Dad placed a hand on my shoulder. His chilly touch shattered the illusion of isolation I'd been feeling. I wasn't alone. I wasn't locked up. I was free ... I was safe. And I was about to partake in something really, really stupid.

Our group paused on the back-porch step. Halina and Gabriel flanked the slider, peering through to see if they could spot any movement inside. It all looked quiet to me. Dad waited with me in the yard. His other hand came up to my shoulder, and he twisted me to face him. Tilting his head, he listened to my thudding heart. "You okay?" he whispered.

Feeling weak and moronic, I nodded and straightened my shoulders. Old memories were not what I needed right now. I needed to be strong and alert. I needed to protect my family at all costs. I needed to be ... my dad.

Seeing strength in my eyes, Dad nodded back. Just as we turned to the porch steps, the faded boards not even creaking under our stealthy feet, Halina blurred the slider open. It ripped from its lock against the wall, partially tearing the frame from the metal. With the force she'd used to open it, the glass door shattered when it hit the other side of its track. I flinched, but that was all the reaction I had time for as everyone was blurring into the house.

Once inside, I stayed near the remains of the slider as Halina and Gabriel blurred throughout the home. Dad was on high alert as he protectively stood in front of me. By the complete lack of sound or activity, I was beginning to think Hunter and his dad had already skipped town. The dining room and kitchen supported that theory. Things were knocked over, scattered, and ingredients for what looked like a spaghetti dinner were strewn over the countertop.

Halina blurred back to us, her face grim. "It's empty. The cowards fled—"

The heat kicked on as she was speaking, and some sort of white powder started billowing out of every vent. In seconds, we were all coated with stuff that looked like flour, flour speckled with something bright and shiny. A hazy cloud of it hung in the air, floating like dust on its slow descent to the ground. Halina cut off mid-sentence. Eyes going wide, she clutched at her throat. As I watched in horror, she gasped and coughed at the same time. Eyes rolling back into her head, she fell to her knees. Then she started convulsing.

Dad was at her side in an instant. "Great-Gran?"

Gabriel blurred back to us, his jade eyes no longer aloof. "Halina?"

Dad held her in his arms as her shaking intensified. Foamy blood bubbled over her lips as she sputtered and shook. I stared in shock, unable to believe what I was seeing. Halina was invincible. A fortress. Nothing touched her ... ever. "Dad, what's wrong with her?"

Gabriel bent to her side, then he started coughing too. It was a much subtler reaction than Halina's had been, but he was obviously uncomfortable. Gabriel's eyes took in the light layer of sparkly flour covering the ground, covering us. Coughing, he faced Dad. "The powder ... it's cut with silver ... the vent dispersed it into the air, into our lungs. We need ... to get ... her out."

Dad and I were the only ones not affected by the silver cloud—it burned my throat and my nose, but that was about it—so I helped Gabriel leave while Dad scooped Halina into his arms. We were outside seconds later, but Halina was still struggling, shaking, foaming at the mouth. Gabriel was still coughing, flecks of blood on his lips. Dad blurred away to the side of the house, then came back with a hose, and began spraying everyone down. The water was freezing, and I felt like I was going to turn into a popsicle before Dad was satisfied I was clean, but I didn't care. Halina and Gabriel were coughing and wheezing; cleaning off the powder wasn't helping them.

Water dripping off him, Gabriel choked out, "Take her home, Teren," then blurred away.

Dad tore off with Halina, leaving me alone in the dark yard, freezing cold and dripping wet. Fear started pressing in on me, but I beat it back. I looked over at Hunter's house, the slider shattered, its glass strewn everywhere. I could just see the thin layer of vampire-deadly dust covering everything inside, could see the remnants of it mixed into the muddy yard where we'd rinsed off. "What have you done to my family, Hunter?" I asked the pitch-blackness.

Only a neighbor's dog's howl answered me, so I tore off into the night after my father.

Our home was a bustle of activity when I got there. Mom's chilly arms flew around me, wrapping a towel around my wet body before squeezing me tight. "What took you so long, Julian? I nearly blurred out to get you!"

I couldn't answer Mom. My eyes were glued on the chaos swarming behind her in the living room. Dad had laid Halina down on the couch. She was still gasping, convulsing. Gabriel was in a chair across from her, struggling to breathe. Dad and Ben looked at a loss as to how to help either vampire. Nika was watching the scene, her hands covering her mouth. Shock and horror filled my sister and over the din of panic in the room, I heard her muttering, "He did this? Hunter did this?"

I pushed Mom away so I could comfort my heartbroken sister. That was when things went downhill with my grandmother. She started to cough up blood ... then she started heaving blood. I froze, halfway to Nika, staring at Halina in disbelief. The once-white couch was quickly coated in pools of dark, almost black blood. I'd never seen someone vomit blood. It was absolutely horrifying.

Dad was squatted by her side, trying to help her. His shirt and hands were soaked with water and Halina's blood, but there was nothing he could do for her but watch. There was nothing any of us could do but watch. Mom blurred away to get some more towels, then rushed to Dad's side. She wiped what she could from Halina's face; the towel and her fingers were quickly stained red. "What happened?" she clipped, her voice laced with panic.

Gabriel, coughing and sputtering a much smaller amount of blood, croaked out, "Silver ... we were coated ... in silver. Teren ... rinsed it off well ... but it's ... inside her. It's still ... inside her."

Mom twisted around to Gabriel. "Inside her? How do we get it out?"

Dad shook his head, a bloody hand running down his face. "We don't ..." he whispered.

Mom looked between Dad and Gabriel, her eyes wide. "Will this kill her?" She said it quietly, like somehow Nika and I wouldn't hear her if she talked low enough. She couldn't possibly talk low enough, though—not with our hearing.

Gabriel wheezed, coughing into his hand. The room laced with tension as we all waited for Gabriel to pronounce Halina's fate. When he could breathe, he shook his head. "I don't know."

Somehow, the fact that Gabriel didn't know what would happen, didn't know what to do ... made all this worse. I felt my knees start to give way as despair rocketed through my body. Nika zipped over to me, holding me up. She gave me her strength while I gave her my comfort. I didn't know how to deal with this. Halina couldn't die. I couldn't imagine my family without her. She was our protector. She was our provider. For all intents and purposes, she was the leader of our nest, our Alpha. Without her ... I just couldn't imagine her being gone.

As Nika and I sank into a chair, Ben put a hand on Dad's shoulder. Dad looked up at him, grief-stricken. "Teren," Ben said. "We should call the others. They would ..." He swallowed, his eyes misting as he watched Halina project even more blood, " ... they would want to be here if she doesn't ..." He closed his eyes, not finishing his statement.

Dad nodded. Standing, he reached his bloody hand into his wet pocket and grabbed his phone. Thankfully it still worked. Dad's hand trembled as he called the ranch. Pressing the back of his blood-smeared hand to his mouth, he visibly shook as the phone rang, and I knew it wasn't the cold that was bothering him. Dad locked gazes with me as he waited. I couldn't look away from him, from the grief and guilt I saw in his eyes. Dad felt responsible. He wasn't responsible for this though. No, this was all my fault.

If I hadn't gone to that party, if I hadn't dropped fang in front of Hunter, Nika wouldn't have realized that her boyfriend knew about vampires. Then she wouldn't have started prying into how much he knew. She wouldn't have uncovered the truth, and Halina would be fine. Some wizened part of me knew that I was taking too much blame, knew that I was only at fault for a tiny portion of the events that had led up to this, but seeing the weight of the world in my dad's eyes made me want to take *all* the blame. Anything to lighten his load.

The line clicked on and Dad's eyes shifted to just above my shoulder. "Mom?" His voice broke. Alanna heard the pain in Dad's tone, and I heard her ask what was wrong. Dad let out a shuddering breath. "You need to come to the house. Everyone needs to come to the house. Something's wrong with Great-Gran."

Imogen responded to Dad. "Something's wrong with Mother? What?"

Dad shook his head. "Just come out to the house. And … hurry." The line clicked dead, and I felt Imogen's presence start to rush toward us. Alanna stayed behind, to wait for the humans who'd have to travel by car. Imogen couldn't wait, though, if her mother needed her.

Dad set his red-tinged phone onto the coffee table. He was a sight to see as he stared at me—straight out of a horror movie. He was soaking wet, his clothes a mixture of water and blood. His face was streaked with blood, and a bright patch shone on his lips from where he'd pressed the back of his hand to his mouth. His fangs were down, too, since any exposure to blood made them naturally drop. It took a great deal of will power to pull them back up once we'd tasted fresh blood—any sort of blood, even our own. Dad obviously didn't care too much about it now.

As we all listened to Halina expelling the very thing that was keeping her alive, Dad flicked his gaze between Nika and me. "Julian, you should take a shower, make sure all that stuff is off you. Then ... you two should go to bed. You have school tomorrow." His voice was tired, lifeless.

Nika and I shook our heads at the same time. Feeling that Nika's feelings matched my own, right down to the guilt, I told him, "We're not leaving her side, Dad. Don't even try and make us."

Not having it in him to argue, Dad nodded wearily and turned back to Halina. Mom was smoothing back her hair, cooing and comforting her like she did with us when we were sick. Our once pristine couch was soaked with red now. It looked like a scene from my favorite crime show, and I suddenly didn't think it was my favorite show anymore. In fact, I might never watch it again.

Imogen showed up to the house moments later. She burst through the door, looking frazzled and frightened. We all looked up at her when she zipped into the living room. She completely froze when she saw her mother, still vomiting blood. Her mouth dropped open, and twin, red teardrops fell from her eyes. "Mommy?" she whispered.

She fell to her mother's side after that, pushing aside Mom and Dad so she could help Halina. Nika sniffled, laying her head on my shoulder. I squeezed her hand, determined to be strong enough to make it through the pain ripping my gut apart.

The rest of the family eventually showed up, and the house was a buzz of grief, tears, and plans. No one knew what to do for Halina, though, other than watch and wait and try to provide as much of a silver-free environment as possible. To make sure the vile stuff was gone from our skin and clothes, every family member who had been exposed to the silver cloud, besides Halina, who was too weak to move, took a shower and changed. Then all the boys were kicked out of the living room so Mom and Imogen could wash Halina as best they could, and put her in new clothes. I could hear Halina heaving blood the entire time they tried to clean her. When they were done, they both showered and changed clothes, just to be on the safe side.

While Dad and Ben talked science with a still-coughing Gabriel in the kitchen, Nika sat with me on my bed. "It's my fault, Julie. It's all my fault."

As I hushed her, my own guilt bubbled to the surface. "No, it's not *all* your fault. I'm to blame too, Nick."

She pulled back to look at me, her eyes bloodshot, her face wan. "I'm the one who fell for a vampire hunter. I'm the one who brought him into our lives."

I shook my head. "And *he's* the one who did this." Hatred brimmed in me as I thought of all the pain, suffering, and ... blood. My guilt burned into anger, igniting the fire that was growing in my belly. No, this wasn't Dad's fault, this wasn't my fault, and this wasn't even Nika's fault. It was *Hunter's* fault.

"Hunter is to blame for this. For *all* of this," I hissed. My hard eyes returned to Nika's. "This is *his* fault. His, no one else's. And he will pay for it, Nika. Trust me."

My sister's eyes widened at my declaration, but she didn't say anything. She couldn't. Her emotions were a mix of jumbled confusion. Mine were finally crystal clear though. Hunter had hurt my family. Hunter was a threat. Hunter had made it clear that he wouldn't tolerate our kind. It was our survival or Hunter's, and, as much as I wanted my sister to get her happily ever after, I wanted my family safe more. *Sorry Hunter, but if it's my family or yours ... I choose mine.*

An hour or so later, Gabriel's discomfort started easing. We all took that as a good sign. It was an even better sign when Halina stopped chucking up blood. Around four in the morning, she was finally calm and peaceful. Her face was sunken, her snow-white skin ashen. She'd lost so much blood. Holding her head in her lap, Imogen stroked her now-dry hair. "We should get her home before the sun comes up," she murmured.

Gabriel examined her, lifting parts of her lifeless, exhausted body. She offered no resistance against him. She hadn't responded to any of us since the silver attack had begun. To a casual observer, she seemed like a lifeless corpse, not even breathing. But Gabriel assured us that she was alive, that she was recovering. How he knew I had no idea, but the fact that he seemed sure gave me hope.

Tilting his head up to Imogen, Gabriel nodded. "Yes, she needs rest and food to fully recover from this." A tired smile on his lips, he twisted to Dad. "But I believe she will."

Dad nodded as Gabriel scooped up Halina. Like a ragdoll, her head fell back and her arms fell to her sides. Gabriel blurred out of the house with her, Imogen close on his heels. I sleepily felt their bodies phasing back to the safety of the ranch. There Halina would be safe and nourished.

There she could recover. Alanna, Grandpa, and Grandma Linda stayed with us until morning.

Grandma Linda was asleep on the smaller couch with Mom protectively watching over her when it was time to get ready for school. I really didn't want to go. It somehow felt like the least important thing in my life. I wanted to be back at the ranch, or out hunting Hunter and his father. Something more productive than learning about isosceles triangles.

As I debated telling Mom that I couldn't go to school since I'd been awake for twenty-four straight hours, Dad sauntered into the living room and clapped my shoulder. "Go get ready for school, Julian."

He was still dressed in the casual clothes he'd changed into after his shower last night. I frowned at his jeans and T-shirt. He typically dressed a little nicer when he went to work. "Aren't you and Mom working today?"

Mom and Dad exchanged glances. Mom had emerged from her shower casually dressed, too, but I hadn't thought much about it since it had been really early in the morning. She was still dressed in jeans, though, as she stroked her fingers through her sleeping mother's hair.

I sighed when I realized what was going on. "You're taking us to school, aren't you?" Dad returned his eyes to mine. Before he could say anything, I added, "And you're going to hang around the grounds, protecting us all day, right?"

As I stood up, my joints tired and almost unwilling to straighten, Dad shrugged and pointed over to the long couch that was now saturated with my grandmother's blood. "Can you blame me for wanting to stay close to you?"

Listening to my sister upstairs, sniffling as she was getting ready for school, I told him, "Hunter thinks we're human, Dad. He won't hurt us." My voice came out in a growl. He might not hurt us, but I couldn't say I'd extend him the same courtesy.

Dad narrowed his eyes at my tone. "That might be so, but I can't risk it. I'm taking you today and staying as close to you as I can."

As I trudged upstairs, annoyed that after everything, school was still on the table, I heard Dad address Ben. "We need to let Starla and Jacen in on this. They need to know there's a threat in the area. They need to be a little more ... cautious."

THE NEXT GENERATION

Sighing, I stomped into my room and started looking around for my backpack. Nika knocked on my side of the bathroom door while I was sifting through piles of dirty clothes. "Come on in," I told her.

She cracked open the door, shoving back clothes and books that were in the door's path as she stepped into my room. Looking down at the ground, to where our parents were calmly discussing guard duty details with our grandparents, Nika said, "I can't believe this is happening." She looked back up at me. "I can't believe Hunter did this to Grandma ... to me. I'm so sorry ..." She let that sentence linger, permeating the house, meaning for everyone to hear it.

Hurt and pain filled her, and I put my arm around her shoulders. "It's okay, Nick," I whispered into her hair. She held me back, the tears in her eyes dropping to her cheeks.

Dad and Ben drove us to school while Mom went to the ranch with Alanna, Grandpa, and Grandma Linda. Dad and Ben seemed to think that they would be safer if they were all together. I agreed. We *would* be safer together, so why weren't we *all* together? Why the hell did Nika and I still have to go to school? If anything justified playing hooky, this was it.

As Dad parked the car in the school's lot, I leaned forward from the back seat. "We should be at the ranch too, Dad. Why are we at school?"

Dad twisted in his seat to look at me. His pale eyes were stern, but warm. "Your education shouldn't suffer because of ... because of small-minded people." He nodded his head over to Ben beside him. "And besides, you've got us as your personal bodyguards, so you'll be fine."

Ben raised his chin, smiling brilliantly. A scar near his eye reminded me that Ben and Dad weren't exactly strangers to violence. Even though I didn't see my dad as scary or imposing, I knew he could be when needed.

We all got out of the vehicle at the same time. Dad stayed near Nika; Ben stayed near me. Their eyes searched the campus, scanning for any sort of threat. Having bodyguards was strange, to say the least. It also felt extremely unnecessary since I didn't think Hunter would hurt us poor, misinformed humans. He was probably a couple of states away by now anyway.

As we walked, I wondered if Dad and Ben were going to take us all the way into class, maybe pretend to be high school students and sit with us during lessons. Dad could pull it off, maybe. He'd be a very old senior ... maybe a fifth or sixth timer. Ben, however, wouldn't be able to hide his middle-aged gray hairs and laugh lines. If Starla hadn't killed off our imaginary father in the personal drama she'd created for our lives, Ben could have played our dad. Maybe he still could ... the bar fight death could have been an elaborate ruse to get out of paying child support.

As we headed for the main building, Dad and Ben on full alert, Arianna approached us with Trey. Arianna gave Nika an enthusiastic wave, one that Nika returned half-heartedly; her mood was still spinning, churning on the events of the last twenty-four hours. I waved at Arianna and Trey—only Trey returned my greeting. Dad narrowed his eyes at Trey as he approached us. He still wasn't happy about my moment of weakness at the Halloween party, and he suspected that Trey had supplied the herbal release. I hadn't told on Trey, but Dad wasn't an idiot.

Arianna avoided looking at me, her eyes only sweeping over Ben, Nika, and Dad. Her gaze stopped on Dad, and she muttered under her breath, "Well, hello again, tall, dark, and gorgeous." I glanced over at Dad and frowned. A part of me, a small part of me, really didn't like her fawning over someone else. I shook off the mood though. Nika was right—it would be pretty shitty of me to start liking her *now*.

Dad didn't react to Arianna's compliment; his eyes were still scouring the area for signs of trouble. Trey clapped my shoulder when he got close enough. "Dude, what's with the escorts?"

I shrugged, not knowing how to explain any of what was going on to Trey. Arianna popped up in front of Dad, appraising him with dreamy eyes. It made me nauseous. "Hi, Teren. It's good to see you again. I'm Arianna, if you don't remember ... *Nika's* friend." She stressed the word Nika, as if to remind me that we were no longer friends. As if I'd forget that I'd lost her respect.

While Dad's eyes never strayed long from his environment, he politely responded, "Yes, I remember you. It's nice to see you again, too, Arianna."

I could practically see Arianna melting, loving the fact that this older man—who she obviously found attractive—remembered her. I wanted to roll my eyes. Of course he remembered her. Mom and Dad knew all our close friends; it was just that none of our friends realized they were being catalogued by them. In Starla's story, "Teren and Emma" lived at the house with us to help with bills and supervision, so it wasn't odd that they were always around when we had friends over. We rarely had people over though. Having friends over meant set-dressing the house—dragging Starla over to be an attentive mom, switching around photos, so it seemed like Starla actually lived there. Even though we could do all that in a matter of seconds, thanks to our super-speed, it was still a pain in the ass—especially wrangling Starla—so we usually spared everyone the hassle, and went to our friends' houses instead.

Arianna tucked her caramel-colored hair behind her ears and giggled at Dad. She actually giggled. Nika grabbed her arm and pulled her forward, away from him. She didn't want to foster that crush either, since our dad was a happily married man, and way too old for Arianna, despite his looks. Ben was softly laughing as his eyes swept the perimeter.

Shaking my head, I muttered, "We'll see you guys after school," and broke free from them to fall in line behind Nika and Arianna.

Dad grabbed my elbow. Stepping into me, he whispered below human hearing, "Ben and I will be close ... watching the grounds. If you see *anything*, you call for me, and I'll be there."

He pulled back to look at me, his gaze intense and worried. I nodded, not able to speak as I remembered the seriousness of the situation. Swallowing, Dad looked around, then pulled me into him for a quick hug. He kissed the top of my head, murmuring, "Be careful, and keep an eye on your sister," then he released me.

"I will," I told him.

Dad paused with Ben at the bottom of the steps leading into the building, and watched Nika and me retreat into the safe-haven of school. Her face solemn and glum, her mood the same, Nika gave them a small wave before disappearing into the building with a still giggling Arianna. I nodded at Dad and Ben, and felt a sense of duty wrap around my shoulders. Maybe realizing that he couldn't pass as a student, that he would have to be a little distant from us, Dad had handed the mantle of Nika's safety to me. It was a heavy adornment, but one I'd do my best to wear. But honestly, Nika and I weren't the ones who were in danger—Dad and my grandmas were. All the undead members of my family were. Shutting the heavy door on my father and Ben, I hoped that Halina was okay. If she didn't pull through ... She just had to pull through.

Trey stared at me as the front door shut with a resounding thud. "That ... was a little weird." His eyes, bright and clean—sober—narrowed at me. "Something going on, Julian?"

Yeah, my sister decided to hook up with a vampire hunter who has it in his head that my kind are evil and need to be put down like rabid dogs. He attempted to kill my grandmother last night, and my dad is worried that he'll come after Nika and me ... possibly here at school.

Not able to say any of that to Trey, I instead told him, "My grandma's sick." I cringed internally after realizing that I'd messed up. Halina wasn't our grandmother to outsiders. She was my grandfather's wife's youngest sister. Oh well, I could have a grandma and she could be sick. It wasn't that suspicious of a comment.

Trey nodded, his eyes compassionate. "Oh, sorry, man. My grandma passed away last year. It sucks."

My eyes stung as I swallowed. She had to be fine ... she just had to be. Nika was waiting for me up the hallway. Arianna was chatting her ear off about how cute Dad was. I could tell Nika wasn't listening to her though. She was swimming in her own problems, problems she couldn't share with her best friend, and all of them revolved around a neighbor boy she'd secretly been dating behind our family's back.

Catching up to her, I slung my arm around her shoulder, giving her what support I could. She leaned into me, grateful for my presence. Arianna wasn't as thrilled. While she still ignored me, she stopped explaining how glorious Dad's eyes were and struck up a conversation with Trey, of all people. Listening to them discuss the last math test we'd taken, I told Nika, "It will be okay, Nick. You'll see."

I tried to be encouraging, but I didn't feel as hopeful as I sounded. Our bond betrayed my true feelings, but Nika squeezed me back, ignoring it. "Thanks, Julie."

Nika and I walked slower than everyone else around us, Trey and Arianna included. I just wasn't ready to part with her. Nika wasn't ready either, I could tell. She wasn't worried or scared for her safety ... she was just sad, confused, and betrayed. We meandered up the stairs to our respective classes, each step slower than the last. It wasn't long until we were alone. I sighed as the bell for class rang, but I didn't move any faster; I doubted Dad cared if we were tardy today, just so long as we were safe.

As we stepped onto the third floor, a feeling crept over me, a feeling that we weren't as alone as I'd believed. I wasn't sure why, but apprehension flooded me. Nika and I stopped on the top of the stairs, and I looked around, trying to find some reason why I felt this way. Feeling my unease, Nika asked, "What is it?"

I was just about to tell her that I didn't know, when I suddenly *did* know. I swallowed a low growl burrowing up from my chest as Nika's estranged boyfriend stepped out from around a bend in the hallway. His dark head was down, and an expression was on his face that almost resembled sadness.

Nika gasped when she spotted him, and I protectively moved in front of her. Hunter lifted his head and then his arms. "I'm not going to hurt you. I just want to talk."

I took a deep breath. The only thing I had to say was my father's name. The second I yelled it, he'd blur up here and take care of this ... thing ... that was threatening my family. Just as I started to make the sound, Nika clamped her hands over my mouth. Shocked, I looked over at her. She was shaking her head, tears in her eyes. "Not yet, don't call him yet. Just give him a minute," she whispered, her head indicating Hunter.

She slowly released her hands from my mouth. Gaping, all I could say was, "Have you lost your freaking mind?"

CHAPTER SIXTEEN

Nika

I TWISTED MY lips at my brother's question. Yes, yes it was quite possible that I *had* lost my mind, but I needed to hear what Hunter had to say. And I didn't believe that he'd hurt me. Not me.

Julian was tense, afraid, but filled to the brim with the desire to protect me. As I stared into his sky-blue eyes, I saw more of our father in him than I ever had before. He still had his moments of weakness, but Julian was quickly becoming a man, setting aside his childish fears to do what he had to do. It was a far cry from the boy I'd had to literally pull from a storage closet just a few weeks ago.

Putting a hand on his chest, I told him, "Stay right here, I'll be fine."

Julian grabbed my elbow. "No way am I letting you leave with him."

I unfurled his fingers from around my arm. "I'm just going across the hall to talk to him." Beneath my breath, I added, "You can call Dad if he tries anything." Julian's eyes flicked to the windows. Dad was out there, walking around the backside of the gym. If we spoke loud enough, he would hear, and he'd be up here so fast that it would seem as if he'd materialized out of thin air.

Julian finally nodded, and walked over to stand by a window so Dad could hear him even clearer.

Relieved that Julian was going to give Hunter a chance, I turned to face my boyfriend. Well, my ex-boyfriend. As Hunter's dark eyes locked onto mine, I felt the flaps of my torn-apart heart shiver. The melancholy and guilt I'd been struggling with all day weighed me down, and each step I took toward him added a metric ton to my body. I was sure by the time I reached him, my wrecking ball steps would punch holes through the floor, showering the students beneath me in plaster and dust.

I'd trusted him. I'd let him into my heart. I'd let him into my life. I'd nearly let him in on my secret, and he'd tried to kill the matriarch of my family. His eyes weren't filled with hatred and anger as I approached him, though. No, those deep brown depths that I had loved to look at were filled with a sadness that matched the jagged edges of my damaged heart. I wondered if he felt anywhere near the level of pain and regret that I felt.

Flashes of our happy times shifted through my head as I closed the space between us. Seeing him for the first time, when he'd hopped out of the moving van right in front of me. Running into him again at the library. The joy in his eyes when I'd shown him the simple beauties of my hometown. Being alone in a dark theater with him. Our first kiss. Everything had been building to something grand and glorious, and then ... it had all been jerked away. It had happened so fast, I still had whiplash. Why couldn't we just go back to the simple times, when our biggest concern was our age difference?

I stopped right in front of him, my heart on my sleeve. He swallowed, then shook his head. "Nika, I—"

There was something in his tone of voice that crawled under my skin. Or maybe it was just the fact that I was my mother's daughter, and I couldn't let him get away with poisoning my grandmother unpunished. With more force than I ever should have used on a human, I brought my hand around and connected my palm with the rough stubble of his jaw. I felt nothing from the hit but cathartic release. Hunter, however, staggered back, then fell to the floor.

Julian's mood lifted, but he didn't move from where I'd left him. Panting, Hunter rubbed his jaw and stared up at me in shock. Standing over him, I felt the strength of my heritage coursing through my veins. More than anything, I wanted to bare my fangs at the hunter before me, show him the true power of what I was. But I wouldn't expose myself. I'd been trained too well for that.

"You son of a bitch," I seethed. "If my ..." I paused, then shifted my wording. Even in my fury, I wouldn't tell him that my direct bloodline was his prey. "If she doesn't recover, I will hunt you down and—"

Hunter leapt to his feet. Understanding my vague reference, he grabbed my arms. Julian let out a low, inaudible-to-humans growl, but I yanked my body away from Hunter with no problem. Hunter kept his distance, but searched my face. "You *do* know a vampire. You sent one to my house?" His face hardened as he lifted his chin. "To get rid of me. And here I thought you loved me."

Even through my anger, his words cut me to the core. "I do love you. I did love you. And no, I didn't send her to get rid of you. I didn't send her at all," I whispered.

Hunter glanced back at Julian, clearly suspecting him of sending an assassin his way. I redirected his gaze to me. "Why are you still here? Shouldn't you be hundreds of miles away by now?"

He looked down at me, his face saddening. "I couldn't leave you here, surrounded by ... them. I just ... I couldn't live with myself if I didn't stay and try to save you."

His eyes were begging for me to see life through his perspective. But I couldn't. My eyes weren't human, and I saw life in a much sharper way than he did. "I don't need you to save me. I'm not a damsel, I'm not in distress."

Hunter grabbed my elbow again. "Yes, you are. You're immersed in bloodsuckers, and you don't seem to think there's anything wrong with that." His hand came up to cup my cheek. "I love you, Nika. It would destroy me if anything happened to you."

I felt Julian's unease growing with Hunter touching me, but my swelling heart was concerning me more. The pain in Hunter's eyes killed me; the pleading in his voice seared me. My anger twisted to sympathy as his words settled around me.

"They're not what you think they are," I whispered, shaking my head in some vain attempt to reprogram his beliefs.

But his beliefs were too well ingrained; I could see the conviction in his eyes as he spat out, "What? Killers? Yes, they are, Nika. I've seen it with my own eyes."

He dropped his hands from my body, like he couldn't stomach touching me anymore. A part of me ached with the loss, both the loss of his touch and the loss of his heart. He'd never accept who I was, not with his beliefs. I could clearly see that now. I'd already known there was no future for us, but the icy confirmation of it socked me in the gut anyway. Tears filled my eyes as I reeled from the blow.

I couldn't help but wonder what horrible event had morphed Hunter's views into the rigid, unyielding mindset he had concerning my kind. Remembering the markings on his sister's urn, I asked, "Is that how your sister really died? Did a vampire kill her?"

Hunter blinked, his expression switching from anger to bewilderment. "My sister? No ... she got sick, just like I said."

I threw my hands up in the air, confused now. A personal attack on his sister would have been an easy explanation that I could have understood. Without it, I was at a complete loss. "Then what happened to you? Why do you blindly hate creatures you don't even understand?"

Hunter crossed his arms over his chest, not liking my question or my tone. His leather jacket creaked open, and I saw bulges in the inner pocket that were unmistakably stake shaped. A slice of fear went through me, but I held my ground. Hunter believed I was human, and therefore, off limits.

"Nothing *happened* to me." He narrowed his eyes. "What happened to you? Why do you blindly love creatures you don't understand?"

I lifted my chin, love for my family burning away the slight fear I felt. "Because I *do* understand. And I respect them."

Hunter scoffed at me. "You really are a child ... a foolish child." As he shook his head at me, contempt clear in his voice, I debated giving him a matching red welt on the other side of his face. Trying to prove that I wasn't a child, I took the high road and resisted assaulting him again.

"I think we're done here, Hunter." Spinning on my heel, I started to walk back to Julian, who immediately strode toward me.

Grunting in exasperation, Hunter reached out for my hand. "Wait!" I paused, but only to jerk my hand away from him. Julian stepped up to my side, minutely standing in front of me as he stared Hunter down. Hunter held up his hands. His voice soft, he again said, "Just ... wait. I need to know ..." he swallowed, his eyes flicking between Julian's and mine. "Are they going to turn you? Is that why you're protecting them?"

Julian snorted, shaking his head. "Turn *us*? No ..." He laughed a little. "Not at all."

Even more confused, Hunter shook his head. "Then why ... ?" Understanding filled his features, and he locked gazes with me. "You're in love with one? Heart and soul in love with one?" His face was crushed, devastated, like he'd just caught me cheating on him.

Sighing, I decided a little honesty was justified. "Yes, I love them." Hunter's eyes watered so drastically, I immediately added, "Like family. I love them like family."

Hunter's expression turned thoughtful as he mulled over my words. Then a cunning light filled his eyes. "Them? How many are we talking about?"

Remembering just what Hunter was, I shut my mouth and shook my head. I'd let too much slip already; I wasn't about to divulge our numbers. Hunter's jaw hardened as he watched me. This was clearly an "us" versus "them" moment, and I was choosing the wrong side in his eyes. "You're right, Nika, maybe we *are* done here."

He strode past me, heading for the stairs Julian and I had just come up. Feeling hurt, confused, and more than a little betrayed, I called out, "Wait! I told you why I love them, now tell me why you hate them."

Hunter looked back at me. His dark eyes were flat, void of emotion. His handsome face seemed so much older than twenty as he stared at me. "I don't hate them, Nika," he whispered. Opening his jacket, he reached inside a pocket and pulled out a long, wooden stake. Julian took a step in front of me, subtly pushing me back, but I held my ground, refusing to cave into the innate fear we had of an inanimate object.

The stake was worn smooth, and had turned a buttery golden color from years of use. Hunter twisted it in his hands until he got to a portion that was black, charred. Focusing my enhanced sight, I could see that a date had been burned into the wood—1793.

His voice reverent, Hunter told us, "My family has been hunting nightmares for hundreds of years, probably longer than your ... loved ones ... have been alive, if you consider them to be alive, which I don't." He held the stake to his heart, his eyes warming as conviction filled him. "Killing vampires has been my family's calling for generations. This is my birthright. This is what I was born to do." The light in his eyes cracked as he watched my horrified expression. "I'd hoped that we could someday ... do this together, Nika. You and me ... ridding the world of horror stories."

I shook my head, speech not possible through the lump in my throat.

Hunter sighed, putting the stake back in his pocket. "Yeah, I see that now. I'm sorry it worked out this way, Nika. I really am."

I felt something then that alarmed me, terrified me for multiple reasons. My dad had been patrolling the edge of the school yard, but he'd apparently caught on to what was happening up here. He was rushing our way, streaking to protect me. He was going to expose himself so he could get the jump on Hunter. He was going to kill my boyfriend. I couldn't handle either event happening. Snapping my head to where I could sense Dad coming, I yelled, "No! Stop!"

Hunter tilted his head at me, confused ... but only for a second. Realizing that I wasn't speaking to him, he backed away from the stairs while he reached into his pocket. I thought he'd pull out another stake, but he didn't. He pulled out a gun. I wanted to scream and cover my eyes, but I was too terrified to do either.

Dad's blurry form paused at the top of the stairs. His concerned pale eyes took half a heartbeat to lock onto Julian and me, making sure we were safe, then he continued blurring toward the man who was threatening his family. Hunter only had a fraction of a second to react, and he couldn't have seen much more than a streaking trick of light coming toward him, but he fired anyway. I screamed as the gun went off, the sound reverberating off the once-quiet hallway walls, hurting my sensitive ears.

Dad's form phased back into solidness right before my eyes, just as Julian tore away from me. As Dad collided into the wall behind Hunter, sliding to the ground and staying there, Julian slammed himself into Hunter, holding none of his strength back as he tackled him. Hunter's head smacked onto the concrete floor, and the gun in his hand clattered to the ground. I kicked the vile thing away, but it was too late, the barrel was smoking from its recent discharge.

Julian growled as he held Hunter down, his fangs bared, poised to strike. I couldn't believe how just a few seconds had changed everything. Hunter had seen the abilities of mixed vampires ... we were exposed, and my dad was injured. God, I hope he'd only been injured.

I heard every chair in every classroom squeak simultaneously, as the students inside realized something horrible was happening. They were probably all standing and crowding around the doors, trying to get a glimpse of what was happening in the hallway; a gunshot going off inside school grounds would *not* go unnoticed.

Hunter's pale face twisted to me. His beautiful skin was a sickly green color, his dark eyes dazed. "What *are* you?" he whispered, awestruck. He seemed completely thrown, like everything he'd known had just shifted on him. And I supposed it had. He now knew that vampires could walk around free during the day. He now knew that some vampires were very much alive. He now knew for a fact that I had vampires close to me, *very* close to me. And he now knew that his original suspicion was correct—my brother was a vampire. And he was about to know that I was one too.

Not having time to answer him, I grabbed my brother, and pulled him off Hunter. We needed to get away. We couldn't be seen by the students timidly starting to come out of their classrooms. We couldn't be linked to a weapon being fired inside a school. That was too big for Halina to cover up ... assuming she pulled through what Hunter had done to her.

Needing to get all our family away, Julian and I blurred over to Dad. He was still slumped on the ground, his shirt covered in blood. He lifted his head as we approached, and I could see pain flashing across his features. Knowing I was doing something superhuman for my size, I reached down and pulled Dad's unyielding body to his feet. Holding most of his weight in my arms, I looked back at Hunter. Shock couldn't even begin to describe his face.

Julian ducked under Dad's other arm, and, as one, we blurred him to safety. We didn't stop until we reached the first-floor landing. His momentary weakness past, Dad righted himself when we let him go. The pain on his face instantly shifted to anger. His eyes roved over our bodies before shifting to the stairs we'd just streaked down.

"Are you hurt?" he whispered, inhaling our scent for blood as his eyes remained locked on the staircase, like he was waiting for Hunter to jog down them.

Needing to get away, I pulled on his arm. "No ... are you?"

Seeing that the stairs were clear, Dad let me pull him to the main doors. "I'm fine. He missed my heart." He swung his eyes to mine. "But getting shot did *not* feel good ... and your mother is going to have to dig out the bullet. The wound healed."

He sighed and cringed simultaneously. Removing the bullet was probably going to hurt worse than getting shot. He couldn't leave it in there though. It could rattle loose from wherever it was lodged, travel through his veins, and puncture his dormant heart ... killing him.

Hearing the students and teachers finally milling about the halls, wondering what had just happened, the three of us dashed across campus. Ben met us near the perimeter, his eyes wide as he locked onto Dad's bloody shirt. "What happened? Did you see him? Did he sneak past us?"

Dad shook his head, trying to cover the blood all over his shirt by zipping up his jacket. "No, he was already there ... waiting."

Dad and Ben scanned the grounds as Dad said, "Why didn't you two call for me the moment you spotted him?"

Guilt went through me as the scent of Dad's blood filled my nose. "I'm sorry, Dad. I just wanted to talk to him ... convince him he was wrong about us."

Irritated, but trying to be understanding, Dad asked, "Why did you warn him I was coming, Nika?"

More guilt pummeled me as I caught sight of the hem of Dad's shirt peeking out beneath his jacket. It was damp with blood, but not dripping. "I'm sorry," I repeated. "I just didn't want anybody to get hurt."

Julian grabbed my hand, supporting me through my misery. Changing the focus, he told Dad, "He knows about *all* of us now, Dad. He saw us blur and he saw my fangs."

Dad looked over at Julian and nodded; his face was grim. He looked about to scold the both of us further, but the sound of sirens filled the air. Wanting to be far away from problems with police, we quickly hurried off to the car. It was definitely time to leave.

"Do you think he got away?" I asked Julian, once we were safe inside the vehicle.

Julian shrugged, his face impassive. Julian didn't much care if Hunter had escaped, or if the sirens in the distance were on their way for him. I knew I shouldn't care either—Hunter had made an attempt on two members of my family now—but, a small part of me did care. He'd been brainwashed to hate my kind since birth. Were his actions really his fault? I knew him to be a good, caring person ... to humans. In fact, in his eyes, he was doing all of this to save humanity. He considered himself an unsung hero. If his actions weren't in such contradiction to how I'd been raised, and I wasn't the target of his lifelong mission, I would have thought him a hero too.

We saw the cops pull up to the school as we turned a corner. Sighing, I laid my head back on the seat. "They're going to notice we aren't at school. Maybe they'll connect us to the incident?"

Dad met my eyes in the mirror. "When I get you safely to the ranch, I'll have Starla call the school and tell them you were both sick and she kept you home. The school won't even realize that you'd set foot on campus this morning."

I lifted my head. "Trey and Arianna saw all of us this morning, remember? They could say something."

"When she's feeling better, I'll send Great-Gran to erase them seeing you, just in case." Dad shook his head, maybe not wanting to dwell on Halina's condition. "But I think it will be fine. There were no witnesses, no victims ... no bullet even. And if Hunter got away with the weapon, then they won't even have a gunman. The entire mystery will be written off as something explainable—a car backfiring nearby, or ... bad pipes in the walls. Something that will make everyone feel better, so they can sleep tonight."

Wishing I could be made to feel better, I whispered, "Will *we* be able to sleep tonight? Or ... ever? Now that Hunter knows what we are?"

Dad exchanged glances with Ben, then his hand came around to touch my knee. "We'll take care of this, Nika. You'll be safe. I promise."

As if to openly oppose Dad's statement, my phone buzzed. My heart heavy, I reached into my pocket. It could have been Arianna asking where I was, if I knew what was going on. It could have been my mom, checking up on me. It even could have been Raquel, asking if Julian was safe, since there were probably a million rumors going around the school. But, no, it was none of those people. It was Hunter.

I sighed as I stared at the screen, unsure if I should read his message or not. Julian leaned over my shoulder and growled, "What's he want?"

Dad and Ben focused on my phone. Ben murmured, "We don't know how tech-savvy the hunters are. We should disable the phone so he can't follow us."

Ignoring them, I read Hunter's message. *'You're one of them, aren't you? That's why you love them?'*

I closed my eyes, hoping Hunter had gotten away, even though I should have been hoping for him to be caught. Typing faster than any human, since Ben looked about ready to chuck my phone out the window, I responded, *'Yes ... and no. It's complicated.'*

'Enlighten me.'

"What's he want, Nika?" Dad asked, while he rubbed his thumbs over the steering wheel. He seemed to be leaning toward Ben's idea of getting rid of a phone that Hunter could track. I knew I'd lose this connection to Hunter by the time I reached the ranch.

"He just wants to know what I am. He's ... confused." I started typing a reply while the men in the car all gave me various suggestions about what I could tell Hunter—most being about where I could tell him to go. I had just enough time to press send before Dad reached back and jerked my phone out of my hands.

Dad read my message, sighing as he did. I'd told Hunter, *'I'm of mixed blood, human and vampire, but it's so diluted in me that I'm basically human. My family is not a threat to you. To anyone.'*

Dad handed the phone to Ben to disable it, right as it buzzed with Hunter's reply. Ben glanced at it, but turned the phone over to take out the battery. I leaned forward in the seat. "What's it say?"

Sighing, Ben flipped it around. "It says, *'All vampires are threats, your family included, and it's my job to get rid of threats. I'm sorry.'*" Ben glanced up at me in the rearview mirror, his eyes apologetic. "I'm sorry, Nika, but he's not going to come around on this one."

I nodded, my eyes watering as Ben took the battery out of the phone. So that was it. I'd confessed my secret ... and Hunter was going to kill me anyway. He couldn't see past the prejudices. He couldn't see the shades of gray that cloaked my life. And if he couldn't, then there really was no hope for the two of us. Some small, romantic part of me died a little as truth wrapped around me. I'd known it. I'd said it a thousand times, but now I knew. We really were over. I wanted to sob.

I managed to contain my feelings while we drove to the ranch, merely sniffling as I watched the cold, dead earth passing by outside our window. The season was starting to turn—days were shorter, nights were longer. It was getting colder outside, and soon, everything would be frozen over. It seemed fitting, since my insides were already weighed down with solid ice.

If all of this had happened during the hot, lazy days of summer, it would have felt wrong, surreal. All it felt now was real—bone-numbingly real.

I didn't say anything as Dad parked the car behind our massive ranch home. There was nothing I could say anyway, except that I was sorry, which I'd already said. It seemed too paltry a word at this point. Julian came over to stand beside me when we exited the car, and I grabbed his hand, needing his support. Mom was in front of us on the cobblestone driveway before Ben had even opened his door.

Grabbing our faces, she looked us over. "Why aren't you at school? What happened?"

Dad walked over to her, scratching his chest. Mom inhaled, then blurred over to him. She had his jacket open in a flash. Her hands flew to her mouth as she gasped at the sight of blood on his shirt. Dad sighed and pulled her fingers down. Eyes watering, Mom shook her head. "What happened, Teren?"

Mouth in a hard line, Dad told her, "Hunter was lying in wait for the kids. I tried to get the drop on him," Dad tossed a quick glance at me, "but he heard me coming, pulled a gun on me."

Mom's hands went to Dad's chest, examining the hole in his shirt that was too close to his heart for comfort. "He shot you?" Her eyes flashed up to Dad's. "He *shot* you!"

Dad smiled at the anger in her eyes, and smoothed back her hair. "He missed, Em." His smile withered into a frown. "But the bullet is still in there. I'll need you to take it out."

Even though it wasn't possible, I swear all the color drained from Mom's face. "You want me to ... what?"

Grandma Alanna was by Dad's side a split-second later, examining her injured son. Dad sighed and patted her back. "I'm fine, Mom."

Alanna gave him a derisive snort. "No, you're not." She grabbed his hand, and pulled him toward the house. Her long black hair flowed behind her in the slight breeze, almost touching Dad as he reluctantly shuffled after her. "You need that bullet removed, Teren. Mom and I will do it."

Shaking his head, I heard Dad mutter, "This is going to suck."

Mom was close on Dad's heels, still looking a little green around the edges, but supporting her husband nonetheless. Ben nodded at Julian and me, then headed into a house that was brimming with people, mostly undead people. Julian squeezed my hand, pulling me after them. I raised my chin as I walked beside him; all of this was sort of my fault, but I had to face the music sooner or later.

Alanna and Imogen had Dad's shirt off when we walked into the kitchen a few moments later. Dad was wincing as he stared at the sharp paring knife in Alanna's hands. Mom was squeezing Dad's hand tight, steadfastly looking up at his face. Noticing her attention, Dad grinned down at her. "Still squeamish around blood? After everything we've been through?"

A small grin crept onto Mom's lips, then she frowned. "It's not the blood, it's the pain. I don't like seeing you in pain."

Dad nodded. "That makes two of us."

Imogen directed Dad to sit on a stool while Alanna tried to figure out where he'd been shot. His chest was perfect. You'd never know anything bad had happened to him. She was using the hole on his shirt as a guide, so she didn't have to dig around too much to find the stray bullet.

Just as my stomach started to roil, Ben smirked at his friend. "You know, Teren, I've never really seen you work out ... other than riding your bike. How the heck do you still have a six-pack after all these years? Don't vampires ever get flabby?"

Dad chuckled and shrugged, while a cocky, half-smile touched his mouth. It fell off his face the minute Alanna poked the knife into his skin. He sucked in a deep breath, biting his lip to not make a word. Mom sniffled, caressing his arm. Julian stared at the operation going on in Grandma's kitchen, but I couldn't. Instead, I watched Mom and Dad's faces. They were staring at each other as Alanna caused Dad more and more pain. His eyes watered and his body shook, but he still kept his gaze on Mom.

Mom stroked his cheek, soothing him as much as she could. It made my heart ache to watch them. Maybe Hunter and I hadn't been connected like my parents were, but we could have been ... maybe. A tear rolled down my cheek while I watched the love and sacrifice playing out before my eyes.

Grandpa Jack put a comforting hand on my shoulder right when Alanna made a noise of exclamation. I wasn't watching her operate, but I could tell she'd found the bullet and was digging in to get it. I could mainly tell by Dad's reaction. He swore and closed his eyes, his face contorting in intense pain. His hand, holding the edge of the marble countertop, snapped a piece of it off. He held the remnant in his hand, pulverizing it into dust.

Alanna muttered something about almost having it, and a wave of disgust and curiosity rolled into me from Julian, still intently watching. Dad cried out as Alanna dug in a bit too far. Surprising me, he dropped his fangs and snarled a warning at his mother. Alanna wasn't fazed by his reaction; she simply pulled her fingers out of his chest, and showed him the bullet she'd retrieved. Dad blinked and stopped the growl emanating from deep inside him.

"Sorry, Mom," he muttered sheepishly.

Alanna patted his cheek. "Don't worry about it, dear. Drink up." She handed him a steaming cup of blood that Imogen had been preparing during the surgery. Dad grasped it with both hands, downing it as quickly as he could. I looked down at Dad's chest just in time to see the ragged hole Alanna had created sealing shut.

Just as Ben murmured that watching that had been almost as bad as watching a heart being cut out of a dead body, Starla and Jacen strolled into the room. Our school-mom must have been given orders by Gabriel to hide out with us here at the ranch, for her own protection, and by the scowl on her perfectly arranged face, she wasn't too happy about it. She did grin, however, when she spotted my dad covered in blood and Alanna holding the bloody knife.

"Ooooh, I had no idea we'd be having vampire boy for lunch." Walking up to Dad, she ran a finger down the blood on his chest and then licked it off, like Alanna had just made a cake and she'd been given the beater to taste. "Yummy."

Mom growled and took a step toward Starla, but Dad held her back. Looking around Starla and Jacen to Gabriel standing in the doorway, Dad asked, "How is Great-Gran?"

Concern swept through me as I felt Halina's presence in the rooms below the earth. She was still, unmoving, most likely sleeping, since it was early morning.

Gabriel ran a hand through his light hair. His eyes were a faded shade of green this morning, exhausted from worrying about the woman he deeply loved. "I believe she will be fine in a few days. She's ... recovering right now."

Dad nodded, his eyes flicking over everyone in the room. "Well, we might have a problem. We might need to leave the ranch."

I stepped forward, not understanding. "What? Leave the ranch? Why?"

Dad locked eyes with me. His earlier pain was gone, but a new, equally intense pain was filling him. "I'm sorry, Nika, but Hunter knows what we are. We need to leave, to keep the family safe."

My eyes widened as I fully understood what he was saying. "You don't just mean leave the ranch ... you mean leave the state."

Starla gasped, grabbing Jacen's arm in excitement. "Are we going back to Los Angeles? Finally?"

Dad ignored her, his eyes still focused on mine. He didn't answer my question verbally, but his silent answer was so loud, it nearly split my head in two. I sputtered for a logical alternative to drastically uprooting our family, but all I could come up with was, "But he doesn't know where we are? I never told him where the ranch was!"

Standing, Dad walked over to me. "Nika, he knows that your family is full of vampires. He knows our family name. How long do you think it will take him to discover where *Adams* Ranch is?"

I wanted to object, but I knew he was right. We weren't safe here. He could find us, stalk us, take us down one by one. A part of me couldn't believe he would do that, but then, I'd just watched my grandmother bury her fingers into my father's chest to remove a bullet that Hunter had put there. He could do ... anything. Tears in my eyes, I shook my head. "Our friends ... school?"

"Can all be established somewhere else, Nika ..."

I thought my heart might explode, but that was *nothing* compared to the shock of pain I felt from Julian. "No," he stated, his voice and face defiant. "No, I'm not leaving town."

His voice shook as rage and pain warred within him. I understood why. He didn't want to leave Raquel and Trey any more than I wanted to leave Hunter and Arianna. But Dad was right, we had to. Dad put his hand on Julian's shoulder, but Julian brushed him off and crossed his arms over his chest.

"No, Dad. There has to be another way. One that doesn't involve us tucking our tails and running away." He dropped his fangs, snarling, "We're not some weak species that needs to live in fear day in, day out. We're vampires. And we have a right to fight for our home."

I stared at my brother in shock. Of all of us, Julian was the one who lived in an almost constant state of fear. His childhood had left him with so many scars ... but staring at him now, he seemed so strong, so able, so confident ... so much like Dad. He was an inspiration, and I dropped my fangs, declaring my agreement with his sentiment, if not his statement. I wasn't quite ready to fight the man I loved; I didn't think I'd ever be ready for that.

Dad glanced between the two of us, looking both proud and flabbergasted. "Safety is our top priority, and the ranch is no longer safe. Where exactly do you suggest we go?"

Julian was about to answer him when we all heard something that sent a slice of fear straight through me. Every vampiric head turned toward the front of the house, to the sound of a car rolling over cobblestones as it entered our driveway. Our entire family was here and accounted for. Whoever had just arrived wasn't welcome at the moment.

Dad slipped on a clean shirt that Imogen had set on the counter for him. Looking over everyone, he whispered, "Stay here." He made to leave, but Mom grabbed his elbow. Eyes fiery, she told him, "I'm coming with you, Teren."

Dad looked like he wanted to argue, but years of marriage must have told him that was pointless. He ended up nodding at her and indicating outside with his head. They slipped out the back door while the rest of us wondered if we were about to go to war ... with my boyfriend.

CHAPTER SEVENTEEN

Julian

FEAR PRICKED AT the edges of my brain, but I drove back the icy terror with the fiery remnants of anger in my belly as I locked eyes with Nika. Her deep brown eyes were also laced with fear, but beneath that emotion was a hurricane of worry swirling within her. She was worried for our parents, worried for our family, and, yes, even worried for her boyfriend, I was sure.

I could feel Mom and Dad's presence darting around to the front of the house, to surprise whoever had just pulled up. I found it hard to believe Hunter and his dad would be stupid enough to drive up to a vampire nest while said vampires were awake, and now that Hunter was aware that some vampires didn't have a problem with sunlight, he had to assume we were prepared for a daylight attack. Hunter's newfound knowledge made the argument for us leaving town a good one. But I couldn't leave. Trey, Raquel, Arianna … they were all intrinsic parts of my life, and I couldn't just cut them out and walk away. Not yet. I was supposed to get until the end of high school with them … then we'd leave. But not now. I wasn't ready.

The car outside creaked to a stop and everyone—those who could—stopped breathing and listened with every ounce of supernatural power we possessed. Mom and Dad were in the front yard, probably getting ready to make their move. The air in the kitchen was so thick with tension, I was having a difficult time pushing back the onslaught of fear. Ben coughed into his hand, and every vampire in the room snapped their heads to him. "Sorry," he muttered, right as I heard the mysterious car's door open.

"Damn, this place is huge!"

Recognizing the voice, I blurred out of the kitchen before anyone could stop me. The ranch had three glass doors encased in heavy, dark wood for the front entrance. Each door was highlighted by a stone arch that supported a balcony on the floor above. My sister and I had mimicked game shows with these triple doors when we were younger, pretending each door led to a unique prize—one potentially priceless, the others potentially worthless. Hoping I was choosing the right door now, I pulled open the middle one.

My sister was instantly beside me as I stepped onto the front patio. A familiar minivan was parked beside the huge fountain of a crying woman that was in the center of our circular driveway. Trey popped out of the passenger's side, his face awed by my impressive home away from home. The only thing that surprised me more than seeing Trey here, was seeing Arianna crack open the driver's side door. My mouth was wide open as they stepped out of the vehicle.

"Teeth," Nika muttered, nudging me in the ribs.

I immediately pulled up my fangs, only then realizing that they were still down. Mom and Dad appeared on the other side of the fountain, holding hands and seeming like they were going for a casual stroll around the property, not stalking my friends. Below what Trey and Arianna could hear, Dad asked, "What are they doing here?"

"Don't know," I murmured back, waving at my unexpected guests.

Faces full of concern, Trey and Arianna made their way over to Nika and me. Knowing I sounded like a parent, the only question I could think to ask was, "Why aren't you guys at school?"

Arianna rushed up to me, throwing her arms around my neck. Her force pushed me back a step, startling me. She hadn't acknowledged my existence much lately, let alone touched me. "Julian, thank God you're okay! I couldn't stay at that place until I saw for myself that you were all right."

Pulling back from our embrace, her eyes flashed to mine and her cheeks filled with color as our gazes locked. It had been a while since she'd purposely looked at me. I'd almost forgotten just how beautiful her eyes were—green, brown, a splash of blue and gray—they were different from every angle, a kaleidoscope of colors. Kind of ... enchanting really.

"Especially after what Trey said he saw in the hallway," she said. "Did someone seriously pull a gun on you?" she whispered, her voice trembling.

"Not at me," I muttered, overly conscious of how close her body was to mine. Pushing back the feeling starting to creep up on me, I looked over at Trey. "What exactly did you see?" Ice tingled up my spine as I realized that he'd, at the very least, seen the gun being drawn.

Mom and Dad stepped up to our group, and Trey eyed Dad with both confusion and trepidation. Arianna switched her position so that she was cuddling into my side. Part of me wanted to push her away, since I was trying to not be misleading anymore, but really, after the last couple of days that I'd had, I wanted the comfort too much.

Trey's eyes flicked between mine and Dad's, but when he spoke, it was directed at Dad. "I went out to the hall to see where Julian was, and I spotted him and Nika talking to that Hunter dude." Trey looked back at me. "Then that crazy mo-fo pulled a gun and fired!" Arianna shuddered as Trey looked back at Dad. "I thought he was shooting at nothing, but then you ... appeared out of nowhere ... slammed into a wall." His eyes scoured Dad up and down. Trey shook his head in disbelief; the hair peeking out from under his knitted cap brushed his shoulders. "I know he got you. How are you not hurt? Or dead?"

Dad frowned, rubbing the spot where he'd been operated on just a few minutes ago. "Maybe we should discuss this inside?" He motioned to the front doors.

Instead of moving toward the doors, Trey looked back at me. "Then you tackled Hunter ... and I saw your face, your mouth. And those fangs weren't props, dude." Scrunching his face, he suddenly looked like he was back in math class, trying to figure out a complicated problem. I would have found his look humorous, except, when he spoke, he asked me almost the same thing Hunter had asked Nika, "What the heck are you?"

Disengaging herself from me, Arianna scoffed. "Trey, knock it off with your stories. He had a gun pulled on him! You don't need to dramatize the situation by adding some crap about Julian being a vampire."

Trey shifted his inquisitive look and glared at Arianna. "Like I said before, I saw it! With my own eyes!"

Standing in front of me, like she was protecting me, Arianna crossed her arms over her chest. "Well, I'm glad you didn't see it with somebody else's eyes, Trey." She sighed, her breath coming out in a puff of moisture. "But you're wrong. All that happened was a gun fired. Luckily no one was hurt, and Hunter, the freaking psycho, ran away."

Trey stepped up to Arianna, glowering. "You weren't there, Arianna. You didn't see what I saw." He pointed back at Dad. "*He* got shot!" His arm swung around to Nika and me. "And they disappeared with him like that!" He snapped his fingers to emphasize his point. "They vanished into thin air, like they ... teleported or something."

I sighed softly. He really had seen everything. Kind of gangly, Trey had always reminded me of a pony who hadn't quite grown into its body yet. I'd always thought the same thing about his mind too, but with how he'd pieced everything together, I had to reconsider. Trey was smarter than he let on.

Arianna gave Trey a look of disbelief. "Have you had anything this morning, Trey?" she asked, miming a joint.

Trey blinked. Looking abashed, he shook his head. "No, I'm sober."

Arianna shook her head. "You're sober, but you think you saw Julian and Nika teleport? You think Julian had real vampire fangs? Do you really think Julian is a member of the walking undead? *Julian?*" She patted my chest, my heart.

Walking around the arguing pair, Dad opened the front door. "I'm pretty sure we can clear all of this up inside," he suggested. He locked eyes with Trey. "We'll tell you everything you need to know."

Trey nodded, and Arianna turned away, muttering, "Vampires ... ridiculous."

I exchanged a long look with Nika while Mom and Dad entered the house after Arianna. Nika's mood was akin to my own. She was a mixture of sadness and elation. It would be easier on some level if our friends knew the truth. But it would be more difficult, too. Our family didn't let a whole lot of people in on our secret. Truly, aside from Ben, it was limited to immediate family only. The theory was that the fewer people who knew the truth, the fewer people who could find out the truth. It was all done to spare our family from being hurt or hunted, to hide mass exposure. Not that it was a foolproof plan, as our current situation with Hunter showed. But letting Trey and Arianna in on the family secret also brought with it the very real possibility of rejection, and they would definitely be wiped if they couldn't handle it. A part of me was really bothered by the idea that the people I was closest to might not be able to accept who I was. Nika was already feeling that ache of rejection, since Hunter had just shunned her in the most violent way he could. She was still reeling from the blow, on the edge of breaking down. Another loss right now might push her over the edge.

I slung my arm over Nika's shoulders, silently supporting her. Trey watched our every move with inquisitive eyes. Of all the days for Trey to come to school completely sober ... With a heavy heart, I headed into the house to tell my friends that I was a ... how did Hunter put it? Right, a bloodsucking nightmare.

Everyone was waiting in the living room when Nika and I arrived with Trey. While the ranch back in California resembled a ski lodge with thick, wooden beams and flat river rocks, this ranch reminded me of a palace. The ceilings were vaulted, with crystal chandeliers and silent ceiling fans, waiting for the heat of summer. Every wall was rich with color, the furniture a deep, dark cherry. Heavy brocaded curtains outlined every set of windows. They were all currently open, to let the bright light of this chilly day filter into the room. A room filled with vampires.

Trey's eyes were wide as he looked at all the youthful faces in the room. He was either thinking that I had a lot of family members who all seemed around the same age, or he was slowly realizing that there were a lot more vampires in the room than he'd anticipated. He paled a little as he found a seat next to Arianna on one of the many plush chairs in the room.

Arianna was checking out the various members of my, admittedly, attractive family. She seemed unperturbed by all the undead around her. Of course, she didn't know yet. She might feel differently in a few minutes.

Mom and Dad were still standing as I found a seat next to Nika. The couch we were sitting on had golden tassels that hung off the buttons. I absentmindedly played with one while Dad stepped up to Trey. Arms crossed over his chest, Dad's face grew deadly serious. "I'll tell you everything that happened in that hallway, Trey, but first, I need to know ... did you tell anyone what you saw? Even just that you saw a gun?"

Trey leaned over his knees, bouncing his heels as nervous energy shot through him; I could smell it. "No, no ... I only told *her*." He jerked his thumb at Arianna. "She freaked out when I mentioned a gun. Dragged me off to go find Julian and Nika before I even had a chance to tell anyone else." His eyes flashed to mine. "Not that I would, man. Your secret's safe with me."

Arianna snorted at his comment, but Trey ignored her. "We left school right as the cops showed up to lock it down. I didn't say anything, I promise. You can trust me."

Dad twisted his lips, considering. After a moment, he shrugged. "You're right. I did get shot. But I ... recover quickly. Especially when they miss my heart."

Arianna's mouth dropped wide open as she absorbed what Dad was saying. My stomach tightened at the thought of her turning away from me ... for real this time.

Trey was only dazed by Dad's pronouncement for a second, then he shot to his feet. "I knew it!" His pointed at me. "You're totally vampires, aren't you?"

Amusement and amazement bubbled into me, both at the look of wonder on Trey's face and the fact that he'd jig-sawed the puzzle pieces of my life together in such a way that he'd come up with the one thing we'd been trying to hide from everyone. A little relieved that the words were out there, I mumbled, "Sort of. We're only a little bit vampire."

"Huh? What do you mean ... little bit?" Trey looked relived that he'd guessed my secret correctly, but dumbfounded too, like the puzzle he'd put together had formed a picture of something that was impossible to understand without guidance.

Arianna turned her head to stare at me. "What?" She still looked confused, but at least she wasn't scared. Yet. Worry passed over her features as she glanced between Trey and me. She seemed to think we were both crazy.

Dad appeared to be about to explain, and even Nika opened her mouth to start talking, but I held up my hand to stop them. I wanted to explain this. It was my fault anyway. I stood up to stand before Arianna and Trey; they both watched me, Trey wondrous and curious, Arianna ... perplexed.

Dad backed up a step, giving me space to admit the deepest, darkest part of myself to people not in the know. My stomach swam with nerves; I'd never confessed this before. I wasn't sure how to begin, or if I even should. But Trey and Arianna had to be told something, especially since they were putting themselves in danger by hanging out with me. If they were going to stand by my side right now, they needed to understand what I was, and what I wasn't.

Inhaling a calming breath, I talked in as soothing a voice as I could. "My great-great grandmother was turned into a vampire while she was pregnant. Her daughter was born half-human, half-vampire. Her daughter was born part-vampire, and so was her son ... and so was my sister ... and so was I. We're all of mixed blood."

Trey's eyes widened to a point where I thought they might pop out of his head. "That's ... possible?"

I nodded, as Arianna jumped up from the couch to stand with Trey. "Okay, I don't know what's going on here, or why you're all making up stories, but I'd like to go home now."

She grabbed Trey's hand, pulling him into her, and searched his face, seeking support in her desire to leave. She was clutching his arm as they stood close together, and a part of me hated how close they were standing. It made an uneasy feeling go through me. Almost ... jealousy, and that was a really odd thing to feel about Arianna. I tried to push the feeling back—someone else touching Arianna should *not* make me jealous. Even still, I reached for her free hand. "I'm not lying ... I'm not making up a story. I'm just telling you what I am, so you can understand why Hunter, well, why he shot my dad."

Arianna's face flushed as she grabbed my fingers and released Trey. Her heart sped up a little, too, but then she shut her eyes and shook her head. "Your dad?" Opening her eyes, she looked over at Nika. "Teren is your ... dad?"

Nika nodded, then shifted her gaze to smile up at Dad. He smiled back at her, adoration clear in his pale eyes. Arianna jerked her hand away from mine and backed up a step. "You're all out of your minds ..."

Starla, stretched out in front of the crackling fireplace, yawned. "God, this is tedious. Just show her already, Julian."

I rolled my eyes at Starla, but I knew she was right. Arianna would have to *see* that I wasn't normal to believe it. At hearing Starla, Arianna snapped her eyes to the woman she believed was my mother. Then she glanced at Dad, and I knew she was wondering how someone as young-looking as my father could have teenage children. I cupped her cheek, and she instantly returned her eyes to mine. Her face was warm under my fingertips, and her heart started racing. A part of me hoped it was my touch that did that to her, not the tension in the air.

"Arianna, watch my mouth as closely as you can."

Her eyes locked onto my lips, and I had the strangest desire to press my lips to hers. But no ... I didn't want to kiss her. I didn't like her that way.

I lowered my jaw and held my mouth open. Arianna shook her head, not seeing anything out of the ordinary. Not yet anyway. Slowly and precisely, I let go of the control on my teeth. My fangs elongated right before her eyes. I let them extend as far as they would go, until they brushed my bottom lip. Watching them grow in such a way made my heritage unmistakable. Like it or not, I was a vampire.

Arianna gasped and backed up until she collided with the couch. She fell back into the cushions and scrunched into the corner of the chair. My heart sank as I watched her face fill with fear. Trey, on the other hand, clapped my shoulder and exclaimed, "Dude! That was freaking incredible! Can all of you do that?"

As I kept my eyes glued on Arianna, I listened to the other vampiric members of my family dropping their fangs. Arianna's eyes shifted to each person as they showed her the beast within. By the time her eyes drifted to Nika, they were moist. She looked terrified. Pulling up my fangs, I sank to my knees before her.

"Hey, I'm still me, Arianna. I'm not going to hurt you. No one here is going to hurt you." Arianna's face was white, and the smell of anxiety was thick around her, like prey realizing it was surrounded by predators. I tried to touch her, but she pulled away from me. I thought she'd burrow into the sofa cushions if she could.

Nika got up from her seat to squat beside me. "You okay, Arianna?"

Arianna stared at Nika blankly, like she was speaking another language. She seemed frozen in shock. I wasn't sure what to do. Carefully patting her leg, I whispered, "It's okay ... we don't bite."

I meant it as a joke, but my comment pushed Arianna over the edge. She scrambled over the back of the couch, trying to get away from me. Nika scoffed and shoved my shoulder, pushing me onto my ass. Her disapproval blazed into me as she blurred over to her friend who was trying to escape. Zipping in front of Arianna, Nika held out her hands. "Wait, please don't leave yet."

Trey let out an impressed whistle while Arianna stopped dead in her tracks. Her eyes flicked from the couch to Nika. "How did you ... ?"

Arianna was shaking, but she let Nika grab her hands. Stepping closer to her friend, Arianna whispered, "You're a ... vampire, Nika? You're all vampires?"

Nika nodded. "Yes, most of us are. But we don't kill people, so you don't need to be scared."

Arianna lifted her chin. "I'm not scared." If her trembling had stopped and her heart rate had slowed, I might have believed her defiant stance.

Nika slowly put her arm around her shoulders and led her back into the living room. "Come on, I want you to meet my parents. My real parents."

Mom cuddled into Dad's side as Nika led Arianna over to them. Of course, Arianna had met them before, but things were a little different now that she knew the truth.

Nika indicated each parent in turn. "Arianna, this is my dad, Teren, and my mom, Emma."

Both had pulled in their fangs, and they looked like a perfectly normal young couple. Mom grabbed Arianna's hand and gave it a light shake. Arianna trembled as Mom's cold seeped into her.

Maybe not wanting to focus on *why* Mom was so cold, Arianna asked Nika, "If she's your mom ... then who is she?" She pointed at Starla.

Arianna had said it quietly, like she didn't want everyone to hear her question, but of course, nearly everyone did. Dad opened his mouth to answer, but Starla beat him to it. Linking her arms around Jacen's neck, she told Arianna, "No relation. I'm still aging, so I got roped into being their designated parent."

Arianna blushed when she realized everyone could hear her whispers. Dad turned and frowned at Starla behind him. She quickly amended her statement with, "And I'm honored to do it."

Trey studied every vampire near him, then asked, "What does she mean by 'still aging'?"

Seeing a scientific question that he could easily answer, Gabriel nodded his head at Nika and me. "All mixed vampires are born alive. They live and grow as normally as humans do. But, the vampiric blood is ... aggressive ... and eventually wears out the human body. Every mixed vampire I've ever known has died sometime before they turn twenty-six."

Arianna twisted to me. Her eyes were moist as she asked, "You're going to die in your twenties?"

I twisted my lips, not sure how to begin answering that complicated question. Starla answered for me though. Waving her hand to get Arianna's attention, she said, "Hey, remember me ... the still aging one?" Arianna's face melted into confusion as Starla popped a bubble with her gum. Jerking her thumb at Gabriel, Starla said, "Father's a genius, developed a shot that keeps us alive for as long as we want to be." She pointed to Julian. "If he decides to take it, he could live and die as a human."

A stillness filled the air as that topic was brought up again. Sensing the sudden tension, Starla looked around the room. "What? I'm just saying he could ... if he wanted to."

While Arianna pondered her statement, Dad took hold of the conversation. "Our lives are a bit complicated, and unfortunately, a bit dangerous. Especially now."

Trey stepped forward, crossing his arms over his chest. "Because of that dick, Hunter?"

Dad frowned, but nodded. "Yes. He knows what we are, and he isn't okay with us. In fact, he wants to get rid of every single one of us."

Arianna locked eyes with Nika. I felt Nika's grief welling as her friend's face turned comforting. "Even you? But ... he's your boyfriend?"

Nika swallowed, and a single tear slid down her cheek in response. Her pain threatened to tear my heart, drop me to my knees, but I stood tall, giving her what strength I could. Arianna threw her arms around Nika, hugging her tight and murmuring apologies.

Walking behind her, Trey put a comforting hand on Nika's shoulder. I stepped up to Arianna, tempted to touch her, but not wanting to startle her. Dad looked over all of us, then sighed and glanced around the room. "We should be discussing what we're going to do, now that Hunter knows about us."

Dad's eyes met Ben's. Ben was leaning against the wall, listening to our confessions. A small smile was on his lips, the faint scar on his cheek crinkling, and I wondered if he was remembering the day he'd found out about my family. Focusing on Dad's statement, he nodded. "He's probably already researched the whereabouts of the ranch. It's only a matter of time before he plans an attack. You're not safe here."

Arianna nodded, catching on quickly, now that her shock was receding. "Yeah, it's not hard to find. We weren't sure where the ranch was, so Trey looked it up online while we drove. Took him two seconds." Scrunching her face, she looked over at Nika. "Did you know there's about seven Adams Ranches around the country?"

Nika smiled, but didn't mention that all those ranches belonged to our family. Grandpa Jack spoke into the quietness as he held Alanna's hand. "So, where do you think we should go, son?"

Dad opened his mouth to speak, but Starla again interjected. "I think we should head back to L.A. There's safety in numbers." She twisted her perfectly coifed head to Gabriel. "And you already drove them out of the city once, Father. They won't touch anyone there again."

As Arianna murmured to Nika, "Is that hot guy really her dad?" I asked Gabriel, "Are they connected to the incident in L.A.? Are they the ones ... answering ads for vampire feedings around here?" Gabriel cocked an eyebrow at me, and I explained further. "Dad told me that's what you and Ben have been doing—hunting whomever has been hunting the vampires. You think it's Hunter and his dad?"

Nika sniffed, hanging her head, and Gabriel thought for a moment. Finally, he impassively told us, "It is highly probable. I would be hard-pressed to believe that there were *two* sets of hunters in the area giving us the same problem. The odds would suggest that they were one and the same."

"I still can't believe Hunter would do this," Nika whispered.

No one answered her. Hunter had already done so much that it wasn't all that shocking anymore. Hunter and his dad had been traveling the country, stopping in towns that showed a high level of "blood wanted" ads. They'd been answering the ads, then staking whatever poor soul tried to feed on them. And since they were both still alive, they must be good at their jobs.

Dad turned to Grandpa Jack and finally answered his question. "I don't know where we should go. We can't stay here, but I really don't want to leave hunters in the city. But the children ..." He looked back at

Nika and me. Bolstering my courage, I raised my chin. I'd meant what I'd said earlier. I would stay and fight for my home, if it came to that. And there were enough of us; we could defend ourselves from two humans.

As I was showing Dad my strength, Arianna put her hand in mine. I clasped it tight, drawing even more courage from her. Dad looked at a loss over what to do, and Trey spoke up in his silence. "You can stay at my place. Hunter doesn't know where I live." He looked over at me. "And even if he tried to find me with my name, he couldn't. The house is in my mom's boyfriend's name."

Dad exchanged glances with Mom, then turned to Trey. "There are a lot of us. Your family won't mind?"

Trey shrugged. "They're usually ... out of it. They probably won't even notice."

Still grasping my hand, Arianna told my dad, "Nika and Julian could stay at my place. My parents won't mind." I smiled as I looked down at her, touched by her offer to hide a couple of vampire kids.

Starla grunted as she popped to her feet. "Well, if we're not going back to L.A., then can I at least go back home? This Hunter guy doesn't know anything about Jacen and me."

Gabriel gave Starla an admonishing look, and she immediately sat back down. Imogen looked between Trey and Dad. "Teren, Mother and I can't travel yet. We have to wait until nightfall."

Dad looked between all the different groups of people around him, some human, some not. Feeling invincible with my family around me, I again told him, "We should stay. Let Hunter and his dad come. We can fight them off."

My words surprised me, as did my lack of fear when I said them. But I'd been living in fear for a long time now, and I was a little tired of it. Dad locked his pale eyes on mine. A smile touched his lips, but then he frowned. "No, I can't risk even one person getting hurt." His eyes moist, he looked around the room. "Every single one of you is important to me. I couldn't handle anything ..." He swallowed, and Mom returned to his side.

"Then we leave, Teren. We all leave together. We all stay safe together."

Dad placed his forehead against hers. "We leave at nightfall. We'll go to Trey's house."

Laughing a little, Trey clapped my back. "All right ... partying with the Adams clan." Mom and Dad frowned at Trey at the exact same time. They looked like they were already regretting their decision, and, despite the seriousness of the situation, I had to smile.

Gabriel started in on a conversation with Ben regarding Hunter's involvement in L.A. Mom and Dad walked over to join their discussion, and soon, all the adults were debating whether Hunter had killed vampires in Los Angeles.

I could see the effect that the conversation was having on Nika. She was trying to be stoic, trying to be strong, but the longer she listened to Hunter's past crimes, the more her chin started to tremble. Not wanting her to dwell, I tried redirecting her focus. "Hey, Nick, since we're gonna be here a while, should we show Trey and Arianna around?"

Sniffling, Nika met my eyes. Her warm, chocolate ones were misty. "Sure ... yeah."

Nika stood, and I grabbed her hand with my free one. Holding both girls, I led our foursome away from the talk of plans and violence. Looking grateful that I was distracting Nika, Dad nodded at me. "Stay inside the house. Stay close," he warned as I left the room with my friends.

Heeding his words, we went back to the main entrance, where a grand staircase led up to the floors above. Trey whistled at the wealth he saw around him, and even Arianna seemed impressed by the fineries.

"Wow, Julian, your family ... does all right, huh?"

I smiled down at her as we headed up the polished granite steps. "Yeah, I guess so." Letting go of my hand, Nika fell back with Trey who was trying to convince her that she should sell a couple of my family's art pieces and buy a Porsche.

Arianna and I ended up on the second floor before them, and I pulled her down the right side of the hallway. Chuckling, Trey pulled Nika down the left hallway. He winked at me before passing around a corner with a grumbling Nika. Knowing he wanted me to make a move on Arianna, I rolled my eyes. I wasn't going to make a move on her. It wasn't like that with us. Although, holding her hand did feel nice.

Shuffling along the hallway with her, I concentrated on her fingers meshed with mine as I pointed out all the various guest rooms and game rooms. She asked me polite questions about my "condition" as we walked, and I told her everything as truthfully as I could—that I was just as alive as she was, but my parents were no longer technically living, that sunlight didn't bother me, but it did bother some of the other members of my family, and that my sister and I, on occasion, drank blood. Arianna cringed when I told her I enjoyed it, but she never once dropped my hand.

As she was peeking into a large room that held a couple of pool tables, I looked down at her caramel-colored hair and sighed, "This is nice."

She looked back up at me with guarded eyes. "What's nice?"

Hating that things were still a little awkward, especially now that she knew the truth, I swung our hands and muttered, "Me and you, hanging out ... talking. I've missed this. I've missed our friendship."

Arianna bit her lip and let go of my hand. She started walking up the hallway, and I fell into step beside her, wondering if I'd just ruined our moment by bringing up the past. Not wanting to broach the topic yet, I instead asked, "Are you ... okay ... with everything? With what we are? With what I am?"

Arianna peeked over at me. A shaft of light caught her eyes, and they glowed with warmth and caring. My heart sped up a little as she slowly shook her head from side to side. "You and your sister are half-breed vampires, and Nika's boyfriend wants to kill you ... I'm peachy."

Reaching down, I again laced her fingers with mine. For some reason, I just couldn't stop myself from being connected to her. I thought she might pull away, but she didn't. She let me hold her. She even let me stroke my thumb against hers. Her eyes inspected the different rooms as we passed them, but my eyes were only on her. "Thank you for coming out here ... for worrying about me. That means a lot to me."

We approached the next set of stairs that led up to the third floor, and Arianna stopped. Eyes locked on me, she said, "Of course I worry about you, Julian. I still care about you ... even when I don't want to."

She started up the stairs, and with a sigh, I followed her. When we got to the top, Arianna looked out the ornate windows. I knew from experience that the view up here was extraordinary, but right now, I didn't care one iota about it. I only cared about the girl in front of me; I needed to know how badly I'd hurt her, and I needed to know if she'd ever be my friend again. I kind of ... needed her to be.

Clenching her hand in mine, I whispered, "Are you still mad at me for ... you know? The party? Our conversation afterward. My feelings about ... Raquel?"

My heart seized when I mentioned *her* name, but I instantly pushed the feeling aside. Arianna twisted to face me, sadness in her eyes. "She doesn't deserve someone like you, Julian." Her tone was completely serious, and a feeling hung in the air between us as her words settled around me. Warmth seeped into my heart, and I wanted to ask her what she thought of me, what she *really* thought of me.

Remembering the fateful party where I'd shoved my tongue down her throat, I shook my head. "I didn't mean to ... kiss you that night. I didn't mean to lead you on. I was high, not that it's a good excuse ..."

Her arms protectively crossed in front of her chest, and the glow in her eyes darkened. "And what about before the party? We were touching, flirting ... talking all the time. I thought ... I thought you were finally letting her go. I thought we were starting something."

"Arianna, I ..." I had no idea what to say.

Arianna filled the silence; her words were laced with heartache. "We finally have a moment—a *real* moment—and then you tell me that you're still in love with her, and you just want to be friends with me. That hurt, Julian. A lot." She sniffed, but it didn't stop the tears from falling.

Not able to look at her pain, I shifted my gaze to the hardwood beneath our feet. Arianna's shoes came into view as she stepped closer to me. "And do you know what sucks the most? The very reason I like you is the very reason she never will," she quietly said.

Confused, I peeked up at her. "What reason is that?"

With a sad smile, Arianna murmured, "You're warm, caring, kind. You're a genuinely decent guy." Her hand started to reach for my face, but then she stopped herself and her fingers fell back to her side. "At least, I thought you were, but maybe I'm just as disillusioned as Raquel."

CHAPTER EIGHTEEN

Nika

TREY WAS OBSESSED with my house. Once he had pulled me in the opposite direction of Arianna and my brother—a not-so-subtle attempt at giving those two privacy to make up—he dragged me through room after room. He gaped at all the fineries, mooned over all the toys. I didn't care about any of it at the moment, but seeing his materialistic joy brought a smile to my face. For a second, anyway. My heart was still stuck on the situation, my mind still replaying the conversation my parents were having with Gabriel. Hunter was killing vampires. I already knew that, since he'd told me as much, but hearing details of just *how* he was killing them was chilling, and confusing. It didn't match the image I had of him in my head—the charming gentleman who'd wanted to be open and honest with everyone about our relationship. The fact that he'd been hiding a secret almost as big as mine was mind-boggling.

In my head, I dissected every conversation we'd had, every smile he'd given me ... every kiss we'd shared. It seemed so wrong to think of his confident swagger being involved in murder. Of course, he didn't see it that way. He was ridding the world of horror stories. Horror stories like me.

As Trey and I stepped onto the third floor, Trey asked his millionth question about vampires. "So, why can you walk around in sunlight?"

Mentally, I sighed. "Because, like I said about ten times already, I'm mostly human. The side effects lessen with each generation. My eyes don't even glow."

Trey stopped and looked at me. "Vampires' eyes glow? Weird." He seemed about to say more, but over my shoulder he spotted something that made his face light up. "Dude, is that a sauna?"

I rolled my eyes at Trey's lack of focus. That was when I felt my brother's mood. He'd been hovering in a stable range of relief and worry, but he'd just darkened into grief and guilt. While Trey had hoped Arianna would sweep Julian into a bedroom and make a man out of him, I knew that wasn't what was happening. Arianna was probably setting him straight about just how much he'd hurt her.

Leaving Trey alone in the steam room, I set off to find my brother. My feet were mere streaks of light across the cracks in the wooden floors as I raced his way. I felt where he was in this massive house, same as I could feel my other family members. He was trudging toward me, barely moving. It only took me a moment to realize why he was walking so slowly.

Arianna was steadfastly walking away from him. Altering my course, I grabbed her shoulders as I blurred to a stop. Arianna screamed when my fingers suddenly encircled her arms. She quieted as soon as she realized it was me holding her, but I cringed anyway. Screaming was super-loud to vampires. But I *had* just materialized out of thin air right in front of her, so I couldn't really blame her for being startled.

"Hey, it's just me."

She hugged me tight, then gently pushed me away. "Please don't ever do that again."

I looked behind her, at where I could see Julian watching us near the stairs at the end of the hallway. "Is everything okay?"

Arianna glanced back at Julian, then back at me. "Everything's fine," she said, her voice sad.

Julian's mood fell a little more, and I gave him a sympathetic smile before turning and walking away with Arianna. "So ... what happened with Julian?"

Arianna mused on her feelings while we walked down the hallway I'd just come from. Giving me a look that spoke volumes about how hurt she was feeling, she leaned in and whispered, "I just don't understand why he chose her over me. She's with someone else, and she just keeps hurting him ... why is he holding onto her?"

Not knowing what to say to her, since I'd often wondered those same things myself, I could only shrug in response. I heard Julian sigh as he fell into step behind us, and I hoped he was finally asking himself that question.

Arianna shook her head, and under her breath I heard her murmur, "Why am *I* holding onto *him*?" Knowing Arianna's crush on my brother might end before Julian's crush on Raquel made my heart break. He could have something here, if he opened his eyes in time.

Arianna walked along in silence after that. We found Trey where I'd left him; he stumbled out of the steam room a little damp. Julian caught up to our group as Trey was telling us that he was officially moving in once everything simmered down. It was a catch twenty-two for me. Even though I wanted everything to simmer down just as much as the rest of the vampires in my family, I didn't want anything bad to happen to Hunter. Right or wrong, I still cared about him, and for one side to win, one side had to lose.

As we headed to our bedrooms here at the ranch, Julian cocked his head toward the living room, where our family was still discussing tactics. I could hear them, too, but I tried to block them out. I didn't want to hear about any plan that either put my family in danger, or put Hunter in danger.

Trey beside Julian seemed to notice his friend's look of distraction. "Dude, can you hear them?" Julian glanced over at Trey and nodded. Trey's impressed face turned inquisitive. "So, what are they saying?"

Arianna tuned in to hear Julian's response, and I let out a weary exhale. Julian looked at me before answering Trey. "My dad is saying that he doesn't want to wage an all-out assault on Hunter and his father. He doesn't want to risk a direct fight." Julian paused, listening. "He wants to catch them unaware, so the chance of anything going wrong is slimmer." He locked eyes with me. "He wants to keep searching the ads, find the vampire who placed it, and then lie in wait with them when Hunter answers the ad."

I tilted my head, listening to Dad's argument. He seemed to think that once Hunter and his dad lost our trail, they'd resume vampire hunting in the way that had worked the best for them so far. They'd keep answering ads and slaying their victims while they were feeding. It was a plausible, if lengthy, plan. For one, Dad and the guys would have to decipher which ad belonged to a vampire, answer it, and hope the party on the other end hadn't already been paid a visit by the hunters.

Just as I was beginning to believe that we might be in hiding for the rest of the year, Trey told Julian, "Why don't they cut out the middle man? Why don't *they* place the ad? You know, like a sting?"

Julian and I both stopped in our tracks to stare at Trey. Our parents had originally been more preoccupied with warning vampires of the potential threat when they'd started searching ads. Their goal hadn't really been to kill the hunter in the area, although they certainly were interested in that outcome. But now that our family was the target, their priorities had shifted. We *had* to find Hunter, before he found us.

Surprise flowed through Julian as he responded to Trey. "Wow, you're sort of brilliant when you're sober."

Trey smirked, then slung one arm around Arianna and the other around me. "I'm always brilliant, that's why the girls dig me."

Arianna and I scoffed at the same time, shrugging ourselves free from his embrace. I had to agree with Julian, though; it was a much better plan than aimlessly sifting through classifieds. Everyone downstairs seemed to think so too. The conversation shifted toward how to best conduct the trap. It broke my heart to listen. All I could think of was Hunter's piercing eyes locking onto mine. The memory of what he'd done was fading as the memory of how he'd cared for me superseded it. I'd never had anyone look at me that way before, and I was doubtful anyone would ever look at me that way again. I couldn't imagine Hunter's eyes dead and lifeless, but the conversations drifting up to me weren't about how to subdue him and wipe his memory. No, they were discussing the best way to get rid of him. And almost everyone's answer was the same—kill him.

While Trey and Julian headed off to his bedroom to discuss vampire lore, I trudged to mine with Arianna. I didn't want to talk about what I was and how amazing my gifts were. I wanted to wallow in the fact that the only man who had moved my soul was now out to get me. Arianna seemed to understand my grief. Either that, or she was dealing with her own, and she remained by my side as my silent, supportive companion.

Neither of us said much as we laid on my bed and waited for the sun to go down. For a long time, the only conversation in my room had been between Arianna and her mom. She'd called her, telling her where she was and that she'd borrowed the car. Even if I hadn't been supernatural, I think I would have heard her mom's concerned reply—there had been a pretty big scare at the school after all. But by Arianna's mom's response, the incident with Hunter had been explained away as nothing. Aside from an early release, nothing in the world of academia was any different. How I wished I could say the same for my world.

After being berated for taking the car without permission, Arianna skillfully manipulated the conversation, and got her mom to agree to let her stay at my house for dinner, although, she had to bring the car home immediately after our meal was done. Once Arianna got off the phone with her mom, I congratulated her on her deception. She could lie almost as seamlessly as I could. I wasn't sure if that was a good thing or not.

About twenty minutes before the sun extinguished for the day, I felt Halina emerging from her rooms. I sat up, curious if she was okay.

"What is it?" Arianna asked.

"Grandma Halina is up." I looked over to her. "I want to go see if she's all right."

Arianna looked pale as she sat up on the bed. "Halina ... the full vampire?"

I nodded, blurring to my feet. Arianna blinked at my rapid change in position. "Yeah, Hunter sort of ... poisoned her. I need to know that she's okay."

Arianna got to her feet. "Okay, let's go see."

Happiness welled in me at my friend's show of courage. I'd thought before that she might be okay with what we were. Well, I'd hoped she would be, at any rate, but she seemed to be handling things fairly well. Grabbing her hand, I hurried with her to the hallway. I could blur downstairs in a second, but I didn't want to leave her behind, and I didn't think she'd be cool with me carrying her.

Julian and Trey met us in the hallway. Trey had an eager look on his face, like he was about to learn how to fly or something. I was sure he was just excited to meet a pureblood until Julian bumped my elbow and murmured, "Hey, Trey wants to know if you'll run him downstairs." I knew by the way Julian said "run" that he meant blur.

My mouth fell open as I looked over at the tall, spindly boy bouncing up and down on his heels. "What? Why me?" I poked Julian's chest. "You do it."

Julian glanced over at Arianna. "I thought I'd take her down."

We all looked at Arianna. Not having heard our conversation, she flushed at the sudden attention. "What?"

A small scowl was on my lips as I looked back at Julian. "Fine, but you owe me."

Catching the gist of our conversation, Trey giggled and held his arms open for me. "Come here, love."

I rolled my eyes, but effortlessly scooped him up. Arianna gasped, seeing my unnatural strength. Then she snapped her head to Julian. He approached her slowly, hands raised like he thought she might run. "If you want, I can get you downstairs really fast."

Arianna's face went a little paler as she realized what was happening, but with Julian approaching her, arms out, she didn't seem capable of saying no. Her heart beat a little harder when Julian slowly bent down to pick her up. When he lifted her to his chest, she laced her arms around his neck. Their eyes never left each other, and again, I thought my brother was an idiot for not seeing what was right in front of him.

"Hang on," he whispered, right before taking off.

Trey whistled as they vanished before our eyes. Then he tried to kick me with the heel of his shoe. "Get a move on, little doggie. They're beating us." I nearly dropped him to the floor right there, but then I'd have to hear him complain all the way down the stairs, so I didn't.

We were back in the living room a split-second later. When I got there with Trey, Julian was tenderly placing Arianna on her feet; his arm remained around her waist, supporting her. I simply let go of Trey. He crashed to the floor with a noisy grunt, and everyone twisted to look at him. Julian frowned at me, but Trey hopped right back to his feet, not looking any worse for wear. He clapped Julian on the shoulder. "Dude! That was freaking awesome!"

Arianna was a little unsteady on her feet after the rapid movement, and she clung to Julian's side. Trey glanced over at her, then whispered into Julian's ear, "You know, whatever freaky thing you are, I think you still got a shot with her."

Julian opened his mouth to respond, but Halina stepped out of her secret door and stole everyone's attention. Dad was right by her side, to help her if she needed him, and for once, she actually looked like she did need his help. She moved slowly, her face wan. She looked a lot better than when I'd last seen her—anything other than throwing up blood was a vast improvement—but she still seemed a little out of sorts.

Imogen stepped to Halina's side, supporting her mother, while Gabriel hovered behind her, ready to assist. The teenage vampire looked really frail with everyone nearby on full alert. The sight set me back; Halina was never frail.

She seemed to agree. After another moment of people asking her if she was okay, asking her if she needed anything, Halina shrugged off her supporters and stepped forward on her own. "Stop that this instant. I am not an invalid who needs to be coddled."

The last of the setting sun's rays stroked Halina's skin, softening the paleness. Gabriel laid a hand on her arm. "Remnants of the silver are still with you, my dear. It will take a while for you to be at full strength again."

Halina lifted her chin as she stared down her boyfriend. "Even still, I do not need to be treated like I'm going to break apart at any moment." She glanced over to the new arrivals in her midst—Arianna and Trey. "Now, who are these two, and why are they here?"

Trey stepped forward, hand extended. Arianna remained glued to Julian's side. Julian held her close and rubbed her arm in a show of sympathy. Halina seemed amused by Trey's boldness as he approached her. "Name's Trey."

A faint smile on her lips, Halina took his hand. "You know what I am?"

Trey's eyes widened as Halina squeezed his hand. I wasn't sure if he was just reacting to her chill or if she was hurting him a little. I knew Halina well enough to know that she wouldn't cause him serious pain, but she would try and intimidate him. It worked too. The color drained from Trey's face as I watched. A protective surge flared in Julian, but he stayed by Arianna's side, watching as well.

Trey nodded at Halina's question, and she asked another one. "And tell me how you feel about that."

THE NEXT GENERATION

I could tell from the way she'd said it, that she'd "forced" him to answer. Whatever he said to her now would be the God's honest truth. His face a little blank, he replied, "I think it's ... freaking awesome."

Exhaling in an irritated way, Halina dropped his hand and twisted to Gabriel. "There was a time when being a vampire meant something. Just hearing the word invoked fear in the hearts of men. But now ... ?" She grunted, exasperated. "Damn pop culture has completely wussified our race."

Gabriel smirked at Halina, happy to see a bit of her spunk returning. Dad cast a nervous glance at the windows as he stepped closer to Gabriel. "As soon as it's fully dark, we should go."

Halina twisted to Dad. "Where are we going?"

Trey raised his hand like an eager school boy who had all the answers. "My house!"

Halina flicked her eyes to him, then back to Dad. "And why are we staying with a human who shouldn't know anything about us to begin with?"

Maybe seeing an argument brewing, Dad crossed his arms over his chest. The sight of him like that—strong, defiant—made me proud to be his daughter, made me want a future that would someday have a man I loved looking as strong and confident as my father. I thought I'd found that in Hunter's confidence ... but I was wrong.

"Hunter showed up at school, pieced together what the children really are. He ... attacked." Dad tapped his chest. "He shot me." Halina hissed and stared at Dad's chest. There was nothing to see of course, but Halina looked ready to tear someone's head off at just the thought of her grandchild being injured. Dad held out a hand. "I'm fine ... he missed my heart. But he knows the truth about our family heritage. It won't take him long to find this place." He circled his finger to indicate the ranch.

Her stance as defiant as my father's, Halina told the room, "I am not afraid of a pair of humans playing at being slayers."

Julian growled his approval of her sentiment. His mood still bristled with the desire to defend his home, but I knew better. Hunter and his dad weren't wannabes, and engaging them head-on wouldn't end well for either side. "He's not playing, Grandma. He showed me. His family has been hunting vampires for generations. They know what they're doing."

Halina analyzed my comment for a moment before answering. "Even still, we vastly outnumber them."

Dad shook his head. "And how many will get hurt in the process?" He pointed over to Julian and me. "Do we risk my children?" He moved his hand to indicate Imogen and Alanna. "Your children?" Halina looked about to argue with his question, but Dad steamrolled over her objection. "And you may have the bravado of someone who can take on the world, but you're struggling to stand up straight. You're not up to a fight yet. And we don't need to fight them so directly. We have another idea."

Trey nudged Julian's elbow. "My idea."

Halina heard him. Voice droll, she said, "Great, now we're letting a teenage human who reeks of pot plan our battles?"

Trey's prideful smile fell. "Hey, I'm sober ... today."

Ignoring him, Halina focused on Dad. "What's next, Teren? We let Olivia handle our finances?"

Starla snorted and popped a bubble with her gum. The apple scent floated past me, along with her chuckles. Dad shot her a glance, but looked back at Halina with determination in his eyes. "It's a decent plan. We'll discuss it on the way."

Halina grumbled and complained while she waited for the sun to set, but she didn't offer any alternative plan and didn't object when it was time to leave. She gave my friends meaningful looks on the drive there as she sat next to Julian and me in Arianna's Mom's minivan. I could tell she was determining just how long our friends would know all our secrets. Now that it was out there, I hated the fact that it would all be taken away. Our friends would never get to remember this moment.

Running a hand through her long, dark locks, Halina finally locked gazes with me. In Russian, she confirmed what I'd been thinking. *"Your friends cannot be allowed to remember this."*

Hating the thought of going back to lying all the time, I countered, *"They're fine with what we are. They won't say a word."* I'd replied to her in Russian, and never having heard me talk that way before, Trey twisted in the front seat to stare at me, wide-eyed.

"It does not matter," Halina said. *"They know a secret that we share with very few. They are young ... and youth talk."*

Julian leaned around me. His emotion was simmering at the same level of desperation mine was—he wanted our friends to remember. He wanted a small piece of normalcy, wanted a friend in this world that he didn't have to lie to. *"They care about our safety, they won't say a word."* Eyes imploring, he added, *"We can trust them."*

Halina stared us both down. *"The only humans we allow to know are those who have gone above and beyond to protect us ... or those we chose as our mates, those who might continue the line."* She cocked an eyebrow. *"Is either of them going to breed with you? Give us offspring?"*

I was already shaking my head, but Julian turned his eyes to Arianna as she drove. Arianna was watching our conversation in the mirror. By the confusion on her face, she understood Russian just about as well as Trey did. And like Trey, she also seemed surprised that we spoke it.

Before Julian could answer, Dad, sitting behind us, leaned over the seat. His voice was heated as he addressed Halina. *"Stop it with the breeding talk. My children are under no obligation to continue the line. You know this. We've discussed it at length."*

I felt my cheeks heat with embarrassment and was instantly grateful that the two humans in the car had no idea what the vampires were talking about. Julian's mood mirrored mine. I looked back at Mom beside Dad. She was concentrating hard on the conversation—trying to keep up with the low and fast foreign language—but she was nodding in agreement with Dad. Gabriel seemed impassive about the entire thing. He probably didn't care either way if a couple of teenagers knew the truth.

Halina's eyes got a little fiery as she held Dad's gaze. *"I'm aware of your feelings on the matter. I was simply making a point."* Her eyes returned to mine. *"If you have no romantic interest in them, then the children will be wiped clean when this is over. End of discussion."*

I felt my eyes sting as I faced front, ignoring her. I knew it was pointless to argue with Halina, but I still wanted to. Julian did, too, I could tell by his mood and the antsy way he kept changing his position. I thought he'd wear a hole in his jeans with all his shifting. Julian's gaze stayed locked on Arianna the entire car ride. I wasn't sure what that meant. Julian wasn't sure either—all I felt coming from him was confusion.

Things were still quiet in the car when we got back into Salt Lake City. We drove past the numerous monolithic churches, our vehicle as solemn as those sacred places. Contrary to the jokes that ran throughout the countryside, not everyone in Utah was Mormon. In fact, I didn't think anyone currently riding in the car was. My own family had a more scientific view of things—an appreciation of nature and the circle of life, and the understanding that there was probably something bigger behind it all. Since my future was potentially infinite, I'd never really dwelled on religion, but as I passed by church after church, I started to wonder if maybe I should say a quick prayer for my family.

The car stopped at a red light as I was staring at a temple about the size of the ranch. The glow from the signal cast an eerie red sheen on everyone's faces. It made the car seemed filled with blood. I was anxious for the light to turn to a cheerier color when a car pulled into the turn lane next to us. It stopped level with the middle of Arianna's minivan, well before the white line painted on the cement, since we weren't the first car at the intersection. The window slowly lowered, and I steadfastly watched it descend. Anything that could shift my thoughts from the darkness I'd been swirling in was a welcome distraction.

There was no one in the passenger's side of the car, so I leaned forward to see what the driver wanted. That was when a flash of light erupted from the vehicle. The window Halina was sitting beside shattered a microsecond later. Shock filled me first, but it was quickly followed by panic. We were boxed into an intersection, a car in front of us, Grandpa's truck behind us, and Starla's car behind him, and some maniac was firing bullets into our minivan! What the hell?

Bullets whizzed through the air. Using a gun was a hard way to kill a vampire, unless you were a really good shot. The person beside us was good, but they were hampered by the bulk of the vehicles separating us, and only a few shots were making it into the car. Even though Halina was protecting Julian and me the best she could, one of those shots nicked my arm, tearing through my jacket and biting into my skin. Crying out in pain and fear, I clamped my hand over the wound. Killing an undead vampire was difficult, but I was still alive ... and a much easier target.

As screams filled the air, Dad yelled, "Drive, Arianna! Go up the sidewalk!" Watching blood ooze between my fingers, staining my jacket, Arianna looked too freaked out to do anything.

As Halina blurred to the shell-shocked Arianna, Dad climbed over the seat to take Halina's spot in shielding Julian and me from the wild, blazing bullets that were still being fired. I smelled blood in the air, and not just mine. Halina looked about ready to toss Arianna outside if she didn't do something soon. Thankfully, she merely tossed my friend onto Trey's lap.

Dad snarled, holding back a pain-filled cry as a couple of bullets hit him in the back. I did pray then, prayed that none of the bullets streaking into the car would hit his heart. That was all it would take to shatter my family forever.

Just as Halina stepped on the gas, smacking our car into the oblivious car in front of us, Grandpa behind us shifted his truck and rammed into the shooter's car. The shooter took off, peeling away as he squealed around a corner. Halina turned the wheel to follow him.

Dad lunged forward. "No! Let him go! Nika's hurt."

That was when I remembered that I'd been shot. I looked at the blood flowing down the back of my hand in utter shock; there was so much. I instinctively removed my hand to look at the wound, and a well of dark-red blood permanently ruined my jacket. The site where the bullet had gouged out my skin burned worse than any injury I'd ever received, and I thought I might be sick. My vision hazed in and out, and I heard voices asking me if I was okay. I couldn't answer ... my world went dark.

When I came to a few seconds later, I was lying down on the seat with Mom sitting beside me, on the very edge of the cushion. My jacket was half off me, and Gabriel was crouched on the floor near my head, inspecting my injury. Tiny shards of glass were everywhere, and an icy wind tore through the car. It whipped Mom's hair around her face as she watched over me. Pain burst through my arm as Gabriel cinched a piece of fabric around my wounded bicep, staunching the flowing blood. I bit my lip to be strong, to not cry out, but what I really wanted to do was cry like a little girl and let Mom comfort me. There wasn't time for that though.

I tried to sit up, but I was dizzy from the blood loss; my head swam and my eyesight darkened. Mom shushed me, and Gabriel made me lie back down. Mom wasn't crying now, but wet tracks were down her cheeks from recently spilled tears. The van was speeding under street lamps, and the alternating lightness and darkness made Mom's face look ill, like she was about to lose her stomach.

"You okay?" I croaked out.

Mom bit back a chuckle. "You've just been shot, and you're asking if *I'm* okay?" She leaned forward to kiss my forehead. "I'm fine, Nika. Not a scratch."

Concerned for everyone else in the car, I looked around with just my eyes. Julian, Trey, and Arianna were all in the very back now, leaning over the seat to see how I was doing. The very back window was shot out, as well, and Arianna's hair blew across her face. Fearing for them, I asked, "Are you guys okay? Did he get you?"

Trey and Arianna both shook their heads. Julian shrugged. "A couple grazed me, but I'm fine, Nick." Wading past the concern he felt for me, I tapped into the tiny amount of pain he felt for himself. It was nowhere near the inferno raging in my arm, but it was there; he'd been hurt. Fury boiled in my belly that another family member had been hurt by my maniac ex-boyfriend.

Sensing my anger, Julian leaned over and ran his hand through my hair. "I'm fine, Nick," he reiterated. Images of my father taking bullet after bullet seared my brain. I looked past Mom, to the front of the vehicle. Dad was in the passenger's side now, debating with Halina on where she should drive us. Face grim, he looked back at me. There was pain in his expression, as surely as it must have been on mine. Hunter had hit him a few times, but thankfully he'd missed the one crucial area. Dad was still alive ... or, still undead.

I could feel the rest of my family following closely in the vehicles right behind us, but I didn't know if Hunter had turned his gun on them in the melee. I had no idea if they were all right or not. Trying to will my body to super-heal, like the rest of my family could, I asked, "How did he know where we were?"

Gabriel, his face stormy, but seeming uninjured, shook his head. "He must have staked out the ranch ... followed us when we left." His cold fingers circled around my arm, feeling heavenly against my heated skin. "Perhaps he thought his odds would be better if he attacked us while we were trapped."

Mom's face darkened. "Like fish in a barrel."

Gabriel nodded, then added, "His choice of weapon was not the best, however. He should have used a much larger caliber, something strong enough to penetrate the body of the car. It would have been noisier than his silenced weapon, but the odds of him killing one of us would have vastly improved. I dare say he would have succeeded if he hadn't acted so rashly."

None of us knew how to respond to that, so the car continued in silence. The sound of glass being crunched beneath shoes on the floorboards was all I heard for a while. Then Arianna murmured, "My mom is going to kill me when she sees the van."

CHAPTER NINETEEN

Nika

DAD DECIDED THAT we couldn't risk the life of Trey's family by continuing to his home. By the way Hunter had sped off once Grandpa had rammed him, we assumed he wasn't following us anymore, but we didn't know for sure. It was entirely possible that Hunter had doubled back and was trailing us again. Our entourage wouldn't be hard to follow, especially with the bullet holes adorning the minivan's side and the blown-out windows. Hopefully no well-meaning citizen had reported our car fleeing the scene of a crime.

Eyes watchful of the road around us, Dad told Halina to pull into the first dark, seedy motel that she saw. Finding an alley nearby, we parked the minivan as close to the wall as Halina could get it, so the violent evidence wouldn't stand out. The rest of our caravan parked in the motel's lot, near the exit but facing a side street, so their vehicles wouldn't be direct giveaways that we were here. Streaming out of their cars, my family hurried to the alley to make sure our group was uninjured from the showdown.

Conscious of another attack, Mom and Dad quickly helped me put my jacket back on and get out of the car. My arm burned, and I was lightheaded, but I was still breathing, and that was always a good thing. As the family groups melded together, I was hugged and inspected by every single friend and relative.

When Julian hopped out of the back seat, he looked at the wreckage with grief and guilt in his heart. Turning to Arianna, he said, "I'm sorry about your car. We'll get it fixed."

His eyes locked on the street, Dad nodded. "Great-Gran will have someone inside clean it up, then take it to a shop. A small, private one." He risked a glance at Halina. "You'll have to go with, to ensure the car is quietly repaired tonight. We don't need anyone reporting this. We've attracted enough attention already."

Halina nodded, her reluctant eyes flicking over all of us. As our guardian, she didn't want to leave our side, but she was also the only one of us who could do compulsion, and covering things up was a big part of our protection.

Seeing her in agreement, Dad told Arianna, "I'll have Starla call your mom, explain that there was a situation with the car and we're getting it fixed. We'll get her permission to let you spend the night with us." He stopped roving the streets to meet Arianna's eye. "I'm sorry, but it's too dangerous to drive you home."

Arianna was too startled by the evening's events to comment; Julian gently grabbed her hand in support. Antsy about being out in the open, Dad started ushering our group to the motel office. On the way, he told Trey, "We should call your parents too ... they'll be worried."

Trey shrugged. "Nah, I doubt they'll even notice I'm gone." Bringing his fingers to his lips, he mimed smoking a joint.

Dad frowned at the reference, while sympathy trickled into me. My parents were so overprotective that it was hard to imagine parents who were so busy getting stoned that they wouldn't notice their only child was unaccounted for. I wasn't sure what that level of apathy would do to a person, but it sure explained why Trey came to school buzzed every day. Well, almost every day.

Dad clapped Trey's shoulder. "We'll tell them that you're with us anyway. They should know where you are." Trey was beaming when Dad removed his hand.

After Dad had Starla make the phone calls, he headed into the office with Halina. One of the fluorescent light bulbs inside flickered off and on in a steady rhythm; it almost matched the blinking of the vacancy sign near the road. I watched my dad through the glass; he was handing the greasy, overweight man at the counter a wad of cash. Both Halina and Dad had bloody smears and streaks on their clothes. I was sure Halina had taken a bullet or two, and I knew my dad had taken several. The clerk on duty didn't notice their appearance, though, thanks to whatever story he was being fed by Halina.

Moments later, they were back with two keys to adjoining rooms and the beefy man was heading out to the van with a gallon of bleach and a handful of rags. Hiding any trace of our vampire blood was of the utmost importance.

Dad unlocked one motel door while Halina unlocked the other. Starla groaned as she peered into the room Halina had opened. "You have got to be kidding me." She twisted to Gabriel behind her. "I am *not* staying in this despot, Father."

Crossing his arms over his chest, the aged vampire stared his "daughter" down. "Until this situation is properly contained, we're all staying together ... so yes, you *are* staying here, Starla. And you will keep your opinions to yourself and be appreciative that none of the bullets in the air tonight hit you." He placed a cool hand on my arm as he said that. The throbbing was better than before, but his touch still felt wonderful.

Starla looked appropriately chastised as she walked into the dingy room with Jacen, who seemed a little unsure how to respond to Starla being scolded. Gabriel was his leader, yet Starla was his girlfriend; it put him in an uncomfortable position.

While Ben, Julian, Arianna, Trey, and Mom entered the second room, Grandpa, Alanna, Grandma Linda and Imogen followed after Starla and Jacen. Gabriel and Halina seemed unsure which room to enter, which family members to protect.

Dad slung an arm around me while nodding at the other door. "We'll be fine. You can stay with the others, Great-Gran."

Maybe seeing that our room was a little human heavy, Halina turned to Gabriel. "You stay with your nestmates. I'll stay with Teren and the children. I'll need to leave as soon as that malodorous man is done cleaning the car anyway."

Gabriel gave her a brief nod. "Be safe, love."

Halina stepped into him, cupping his cheek. "And you as well."

THE NEXT GENERATION

Leaning in, Gabriel gave her a brief peck. "And try to remember that you are not at full strength yet." He gave her a pointed look. "Regardless of what you believe, you are not invincible."

Halina smirked. "So you say."

Gabriel's normally passive face was amused as Halina sauntered into our room. Dad shook his head at his great-grandmother and her super-old boyfriend as he urged me inside. I cringed when Dad closed the door. Starla was right, the place was a dump.

There were two beds with rumpled, mismatched comforters; I instantly wondered when they'd last been washed. Between them was a table that was missing a leg. The top of the table was resting on a nail driven into the wall behind it. It looked ready to topple at any moment, which would surely break the gaudy lamp sitting atop it that was the only point of light in the room.

The wallpaper was cracked, and a faded grayish-yellow color that made the room seem sickly. There was a door leading to a bathroom in the back of the room; I was a little afraid to go in there. But Dad had wanted discreet ... and sometimes discreet meant decrepit.

There were no chairs in the room, so everyone was seated on the bed or standing around. Dad helped me to the bed where Mom was sitting, and even though I was feeling better by the moment, I sat down beside her. Julian and Arianna were sitting on the edge of the other bed, still holding hands. Arianna was paler than I'd ever seen her and Julian was filled to the brim with worry. Ben was on full alert at the window, peering through the blinds.

Halina's eyes were on Dad as he stepped up to Ben and clapped him on the shoulder. "I was only grazed, Teren, but you took a few," she said. "How many times were you hit?"

Remembered horror sent a shiver down my body as Dad twisted his dark head to Halina. "I don't know ... a few times."

Dad shifted his gaze to meet Mom's eyes. Standing from the bed, she walked over to him. A stuttered exhale escaped her as she wrapped her arms around her husband. He held her tight and rested his head against hers. In the silence, I heard Mom murmur, "That was too close, Teren. Much too close."

Over Dad's shoulder, Mom locked eyes with me. They began to water as she shifted her gaze to stare at the blood-stained sleeve of my jacket.

Dad was about to respond to her when Halina interjected, "Those bullets will need to be removed, Teren."

Dad sighed as Halina walked over to Ben and pulled a switchblade out of his pocket. My eyes widened at the thought of having to witness another operation like I had earlier. I really didn't think I could right now. The shock and fear were wearing off, and a feeling of peace was starting to come over me. Watching my dad in that much pain would surely undo that calm; it would probably unhinge me.

Arianna too. She shot up off the bed. "What are you going to do with that?"

Dad looked over the many young adults in the room, then indicated the bathroom door. "Maybe we could do this privately?" Halina nodded and grabbed his hand, leading him away; Mom hurried after. Before they disappeared into the bathroom, Dad locked eyes with Ben and pointed at us. "Watch them for me."

Ben straightened, and his expression hardened as the weight of his newfound responsibility settled around him. When the bathroom door closed, Ben turned back to the window, all the more vigilant. Someone in the bathroom turned the faucet on full blast. It wasn't enough to mask all the noise, but it helped. The conversations drifting from the room were muted under the surge of water.

Standing up, I walked over to Arianna; her wide eyes were glued on the bathroom door. Slightly shaking, she asked me, "Nika ... are they doing what I think they're doing?"

Putting a comforting hand on her shoulder, I nodded as I sat on the bed with her. "Yes, they need to get the bullets out. But it's okay, my dad will be fine."

I heard Dad inhale a quick breath, and I figured the operation had started. Maybe to distract us, or maybe to distract himself, Ben murmured, "I'm glad Olivia is with her mom right now."

Sympathy bubbled to the surface as I watched Ben diligently scanning for trouble. The neon sign outside cast a reddish light across his skin where it shone through the blinds. The light enhanced the slight scars that marred his perfect face, scars he'd received over the years either protecting or confronting our species. It made me think maybe Mom was right, maybe Ben should be wiped and set free. Maybe my friends should be wiped and set free too. "I'm sorry you got wrapped up in all of this, Uncle Ben," I told him.

Ben shook his head without looking at me. "Protecting your family is an honor, Nika. There's no place I'd rather be right now."

Hearing my dad's muted attempts to contain the pain he was feeling overwhelmed me with guilt. This was all my fault. Well, no, if I were to place the blame properly, this was all Hunter's fault. He'd overreacted to the situation, acted out of fear and prejudice, not reason. My family wasn't a threat to humanity. We just wanted to fit in, to belong ... even if we never really could.

Needing an explanation, needing to vent, scream, question, and maybe break something, I turned to Arianna. Seeing her purse securely fastened across her chest, I whispered, "Let me see your phone."

Wrapped up in guard duty, Ben didn't hear me. Julian did. As Arianna's still shaking fingers dug through her small bag, his expression darkened. "What are you doing, Nika?" he asked, equally as quiet.

I didn't answer him. There was nothing I could say, no rational explanation for the risk I was taking. I wasn't sure just how tech-savvy Hunter was, wasn't sure whether he could track Arianna's cell phone once he knew her number. There was a lot I wasn't sure about. But I knew my parents were wrapped up in Dad's situation, and this was the only chance I would get to talk to Hunter again. And I had a few things to say to him.

Luckily the vampires next door weren't paying any attention to me either; a lively debate about whether or not placing an ad was still a viable solution to the problem was being tossed around the room. Time seemed to be the biggest factor in the con column. It would take a considerable amount of time for Hunter and his father to assume we'd left the area, to feel comfortable enough to fall back into their old ways and again start answering vampire blood ads. In the meantime, we'd be in a constant state of worry, anxiety, fear, and hiding. We'd have to put our entire lives on hold—like we'd been put in the vampire protection program.

Ignoring my brother's anxiety, I quickly called Hunter. He answered immediately. "Hello?"

I paused for a moment as his voice washed through my brain. Even though it hadn't been that long since I'd talked to him, it felt like forever since I'd heard his voice. Or at least, since I'd heard it without the sting of rejection added to it. When I didn't answer him immediately, he whispered, "Nika? Is that you?"

Needing some additional background noise to hide my conversation from Ben, I turned on the ancient TV bolted to the wall. It flashed on and some Spanish telenovela started blaring. Ben cocked his head, but didn't turn to look. He was more concerned about things outside of our room than inside. Covered by some shrill, irate woman, I focused *my* anger.

"You open fired on my family? What the hell were you thinking?"

Julian leaned forward on the bed, intently listening. His mood was stormy, and he was clearly restraining himself from either ripping the phone from my fingers or launching into his own tirade.

After a microsecond of silence, Hunter's voice hit my ear. "Open ... what? What are you talking about?"

Rage roiled in my stomach as I remembered the incident he was playing dumb about. "Don't. Don't even try that innocent crap. You followed us from the ranch, then pulled up beside us at a red light. You started firing ..." My throat dry, I had to swallow before I could continue. "There were humans in the car, Hunter."

"Oh my God, Nika ... I didn't. Are you okay?"

The true concern in his voice seared my heart, but the fire in my belly quickly obliterated it. "No, I'm not. You hit me!" I didn't elaborate on that, didn't tell him that he'd only nicked me.

"Jesus! Are you okay? Are you at the hospital? Where are you?"

The panic in his voice muddled my mind, and I clarified my situation. "It was just on the surface ... I'm fine."

I eyed Ben, but the television was doing its job, and he wasn't paying any attention to my conversation. So far, no one else was either. The vampires next door were still in contemplation, Mom was sniffling in the bathroom, and Dad was snapping at Halina that there wasn't a bullet in his spleen so she could stop digging around in there. Hearing that made me gag a little.

Hunter sighed. "Thank God ... you scared me."

The temperature increased in my stomach, evaporating the confusion in my head. "I scared you? You're the one who freaking shot at me!"

I could hear Hunter sputtering, then he said, "I have no idea what you're talking about, Nika! I've been at home, cleaning up, and wondering what the hell I'm supposed to do about you."

That deflated my anger a bit. "Then who ... ?"

Hunter gasped as he made the only logical conclusion left to make. "No ... he couldn't have. He said he wouldn't ... He said he would leave you alone until I ... Oh my God ..."

"Your dad did this, didn't he?" I whispered, awed by the shock in his voice. "He followed us, and fired on us ... and you, you didn't know?"

"I swear I didn't know he'd do that, Nika. I told him ..." he paused, and I couldn't help but picture his dark brow compressed in puzzlement, "I told him I couldn't hunt you ... that you were different, that you were basically human. I told him I couldn't kill you, and I begged him to leave your family alone. Just until we figured out what your kind was."

"You ... couldn't kill me? But you said ... you said I was a vampire and it didn't matter?"

Hunter sighed, the sound as conflicted as his voice. "I know what I said. I was in shock. I still am. I just didn't expect ... All of this has turned my world upside down, Nika. You have to understand that. But the thought of anything happening to you ... I just can't ... handle it." His voice full of worry, he again asked, "Are you okay?"

My heart melted at the love I felt coming from him. He still cared. Regardless of what I was, he still cared about me. Julian frowned as my feelings leeched into him, but I ignored his disgruntlement. "Yes," I whispered, lightly rubbing my wound. "I'm fine."

"Thank God," he reiterated. "Dad was pissed at me when we parted ways after the incident at school, but I never thought he'd ... He really shot at you?"

Just then, the water shut off in the bathroom. There was some light laughter from my dad, and I knew I only had moments before my parents reemerged. "Yes, but I'm fine," I breathed into the phone.

"I can't believe he did this to me," Hunter mused. I thought to say goodbye to him, even though that idea killed a part of me, but before I could, he added, "I need to see you, Nika. Where are you?"

The bathroom door creaked open, and I knew I should disconnect the phone and hand it back to Arianna. I couldn't though. I couldn't sever this moment with Hunter ... not yet.

"I can't tell you that, Hunter."

Dad's eyes snapped to mine as he stepped into the room. His expression was dark as he took in the sight of me making a secret phone call behind his back. I was sure I had guilt plastered all over my face as I locked gazes with him.

Dad looked about ready to blur over to me and smash the phone against the wall. Halina, too, for that matter. Cognizant of the tension in the air, Ben turned from his post at the window. My guilt tripled as his mouth dropped in shock. He seemed stunned that I would call the enemy right after being shot at by him. But I hadn't been shot by Hunter. He still loved me ... I was sure. He confirmed that while shock froze my family.

"I love you, Nika ... and I'm not going to hurt you. I just want to see you, talk things out. Surely we can find a way to figure this out?"

My dad tilted his head, and hurriedly, I finished up my conversation with Hunter. "That's not a good idea. You and I shouldn't be around each other ..."

I was interrupted from my train of thought by Dad. Shaking his head, he whispered, "Say yes."

As I puzzled over Dad's response, Hunter asked for the same thing. "Please, Nika. I'm not going to hurt you. I just need to make sure you're okay. I just ... I need to see you. My dad won't be there, it will just be me, I promise." When I still didn't respond, he added, "Please? We can meet somewhere neutral. The library?"

Wondering why my father was giving me the go-ahead, I told Hunter, "All right. The water wall, at midnight."

The relief in Hunter's voice was palpable. "I'll be there, Nika. Just me."

Staring at my father, I responded, "Okay ... but you better not kill me, Hunter."

A soft laugh escaped him, and I immediately pictured his warm smile. "I won't, I wouldn't ... ever. I'm in love with you, remember?"

I bit my lip, not able to respond. Instead, I ended the call. Dad had his arms crossed over his chest, but he was smiling. I had no idea why. Nerves spiking, I asked him, "Why did you say it was okay? I thought you'd never let me see him again."

Lifting his eyes to Ben, Dad calmly said, "Because it's a lot easier to trap a hunter, when you know exactly where the hunter will be."

I shot up off the bed. "No! It wasn't him, Daddy. He didn't fire at us!"

Dad lowered his eyes to mine. There was remembered pain in the pale depths. "He shot me at the school. *That* was most definitely him."

I violently shook my head, but Mom objected first. "Teren, we can't use our daughter as bait."

Dad turned around to face her. "We'll all be there, waiting. She'll be safe. Besides," Dad twisted to face me again, "he's in love with her. That will give us an edge."

Furious, I stormed past him into the bathroom. I slammed the door shut behind me, cracking the frame. My destruction didn't alter the look of the room much, but it made me feel better. Ignoring the tinge of blood in the air, I sank down the wall and sat on the floor. It was filthy, but I didn't care. My family was about to take a much more proactive step to finding Hunter and his father. It twisted my gut in fear and revulsion. I didn't want this ... any of this. I just wanted to sneak out of the house to go see a movie with Hunter. I wanted my biggest problem to be that my brother was in love with someone he couldn't have, and my boyfriend was too old to openly date. I'd give anything to have those simple problems again.

In the other room, I heard Halina making plans to temporarily leave us. She was as reluctant to go as Dad was to let her leave. But we had to fix Arianna's car before some curious person saw it, and Halina was the only one who could make that process happen this late at night, with no questions from the repair shop about why there were bullet holes in the car. There would be no record of it either. Halina could make all of this happen in a blink of an eye with no one the wiser. Being a full vampire did have some perks.

In the end, Halina took Imogen with her so she wouldn't be out there all alone. Gabriel wanted to go, too, but he couldn't pull himself away from protecting Starla and Jacen. Starla was just as human as Julian and me; unlike my dad, she wouldn't pull through being shot or stabbed.

Before leaving, Halina told Dad, "I'll be back as soon as I find someone with the parts we need. Do *not* go off to meet that boy without me."

I cringed. That *boy* was my boyfriend.

I heard Dad respond, "I won't ... you need to be there." I pictured Halina giving Dad a cocky smile. Just as I felt frustrated tears stinging my eyes, Dad added, "And please be careful. No showboating, you're still weak."

Halina sniffed indignantly. "I am not ... weak. But I am a little ... run down. Maybe I'll grab a bite while I'm out."

Arianna gasped and a burst of something warm and protective sprouted in Julian. He murmured to her, "It's all right, she won't hurt anybody."

I knew that wasn't the case. When Halina hunted in the city, she generally hunted people. A bite, regardless of how small, would hurt. But what Julian really meant was that Halina wouldn't kill anyone. While I would never contradict that statement in front of Arianna, that wasn't always true either, and with Halina not feeling up to her usual level of fitness tonight, she just might take a life.

Halina was pretty good about only killing people that most of society wouldn't miss, but how could I explain that without sounding horribly callous? Whether her meal choice was right or wrong, I couldn't say, but I knew that it was a choice I would never make. I was never going to kill anybody. Ever.

The two motel room doors opened simultaneously as Halina and Imogen left together. Once the doors shut, I heard a knock on the bathroom door. Having felt her approach, I knew who it was. "Come on in, Mom."

She opened the door and entered the bathroom where I was sulking. I spotted Dad standing near Ben through the open door. He was looking back at me, his face apologetic. Dad didn't want to set up my boyfriend, but he needed this over with. I dropped my eyes from his as Mom took a seat beside me.

She put a chilly hand on my knee. "We're all very sorry that it has to be this way, Nika."

I felt Julian's feelings shift to sympathy as he listened. "I know, Mom. I'm not really mad. Just ... frustrated." Meeting her eyes, I shrugged. "Does that make sense?"

Sighing, Mom cupped my cheek. "Perfect sense."

I shivered as the chill from her hand traveled down my spine. Laying my head on her shoulder, I whispered, "I'm sorry I kept him from you guys. I just didn't want ... I didn't want you to tell me that I couldn't see him."

Mom put her arm around me. "We understand that, Nika." Giving me a knowing smile, she added, "Your father and I didn't always share our secrets with our parents either. What matters is that you told us when you had to. When it got dangerous, when you got scared, you told us. That's what's important."

I nodded, feeling a small bit of relief from her words. As I stared at the woman who had given me so much of her appearance, I wondered if her personality had been passed down to me too. Mom was brave, strong, and a little feisty. She was every bit the hero my dad was. But I really wasn't sure if I was anything like her, even though Julian assured me I was.

Mom and I were silent as we felt Imogen and Halina drifting away from us. They were in the abused minivan with the pudgy man from the front desk. I'd heard Halina compel the man to take them somewhere that could repair the damage to the car in one evening. The man had immediately started spouting something about knowing a guy who owned a junkyard and could fix just about anything. Luckily, Arianna's Mom's car was pretty common; finding the parts to repair it wouldn't be too much of a problem. Especially since Halina could breeze around town and have any needed part delivered by ... well, literally, anyone. Unless a human had vampire blood mixed into them, there was no protection from compulsion that I was aware of.

They wouldn't be gone long, and when they got back, we'd be heading out to trap a hunter ... *my* hunter. It made me ill to think about it. He might have shot my dad, he might have insinuated that I was a monster, but ... I still had hope that our star-crossed love would somehow work out. The logical part of my head knew that was rarely the case. Romeo and Juliet were shining examples of just how badly our type of love could end.

I never imagined that my first real relationship would turn out this way. I'd always pictured flowers and poetry, dramatic declarations of love, followed by a beautiful wedding and equally beautiful children. Never in a million years did my fantasy include bullet holes.

After my mood cooled, I rejoined the others in the motel room. Mom left me to drape her arms around Dad. Dad never lost his vigilant stance as he tenderly embraced her. Trey was lying on the bed with his eyes closed. His heartbeat was slow and steady as he slept. I didn't understand how anyone could nod off after what we'd been through tonight. I was sure I'd be awake for days.

Julian patted the corner of the bed where he was sitting. Arianna was still right beside him, clenching his hand for support, like he was the only thing keeping her grounded. I sat beside the pair, my mood speculative. Julian's was sympathetic as he watched me. After a long moment of silence, his hand closed over mine. "It will be okay, Nika. If they can wipe him without killing him, they will."

I lifted my eyes to my brother. He wasn't sure if what he'd just said was true; I could feel it in his emotions. Not sure either, I wrapped my hand around his. "I know." We both knew the odds of that happening were slim, but I appreciated his attempt to comfort me anyway.

The hours ticked by, and yet, at the same time, the hours blurred by with a speed that matched a pureblood vampire's. My two absent grandmothers returned just as the clock on the wall moved into the eleventh hour. Imogen went straight to her room, to check on her daughter waiting with the others. Halina sauntered into our room. She gave Dad a businesslike nod.

"The vehicle will be delivered in the morning in near-perfect condition."

"That's fast ... good." A slight frown marred Dad's features as he absorbed her words. "I don't suppose you allowed the mechanics to give themselves short breaks while they work on the van?"

Halina raised an eyebrow. "Speed was of the essence. They can take all the time they need when they're done."

Dad sighed. "I know, but if they work themselves to death ... ?"

Halina waved off his concern with her hand. "The mechanic the fat man knew was young, strong ..." she wiped the corner of her mouth with her thumb, " ... tasty. He'll be fine."

Dad let his concerns over the mechanic's welfare go. Arianna shivered and buried her head into Julian's shoulder. He patted her back while Trey let out a lumberjack snore. All the vampires twisted to look at the sleeping teenager.

"I see he's terribly upset by everything that has transpired tonight," Halina mumbled.

Julian lifted his chin. "I told you they could handle it, Grandma."

Halina eyed Arianna trembling in Julian's arms. "We'll see." She focused her attention on Mom, Dad, and Ben. "Now, let's go over our plan."

I tuned them out as they started discussing what to do. I didn't want to listen to them making plans that would harm someone I cared about. In fact, if there was a way to sneak off and meet up with Hunter alone right now, I might do it. But escape was impossible, not with my internal GPS telling every family member where I was at all times. If it only came with an on/off switch ... but the person who knew how to do that died a long time ago.

At quarter to midnight, Dad squatted in front of me. "It's time, Nika." His face was both apologetic and determined. Regardless of my feelings on the matter, this was happening.

With a sniff, I stood up. Surprisingly, Julian stood with me. Dad immediately started shaking his head. "No, son, you stay here with the others." It had already been decided that Alanna and Imogen would stay behind with Starla, Jacen, and all the humans, sans Ben. He was joining the hunting party of Mom, Dad, Gabriel, and Halina.

As Julian stood tall and proud, Arianna slowly raised herself to stand next to him. "I'm going, Dad. I'm not letting Nika do this alone."

A faint smile lifted Dad's lips, then it faded. "She won't be alone. Your mom and I will be right there, along with the others. Nothing will happen to her, I promise."

A level of determination filled Julian; it was stronger than any protective emotion I'd ever felt from him. "You'll be in hiding while she's exposed. I'm not going to let her be exposed all alone." My brother looked over to me, fear and concern washing over him. "If you're going to be in danger, I'm with you." He held out his hand for me. "I'm with you to the end, Nick."

A knot formed in my throat as I took his hand. "The very end, Julie."

Julian looked back at Dad. "Besides, it won't be odd to Hunter if Nika brings me along." He shrugged. "We're best friends." Arianna let out a small sigh as she stared up at Julian. I couldn't feel her emotions like I could feel my brother's, but it was clear by the look in her eye that her crush on him had returned in force. If it had ever truly gone anywhere to begin with.

Dad seemed like he wanted to argue, Mom did too, but Halina stepped right in front of us. She appraised us with a calm, almost detached expression, but I knew that she loved us and worried about us, even if she didn't express it as freely as our parents. Tilting her head toward Julian, she asked in Russian, *"Can you handle being her first layer of protection? I won't put you out there if you are not strong enough. We cannot risk you having a ... moment."*

Julian swallowed. We all knew that a "moment" was really a panic attack. Given enough stress, Julian could freeze up. And if tonight went badly, and he froze up ... he would be the one in the most amount of danger. But as surely as he would be protecting me tonight, I would be protecting him. And I knew he could do this with me by his side. We were stronger together.

I shoved as much of my encouragement into him as I could, and he stood a little taller. Unwaveringly, he answered Halina in her native tongue. *"I'm ready. I will not fail her ... or you."*

Halina smiled and responded to his statement in English. "Then you may go with Nika."

Dad bit his lip, not happy. "Great-Gran, I don't think—"

Halina merely looked over at him, but Dad immediately stopped talking. There was something in the power of her presence that made arguing with her pointless. Like it or not, she was the matriarch of our nest, and that generally meant that she had the final say over our lives.

Arianna looked unhappy as her eyes darted between Julian and me. "Just how dangerous is this?" she asked, fear for us evident in her expression.

Julian gave her an untroubled smile that I did my best to match. "We'll be fine, Arianna," I told her. "Hunter won't hurt us." And hopefully, none of *us* hurt him.

Lips set in a hard line, Arianna shook her head. "I don't like this." From the way Dad sighed, I could tell he agreed with her.

Grabbing her hand, Julian repeated my words of reassurance. "We'll be fine ... just fine."

Turning to face Julian, she quietly said, "Please be careful." Her heart was in her eyes as she locked gazes with my brother, and it took her a solid ten seconds to look over at me. "Both of you," she said, extending one of her hands to me.

Taking her hand, I gently squeezed her fingers. I was so glad she was staying here at the motel with the others; I wasn't sure exactly what might happen tonight, but I knew I didn't want my friend in the middle of it. Julian was just as relieved as me that Arianna was staying behind, but as he kept holding her hand and staring into her eyes, his relief began shifting into something deeper. He was swirling with confusion over those feelings, but they were crystal clear to me. He cared about Arianna, and not just in a friendly way, and while he couldn't quite see it yet, I thought maybe he was beginning to.

Shaking himself out of his thoughts, Julian finally released Arianna. Walking over to Trey, he thumped his leg to wake him up. The dozing boy woke with a start. "What? What I'd miss?" Looking around with hazy eyes, he murmured, "Are we still at the motel?"

I rolled my eyes at Trey, and Julian let out a small laugh. "Yeah, for now. But Nika and I are leaving with some of the others."

Trey sat up as our family started to rendezvous outside the motel rooms to say goodbye to those of us who were leaving. Listening to my mom say goodbye to Grandma Linda made my eyes sting. Standing, Trey clapped Julian's shoulder. "Where we going?"

"You're staying here with Arianna and the other humans," I answered.

Trey frowned. "What's with the species-ism?"

I pursed my lips, trying not to be annoyed. Sensing my mood, Julian interceded. Leaning in, he whispered, "Hey, man, I need you to stay and protect Arianna for me." He paused, genuine concern filling him. "I need you to keep her safe for me. I'm counting on you."

Trey beamed with his protection assignment. "You got it, man." His expression clouded over as he glanced between my brother and me. "What are you guys doing though?"

Sighing, I pulled on his elbow. "I'll fill you in outside." I tilted my head at Julian and Arianna, hoping Trey would understand that I wanted to give them a moment alone to say goodbye. It took him a second, but eventually Trey got it. Nodding, he followed me out the door.

Once outside, I quickly got Trey up to speed, then hugged every family member who wasn't coming with us. As I tearfully said goodbye to Grandpa Jack, the tender conversation between Julian and Arianna filtered out to me. I tried not to listen to them, but Julian's emotions were so strong, they pulled me into the conversation.

"Are you really going to be okay?" Arianna asked, a tremor in her voice.

"Yeah, of course." Quietly, Julian added, "I'll worry about you though."

"You will?"

Julian sighed, the sound full of caring. "Yeah, you'll be in the corner of my mind the entire time I'm gone." He paused, then added, "I'm so sorry you got dragged into this. I never wanted ..."

"I know, Julian ... but ... I'm glad I know what you and Nika are."

Julian's spirits soared. "You're...happy that you know?"

Arianna sighed. "Yeah, I mean, it explains a lot about why you're ... aloof. Why you sometimes seem unhappy. Why you look like you don't think you belong. But, no matter what you are, you *do* belong, Julian. You fit. Even if you're a ... vampire, you fit."

Julian was awed by her comment, and my heart lifted for him ... for them. "Arianna ... I ... I don't ..."

Julian's rising emotions boiled over, and I had to pause a moment while saying goodbye to Jacen. As I breathed through the intensity, Jacen asking me if I was all right, I heard a noise cutting through the night—the sound of two people exchanging sweet, soft kisses. Julian's mood leveled off as he shared an intimate moment with Arianna. Smiling, I told Jacen, "I'm fine ... everything's fine."

Mom and Dad glanced at the motel room where Julian and Arianna were kissing, but they didn't interrupt the pair's innocent pecks. Even with my abhorrence of what was about to happen tonight, I wished Julian and Arianna well. If my pig-headed brother had truly opened his eyes, maybe they could finally be together.

When they emerged from the room a moment later, Arianna's eyes were bright, and Julian looked a little dazed. Halina smirked at him, but surprisingly didn't comment. I hugged Arianna when she walked over to me. She giggled when we pulled apart, then her face turned serious. "You be careful, Nika."

My nerves spiked. This was it. Either way, this was the last time I would ever see my boyfriend.

"I will. I'll be perfectly safe."

I hoped so, anyway.

CHAPTER TWENTY

Julian

GABRIEL AND HALINA blurred away, streaking toward their assigned hiding place. Dad started Grandpa's truck and drove the rest of us to the library in silence. Nika's mind was spinning, her emotions shifting from one extreme to the other. I could scarcely imagine how I would feel if I were in her position. If Raquel turned out to be a vampire hunter hell bent on destroying our family ... or if Arianna was a hunter ... well, torn wouldn't even begin to describe my feelings.

Thinking of both of those women in that context gave me pause. In a way, I was just as conflicted as Nika, but on a much smaller scale. Try as I might, I couldn't deny that I felt something for Arianna. I wasn't sure what it was, but it was growing with every passing second that I spent with her. I ran a finger over my lips, remembering the softness of her mouth pressed against mine; I was still tingling from the contact.

Unlike Raquel, Arianna knew what I was, and even more shocking than that—she'd accepted me, told me I fit, told me I belonged. I didn't know if Raquel would feel the same if she knew. There was a nagging knot in my stomach that told me she wouldn't.

Nika was right. Raquel would most likely never accept me. But Arianna ...

We arrived at the library while my thoughts were still spinning as rapidly as my sister's. Dad drove past the library and parked the truck nearly a mile away. He didn't want our vehicle to tip off Hunter. Not that Hunter knew what Grandpa's truck looked like, but better safe than sorry. Besides, with our super-speed, it didn't matter how far away we parked. We could be there in seconds.

Keeping to the shadows as much as possible, we blurred toward the plaza. When we got there, we stopped across the street, where the cathedral-like county building was nestled in a clump of trees surrounding Washington Square. Ben couldn't move as fast as the rest of us, so Mom carried him. After she set him down, he grinned and said, "I'll never get used to that."

Dad smirked at his friend, then reconfirmed the plan. "Gabriel and Great-Gran are checking out the area to make sure Hunter is alone." I couldn't feel Gabriel, but I felt Halina, and Dad was right, she was flitting over the property, checking every nook and cranny she came across.

Dad's jaw clenched as he studied Nika and me. "You two stay close together, watching each other's backs." He put a hand on my shoulder. "Your mother and I will be right there with you, as close as we can get. You'll be perfectly safe."

Even though butterflies were tickling my stomach, I nodded. Nika raised her chin. Her voice loud enough that our grandmother would hear, she told Dad, "Since he's my boyfriend, I think I have the right to say ..." her eyes shifted to lock onto the spot where we all felt Halina, "no one touches him until I give the word."

A low growl in the night air lifted the hairs on the back of my neck. Clearly, Halina didn't like Nika's command. Nika didn't back down though. Determination in her eyes, she turned back to Dad. "Unless I'm in danger, no one makes a move on him without my permission."

I could feel the fear and desperation coming from Nika, but I couldn't see it. On the surface she was calm, focused, in control ... powerful. She was a force to be reckoned with as she bravely stood her ground. She made me proud.

Dad glanced back at Mom, a small smile on his lips. "She remind you of anyone?" he whispered to her.

Mom returned his knowing smile. "Every day," she answered.

Dad briefly grinned at Mom before schooling his features. His pale eyes as determined as my sister's, he nodded. "All right, Nika. We'll play this your way. As long as you're safe, we won't touch him ... until you say the word."

Relief melted Nika's rigidness. Our parents vanished with Ben into the darkness, leaving Nika and me alone. Well, they left us to ourselves, since we weren't really alone. I felt our family's presence shadowing us as we walked along the path that led to the meeting place.

In the plaza next to the impressive steel and glass library was a wall of steps where water continuously flowed. Even I had to admit it was a beautiful piece. I might not be into art and nature like my sister, but I still appreciated the calming rhythm of the cascading water, enjoyed the sparkle of the spotlights reflecting off the fine layer of mist hovering near the bottom of the fountain.

Nika's eyes were contemplative as she stared at the slick stones. Her mood turned dark and I squeezed her hand. When she looked up at me, a tear fell to her cheek. She didn't have to explain why she was crying ... I knew. I knew all too well how jumbled her insides were, how badly she wanted to see Hunter, how badly she wanted to run from him. It was our gift, our curse—I knew it all.

Feeling my sympathy and support, Nika nodded at me, and we silently watched the fountain while we waited for Hunter. The water seemed like a solid sheet as it washed down the steps, but my sharp eyes caught cracks and separations in the stream, where one section deviated from the rest to run around an obstacle in its path. As I picked out more breaks in the continuity, I began to see a violent pattern churning under the surface. Maybe Nika's turmoil was darkening my thoughts, but the soothing fountain suddenly seemed metaphoric of our situation, an omen. No obstacle could stand in the water's path. There was no deterrent that it couldn't find a way around, no barrier that it couldn't eventually penetrate. In the end ... water always found a way.

"Nika?"

A voice behind us drew our attention from the fountain, and I immediately twisted around. Nika hesitated before she turned to look at her boyfriend. Hunter's eyes were pitch-black in the night. The thick jacket he wore was dark, as well, and there were bulges in the pockets that I assumed were weapons. Stakes maybe, although it wouldn't surprise me if he still had his gun on him. His brow was creased as he took me in. "Julian? What are you doing here?"

Feeling my family start to close in, I stood tall and straight. "I wasn't about to let Nika sneak off and meet you on her own." Glancing at Hunter's empty hands, I added, "Who knows what you might have done to her."

"I'm not here to hurt her." He exposed his palms to me. My eyes locked onto the odd jewelry he was wearing. Every finger had a ring on it and every ring was connected to the bracelet around his wrist by thin chains that gleamed silver in the moonlight. I hadn't spent a whole lot of time around Hunter, but I was sure I'd never seen him wearing those before. "I only want to talk to her," he said.

Nika dropped my hand and stepped up to him. I had to restrain myself from pulling her back. "Well, here I am. Start talking."

Hunter sighed as he ran a hand through his hair. "I ..."

He faltered, seemingly at a loss for words. My sister wasn't. Anger surging through her, she spat, "You shot my father! In a high school!"

Hunter flinched at the menace in her tone, but he didn't back down. "A vampire was coming at me. I panicked ... it was instinct."

Nika crossed her arms over her chest. "He wasn't going to hurt you."

Hunter mimicked her position. "He was only going to erase my mind, right? Destroy everything about me that makes me who I am." He shook his head. "How can you say that's not hurting me?"

Nika deflated a little under his reasoning. "You would have lived ..."

Hunter's expression turned inquisitive. "Would have? Is letting me live not an option anymore?"

Nika's chin dropped, along with the rest of her anger. "I don't know. It's not my decision." She peeked her eyes up at him. "Would *you* let us live?"

Hunter turned his head away from Nika, surveying the plaza. He looked like he was pondering Nika's question, but I knew he was searching for signs of trouble. He wouldn't find any, not yet. My family was well hidden, waiting for Nika to give the command to put her boyfriend down. Sympathy welled in me. Nika's situation gave a whole new meaning to the expression stuck between a rock and a hard place.

Twisting back to face her, Hunter whispered, "It's not my decision either, Nika. I'm sorry."

Nika nodded, the moisture in her eyes thickening. Wanting to provide comfort, I took a step toward her. She discretely held up her hand to stop me. Hunter surveyed us for a moment, then said, "I'm sorry my father fired on you." Genuine concern softened his face as he focused on Nika's bloodstained jacket. "Are you okay?"

"I'm fine," she whispered, not looking him directly in the eye.

"Nika ... I need to know how badly you were hurt. Show me, please?" he pleaded.

Nika hesitated, then slowly unzipped her jacket. Shrugging it off her shoulder, she exposed her injured arm. Gabriel's bandage around her bicep was thick, but a trace amount of blood was seeping through it. The pain from it still burned through Nika, and I grit my teeth. What she referred to as a "graze" was much deeper than that, almost a through and through.

Hunter inhaled a quick breath as he took in her wound, then he shut his eyes, like he couldn't bear to look at it anymore. "I can't believe he ... I'm so sorry, Nika."

Ignoring his apology, Nika slipped her jacket back up and changed the subject. "Are you and your father the ones who are answering ads for feeders?"

Hunter's jaw dropped as he opened his eyes. "You know about that?"

Nika swallowed, getting her answer in his question. "So, you *are* killing vampires ..."

Hunter took a step toward her, and, from somewhere in the night, a low growl filled the air. Hunter's eyes snapped to me, and that was when I realized that I'd made the intimidating sound. Abashed, I straightened from the half-crouch I'd unknowingly ducked into. Keeping his distance from Nika, Hunter responded, "I'm hunting monsters. That's what I do."

Nika settled her hands on her hips. "They aren't running through the night ripping out throats, Hunter. They're taking small amounts of blood from willing participants. You're oversimplifying things again."

Hunter narrowed his eyes. "And you're being naïve again. You think all of those 'willing' participants get to leave? You think they *all* realize what they're giving up when they walk in the door? Vampires don't come out and ask for blood. It's a lot subtler than that."

Face defiant, my sister snapped, "You would know."

Hunter gave her a stiff nod. "Yes, I would know. I've been doing this a really long time, and I've seen things that would make you change your mind."

"Like what?" Nika challenged.

"Like children."

The words hung in the air, and Nika and I both stared at Hunter in disbelief. I wasn't sure what he meant by his statement, but it sent a shiver down my spine. Nika's too. Shuddering, she asked, "What do you mean?"

Seeing Nika's anger diminish, Hunter stepped toward her again. This time I let him. In a low, comforting voice, he said, "I knew this girl who was obsessed with vampires." He smirked. "'Twilight-crush' is what Dad and I call it. Anyway, she came across an ad that we found, and she snuck out to meet the bloodsucker ..."

Hunter's eyes misted over and his lip began to tremble. Nika raised her hand to touch him, then stopped herself. "By the time Dad and I got there ... she was dead ... drained." Hunter sniffed, then lowered his head. "She was thirteen, Nika, and completely—"

"Innocent?" Nika whispered, cutting him off. "She was the innocent girl your dad was referring to last night, wasn't she?"

Hunter lifted his head, then nodded. "I tried to get her to see what they really were, but I failed, and she paid the price." Dark memories clouded his face, as he looked out over the empty plaza. Well, empty to him. I felt the pinpricks of my family out there, waiting to pounce. I also felt Nika's turmoil. She wasn't sure if she could do this to Hunter. A part of her wanted to tell him to run.

Unaware, Hunter continued reminiscing. "Dad and I tore up the city after that, destroying any nest we could find." He looked back at Nika. "We would still be down there, but things got a little ... hot, and we had to make a run for it." His jaw clenched, and it was pretty easy to see he didn't enjoy running from a fight.

Knowing what he was referencing, I asked, "Los Angeles, right? You got kicked out of L.A.?"

Hunter's irritated eyes snapped to mine. "We didn't get kicked out ... but, yes, we had to leave. They got too close to ..." His eyes narrowed again. "How did you know that?"

A surge of cockiness hit me, and I crooked a grin. "You have your sources, I have mine."

Hunter let out a controlled exhale. "That prick vampire is here, isn't he?" His dark eyes shifted between my sister and me. "The ancient one. The one who leads the largest nest in Los Angeles. They say he's well-connected, almost impossible to kill. You two know him, don't you?"

I bit my lip and glanced at Nika. I'd said too much, and now Hunter was aware that Gabriel was here in Salt Lake. I doubt he knew Gabriel was currently lurking in the plaza with my grandmother, but he knew that the vampire who'd chased him out of L.A. was close by. It didn't matter, though. After tonight, what Hunter did or didn't know would be irrelevant. He'd be a clean slate once Halina was done. He might not even remember his own name.

Nika took a step forward, until she was directly in front of Hunter. Hunter's scowl evaporated at her nearness. My family members all surged forward, but Nika held up a finger behind her back, and they stopped. I wasn't sure what to do. It was my responsibility to keep Nika safe; I was her first layer of protection. But she was so close to him now that he could potentially drive a stake through her before I could yank her away. Nika clearly didn't think he would, but I wasn't as convinced.

Even though her expression was calm, Nika's heart was racing. Whether that was from excitement or fear, I couldn't tell. I was on edge when she asked, "What really happened to your sister?"

Hunter closed his eyes. "She died. I don't know how many times you want me to say it."

"By a vampire?"

Hunter opened his eyes, a frown on his lips. "No ... cancer."

Perplexed, Nika asked, "Then why are there fangs on her urn?"

Hunter's lips curved into a slight smile. "It's tradition in my family. A badge of honor, so to speak. All hunters' graves or urns are marked with the symbol." He shrugged. "Mine will be too, some day."

Nika's face fell. "So, she was a hunter, like you?"

Hunter scoffed and shook his head. "No, she was much better than I'll ever be. She was amazing."

"Oh." Nika swallowed and backed up a half-step. A small smile on his face, Hunter didn't seem to notice she was retreating.

"Yeah, she's the one who realized vampires were placing ads for victims. She's the one who came up with the idea of answering the ads." A prideful smile on his face, Hunter shook his head. "And she's the one who realized they'd be easier for us to stake if they were busy eating. She volunteered her blood, let them bite her." Hunter's smile faltered. "I didn't want her to take that chance, but she was already dying so she said it didn't matter if they killed her. She told me that if it meant Dad and I could destroy the monsters without a fight, without us even getting a scratch ... then she'd gladly die."

Expression solemn, Hunter whispered, "She was a hero, Nika." Grabbing the collar of his shirt, he pulled the fabric over to expose his shoulder. Above his collarbone was a vampire bite. It was faded, nearly-healed, but my sharp eyes still knew what it was. "I only hope I can be half the hunter she was someday."

Nika gasped, her hands flying to his clothes to examine the aged wound more closely. I bristled at her touching him, but Hunter didn't move as her fingers traced the bite mark. "Are you insane, Hunter?" she murmured. "You're letting them bite you?"

Hunter shrugged. "With my sister gone, someone has to be the bait." Ducking down, Hunter met Nika's eye. "And what's the problem? You seem concerned that I'm letting 'harmless' vampires take a small amount of blood from a 'willing' participant."

Nika froze and removed her fingers from Hunter's shirt. Irritation flared in her at hearing Hunter use her words against her. Just as she seemed about to respond, Hunter's expression shifted to confusion. He grabbed her hand when she pulled away, clenching her tight. My reflexes kicked in, and I blurred to her side. Fangs lowered, I shoved Hunter away from her. Another one of my growls ripped through the night as Hunter was propelled backward a few feet. Nika turned to me while Hunter crashed to the ground.

"He wasn't going to hurt me, Julian," she reprimanded.

As I gaped at her, she rushed to Hunter's side. I looked over to where I could feel my father. Even though I couldn't see him, I lifted my hands in a *What the hell?* expression. I had to believe Dad wasn't happy that Nika was tending to her injured boyfriend. If she got too close to Hunter, Dad might go back on his word and attack him without her permission. Actually, I was a little surprised they were still holding back ... especially Halina; I could sense her pacing in agitation as she waited for Nika's word.

Kneeling beside Hunter, Nika helped him sit up. Hunter glared at me, then shifted his focus to Nika. "I don't understand you," he whispered. He held up his hand, showing me his bare palm. Well, bare except for the slim metal chains that connected his rings to his wrist. Slowly, deliberately, he placed his palm against Nika's cheek. Other than furrow her brow, Nika didn't react. Hunter shook his head, even more confused than before. "You're a vampire, I've seen that much, but why don't you react to silver?"

Removing his hand, he grabbed a metal strand. "All vampires react to silver. That's a basic fact that even the most simple-minded person knows. It's Vampirology 101."

My eyes widened as I stared at his jewelry. It wasn't just jewelry ... it was another weapon. If a vampire was close enough for him to touch them with those silver chains lacing his palm, he could hurt them enough that they'd back away. A hazy memory formed as I stared at those chains. A vague recollection of Hunter touching my face with them broke through my drug-induced fog of the Halloween party.

Irritated, I pointed at his hand. "You touched me with those! You tested me!"

Hunter looked up at me. "Your fangs weren't plastic knockoffs. They looked so real ... I had to know if you'd been turned." His brow scrunched. "But you didn't react to the silver." He looked between Nika and me. "I've seen both of you in the sunlight, I've watched both of you eat food ... Vampires aren't supposed to be able to do either of those things. I don't understand ... what are you?"

Nika sighed as she sat back on her heels. "I told you, I'm a mixed species ... a half-breed." She pursed her lips. "Or a sixteenth breed ... something like that."

Hanging his wrists over his knees, Hunter shook his head. "I've never heard of such a thing. Ever. I'm blown away by you."

Nika flushed, taking that as a compliment. Hunter glanced at me, then slowly reached out to touch her again. I was on high alert, but I let him. Nika held her breath as his fingers touched the artery in her neck; it was surging with blood as her heart pounded in her chest. I was pretty sure it was from excitement this time.

Amazed, Hunter whispered, "You have a heartbeat. You're alive?"

Nika grabbed his hand, holding it in hers. "I told you I was. I'm completely alive, Hunter."

His face fell into despair. "But you have fangs? You drink blood?"

Nika averted her eyes for a moment. When she returned her gaze to his, her fangs were lowered. Hunter instinctively shot to his feet and backed away from her. She stood with her hands out in placation. "I've never had human blood, and I've never bitten anything. But yes, it's in my nature. It's a part of who I am ... but it's not *all* I am."

Hunter grunted and ran his hands through his hair. "This wasn't supposed to happen. You were just supposed to be this sweet, beautiful girl I was falling for ..."

Nika grabbed his hands, her heart in her eyes and pain in her chest. "That's who I am! I've never lied to you!"

Hunter jerked his hands free, and I felt Nika's heart crack. "All you've ever done is lie to me!"

A tear rolled down Nika's cheek as she lamented, "This is how I was born! I haven't hurt anyone! Why do I deserve a stake in my heart when I haven't done anything wrong?"

Hunter flinched at her words, but raised his chin as he answered her. "You're ... unnatural."

Pain and anger battled within my sister's soul. Pressing her body against Hunter's, she bit out, "Does this feel unnatural? Did it feel unnatural when you were kissing me? When you told me you wanted to rip my clothes off and take me?"

I heard a low growl in the night that didn't come from me this time. Luckily, Hunter was so absorbed in Nika that he missed it. I was pretty sure Dad was restraining himself from zipping over here and tossing Hunter into the next county.

It was clear by his befuddled expression that Hunter was at a loss. Their bodies still flush together, he finally sputtered, "It didn't feel unnatural then. But it does now ..."

Nika choked back a sob as she stepped away from him. "I thought you said you were in love with me?"

Looking like he was holding back a sob of his own, Hunter told her, "I *am* in love with you. I love you so much ... and I hate myself for it."

Shaking her head at him, Nika whispered, "Go ahead, Dad. We're done here."

I instantly felt the multiple streaks rushing toward Hunter. Now that Nika had given my family the okay, Hunter would be taken down and erased in a matter of seconds. He'd be out of our lives for good. Nika's heart was shattering. She'd opened herself up to Hunter, and he couldn't accept what she was. Hunter couldn't see past the fangs, to the beautiful person Nika was underneath. No, that wasn't entirely true. Hunter *could* see the person Nika was, and he did love her, despite her heritage. But he resented himself for loving her. He couldn't accept *himself*... and that was almost worse than him not being able to accept my sister.

I started to move toward Nika, to offer her whatever consolation I could, but somewhere in the night, a strange twang sounded. A breath later, a heavy shaft of wood sailed through the air. Frozen in curiosity and terror, I watched its flight. Even though my family was a hairsbreadth from my sister and me, they weren't close enough to protect us, and my sister screamed when a crossbow bolt lodged into her shoulder. Her pain brought me to my knees.

Mom and Dad were instantly at Nika's side, while Gabriel rushed over to help me to my feet. I couldn't see my sister as my parents hovered around her, but I smelled her blood in the air and I felt the pain rocketing through her body. Another twang and whistle floated through my brain. Gabriel snarled as he snatched an arrow out of the air, right before it penetrated his chest. Another foot, and it would have hit *my* chest.

Frantically searching the skyline around the plaza, Hunter yelled, "Father, stop!" but I heard the telltale sound of another arrow being released. This one hit my mother in the back as she kneeled over Nika. She let out an anguished cry, and Dad blurred to her side. He immediately pulled out the arrow, his eyes wide and fearful. A centimeter or two to the left, and the arrow's sharp point would have punctured my mother's heart. Hunter's father was an excellent marksman, and he was swiftly correcting his aim. Somehow, I knew his next shot wouldn't miss.

Slower than the vampires, Ben finally ran into the plaza. Ducking under the footpath that led to the library's garden rooftop, Ben hid as much of his body as he could. He scanned the area, searching for the source of trouble, but it was difficult to pinpoint exactly where the attack was coming from. My heart thudded in my ears as I waited for the next barrage. Instead of a twang and a whistle, though, I heard a man scream in pain. My head snapped over to Hunter. Halina was behind him, her mouth firmly attached to his neck. Hunter struggled beneath her, but she was much stronger. Acting fast, Hunter reached up to burn her face with his silver-laced palms, but Gabriel rushed over to him, grabbed his wrists, and yanked the cursed metal contraptions from his body. The silver stinging him, Gabriel immediately tossed the weapons to the ground.

Not giving up, Hunter tried to pull Halina off him with his bare hands, but in the span of a few heartbeats, she drained enough blood from him that he didn't have the strength to fight her. Hunter's eyes rolled back as his knees gave way. Holding him upright, Halina pulled her mouth away. Dark red blood flowed from the gash at his jugular, making his black T-shirt glisten in the moonlight. His blood ran in rivulets down Halina's chin. The gruesome sight made my skin crawl, gave me goosebumps.

Eyes lifted to the night sky, Halina snarled, "Launch another arrow at my family, and I will drain him dry!"

The answering silence was deafening.

CHAPTER TWENTY-ONE

Nika

HEARING MY GRANDMOTHER'S pronouncement of my boyfriend's fate, I struggled to get to my feet. Strong, cold hands held me down, urging me to lie still on the ground. Pain burst through my shoulder whenever I moved, causing my vision to fade in and out. In my hazy peripheral, I could see a thick shaft of wood erupting from my skin; my stomach churned with nausea.

I'd been shot … with an arrow. Even in my pain and fear, I was struck with the oddity of it all. *Who the hell gets shot with an arrow?* I reached up to tentatively touch the shaft and screamed as an explosion of electric pain sizzled through my body.

"Nika, stop moving."

My mother's voice was tight, pained. I tried to focus on her features, but my basic bodily functions weren't responding like I wanted. What I wanted was to rip that damn arrow out of my shoulder and jump to my feet. I wanted to blur over to Hunter and make sure he was okay. I wanted to believe that all of this was just some horrible nightmare that I would soon wake up from.

"Mom," I croaked out, "it hurts …"

Shushing me, her cool lips graced my forehead. "I know, baby. It will be okay, just try not to move." As I gritted my teeth, trying to stomach the torture, Mom's voice shifted to panic. "What do we do, Teren? Leave it in, or take it out?"

Focusing my vision, I concentrated on Dad's face. His pale eyes were wide as he shifted his attention from me, to the sky, to the others in the plaza. My father was my rock. He always knew what to do. He always knew what to say. He never lost control. Seeing the confusion in his eyes, the distress in his features, I almost didn't recognize the man leaning over me. He was so lost, so scared, so … human.

"I don't know … I just don't know …"

"Dad?" I whispered. "Is Hunter okay?"

Dad gave me a smile that I was sure was meant to be comforting. It wasn't. "Don't worry about him right now, Nika." His worried eyes flashed over my wound, then his head snapped up. "Gabriel! What do I do?"

The youthful, blond vampire was suddenly hovering over my vision. Green eyes intense, he scoured my shoulder that was radiating with pain. He examined me for a few seconds, then reached down and snapped the arrow at the base. The sudden influx of pain was so strong, all I could do was gasp.

His jade eyes turned to my father's. "She may bleed out if we remove the rest. Leave it for now."

Dad nodded, then looked over Gabriel's shoulder. "Julian! Take your sister somewhere safe." His focus shifted to the left. "Ben, stay with them."

Dad stood. By the set of his jaw as he scanned the area, I knew he was about to take off. The assault had stopped once Halina attacked Hunter, but the arrow-wielding maniac was still out there, watching us. As Julian squatted beside me, I grabbed Dad's pant leg. "Don't leave, Dad."

He smiled down at me, his face softening for a moment. Then his eyes shifted to my brother. "Take her inside. Keep her down, keep her safe … and don't come out here again."

Julian nodded, while Mom kissed my forehead. Standing, she clasped Dad's hand. They exchanged a look of such love and devotion that it warmed my heart and broke it at the same time. They were silently saying goodbye to each other … just in case.

Julian helped me sit up as they blurred away. "No! Don't go ..." I knew it was pointless. I knew they wouldn't let a man who was set on destroying our family slip away, but I couldn't stop the words from leaving my mouth. I couldn't lose my parents. I just ... couldn't.

Gabriel stayed in front of us, surveying the land while Julian got me to my feet. My head swam as the pain intensified. I could smell blood in the air—some from me, some from the others. A particularly fragrant whiff of blood got my attention, and dazed, I finally spotted Hunter.

He was slumped over in Halina's arms, unconscious. By the blood I could see on his body and on her mouth, it was clear that she'd been feeding on him. His heartbeat was thready as she held him upright; there was barely any life left in him.

My pain was suddenly nothing. I jerked away from Julian. "No, no, no ... Hunter!"

I tried to run to him, to save him somehow, but my body wasn't up to the task, and my knees gave out. Julian caught me before I completely fell to the ground. Pain made me cry out, both physical and emotional. "No, please, don't kill him!"

His voice rough with emotion, Julian told me, "We need to go, Nick. It's not safe here ... please."

Sobbing, I ignored him. All I could see was Hunter's dark eyes, his confident swagger, his boyish grin. I couldn't picture a world without him in it. I'd been ready to part ways with him, to let him go, but I'd never be ready for him to die. I loved him.

Halina looked back at us and snarled. Turning her head to Ben, she snapped, "Get the children out of here!" With her chin coated in Hunter's blood and her fangs extended to full drinking length, she was the very image of a monster.

I began to beg for his life again, but Ben yelled, "Go!" and shoved Julian forward. My brother blurred away with me before the words could leave my mouth.

He stopped us across the street on the far side of the plaza. A red-bricked church occupied the corner lot, its windows dark and vacant. Holding me in his arms, Julian murmured, "Please don't have an alarm," as he kicked in the back door. We both waited for the piercing cry of a security system to go off, but the only sound was the heavy door hitting the far wall.

Stepping into the sanctuary, Julian tenderly set me down in the hallway. I tried to stand but he stuck his finger in my face. "Stay there!"

As I blinked in surprise, Julian blurred away. Fear tore through my chest as I felt him leave me, but his presence started returning almost instantly. Zipping through the door a second later, he carried Ben in his arms this time. Seeing me on the floor, Ben freed himself from Julian and squatted at my side.

"Thank you," he tossed over his shoulder at my brother. Julian nodded as Ben turned to me. Examining my shoulder, he asked, "You all right, Nika?"

Tears stinging my eyes, I shook my head. "She's going to kill him. We have to do something!"

Julian squatted on my other side. "There's nothing we can do, Nick. I'm so sorry." He cradled my head into his shoulder. I fought back the sobs as Julian's compassion poured into me. His sympathy only deepened my anguish.

I pushed him away from me, my shoulder screaming in protest. "That's bullshit! There has to be something we can do!"

Only using the power of my legs, I slid my back against the wall until I was standing. Ben had his hands outstretched, ready to catch me if my strength gave out. Shaking his head, he agreed with my brother. "The only thing we can do is stay here, where it's safe, until your parents have found and contained the threat."

My eyes snapped to his. "The threat? You mean my boyfriend's father."

Ben pursed his lips. "You need to let the familiar association go. All he is to you now is a predator." His face softened. "Don't let yourself feel anything for him. He doesn't feel anything for you."

I swallowed a hard lump in my throat. I wasn't sure if Ben was talking about Hunter's father, or Hunter. I was about to respond when I heard glass breaking. Tilting my head, I listened harder; Julian mimicked my posture, listening as well. Ben, used to being around people with far superior hearing, said nothing as he studied our expressions. After the initial sharp crack, I heard glass falling, shattering as it hit the floor. A scuffling sound was next, then the crunch of a boot.

Julian and I looked at each other and simultaneously said, "Someone's inside the church."

Always the protector, Ben surged in front of us. Him being our shield was ridiculous, since he was weaker and slower than we were, but a man who routinely ran with vampires wasn't a man to be trifled with, and Ben made for an imposing figure as he blocked our path.

With one hand behind his back, he motioned for us to leave the church. Well-trained, Julian and I quietly inched our way toward the door. My heartbeat surged in my ears, along with Julian's and Ben's. I listened for the intruder's, but I couldn't hear him anymore, and I cursed my mixed blood. A full vampire would have heard him easily, would have smelled him.

Julian and I clasped hands as we neared the door. We could have blurred to safety in a second, but we both loathed leaving Ben behind. Ben was backing up with us, a knife ready in his hand. I prayed he didn't have to use it.

The cool night air hit my back, and I shivered; freedom was within my reach. Julian looked back at the open door, then whispered, "Uncle Ben, let me take you ..."

Ben looked back at us. His face was framed by moonlight streaming through a window across the hallway. The gray streaks in his hair weren't noticeable in the shadowy light, the scars along his skin weren't as defined. His rigid jaw was set with determination, but his lips softened into a smile. He seemed younger as he stood before us, almost boyish, but at the same time, wise beyond his years. While I'd always thought my adopted-uncle was handsome, in that moment, he was stunningly beautiful.

Just as he was about to tell us something, a gunshot shattered the quiet.

Ben's head jerked to the side, and he collapsed to the ground. Fresh blood hit the air, and a pool of it started forming around Ben's limp body. Stifling a scream, I clutched Julian tight. There was no way that just happened. Ben couldn't be ... dead. He just couldn't be.

I tried to blur to his side, to check his vitals, to stop the flow of blood from his head, but Julian cinched his arms around me, holding me in place. In my ear, he whispered, "Don't move, Nick."

Confused, I glanced up at Julian's face. If we weren't helping Ben, then shouldn't we be fleeing? Julian's eyes were glued on something in front of us, and my slow mind instantly caught up. Ben was shot, and bullets don't just magically appear. Bullets came from guns, and there was only one person I knew who wanted to put down every member of my family.

My shoulder radiating with pain, I struggled against my brother as I snapped my attention to the threat in the room. "Connor! Stop this!"

Eyes wide, Hunter's father look like a man possessed, or unhinged. His hand shook as he pointed the gun between Julian and me. "My son," he croaked. "What have you done to my son!" His lips frothed with spittle as his voice gained strength.

He started storming toward us, and I reflexively raised my hands. I honestly didn't know if Julian and I could outrun bullets. We were fast, darn near supersonic, but our vampiric gifts were very diluted. And dodging a bullet was something you needed to be sure you could do before you tried it. My father was stronger than we were, and he hadn't been able to avoid being hit by one...and for us, one hit was all it would take.

As Connor stepped right in front of me, I violently shook my head. I still felt weak from the wound in my shoulder; my legs were trembling, threatening to give out on me. I knew that if they did give way, Connor would think I was attacking, and fire a bullet into my brain. Fear, and my brother's strong arms, gave me strength. "My brother and I didn't do anything to Hunter. Please, Connor, we're not a threat. Let us go."

Connor pressed the barrel of his weapon against my forehead; it was still warm from its recent discharge. Julian growled, adrenaline pumping through him. "Not a threat? As far as I'm concerned, you're the biggest threat of them all." He leaned into me, his breath washing across my skin. "You're blood-sucking day-walkers. You're ... succubus ... luring victims to you so you can spread your filthy seed. I knew following my son would lead me to you, since you've somehow poisoned him with your seductress ways."

A tear dropped to my cheek at hearing his vitriol. "I'm just a girl, and I'd never hurt your son."

"You already did ..." Sadness marked Connor's features, and, for a second, I felt sorry for him. What my grandmother had done to Hunter would be hard to recover from, especially the longer it took to get Hunter medical attention. Connor pulled back from me, lowering his gun from my forehead. "But you can fix this, you can save him." A hint of madness in his eyes, he gave me a cold, calculated smile. "You can bring him back."

I had no time to contemplate what he meant by that. My family had heard Connor's gun go off, and streaked to the church. They'd been right outside the church, debating how best to proceed, but my father couldn't idly stand by while a gun was being waved at his children. Once Connor lowered the gun, Dad blurred into the room.

I had to give it to Hunter's dad ... he was fast. He must have known that discharging his weapon would alert the rest of my family. He must have been expecting them to swoop down on him. Maybe that was the real reason why he hadn't killed Julian and me right away. He tore me from Julian and held me to his chest while he pressed his back against the wall. Dropping his weapon, he pushed his fingers against the arrow shaft still imbedded in my shoulder. I screamed.

Dad froze as his pale eyes surveyed the chaos around him. Ben was bleeding out on the floor, and Julian was staring at me in disbelief while I forcefully stopped myself from wailing. I would *not* scream for this bastard. Switching his fingers to my neck, Connor grabbed a sharp knife from his belt. The metal glistened in the moonlight as he pressed it against my throat. A sharp zing of pain was followed by a warm trickle of blood. I held as still as I could, so I didn't inadvertently slit my own throat.

Dad held up his hands. "Don't ... We'll let you go, I promise. Just ... release her ... please."

The knife dug in a little more, and I struggled to maintain my composure. Falling apart now wouldn't do anybody any good, least of all me. "I don't want to be let go," Connor growled.

Dad furrowed his brows. "Then what do you want?" His eyes darted from Julian to me. He clearly wanted Julian to leave, but didn't want any sudden movement to spook Connor.

"My son. Tell that bitch to bring him to me."

Dad didn't do or say anything. He didn't need to. Halina blurred into the room before Connor even finished his sentence. Long, black hair, wild and free, wet blood dripping down her chin, she was the epitome of a woman enraged. Dad grabbed her hand as she stormed past. Fangs out, she hissed at Dad, then shifted her attention back to Connor. Muted, driving rock music suddenly pressed against my sensitive ears. I couldn't turn to look, but it sounded like Connor had just turned on a music player. I had no idea why, until he spoke.

Louder than was necessary, he told Halina, "I can't hear you, so don't bother with the mind control crap. Now, unless you want this child covered in her own blood, you bring me my son!"

Halina growled, but didn't move. That was when Mom entered the church with Gabriel a few steps behind her. Mom was holding Hunter's limp body in her arms. Her eyes darted to Ben's equally limp form, and she swallowed a sob. Seeing Hunter's bereft body, his neck and chest stained red, I bit back my own cry. I couldn't hear his heartbeat over mine, Connor's, and Julian's. I had no idea if Hunter was even still alive as Mom held him.

Gently laying him at Connor's feet, Mom pleaded, "Please, let my daughter go now."

Connor couldn't hear her, but I was sure he understood what she was saying. Pushing the blade deeper into my neck, he spat out, "I'm not going anywhere until he's recovered."

Sitting back on her hip, Halina cocked a smile. "Well, that may be a problem, since I got a little carried away. Barring some miracle, he's going to die any minute."

I closed my eyes for a second, both relieved that he was still living, and despaired that he was moments from dying. Connor, not having heard her, barked out, "I said, save him! Or I shove this through her windpipe!"

Halina blinked, then looked around. "None of us are doctors with blood bags at the ready. What exactly do you want us to do? Speed him to a hospital ... so he can die there? It's too late for him!"

Seeing her clear bewilderment, an enraged Connor pointed at the body at his feet. "I know he's dying! I know nothing can be done to revive him! So, do what your bloody kind is meant to do, and bring him back! Turn him, now!"

I felt the madness in Connor's voice. Whatever hold he'd been keeping on his sanity, seeing his son's prostrate body had clearly pushed him over the edge. I doubt he was even cognizant of what he was asking my grandmother to do. He just wanted his son back, regardless of the price. I understood; I wanted him back, too, but I couldn't believe that Connor, a devout hunter of our species, would truly consider vampirism as a viable solution to death.

Halina's face was paler than I'd ever seen as she shook her head. "No ..." she whispered.

THE NEXT GENERATION

The knife in my throat jerked backward, and a sheet of blood flowed down my throat. Too scared to cry out, I sucked in a deep breath and held it. I didn't want to move a centimeter, lest it be my last.

"Do it!" Connor yelled. "Or I slice open the girl and move on to the boy. Think you can kill me before I kill them both?"

"Just give him what he wants," Dad begged, his eyes watery.

Halina snapped her head to Dad. "I don't change people—ever!" Her expression softened. "This is not a life I pass on."

Dad swallowed as he nodded. "I know ... but he'll kill Nika if you don't. None of us are fast enough to prevent it. You know I'm right. Just give him what he wants."

Halina stared at the body at her feet. Tears clouded my vision, then streamed down my cheeks. I didn't want this. I didn't want him to die, either, but this ... ? Being forced to be something he hated for ... eternity? He wouldn't want this. He'd rather be dead than undead. With the knife pressing on my vocal cords, I didn't dare voice my opinion. My tears spoke for me ... and so did Julian.

When Halina bent down to Hunter's side, he took a step forward. Connor tensed in anticipation, but my brother wasn't paying attention to Connor. He was focused purely on Halina. "Don't," he whispered. "Nika doesn't want this." His eyes flashed to mine. "She'd rather die for him, than condemn him for all eternity."

Halina growled and Julian looked back at her. Fangs bared, she held out her wrist. Under the snowy skin, I could see the bulging veins flowing with pure vampire blood. "Trust me," she murmured, "he won't get an eternity." Her eyes narrowed. "But no child of mine is going to die today."

With that, she tore into her body, exposing her blood. Eyes locked on Connor's, she brought the gaping wound to Hunter's lips. When his mouth filled, he instinctively swallowed. The sound broke my heart. It was done. He'd turn now. He'd be forced into darkness, into shadows. There was no cure for vampirism. He'd hate himself. He'd hate me ...

As Hunter gulped more and more of Halina's blood, her pausing on occasion to reopen the wound at her wrist, reason seemed to return to Connor. Releasing the knife's tension at my throat, he muttered, "Dear God ... what have I done?"

Dad moved an inch to the left, and Connor's rigidness returned. The knife bit into my flesh, and I forced myself to not cry out. Dad held up his hands, then pointed to Ben's body. "I just want to check on my friend."

Connor must have nodded, for Dad continued moving toward Ben. Eyes wide, I watched my father squat next to the fallen hero. Dad tilted his head, listening, then placed a couple of fingers along his jugular. Anxious, Mom whispered, "Is he okay, Teren? I can't hear his heartbeat." There was a lot of blood on the floor around Ben. I didn't see how anyone could survive a head shot like that, but I also couldn't imagine Ben dead. He'd been a fixture in my life for too long.

Face grim, Dad looked up at Mom. "It's there ... barely." He swung his head to Connor. "We gave you what you asked for, now please, let my daughter go, and let us take him to a hospital."

Connor's grip on me tightened as he considered Dad's proposal. Halina, finished with her assignment, stood and licked the blood from her closing wound. Her pale eyes burned holes into the man holding me captive, and her fangs were still extended. She seemed a little steadier than she was at the motel. I figured that the massive amount of human blood she'd drank tonight was the reason.

Lying prone at her feet, Hunter looked the same as before. Well, no, he did look a little different. There was no slight rise and fall to his chest anymore, no involuntary muscle twitches. He was stone still ... dead. Tears ran down my cheeks.

Connor's free hand pointed at his son's body. "Why isn't he waking up? Why isn't it working?"

His music was still blaring through his headphones, keeping his mind protected from my grandmother's hypnotizing words. Realizing this, Halina lifted her wrist, miming like she was checking the time on a watch. "It is not instant, you imbecile. Pureblood conversions take time."

She showed him her fingers, curled them, then reopened them. She repeated the process, only flashing four fingers. Twenty-four. That was how long Hunter's conversion would take. Connor understood her game of charades. Of course, he had probably known that all along, having come from a generations-old vampire-slaying family. Indicating outside, he told her, "I need to speak with your nestmates ..." he tapped his ear, "so you need to leave."

Halina rolled her eyes. "I won't compel you." A small smirk was on her lips after she said it, and I knew she was lying.

Connor couldn't hear her, but he got the gist of what she was saying, and he also questioned her sincerity. With more force, he reiterated, "Leave! Or I add one more lifeless body to this room!"

Mom grabbed Halina's elbow. "Halina ... please? Teren and I can handle this. You and Gabriel take Ben to a hospital." She swallowed, and her voice warbled. "He's going to die, Halina, for us ... and he's sacrificed so much already. We owe him."

Halina looked back at Ben, her eyes compassionate. They hardened again as her head snapped to Connor. "*He* does not get to walk away from this," she snarled.

"He won't," Dad whispered, his eyes locked on Halina's.

Halina appraised her grandson for a moment, then nodded. Giving Connor a warning hiss, she slinked her way over to Ben. Connor watched her apprehensively, his body tight with tension. Halina effortlessly scooped Ben into her arms, then backed toward the exit. Stepping next to Gabriel, she gave Connor an icy glare.

In Russian she told him, *"After my grandson kills you, I am going to pull off your head, place it on a platter of fine china, and rest it on my nightstand. Every night before I retire, I will smile at your vacant eyes, knowing you are no more."*

Gabriel's lip twitched as he followed Halina out the door. I felt Halina's presence streaking away, getting Ben some much needed help. I prayed that he made it ... that we all made it.

Julian turned to Connor once she was away. "She's gone."

The rock music abruptly ended, and Connor let out a long exhale. "I'm assuming none of you can control people's minds ... otherwise the girl would have compelled my son ages ago."

Dad stood. "Her name is Nika, and she's only sixteen years old." Carefully avoiding the pool of Ben's blood on the floor, Dad made his way toward me. I wanted to reach out for him, but the metal pressed into my neck frightened me so much, I couldn't even lift a pinky. "Your son will live now. Please let her go."

"Live? Is that what you call it?" Connor's voice was full of despair, but my well of sympathy for him had run dry a while ago.

Dad reached out a hand for me. "If you give her to me, I'll let you leave with your son. You have my word."

Disbelief flowed into me from Julian. Underneath my mountain of fear, I felt the same way. Dad had told Halina that Connor wouldn't get to walk away. Dad was either lying to Connor right now, or he'd purposely misled Halina so she would leave. I wasn't positive which direction he was headed, but by the sincerity on his face, I was guessing that he really was going to let Connor leave. Halina was going to be pissed.

Connor's tone was hard when he responded. "Your word? What good is the word of a monster?"

Dad clenched his jaw. "I'm no more monster than you. But when I give my word ... I keep it. You and your son are free to leave." Dad glanced over at Mom. She was scowling, but she nodded. She wouldn't go against Dad's act of amnesty.

Slowly, I felt the sting of the knife retreating. The warmth of fresh blood trickled down my neck as I inhaled a deep breath of relief. My initial reaction was to turn and strike Connor in the nose with my elbow, but I knew how dangerous he was, and I wasn't about to risk getting knifed in the stomach. I'd had enough of knives ... and arrows ... and guns. I'd had enough of violence. I never wanted to see blood again, and that was saying a lot, considering how much I loved the stuff.

Julian's arms were instantly around me when Connor backed away. The relief coursing from my brother nearly drowned me, but I buried my head in his shoulder, grateful and tired. Mom urged us both to back out the door with her, but my eyes were transfixed on Hunter's body. I was assaulted by memories of his warm smile, of the sunlight reflecting in his dark eyes. He would never again feel the heat of the afternoon sun on his body. His favorite time of day was now forbidden to him, along with silver ... and food.

He would live in a world of deceit now, where he was forced to lie to every person he encountered. Then again, he was born and raised to be a vampire hunter ... he'd been lying to people for a while. But he would live in a world of thirst, where blood ruled his senses. The urge to drink was pretty mellow for my family and me, another one of the benefits of having diluted blood, but to Hunter, a newborn pureblood, the desire for blood would be profound. Especially when he first woke up.

I lifted my head and stared at Connor inching his way to his son, his knife protectively held in front of him. "He'll need to eat right away," I murmured, my voice scratchy, my throat feeling bruised. Connor snapped his eyes to mine. He paused as I continued. "If you want him to live ... he'll need to eat as soon as he wakes up. And he'll be hungry, *really* hungry, so if *you* want to live, you better have something ready for him."

My eyes drifted to my father. The story of Dad's conversion was legend in our home. It was a horrific warning of what could happen to my brother and me if we walked into our own conversions overconfident. There were some things about our lives, about our bodies, that needed to be handled with the greatest of care and planning. Conversions were at the top of that list; they were not to be taken lightly.

Connor's face paled as he looked down at his vampire son. His words reverberated in my mind: *Dear God ... what have I done?* I couldn't help but think the exact same thing.

Eyeing my mother and father, Connor tucked his knife back into his belt, bent down to retrieve his discarded gun, and then picked up his son. He didn't have our super-strength, so it took him a moment to lift him. Once he was carrying Hunter, he cautiously made his way toward the door. He passed close by me, and I absentmindedly reached out to stroke Hunter's cheek; it was cool to the touch.

Connor hesitated, and I peeked up at his face. His eyes were brimming, the earlier madness in them gone. His hope seemed gone, too, as he held his limp child. Swallowing my grief, I leaned over and placed a light kiss on Hunter's forehead.

"Goodbye, Hunter," I whispered, not sure if he could hear me. "I'll always love you."

Tears fell on Connor's cheeks as he carried his son away from me.

CHAPTER TWENTY-TWO

Julian

MY SISTER WAS barely holding it together. Her neck ached, her shoulder throbbed, her arm burned, but the hole in her heart was more excruciating than any of those pains. She watched her boyfriend being carried away from her with stoic resolve, but she couldn't hide her feelings from me. She was wrecked, physically and emotionally.

After Hunter and his dad were gone, Mom and Dad cautiously made their way over to Nika. "Honey ... you okay?"

Nika turned her head to answer Mom, but instead of speech escaping her lips, her knees buckled.

My arms were already around her, and I cinched her tight to keep her from crashing to the floor. Her head dropped back as she lost consciousness. I wasn't sure if her injuries had finally pulled her under, or if she'd finally snapped from the strain. Either way, I swooped her into my arms as Mom felt her forehead.

"She's hot ... does she feel hot?" Mom twisted to Dad.

Dad felt her forehead, too, but shrugged. "She always feels hot to us, Emma." His expression grave, he lifted his eyes to mine. "We need to get her to a hospital ... have that arrow removed." He paused, then added, "And check on Ben."

A solemnity filled the church as we all looked at the bloodstain on the floor ... Ben's blood. Halina would have to send someone out here to clean it up. I wasn't sure why that thought popped into my head. I guess concealment was so ingrained in me that covering things up was instinct now. If only those instincts had served me better earlier, when I'd decided to let my guard down at that Halloween party, then maybe I wouldn't be staring at a puddle of blood on a once-pristine tile floor.

The three of us dashed away with Nika moments later. Dad unlocked Grandpa's truck, and I gently laid Nika down on the back seat. She cringed as her shoulder compressed against the seat, but the stress and exhaustion had a firm hold on her, and she didn't wake up. I folded her knees to make room for me, then sat beside her.

Dad started the truck and we drove to the hospital. We could have chosen to forgo the truck, zipping there in seconds with our super-speed, but Nika wasn't in mortal danger ... and I didn't think any of us wanted to return to this spot once we left. Now that the library was receding in the rearview mirror, I knew I didn't feel like ever going there again, and I had to believe my parents felt the same way.

The hospital was quiet when we pulled into the lot. That surprised me for some reason. I guess so much had happened in the past several hours, I expected everyone else's lives to be equally turbulent. But no patients were waiting in the emergency room when we walked in.

The nurse on duty did a double take when she noticed Nika snuggled in my father's arms; most people probably walked in on their own accord. My sister was still out, though. That was probably a good thing, since she would've been really anxious about what they were going to do to her if she'd been awake. Even though it was a little selfish of me, I was grateful that I wasn't feeling her anxiety. I was wound up enough on my own.

I was still reeling over what had just happened. She'd turned him. My grandmother was adamantly against turning anyone ... and she'd turned Hunter. True, she hadn't had a choice—Nika's life had been on the line, and maybe mine too—but still ... turning someone into a vampire went against everything Halina believed. Even if I couldn't feel her emotions, I knew she had to be sick to her stomach over her actions.

Halina loved us, and loved our family, and I think she even loved her life, but she viewed vampirism as a curse, a plague, a weed that we were trying to purge from our family tree. I never thought I'd see the day when Halina put another pureblood on Earth. And a hunter to boot. I had no idea what a vampire hunter turned vampire would do, but from Halina's ominous last words before she'd turned him, I was certain she wasn't going to let him do very much. Hunter wasn't going to have a long afterlife. Nika was going to lose him twice. And she knew it ... that was why she'd made sure to say goodbye at the church.

It didn't take long for Nika to be checked in and assessed. She started to wake up when the nurse began examining her injuries. "How did this happen?" the severe-faced woman asked us, indicating the arrow shaft.

Dad's face showed only concern for his daughter, as he told the nurse, "Hunting accident." For once, he wasn't lying; only, we were the prey, so it wasn't really an accident.

The nurse pursed her lips but didn't offer any additional comment. I wasn't sure if she believed my dad, but it *was* an arrow in Nika's shoulder, and what other explanation was there for getting shot with an arrow?

Nika stirred as her jacket was cut away from the wound. "Mom? Dad? Where am I?" she muttered, squinting her eyes.

Mom and Dad quickly glanced at each other, then Mom laid her hand on Nika's arm. "You're at the hospital, dear ... and your mother is on her way. *Teren* and I are here with you and your brother ..."

Mom stressed Dad's name, subtly reminding Nika, and me, that we were back in the real world, and our "scripted" personas had to be put back on. Nika and Julian Adams were the offspring of Starla Adams, and our father was dead; Dad had called Starla while we were checking in Nika, and she was coming down here to sign the admittance forms.

Nika frowned as she looked at Dad. "Oh ..." Then she winced and bit her lip to try and contain her agony; it washed through me, tightening my stomach.

"Stop, you're hurting her," I snapped at the merciless nurse who was now cutting Nika's T-shirt away from the arrow. I tried to calm my expression when she looked up at me, but Nika's pain was flashing through me in waves, and I couldn't stop cringing.

The woman in scrubs didn't seem sympathetic as she returned her attentions to Nika; she almost seemed ready to kick me out of the room, since, to her eyes, I looked to be bothered by the gory sight. "The doctor needs to be able to see the injury to know how to best proceed." She paused, considering. "But I'll get her something for the pain."

She swiveled her stool around and left the room. Nika let out a low groan, and I squeezed her hand. Her moist eyes locked onto mine, grateful. Dad looked at us thoughtfully for a moment, then twisted to Mom. "Once she's taken care of, I want to go check on Ben."

Mom gave him a solemn nod. I could feel Halina's presence upstairs. She was most likely close to Ben, awaiting his outcome. I fervently hoped he survived ... and wondered if maybe one of us should call his wife.

Halina was pacing, and I figured she was torn between sticking to her assignment and rushing to us. Eventually, her desire to make sure we were safe superseded her sense of duty. When the nurse came back with Nika's drugs, Halina stormed into the room. The nurse looked over her shoulder and snipped, "There are too many people in here. Why don't you wait in the lobby?" Snatching Nika's hand from me, she shoved an IV needle into a vein. Nika hissed in a sharp breath.

Halina narrowed her eyes. "I'm fine here ... and be gentler with her."

The nurse instantly obeyed Halina's command, softening her touch when she resumed cleaning and preparing the wound. Nika relaxed as the IV medicine kicked in. I felt it, too, and my head started to swim a little. I pushed it back as best I could.

Dad stood and faced Halina. "Ben?" he asked in a hushed voice.

Halina looked at the floor. "He's ... They're still working on him. The bullet ran along the edge of his skull, but didn't penetrate his brain. They're removing it, but ... he lost a lot of blood." Eyes shimmering with red tears, Halina shook her head. "His heart stopped on the table more than once. The last time it did, they had trouble reviving him."

The nurse heard Halina and twisted to look up at her. "They're still working on him? The doctors don't usually give updates until the patient is off the table. How do you know all that?"

Halina let out an exasperated grunt. "Because I can hear almost everything that's happening in this damn hospital, from the person with the incessant cough down the hall, to the couple having sex in the on-call room. It's infuriating, having to weed through all the crap to hear the things that I *need* to hear ... especially when they're not things I *want* to hear! So, quit eavesdropping on my conversation and get a doctor in here to pull out that goddamn arrow!"

The nurse immediately fled the room. Halina closed her eyes and squeezed her hands into fists. My eyes were huge as I stared at her. I'd never heard her go off on someone before. She was having a rough night, and was understandably on edge, but, damn ... Thank God she wasn't mad at me.

Starting to get a little high, Nika giggled while everyone stared at Halina. Opening her eyes, Halina glanced up at the ceiling. "I know ... I'll take care of it," she muttered, her expression sullen. Mom and Dad looked at each other, small smiles on their faces. Gabriel must have said something admonishing to Halina, something my weaker hearing couldn't pick up.

Still on edge, Halina snapped her head to Dad. "What of the hunter and his ... son? Did you take care of them?"

While Dad didn't look away from Halina, it was clear by his expression that he didn't want to answer her. He did, albeit very slowly. "I let him go."

Halina didn't like Dad's answer. Zipping over to him, she grabbed his neck and lifted him into the air with one hand. I glanced at the door, but a privacy curtain was in place and no one could see the super-human act. "He was not supposed to leave that church alive, Teren! I thought you understood that, or I wouldn't have left you in charge!"

Dad kicked his feet and tried to remove her fingers from his throat, but he couldn't break free from the pissed-off pureblood. I was sure he couldn't breathe ... not that he needed to.

"Halina! Knock it off! The children ..."

Mom indicated us watching Halina manhandle our father. Nika giggled, cooing in a sing-song voice, "Daddy's in trouble ..." Slightly buzzed by the painkillers flowing through my sister, I snorted.

Halina reluctantly lowered our father to the floor. He backed away from her, massaging his neck. "I didn't have a choice! He wasn't going to let Nika go without some assurance that I would let him take his son!"

Halina gave him a dry look. "Then you give him whatever assurance you need to ... and you rip his heart out while he's walking away."

Dad straightened his stance and raised his chin. "When I give my word, I keep it."

THE NEXT GENERATION

Halina stepped up to him. Voice low and menacing, she snapped, "Then whatever blood he spills from here on out is on *your* hands!"

Dad's jaw tightened. "I know," he told her, a quaver in his voice.

Halina looked over Dad's stoic but tortured face. Her expression softening, she placed a hand on his cheek and spoke to him in her native language. *"I'm sorry for the choice you had to make. I would not have made the same one ... but that is why I love you so much. You're a far better person than I'll ever be."*

Dad nodded, a slight smile touching his lips. Frowning, Halina dropped her hand and placed her fingers on her stomach. "I apologize for being ... on edge. It's this feeling. I can't stop ... worrying."

Putting a hand on her shoulder, Dad said, "It's natural. Nika's hurt, the hunters are still out there, and Ben's ..." His throat closed, and he swallowed.

Halina shook her head. "No, that's not what I'm ..." Blue eyes pale and wide, Halina grabbed both of Dad's forearms. "I'm worried for the child."

Dad furrowed his brows, not following her. I didn't either. Nika's high was slowing down my brain, making it hard to concentrate. Did Halina mean Nika when she said child? Because aside from being pumped full of endorphins, Nika was fine. I was fairly certain the doctors would be able to remove the arrow shaft and seal her up. Or did Halina know something I didn't about arrow injuries? Should I be more concerned about my sister's health?

Halina looked around the room, seemingly at a loss as to how to explain herself. Oddly, my drugged sister was the one who came up with the answer. "Ah, she's worried about Hunter. How sweet." She giggled again, and everyone shifted to stare at her, then Halina.

"You're worried about the ... vampire?" Dad whispered.

Halina bit her lip and nodded. Another figure blurred into the room, and Halina spun to face him. "I don't understand, Gabriel. Why can't I stop thinking about him? Why am I concerned? Why am I ... scared?"

Gabriel surveyed the room, assessing Nika's condition and my pseudo-high with his scientific eyes as he casually answered my grandmother. "You sired him, dear." His eyes returned to hers. "That creates a permanent bond between you."

Dad snapped his head to Mom. I watched them while my mind tried to hold onto Gabriel's words. Halina was now bonded with my sister's boyfriend. She'd be able to feel his presence, just like she could with our family ... and I supposed, we'd be able to as well, since he had our family's blood in him. But a sire bond was a little different than the familial bond we shared. When Dad had sired Mom, their bond had driven them to be together; even now, they got kind of a high when they came near each other. God, was Halina going to get buzzed by being around Hunter now? Nika wasn't going to like this.

Looking back at Gabriel, Dad shook his head. "But Starla told us the sire bond varied in strength. That it depended on the connection between the pairing pre-turning. It was strong for Emma and me in the beginning because we were married, deeply in love before Emma changed." He pointed at Halina. "She doesn't even know Hunter. She shouldn't feel anything for him."

Gabriel shrugged, "While what Starla said is true, the strength of the bond is also dependent upon the individual." Walking up to Halina, Gabriel grabbed her hand. "And you, my dear, have a deep place in your heart for children, for *all* children. And Hunter is now essentially your child. I could be wrong about this, but I believe your feelings for him will rival your feelings for your own daughter."

Halina's mouth dropped open. "This was *not* supposed to happen." She shook her head; her long, black locks swirled around her, enhancing her frustration. "I was going to turn him, then kill him!" She gasped, holding a hand to her heart. "I can't, Gabriel. I can't kill him." Anger flooded her features. "And if his idiot father doesn't take proper care of him, he's going to die tomorrow night!" Her mouth set in a hard line, and her entire body stiffened with tension. "He should be with me! I can feed him. I care take care of him." Her lip trembled. "I can't lose him, Gabriel ..."

A bloody tear rolled down her cheek, and Gabriel wiped it away. Enfolding her in his arms, he rested his head on hers. "I know, love."

Our room was quiet after that. I could hear activity in the rooms beside me; another patient had been brought in, an orderly was complaining about mopping up vomit, and a nurse was cussing out a doctor for being too busy in the on-call room to remove an arrow from a poor teenage girl who'd been in a hunting accident. I flushed a little, remembering Halina's earlier comment, then, still high off my sister, I chuckled to myself.

When the doctor finally arrived, and Nika was whisked away (and the nurse's memory was modified), our group shuffled off to wait for both of our hurt family members to recover ... assuming they would. Halina paced while she waited, her anxiety over Hunter too great to contain.

With Nika farther away from me, some clarity returned. I still couldn't wrap my mind around the change in my grandmother. Just hours ago, she'd been dead-set on ending Hunter's life, and now she was more worried about his conversion than Ben's surgery. Was Hunter really going to be as important to her as Imogen? That seemed bizarre to me. Those two were almost best friends more than mother and daughter ... how would Hunter fit in? Would he feel the same way toward Halina?

There were so many unknowns about this that it boggled me. I was having a hard time picturing anything but the man who'd fired a gun on my father. But, I supposed I needed to stop seeing him that way. Hunter wasn't that person anymore. He was a vampire now, a pureblood vampire. Everything was different.

We received news that Ben was stable and in recovery right as Starla and Jacen arrived at the hospital. Mom and Dad went to check on Ben, while I went downstairs to greet my "mother" so she could formally sign in Nika.

Gabriel came down with me to see Starla, and her face lit up when she saw that he was all right. Turning from the nurses' desk, she ran over to Gabriel and slung her arms around him. He held her back, his hand patting her reassuringly. "Father," she gushed, "I'm so glad you weren't hurt."

As her grip tightened, the smile on Gabriel's face shifted to a frown. "No, I made it out unscathed, but others didn't." His blond head lifted to where Ben was unconsciously resting.

Starla pulled back at hearing his tone. She nodded, her face, for once, remorseful. "I heard about Ben, I'm so sorry."

Gabriel nodded, then his smile returned and he cupped her cheek. "Your face brings me joy, child." He kissed her head. "I am glad to see you in one piece." His emerald eyes swung over to Jacen. "Both of you."

Jacen smiled and nodded. The poor nurse on duty didn't appear to know how to take in the dynamics of my expanded family. She kept looking between Starla and Jacen and Gabriel. She had to have noticed that Starla and Jacen were an item when they came in together. Even though the two were similar enough to be related, they were usually affectionate enough that it was clear they weren't. But with how Gabriel was holding Starla, it must seem like they were together too. And the fact that both men looked twenty-something and Starla was creeping up on forty didn't help. To the nurse's eyes, Starla had two younger men wrapped around her finger. Considering both men's actual ages, that was pretty laughable.

When Starla finished with Gabriel, she walked over to me. "Hey, Julian. You all right, kid?"

I nodded, then frowned. "Nika got hurt ..." I knew she was already aware of that fact, but I couldn't stop myself from saying it. From what I could tell of Nika's emotions, she was still feeling no pain. They were keeping her pretty medicated while they worked on her shoulder; her exhaustion made me a little sleepy, or perhaps that was my own. Sometimes it was hard to tell.

Starla's face softened as she took in my expression. "Yeah ... I heard." Thinking of something, she said, "You can feel everything she feels, right?" I nodded, and she asked me a question that no one else had. "So, you felt her pain all night?" I nodded again, and she frowned. "God, that bond sucks. Father needs to do something about that soon." She rubbed my arm in sympathy, and I smiled.

It wasn't too much later that Nika was all patched up. I carefully put my arms around her as she lay in her bed, recovering. Still a little groggy from the pain meds, she blinked up at me. "Ben?" she asked, her throat dry.

Mom and Dad sat on the other side of her bed. Grabbing her hand, Dad reassuringly told her, "He'll be fine, honey. Don't worry."

I wanted to believe that, but there had been a touchy moment with Ben not too long ago. Alarms had gone off and nurses had rushed in. I'd been outside his room at the time, waiting while Starla and Jacen had checked on him. There had been so much chaos. His room had been cleared out, and a bunch of medical jargon had stung my ears while the frantic staff had tried to keep his heart going. Eventually, they got him back, but I was still on edge, waiting to hear those alarms again. The next time they went off ... he might not come back.

Mom and Dad were checking on Nika when it happened, but they knew about it; they'd been listening. None of that showed on Dad's face as he patted his daughter's hand. She weakly clenched his. If she were more alert, she might have caught the slight crease of Mom's brow, but Nika

THE NEXT GENERATION

was too tired and closed her eyes. Her peace flowed into me, and I tried to let the horrible evening slip from me. I yawned.

Dad looked over at me, then up to Starla and Jacen standing with Halina and Gabriel. "Will you take him home? We'll stay here with Nika."

Halina nodded, but I shook my head, wide awake now. Staring at my limp sister, a bandage over her neck, another around her arm, and a huge piece of white gauze on her shoulder, I knew I couldn't leave her. She'd endured so much tonight. Our bond was stronger the closer together we were. I had to stay with her, to give her my strength. I'd promised her that we were together until the very end, and I wouldn't leave her now. "No, Dad, I'm not—"

Dad's mouth set in a parental line of rigidness. "I'm not arguing this with you. You're exhausted, you need rest, and your sister needs rest. You can return after school."

Shock hit me like a brick wall. "I have to go to school? Are you serious? What about ... ?" I flung my hands to the window, indicating the maniac who was still out there.

Dad inhaled a deep, calming breath. "He's ... preoccupied with his situation. I don't expect him to be a problem for a while." His eye line returned to Gabriel's, and his face asked a question while his tone gave an order. "Keep him safe."

Gabriel gave him one curt nod in answer, and Dad relaxed. Fury built in me. It was so unfair! I should be allowed to stay. She was my sister, my bonded twin. They couldn't make me leave her side. They couldn't make me do anything. I was sixteen years old, practically a man! Dad should understand that. I mean, he'd almost fathered a kid when he was my age!

Exhaustion, anger, and fear all swirled within me. I wasn't sure if I had a good argument, but I was going to start in on it. Especially when Dad looked back down to Nika, effectively dismissing me. I sat up straight on the bed and opened my mouth to start ranting. That was when Nika touched my face.

I looked down at her instead. Her eyes begged me to relax as she sent calm feelings my way. "It's okay, Julian. You're on edge, you're tired ... go rest. I'll be fine ..." Her eyes fluttered closed, and her hand dropped from my skin.

My anger melted away as I looked down on my brave, heartbroken sister. I couldn't deny her request, not now. Glumly, I looked back at Dad.

"Fine," I sulked. I might have to leave, but I didn't have to be peppy about it. Especially since I had to go to freaking school in a few hours. You would think being involved in a drive-by, getting shot at with arrows, being held hostage, and being awake for the past forty-eight hours would buy a person a few days off.

I left with Halina and Gabriel not long after that. Starla and Jacen left, too, following behind Grandpa's truck in Starla's sporty car. It felt strange to leave my immediate family behind. After everything we'd been through tonight, their presence being stretched from me was unnerving. And Nika was right, I was on edge. Having multiple attempts made on your life did that to a person.

It was getting close to dawn when we got back to the seedy motel. Arianna's mom's minivan was parked outside the door when we pulled up. Surprisingly, it looked exactly as it had pre-bullet holes. I marveled at how quickly and easily my grandmother's compulsion had taken care of that little problem. I also wondered if Dad was correct—had the mechanic nearly worked himself to death to fix this thing?

Everyone greeted me when I stepped out of the truck. Imogen and Alanna inspected me for injuries, but aside from the few grazes I received during the shoot-out, I was fine. As Grandpa Jack warmly enclosed me in a hug, I spotted Arianna. She was standing in the motel room doorframe, biting her lip. Her eyes were red, and she looked on the verge of losing it. I furrowed my brow, trying to understand why she looked so upset. Had something happened?

When my family backed off, I took a step toward her. "Arianna? You oka—"

I didn't get a chance to finish my question. She barreled into me, tossing her arms around me like she was trying to prevent me from falling off a sheer cliff face. Burying her head into my neck, she exhaled, "Thank God ... I was so worried about you."

Warmth burst through my chest, and as I protectively wrapped my arms around her, something else opened inside me. Feelings I'd been masking, blocking, all tumbled out. I couldn't contain them anymore. I didn't want to. I felt the fog lifting from me, and I suddenly understood everything I'd been confused about.

I liked her. Truly, deeply, I wanted-to-be-with-her liked her.

It was so painfully clear to me now that I didn't understand how I'd missed it earlier. I guess I'd been holding onto Raquel for so long that I'd convinced myself I couldn't like anyone else. But that was ridiculous. Of course I could. Especially since Raquel had never shown me more than the slightest glimmer of hope that she might care for me. Arianna had never tried to hide her feelings. And she'd never played games with me. She'd always cared about me, and even after learning what I really was, she still cared about me.

I kissed her head and breathed in her comfort. "I was worried about you too," I murmured.

She pulled back to look at me, her eyes soft with warmth. "You were?"

She looked about to ask me more, but Trey bounded up to us, clapping my shoulder and inadvertently breaking us apart. "So, you guys put down the baddies?" He looked around, his grin dropping. "Where's Nika?"

My head fell forward as I felt my sister. "She ..."

Arianna's eyes watered, and I couldn't finish telling her about her best friend's injuries. She understood my expression. "Is she going to be okay?" I nodded, and she asked, "Did Hunter hurt her?"

I shook my head to tell her no, right as Halina walked up to me. "Come, Julian. We're taking everyone back to your house in the city." Her pale eyes scanned the sky. "I can't stay here, and Teren is right, we'll be safe. Hunter's father has too much to do to worry about us right now ..." Her voice trailed off, and she chewed on her lip. It was clear by the look on her face that she would love to be with Hunter instead of leaving him with his father.

I nodded at her, and her dark head twisted to my friends. "I suppose I should clean them now."

Trey looked down at himself, inspecting his clothes. Arianna looked back at me, a question in her eyes. With great sorrow, I supplied her with an answer. "Clean your mind of any knowledge of what happened tonight."

Clutching my hand, Arianna shook her head. "No, I want to remember."

Halina curled a corner of her lip in an expression that clearly said she didn't really care what Arianna wanted ... she had a job to do. I stepped in front of Arianna, blocking her from Halina. "She's accepted us, and she won't say anything. Please, Grandma ... let her keep her memories. Let her know what I am."

Halina examined the dark clouds above us. "I don't have time to argue this with you, Julian. You know the rules."

In Russian, I quickly told her, *"But I want to be with her. You've always allowed people our family was dating to know ... so long as it was going well. And, I want ... to date her. I want to see if I could have a future ... with her. Who knows ... maybe we'll give you children one day."* My cheeks felt red-hot, but now wasn't the time to beat around the bush. I had to be blunt with her.

Halina answered me in her native tongue. I felt my other grandmothers staring, but I ignored them. *"You think you might continue the line with this one?"*

I shrugged as I shook my head. *"I don't know ... but I'd like the freedom to find out—with her knowing everything. Just like Mom and Dad."*

Halina raised an eyebrow, then nodded. *"All right, Julian. So long as she is your potential mate ... I will not take her mind."*

Smiling, I nodded. "Thank you."

She paused a moment, then added, *"But if you end the relationship, even amicably, I will wipe her. And I'll take it all, Julian. She won't even remember you."*

Tears in my eyes, I nodded again. All or nothing, that was what she was offering me ... and I would take it. Guilt poured into me as I thought of my sister. I'd just given her an all-or-nothing relationship with Arianna too. If things ended between us, and Halina wiped her mind of me, she'd surely wipe her mind of Nika as well. We'd both lose her. I really hoped Arianna wanted this.

Arianna had a questioning tilt to her head when Halina turned away from me. "What was that about?"

With a nonchalant half-shrug I told her, "Nothing." My heart was beating harder as she stared at me. Her hazel eyes were drinking me in, the disbelief in them obvious. Tucking a golden-brown strand of hair behind her ear, she said in a droll voice, "Nothing? You were having a conversation in Russian over nothing?"

I blinked. "You knew that was Russian?"

She nodded. "This lady my mom knows speaks it, so I recognize the accent. Why do you speak it? And what were you saying?"

I rubbed my chin, not sure what to tell her, when I suddenly noticed that Halina was talking to Trey ... and he was hanging on her every word. "When we get to Julian's house, you won't remember anything that happened tonight. You won't remember anything odd happening at school. You won't remember anything about vampires, or being shot at, or hiding out in a motel. In your mind, you went to visit Julian after school, got tired, and spent the night. You spent the evening playing video games and ... looking through women's underwear ads."

Trey's lips lifted into a smile, but his eyes remained dazed and dreamy. My mouth was agape when Halina finished with him and twisted my way. "You wiped him? Why?"

Icy blue eyes flicked up and down my body. "You're not going to date him, and Nika will never be interested in that one." She closed her eyes for a minute and shook her head. "Plus, he's a chatty teenage pothead ... not exactly a secure vault." She lifted an eyebrow. "And our secrets must stay secret."

Halina's eyes drilled holes into Arianna. Arianna clenched my hand tight, but bravely nodded. "I wouldn't say anything, ever."

Resting a chilly hand on her shoulder, Halina leaned in and whispered, "I know you won't."

A shudder went down Arianna's spine as Halina walked over to Gabriel. She slung her arms around his waist and pulled him toward Grandpa's truck. While she had mostly recovered from her exposure to silver, she still seemed a little off her game to me—a little slower, a little stiffer—but still a force to be reckoned with. As I watched Halina get into the vehicle, I was both irritated and relieved. I supposed one friend keeping their memory was better than neither friend. And ... Arianna was sort of my girlfriend now in Halina's eyes. Crap. I should probably ask her out. My palms started sweating. Hopefully Arianna wouldn't notice.

Arianna relaxed as I pulled her to the minivan. "So ... Trey really won't remember tonight?"

I let out a weary exhale as we passed by the perfectly repaired door. "No, as soon as we get to my house, he'll think nothing out of the ordinary happened."

Arianna frowned as she opened the driver's side door. "And there's nothing you can do?"

I shrugged as she climbed inside the minivan. "Aside from tell him again?" I paused as I thought for a second. "Or never go home?" Glancing over at the truck, I saw that Halina had heard me. She narrowed her eyes in warning, and I quickly turned back to Arianna. "No ... once you're tranced, you're tranced."

Arianna examined the wheel before looking over at Trey getting into the second row. He seemed completely oblivious to the fact that soon he wouldn't remember tonight. She returned her eyes to mine; they were slightly moist. "Did she do that to me? Will I forget?"

Her eyes searched mine, and my pulse quickened. The dome light cast a soft glow on her hair as it backlit her face. She was so beautiful ... how did I miss that? Shoving my hands into my pockets, I kicked a rock on the cement. "Ah, no ... she won't ... do anything ... as long as ..." I peeked up at her, a small smile on my lips, "If you'll go out with me ... if you'll be my girlfriend, then you can remember." My words came out a little strangled, and I had to swallow the knot in my throat.

Arianna gave me a blank look, and I started to think she hadn't heard me. Then she said, "What about ... Raquel?"

Biting my lip, I wished I had the words to clearly explain how and why my feelings had shifted. Translating it into any kind of coherent speech seemed impossible. "I don't ... It's just ... Raquel will never accept me like you did. She'll never care about me like you do. I'll always be a 'maybe' to her, and I want more than that. I want to be with someone who likes me as much as I like them. I want my feelings to be ... reciprocated. And you ..." With a sigh, I lowered my gaze to the pavement. "I like you, Arianna. I think I've always liked you." I lifted my eyes to hers then. "I resisted it for so long ... But I'm done ignoring it, or brushing it off, or whatever the hell I was doing." Heart in my eyes, I shook my head. "I just really want to be with you, and I hope you want to be with me too."

I thought I might throw up while I waited for her to say something. As she wordlessly studied me, I saw myriad emotions pass through her eyes. *God, I'm so sorry I ever hurt you.* Like she heard my silent apology, she smiled, then nodded. "Okay, Julian ... we can date. But *just* date." My immediate joy faded, and I frowned. What did she mean by that. Seeing my confusion, Arianna explained. "I won't be your girlfriend. Not yet. But if all goes well, and I'm *completely* sure you're over her, then maybe, just maybe, I'll agree to be your girlfriend."

She gave a one-sided grin, full of teasing promise, then she leaned forward to kiss me. My heart soared as her lips met mine, and I melded into her skin. I was fine with dating first, and if I had to prove to her every day that I was over Raquel, then that was what I would spend every day doing. Gladly. I'd never felt such joy in a woman's arms, and knowing it was reciprocated—100 percent—made all the difference in the world.

Even though the night had been disastrous, I smiled the entire ride home. I wasn't even bothered by the fact that I had to go to school in a few hours. Once we got to our quaint Bavarian-style, two-story house, Arianna and I flopped onto the couch to watch a little TV before school. There really was no point in sleeping now, and I was too wired to sleep anyway. Trey wasn't, and passed out immediately on one of the other couches. It saddened me that he wouldn't remember ... that he'd already forgotten, but as I squeezed Arianna's hand, I took comfort in the fact that she still remembered, and more amazingly, she still wanted to be with me. And I wanted to be with her too.

A huge blanket was draped across the massive white couch that I was sitting on; its deep red color was the same shade as the blood it was covering. Halina's blood, from her night of being poisoned with silver. This couch would eventually have to be tossed. Seeing that I was safe and settled with my girl, Halina escaped to an underground cellar that Dad and Gabriel had put in for her. It wasn't as spacious and luxurious as her rooms back at the ranch, but it was better than sleeping in the ground. And while Halina had time to zip to the ranch before the sun came up, from the look on her face when she slipped away, it was clear she wanted to stay close to us tonight. Or, to be more accurate, today.

The rest of my tired family shuffled upstairs. Except Starla and Jacen. Once they received Gabriel's permission, they headed home. Gabriel stayed on the couch in the living room, watching me with curious, scientific eyes. I knew he was examining my bond with my sister. That was usually the reason for him studying us. He was fascinated with our connected feelings, and he was probably wondering exactly what I'd gone through tonight. Normally I'd talk to him about it, answer all his questions, but I was too emotionally tired, the stress too fresh. Being terrified, heartbroken, scared, and in pain was hard enough to face on your own. Having it amplified by my sister had been excruciating. But we'd done it, and we were fine now. Nika was resting peacefully, and I was content with Arianna by my side. All was well ... for now.

CHAPTER TWENTY-THREE

Julian

GOING TO SCHOOL was ... strange. So much had happened to me recently that it felt surreal to be on campus. And none of the students around seemed to realize just how climatic yesterday had been. Everyone was milling about, having conversations about mundane, trivial stuff. It was a kind of disheartening. I wanted someone to know, someone to care, someone to acknowledge just what my sister and I had gone through.

Arianna squeezed my hand as she leaned into my side. Looking down at her, I saw the encouragement in her eyes and remembered that, for the first time ever, I *did* have someone on the outside who knew, someone who cared. Smiling, I whispered, "I'm glad you know everything." My eyes indicated the school grounds, so she would understand what I meant.

Her green-brown eyes surveyed the students around us. Looking as shocked as I felt, she muttered, "It's so strange that they don't realize ..." Her mystified eyes returned to mine. "They all think a car backfired yesterday. None of them suspect ..." She didn't finish explaining, but her eyes spoke volumes.

Loving that I wasn't alone, I leaned down to briefly press my lips to hers. Her hand tightened in mine. As I pulled away from her, my shoulder was violently shoved. I glanced back to see a very confused Trey staring at me. "Dude? Are you two gettin' it on now?"

Arianna scoffed at Trey's comment while I rolled my eyes. "We're dating, if that's what you mean."

Trey's jaw dropped to his chest. "When the hell did that happen?"

Arianna and I looked at each other and laughed. When indeed. Glancing up at Trey, I muttered, "Don't worry about it, man."

He shrugged; it was already forgotten. "Where's Nika?" he asked, his bright and sober eyes searching for her.

Again, marveling at the power of compulsion, I told him she was sick, and it wasn't really a lie either. She *was* sick, in a way. Trey adjusted the backpack on his shoulder. I'd left mine in my dad's car at the ranch. I felt naked without it, and I knew I was going to get "talked to" in every class today for forgetting it. If the teachers only knew what had happened last night, they might understand, but I couldn't tell them, and I'd have to look like an idiot every period.

Trey's face sympathetic, he told me, "That sucks. Tell her I hope she gets better." He grinned. "We need her hot body back on campus."

Cringing, I pushed him away from me. "Dude, she's my sister."

Trey chuckled as he walked beside me. Arianna stared at him like he'd just sprouted wings. It must rock her to the core to witness the result of a mind wipe. I'd seen my grandmother steal memories my entire life. I was impressed by it, but I was used to it. I could tell it was going to take Arianna a while to get used to it.

As we approached the main building, a feeling of anticipation went through me. Recognizing it, I glanced to the side and instantly spotted Raquel. She was alone, walking to class by herself. Her head was down, and her dark sheet of hair obscured her face. I couldn't tell if she was happy or not, and … I wasn't as concerned about it as I used to be. Raquel's happiness wasn't up to me. And if she continued to stay with a man who made her miserable, well, I wouldn't let myself feel bad about it anymore. She'd made her choice, and I'd made mine, and while Raquel might regret her decision later in life, I felt great about my future.

Turning away from the sight of her, I focused on Arianna instead. She was watching Raquel, too, and when she looked up at me, her expression was guarded. Not wanting her to worry about that old obsession, I stopped, cupped her cheek, and leaned in for a nice, slow kiss. Trey slapped my back as he walked by and congratulated me on becoming a man ... which technically I wasn't, not in the way he meant anyway. Ignoring him, I concentrated on the warm, luscious lips beneath mine.

And that was when I heard a soft voice beside me say, "Julian?"

Reluctantly, I pulled away from Arianna, and twisted to face the person who'd interrupted us.

Raquel's eyes were wide as she stared at us, her tan cheeks pale. Guilt went through me at seeing the pain in her eyes, but I forced the feeling aside. Still holding Arianna's hand, I told Raquel, "Hey ... what's up?"

Raquel blinked in surprise at my casual question. Closing her eyes for a second, her cheeks flushing with color, Raquel sputtered, "Ah, nothing, I just ..." She opened her dark eyes, her expression was overflowing with pain. "I didn't realize you two were ... together," she finished, her voice cracking.

Confused over her reaction, I stammered with my response. "Yeah, we ... uh ... started dating last night." Arianna's hand tightened in mine, and I stroked her thumb in reassurance; I hadn't changed my mind—she was who I wanted.

Raquel's eyes dropped to the ground. "Oh, I see ..." Peeking up at me, she whispered, "I broke up with Russell last night." Her eyes watered as she said it.

My heart stopped, and for a second I couldn't breathe. I'd been waiting for those words for so long ...

I felt Arianna minutely pull away from me as I stood there, gaping. I couldn't stop my stunned expression. If this had happened a few days ago, I would have immediately asked Raquel to be mine, but things were so different now. I was with Arianna, fully and completely, and I just didn't feel the same way about Raquel; the feelings really had vanished.

Snapping my mouth shut, I moved closer to Arianna again. "I'm really sorry to hear that, Raquel. I know you cared about him. The light of hope in Raquel's eyes faded as my words sunk in. Keeping my voice friendly, but sympathetic, I told her, "But honestly, I think it's for the best. He was a jerk who didn't deserve you. I'm sure you'll find someone else soon who actually makes you happy."

I started to walk away, my heart pounding in my ears, but Raquel grabbed my arm. Tears dripping down her cheeks now, she said, "Can we talk for a minute alone, Julian? Just you ... and me." Her dark, watery eyes darted between Arianna and me, and there was almost an edge of panic in them.

The pain on her face was difficult to witness, but there was nothing more I could say to comfort her, and going somewhere with her alone felt wildly inappropriate. I wasn't about to play those kinds of games with Arianna. "I'm sorry, Raquel ... but no, I can't go somewhere private with you. And I'm sorry you're hurting, but I can't be your shoulder to cry on. Not anymore. Just know that you did the right thing, and you'll be okay."

I turned again to walk away, but before I could, Raquel said, "But I left him for you. I finally made a choice. I want *you*, Julian." She looked embarrassed to be saying that in front of Arianna, but she looked desperate, too, like she saw me slipping away. What she didn't realize was that I'd already slipped ... I was already gone.

I could feel the anger building in Arianna as she tightened her grip on my hand, and I figured she was about three seconds away from going after Raquel. Putting a comforting palm on Arianna's shoulder, I whispered, "It's okay," and turned back to Raquel. "You're too late, Raquel. You broke my heart after the party. Before that even. You chose Russell every *single* time, and I made a choice to stop holding onto something that wasn't mine. I moved on ... and I'm happy, truly happy. And I know you'll be happy one day too, but it won't be with me. We're not meant to be." I squeezed Arianna's hand, letting her know that *she* was my "meant to be."

Raquel's lip quavered as she absorbed what I was saying. Shaking her head, she turned around and walked away. A weary exhale left me as I watched her leave. I hadn't wanted to hurt her. And she probably hadn't wanted to hurt me either. But that was what happened when feelings were one-sided. Hopefully, she let her crush on me go, and found someone who liked her back. Someone better than Russell.

Arianna's arms circled me, and I twisted to look at her. Eyes glossy, she rested her head on my shoulder. "You turned her down ... for me. You really are over her, aren't you?"

Nodding, I smiled. "Yeah, I am. You're the one I want, Arianna."

She kissed the sleeve of my jacket. "Good, because I've wanted to be with you for forever, and it's about time you caught up."

She gave me a wink, and my heart beat harder. God, she was so beautiful, so accepting, so ... amazing. Why had it taken me so long to realize it? I had a goofy grin on my face as I walked through the door, and even though I *did* get reprimanded by every teacher for not having my stuff, I'd never enjoyed school more.

I was exhausted by the end of it. Going for two days on little-to-no sleep was messing with my head. I was so tired that I would start to laugh for no reason during class, then, moments later, I would begin to nod off. Arianna and Trey smacked me awake on more than one occasion. When Starla picked me up at the end of the day, I was practically asleep on my feet.

After giving Arianna a long kiss in the parking lot, I told her that I'd call her later tonight. With a half-smile on her lips, she looked over my sleep-deprived eyes and told me she'd see me tomorrow. I supposed she was right. Once I found a bed, I probably wouldn't rise from it for a while.

I didn't even make it to a bed—I fell asleep in Starla's car on the way home. When I woke up, I was in my bedroom and there was a lively debate going on downstairs. Wishing I could sleep until morning, I yawned and stretched. Sensing my sister's presence back at home made me smile. She was feeling better—sore and in pain, but better. Her heart, though, was another matter. It was broken, mangled, and would take much longer to heal than her external wounds.

Rising from my bed, I decided to change my clothes before joining the fray in the living room. The debate going on was about Ben. He'd survived the night, and his condition had stabilized throughout the day. He'd woken up a few hours ago and was finally well enough to have visitors. I was anxious to see him, to thank him for trying to protect my sister and me, but, with the heated conversation going on downstairs ... I didn't think I wanted to see him anytime soon.

They were going to wipe him. They were going to set him free.

Sighing, I stripped off my shirt and examined myself in the mirror. I had scrapes and bruises, and there was a long, angry red line down my forearm from where a bullet had nicked me. I wasn't nearly as beat-up as Ben and my sister, but I couldn't deny that my life was dangerous. My family wanted to give Ben a chance at a less dangerous life.

I couldn't contemplate it. He'd been a rock in our family since before we were born. He was my dad's best friend. Those two turned into teenagers whenever they were around each other. And if our family was ever in trouble, Ben was there in a flash—no matter the personal cost. And that price had been high. Ben had scars much deeper than mine. He was constantly worried about the safety of his daughter. And his wife ... their troubles really bothered my parents. But wiping him? It seemed so ... drastic.

Dressing, I hurried downstairs. Maybe I could stick up for Ben, for his memories. He was too important to our family to just cut him loose. But I had my work cut out for me, since the person who wanted him erased the most ... was my dad.

"He's done enough for this family. We can't ask him to risk his life anymore."

Dad stood in front of the TV, arguing with Alanna. Mom was cuddled on the couch with Nika. She peeked up at me when I entered and patted the space next to Nika. I sat by my sister, giving her a quick hug before returning my attention to Dad.

Dad's gaze swept over me. I could tell from his expression that he hated what he was saying, but he needed to say it. "We owe him ... everything." His pale eyes flashed to Alanna's. "Giving him a fresh start is the least we can do."

Alanna sighed. "I know, son, and I know how difficult this is for you. I'm just saying that it doesn't have to be all or nothing." She pointed out the window, to the direction of California. "Send him home, send him back to his wife ... there's no need to erase him."

Dad crossed his arms over his chest. "He's better off not remembering. He's better off not being in constant danger. And sending him home won't keep him from danger ..." Dad sighed and rolled his eyes. "He'll just find more."

Standing, Alanna walked over to Dad. "I love Ben, I really do, but my main concern here is you." She cupped Dad's cheeks. "You don't need to let him go, Teren. Don't let your guilt punish you like this. Ben loves you, and he made a choice to defend you and your family with his life. Don't take that choice away because you're scared." Sighing again, she ran a hand through Dad's hair. "Let your guilt go, son ... you hold onto it much too tight."

Dad looked away from Alanna, the guilt she was referencing clear in his eyes. Shaking his head, he reiterated, "He almost died ... because of me." Eyes watery, he turned back to her. "I won't let that happen again."

Sniffing, Dad walked away from his mother. Halina paced back and forth in front of the sliding glass doors that led to the backyard. Oddly, she was ignoring the conversation, her eyes fixated on the dark skies instead. She glanced at Dad when he blocked her view. "You know what to do," he murmured. Halina frowned, but Dad stormed off to the kitchen before she could respond.

Mom waited a moment, then patted Nika's knee and followed him. I tried to tune out Mom's quiet words of comfort as I slung my arm over my sister. As everyone in the living room felt the weight of Dad's words in the air, a growl burrowed up from Halina's chest. "I can't be here. I need to leave," she said.

Gabriel took a step forward and placed a hand on her shoulder. Her head snapped around at his touch. She seemed on edge, and I didn't think it had anything to do with Ben's condition. "He'll be fine, love."

Halina narrowed her eyes. "He's going to wake soon. I should be there." Her fingers clenched Gabriel's arms. "I need to go to him, Gabriel." Her voice was pleading with him, and a wave of surprise went through me. Halina didn't plead with anyone. If she wanted something, she took it.

Gabriel sighed. "It is too dangerous. Let his father handle it, Halina."

Halina shoved him back. "His father is not equipped to handle a newborn vampire!"

Gabriel's face was like stone. I had the feeling he'd had this argument with Halina before. "A newborn vampire who is not going to be happy that he *is* a newborn vampire." He raised a pale eyebrow at her. "Do I need to remind you what you did to your creator, my dear?"

Turning from him, Halina resumed her pacing. "I know how to be careful ... he won't stake me."

Imogen watched her mother from a chair in the corner. With a frown on her face, she told her, "He was a hunter before you turned him, Mother. You can't underestimate him." A spike of heartache sliced through Nika, and I held her tight to my shoulder. Hunter's upcoming awakening was just as hard on her as it was on Halina ... maybe harder, but she was silently dealing with her pain.

Halina wasn't so silent. She snarled and tossed her hands in the air. "Fine! Then let's go wipe Teren's hot friend so I can get my mind off my child who is waking up all alone!"

Imogen frowned at her mother's choice of words, then she crossed her arms over her chest. Halina looked back at her, and her face softened. In a flash, she was kneeling in front of her with a hand on her cheek. In her native language, she told her, *"You will always be my firstborn, my daughter, my heart incarnate. Without you, I am not complete."* Standing, she added in English, "I'm just a little ... testy ... at the moment." Her daughter smiled and nodded.

When Dad collected himself, he walked back into the room with Mom. His pale eyes were shining as he turned to Halina. "Let's get this over with," he murmured.

Halina, agitated at her own situation, softened her expression as she regarded her grandson. "Are you sure you want to do this, Teren?"

Dad looked over at me, heartache all over his face. "Yes, I should have done this ages ago. Maybe from the very beginning." Mom rested her chin on Dad's shoulder, supporting him.

I wanted to look away from his pain-filled gaze, but I made myself keep eye contact with him. "I want to be there, Dad. I want to say goodbye." The words felt hollow in my ears, surreal. We weren't actually going to say goodbye to our uncle, were we?

Nika sat up straighter beside me. "Me too."

Dad frowned as he glanced at Nika's many healing wounds. "No, you stay and rest. Your mother and I will handle this," he returned his gaze to me, "with Julian."

Nika was about to protest, but I leaned forward and kissed her hair. "You're tired and need your rest." She gave me a dry look at hearing her words at the hospital being repeated back to her. Before she could start in on me, I added, "I'll say goodbye for you. I'll *feel* goodbye for you."

She bit her lip, understanding; it would almost be the same as being there. *Almost*. With Nika accepting Dad's decision, and the rest of my family finally conceding to Ben's fate, I returned to the hospital with Mom, Dad, Halina, and Gabriel.

Walking through the halls filled me with dread. I didn't want to do this. I didn't want to be a part of this. But Ben meant something to my family, and seeing him off was the proper thing to do. Dad was equally glum as he walked in front of me with Mom. She rubbed his back encouragingly, but his head was down in contemplation. Even Halina seemed less self-assured as she followed behind me with Gabriel. No one really wanted to do this, but giving Ben a fresh start ... before this life killed him ... was the kindest thing we could do for him. It was our gift to him, in a way.

Dad paused before Ben's door. Resting his hand on the smooth wood, he inhaled a big breath. He took another second of reflection, then he swung open the door. Ben had always been so full of life and strength ... seeing him in that hospital bed, his head wrapped in gauze, his body hooked up to beeping machines ... it was jarring, to say the least. His confidence was still intact, though, as he smiled at our group of well-wishers. My heart sank at seeing the warmth in his smile. I was going to miss him ... a lot.

Ben tried to sit up on his pillows, but it seemed to hurt him so he stayed where he was. Pointing a finger at the TV bolted to the wall, he smirked. "Thank God you're here ... there's nothing good on." He pressed a button on his bed, and the television instantly snapped off. The sudden disappearance of the background chatter made the tension in the air seem thicker. Swallowing nervously, I stared at my feet.

I looked up again when I heard Ben ask, "So, we get 'em?" His light blue eyes flicked between all of us. When none of us answered, Ben frowned. A faint scar line along his lip deepened. "Why do you guys look so glum? I made it, I'll be fine."

Dad sat down on the edge of Ben's bed, his eyes moist. "Ben ..."

Ben let out a soft groan. "Damn, he got away, didn't he? After all that, he—" Cutting himself off, he looked up at me. "Is Nika all right? Is she safe?"

A sad smile was on Dad's face as he nodded. "She's fine, Ben, and yeah, he got away ... but he won't be an issue for a while."

Ben looked back at Dad. He was clearly confused, but he trusted Dad, so he didn't question him any further. Lying his head back down on the pillows, he closed his eyes for a second. "That's too bad. I was hoping you got the guy. He did shoot me, after all," he whispered, cracking open an eye.

An amused grin was on Ben's face. Mom sniffled and lowered her head, and Ben frowned again. "Seriously, what is with you guys?" His concern deepening, he asked, "Did someone ... die?" His voice wavered as he spoke, overcome with just the idea of someone in my family not making it.

Dad shook his head. "We're all fine ... everyone is fine." Dad swallowed, overcome by his own grief. "You did great, Ben."

Still feeling despair in the air, Ben's expression grew even more bemused. "Then what?" Eyes widening, he tried to sit up again. "Is it Olivia? Tracey? Did something happen?"

Dad put his hands on Ben's shoulders, urging him to lie down. "No, no, they're fine, Ben. It's not them ..." Sighing, Dad averted his eyes from his friend. "We've decided ... that you ..."

"That I what, Teren?"

Dad inhaled a big breath, then looked up at his friend. "You've done enough for our family ... and we need to let you go."

Ben's jaw dropped as he looked between all of us. My heart broke watching his eyes fill, and I was instantly glad Nika wasn't here for this. She was despondent over the loss of Ben, over the pain she could feel blossoming in me, but actually being here to see it happen ... was almost too much. I bit my cheek to try to rein in my turmoil. Mom couldn't hold back hers and was softly crying as Ben examined us.

His eyes swung back to Dad's. "You're wiping me? After everything we've been through ... you're wiping me?" Dad hung his head, and I saw a sparkle of moisture fall to his lap. Ben's face hardened. "After everything I've done for you? Every sacrifice I've made?"

Dad snapped his head up. "Yes, because we never should have let you make them in the first place. How many times have you almost been killed because of me? How many times have you lied to Tracey because of me? Your marriage is a mess, you're being kept apart from your daughter." He flung his hand towards Ben's injury. "You were shot in the freaking head, Ben! For me!" His voice lowered as he shook his head. "I won't let you do it anymore. I'm not worth it ..."

Ben grabbed Dad's arm. "That's not your call to make. You don't get to decide who loves you, Teren. You don't get to decide what people are willing to risk for you."

Seeing that Dad wasn't moved enough to change his mind, Ben's eyes flashed to Halina's. "I've earned the right to keep my mind, and you know it."

Halina sighed. "I do, and you know that I respect you, but this is Teren's wish, and I have agreed to it. But have no fear, I'm going to give you the best life possible. You will have it all, Ben. A loving wife, a loving daughter, riches, security ... friends. I'm going to give you the world."

Ben looked back at Dad. "All I want is to be a part of your family." A tear dropped to his cheek. "I'll stay out of it, I'll leave the vampire business to you, if that's what you really want me to do ... but I want to remember, Teren." Dad closed his eyes, and Halina took a step forward. Ben looked between them, then looked up at Mom. "Emma ... please?"

Mom started sobbing; it cut me like a knife, and I couldn't hold in the tears anymore. "I'm sorry, Ben," she said. "I don't want you to die. I'm so sorry."

Seeing that not even pleading was going to save him, anger heated Ben's expression. Eyes narrowed, he looked back at Dad. "You can be a real prick sometimes, you know that?"

Dad frowned at Ben's comment. "I'm not enjoying this."

Ben crossed his arms over his chest and looked up at the ceiling. "I won't forgive you for this, Teren. I may not remember it ... but you'll never have my forgiveness ... and you'll have to live with that."

Dad sighed as he stood from the bed. "I know ..."

Mom took his place, flinging her arms around Ben and sobbing into his shoulder. Ben wasn't really in the mood to comfort her, but he loosely patted her back. Even though his face was stormy, I could tell he was trying to not break down. When Mom backed away, I tentatively walked over and gave him a quick hug.

"Bye, Uncle Ben," I sniffled in his ear.

His face softened as he looked up at me. "Bye, kiddo. You keep your sister safe, all right?" I nodded, and Ben looked over my shoulder at Dad. "And make sure you give your pops some gray hairs for me." Ben smirked, and my dad softly chuckled.

When I stepped back, Gabriel gave Ben a firm handshake. "It was an honor," he intoned, slightly inclining his head.

"For me as well." Ben sighed as Gabriel released his hand. "Tell Jordan and the others to ... keep doing what they're doing."

Gabriel told him that he would, right as Halina stepped up to the bed. Ben swallowed as he looked up at her. "I gotta say, I'm surprised you agreed to this. I thought we had an understanding."

Leaning down, Halina kissed the bandage over his injury. "We do ... but you are only human, and will only ever be human, and at some point, living our life will kill you." She smirked and patted his cheek. "And you're far too attractive for that."

Ben gave her a wry smile. Halina stared at him for a moment, then spoke in the foreign language she often used when she wanted to say something profound. *"From one warrior to another, I thank you for your service to my family. Your sacrifices will not be forgotten ... you will be missed."*

The look on Ben's face was both touched and confused. He didn't understand what she'd said, but he could tell by the look on her face that it was something meaningful. Grunting a little, I wiped my cheeks dry with my sleeve. I wasn't crying as hard as Mom, but any sort of blubbering was embarrassing, and I wanted to be strong for Ben. Of course, I did have Nika's heartbreak amplifying my own.

Dad looked away when Halina started in on the speech that would obliterate Ben's mind. His remorseful eyes locked onto mine, and I saw the hard decision he'd just made in his morose expression. I wondered if I'd be able to make the same decision in his place. If Arianna's life was in danger by knowing me, could I wipe her to protect her? Could I be that selfless?

"Ben, you have fought well for our family, but when I am done speaking, you will not remember a moment of it. You will remember nothing of vampires. You will remember nothing of Teren, Emma, and their children. You will remember nothing of the nest in Los Angeles. You will not remember any of us. You will think that you were in Salt Lake City on a business trip, and that your injuries were from a mugging. You will go back home, and you will stay there. You will never again return here."

Dad sniffed and stared at his hands. Mom swallowed her grief, sat beside him, and put a comforting arm around him. Ben's eyes were glued on Halina as she continued.

"You will stop your incessant lying to Tracey and find a way to fix the distance in your marriage. You will become a loving, devoted, and *honest* husband. You will shift your focus from protecting vampires to raising your daughter. You will put her needs above everyone else's, save your wife's. You will pursue a career that you love, but that will also sustain your family. You will excel at it without letting it overrun your life. You will find wealth and balance. You will be happy and have a good life ... and vampires will only be a myth in your mind, easily discounted and dismissed."

She finished with a warm smile. "Goodbye, Benjamin. It has been an honor." She gave him a slight incline of her head, then twisted on her booted heel.

We all started to follow her out the door, since there was no point in staying anymore. Ben didn't remember us. As I walked through the doorframe, a step before my dad, I heard Ben say, "You really stressed that honesty part. You think I ought to tell Tracey what you really are?"

Every single one of us froze in our tracks. Dad swung his eyes back to Ben; Ben was grinning. Dad snapped his head to Halina as she pushed me aside to storm back into the room. "He remembers? I thought he would forget the minute you were done talking?" Dad said.

Halina's brows were furrowed as she stared at Ben's cocky expression. "And so he should have." Hands on her hips, she hissed out, "What did you do, Benjamin? Aside from insanely loud rock metal, there is no protection from compulsion."

Ben shrugged and chuckled. "I don't know, but I remember everything." He frowned at Dad. "And you're still a prick for trying to wipe me. Not cool."

We all walked back to Ben's bed. I was stunned. He shouldn't remember ... but he did. I didn't get it. Mom didn't either. She turned to Dad. "Teren ... why does he ... ?"

Gabriel's amused voice overlapped her question. "Interesting," he murmured.

Dad leaned around me to look over at him. "You know what happened?"

Gabriel stared between all of us. "Of course, it's quite obvious."

Dad's expression grew tight. "Mind filling us in?"

A small smile touched Gabriel's lips for a fraction of a second, then the cool, detached scientist returned. Splaying his hand toward Ben on the bed, he matter-of-factly said, "Halina is correct in there not being protection for humans from compulsion." He frowned for a second. "Besides complete deafness." Shaking the thought away, he looked back to the bed. "That only leaves one logical reason as to why Ben appears to be immune."

I studied Ben as Gabriel spoke, trying to think of any possible reason that Halina's mind control wouldn't work on him. It worked on all humans, it should have worked on him too. Unless ...

Dad gasped at the same time my mind pieced it all together. We both stared at Ben open-mouthed. Ben looked between us as Halina scoffed. "Please, there's no way, Gabriel." She'd figured it out, too, then.

Ben still seemed clueless as he examined each of us. I heard Mom lean over and ask Dad, "Is he saying that Ben's ... a ... a ..."

Irritated and concerned, Ben snapped out, "A what? Why are you all looking at me like that? So I have some super-secret blocking power. No need to bug out."

Halina leaned forward and stared Ben down. "Bark like a dog."

Ben raised his chin. "No."

Frustrated, Halina clipped, "Get your broken ass out of bed and hop on one foot."

"No, I don't feel like it."

A scowl formed on Halina's face; she wasn't used to a human denying a direct request. "Tell Teren that you fantasize about the time you caught him and Emma going at it in your SUV."

A flush swept over Ben's cheeks at the same time it swept over mine. He looked past Halina to Dad. "I so ... *so* ... don't, Teren." Ben's eyes reconnected with Halina's. "And if you *could* take that one, that would be great."

Dad sighed and put a hand on Halina's shoulder. "It's not going to work, Great-Gran. He can't be wiped." With a heavy exhale, Dad shook his head. "He's of mixed blood...several generations old, I'm assuming ... but still mixed, still there." He crooked a grin. "He's a little bit vampire ... just like us."

Halina stood straight and looked over at her grandson. "Well, damn. I didn't see that one coming."

CHAPTER TWENTY-FOUR

Nika

THE GRIEF THAT I'd been feeling from my brother shifted to astonishment ... and I had no idea why. He was saying goodbye to Ben at the hospital with my parents. Nothing about that should have been remarkable—just sad. But I was definitely feeling shock from him. If he came home and told me he saw a gaggle of pigs in the sky, the feeling of surprise and disbelief wouldn't come close to what he was feeling now. Whatever had happened, it was big. But Julian didn't seem scared or worried, so I tried not to think too much about it.

I had my own problems anyway.

Hunter. As the night stretched on, he filled more and more of my thoughts. Now that Hunter had my family's blood running through him, I could feel his location, like I could feel everyone else's. The familial bond had activated a couple of hours ago, before darkness had fallen. Not rushing to him when it had kicked in was a challenge; not rushing to him now was equally challenging. He would be waking up soon, and I didn't know what to expect from him once he was fully converted. I honestly didn't know if he *would* convert. It would be just like him to stoically refuse to eat.

There were rumors in the house that Dad had almost died on the night of his conversion for just that reason. It wasn't something my family talked much about, but I'd gleaned enough to realize that Dad had woken up when Mom was around, and she'd nearly become his first meal as an undead vampire. I couldn't imagine the horror that Mom had felt, or the guilt that Dad would have felt if he'd accidentally killed her that night.

I laid my aching body down on Grandma Linda's warm lap and tried not to think about that either. Grandma stroked my hair, murmuring that everything would be all right. Grandpa and Alanna were sitting on the other small couch, absorbed in their own quiet conversation; they were reminiscing about Ben. I tuned out their words as I watched my old, gray-haired grandpa sling his arm around his youthful, beautiful wife.

To the outside world, they seemed an odd pair. Some people called Grandpa a cradle-robber, said his relationship with his wife set a bad example for his grandchildren. If they only knew the truth—that Grandpa was one of the most moral and honest men I'd ever known. If people knew that he'd adored, loved, and remained faithful to his wife for several decades now, they'd change their tune about him.

Imogen paced before the sliding glass doors. I wasn't sure if she was anxious over Ben's fate, or concerned about her mother's unseemly bond with my boyfriend. Probably both. I was a little ... confused ... about Halina's link with Hunter. In one regard, it was sweet that she was just as worried about him as I was. In another, it was strange to have someone else care so much about him. I didn't want to be jealous, but, yeah, I kind of was.

As time ticked by, Julian's level of shock evened out. I relaxed as his mood improved. For some reason, he was happy now ... content. I wasn't sure why his mood had shifted again. That was the annoying part of our bond. We felt each other's emotions, but we couldn't feel the reason behind the emotion. It could be incredibly frustrating at times. All I could assume was that Ben had been successfully wiped, and Julian had finally accepted it. I hoped I could be as accepting of it as Julian one day, but I was still feeling a little bitter about the whole thing. Especially since I wasn't allowed to be there for it.

Just as I yawned, and considered heading up to bed, Halina's form streaked away from the hospital. It happened so fast it sent an electric zing through me, like someone had snuck up behind me and slipped an ice cube down my back. I shot up from my grandma's lap and stared out the window, to where I could feel Halina blurring away. Imogen and Alanna were staring as well.

"What is it?" Grandma Linda asked, touching my shoulder.

Imogen looked back at her, her brow furrowed. "Mother left the others."

Ignoring the ache in my shoulder, I stood up. "She's going to Hunter." In a whisper, I added, "He's awake."

Imogen walked over to me. "You can't know that, child."

I looked up into her pale, sky-blue eyes, eyes that were inherently common in my family. "But *she* could, right? Grandma Halina would know ... she'd feel it?"

I looked around at everyone, but none of them answered me. Truth was, we didn't know. No one in my family, save my father, had ever turned someone. I wasn't sure if Dad had been aware when Mom awoke from her conversion. But, then again, Mom's conversion wasn't your typical vampire turning. Hers had been more along the lines of what mine would be like. A pureblood conversion was completely different; our species were more like cousins than direct descendants.

I looked back to where I could feel my grandmother. She knew, and she was running to him ... to try to save him. It warmed and terrified me all at the same time.

Mom and Dad returned with Julian not too much later. Dad had a big grin on his face. Shaking his head, he told the room, "You are not going to believe what happened with Ben."

As Dad relayed the story, I had to agree with him. It *was* hard to believe. Ben had vampire blood in him? He didn't have any of our "gifts," so it was very, very diluted, but it was in there somewhere, buried deep. I supposed that would explain how he held his own against vampires. He had a tiny, tiny edge.

Imogen and Alanna were ecstatic over the news, and not just for the fact that Ben would get to keep his memories. No, they were overjoyed that returning our line to humanity was indeed possible. Breeding out the vampiric blood was one of the many reasons why they had all chosen to have children.

As the news sunk in, Julian twisted his lips. "Uh, Dad, that means Olivia ..."

Dad's smile fell a little. "Right ... we won't be able to wipe her either. I guess we'll just have to be extra careful around her, to keep her in the dark for as long as possible." His eyes scanned Julian and me. "No need for her to grow up before her time." His tone was remorseful, and I knew it was because he regretted how quickly our childhood had been taken from us. It wasn't his fault, though.

Walking over, I looped my arm around his waist and rested my head against his shoulder. After a moment of silence, I asked him the question that was pounding through my brain. "Dad ... do you think Hunter will be all right?"

Dad took a moment before he answered me. "I don't know, kiddo. I'm sorry."

With trepidation, I asked, "Can I go to him?"

Dad smiled and tucked a strand of hair behind my ear. "You already know I would never agree to that. It's too dangerous, Nika. *He's* too dangerous." My heart sank, but I wasn't surprised.

Halina stayed away all night long. Dad eventually made Julian and me go up to bed, since we had school in the morning. After giving me a warm hug, Julian sauntered off to his room and crashed onto his mattress. He was asleep in seconds. I stared at his form sprawled across his bed for a moment before I closed our mutual bathroom door.

I took my time brushing my teeth and washing my face. My stomach had a huge knot in it, though, and I couldn't stop thinking about Hunter. I couldn't help but worry about him. He would have woken up starving, near death. If he didn't get food right away, his body wouldn't complete the changeover, and he would die. He could be dead already. Maybe Halina was staying away out of grief. I wasn't sure what I would do if he died. I wasn't sure what I would do if he came back to life either.

I woke up the next morning feeling like I hadn't slept at all. I must have fallen asleep at some point, though, since the last thing I remembered was staring at my dark ceiling. The dull grayness I woke up to told me it was morning. I could hear Julian lightly snoring as I got ready for school. I let him sleep in; he hadn't gotten the drug-induced rest that I had yesterday. Poor guy had been forced to go to school on practically zero sleep. I thought if Dad hadn't been so worried and frantic, he would have let Julian skip. Dad had just needed one thing to return to normal I guess.

I meandered downstairs once I was ready for the day. Mom and Dad both looked up at me when I entered the kitchen. Noting the quietness of our home, I took a second to pinpoint the rest of my family. Everyone was back at the ranch except Halina. She was still miles away from us with Hunter ... or Hunter's body. Not ever having lost a family member, I had no idea if I would stop feeling Hunter's location if he died, or if he would forever be a blip on my internal radar. I never wanted to find out the answer to that question.

Mom stood and examined me as I poured a bowl of cereal. She felt my forehead, cupped my cheeks, checked my eyes. "I'm not sick, Mom," I grumbled, batting her hands away.

Sighing, she turned her attention to my bandages. I'd removed the one from my throat, opting for a high turtleneck to cover the raw, red line instead. The bandages on my shoulder and arm were clean, the wounds no longer bleeding. Mom would have known all of that just by smelling me, but she needed the reassurance, so she thoroughly inspected each injured area on me. "Are you done?" I asked, feeling grumpy and out of sorts.

Kissing my cheek, she murmured, "I suppose so." She pointed to the counter, where a carafe of steaming blood was waiting. "I want you to drink up before you go, though."

The smell emanating from the stainless-steel container made my mouth water. It had been a while since I'd had blood. Forgetting my bowl of sugary goodness, I got a glass from the cupboard and poured myself a cup. My fangs were down before I even finished pouring. Closing my eyes, I tilted the cup to my lips. It was heaven. I might not need blood like the others, or even crave it like they do, but I was still recovering, and my body wanted it right now; I savored the metallic sweetness as I gulped it down.

Gasping for air when I was done, I immediately poured a second glass. A low growl escaped me as I tipped that one back. Blood for a vampire was a natural, revitalizing painkiller. Gabriel said the introduction of blood into our system released endorphins, much like drugs do with humans. It was why some vampires got carried away with drinking. Whatever the reason, I instantly felt more alert and a lot less sore.

When my thirst was satiated, I finished my less-satisfying breakfast. Julian rolled out of bed and joined our group right as I was putting my bowl in the sink. He looked a little worn down, but he had a huge smile on his face and his mood was buoyant. Even though I'd been in and out of it yesterday, his mood had been similar. He was excited to go to school ... and Julian was never excited for school. I had to assume that it was a person who was boosting his spirits, and not what he was being taught.

As he poured himself a glass of blood, I cautiously asked, "Why are you so peppy?"

Smiling around his fangs, he shrugged. "No reason."

He was practically bursting at the seams now, and even Mom and Dad noticed. "Something going on, son?" Dad asked, a knowing smirk on his face.

Julian glanced at everybody, then lowered his cup from his lips. "Well, besides the fact that Ben is sort of one of us?" He paused as Dad's grin grew. "Grandma let Arianna keep her memories."

The smile fell from Dad's face. "Why would she let her remember?"

Julian brought the cup back to his mouth. Under his breath, he murmured, "Because she's sort of my girlfriend."

My head snapped around to Julian so fast it made my shoulder ache. "You asked her out?" Shock swept through me as I analyzed my brother's joy. He was feeling that for ... Arianna? Finally? Eyes narrowing, I asked, "What about Raquel?" If my brother was playing some kind of game with my best friend, well, I would give new meaning to the word Mom-zilla.

Seeing the seriousness in my expression, Julian set his cup down on the counter. "I don't feel for Raquel what I used to feel." He gave me a soft smile. "Arianna has my heart ... and I told Raquel as much."

I was floored. Not only had he chosen Arianna, but he'd confessed his feelings for her to the woman he'd been drooling over for months, if not years. This was huge for Julian. I automatically swept him into a hug, and my parents chuckled. Then a thought struck me. Pulling back, I told him, "You better not break her heart. I would have to stake you."

Julian sighed in a clearly love-struck way. "I'm not going to, Nika."

Mom stood and gave Julian a kiss on the head. "That's wonderful, honey. Arianna is a great girl."

Dad walked over and put his hand on Julian's shoulder. "Congratulations, Julian. I told you that you would find someone who'd accept you for who you really are." Pride blossomed in Julian's chest at Dad's words. It was instantly replaced with embarrassment when Dad said, "And I think we should have the sex talk, now that you're seeing someone."

Julian flushed with color as he groaned. "Dad ... I know how it works."

Dad shook his head. "It's not the mechanics that we need to talk about. There's a lot more to sex than ... sex."

I giggled at Julian's mortification when Dad swung his eyes to mine. "That goes for you, too, Nika. With Hunter still out there ..."

My laughter died along with his sentence. Melancholy filled me as my thoughts turned toward my wayward boyfriend. In a whisper, I told him, "Don't worry, Dad. I don't think I'll be having sex anytime soon."

I sighed and Dad wrapped his arms around me. He murmured in my hair that everything would be all right, and I hoped that was true. We just didn't know anything yet ... and it was maddening.

Watching Arianna and Julian at school was sweet, and a little annoying. I was used to my brother brooding and pining for a girl he couldn't have. Not that I wanted him that way, it was just how things had been for a long time. I was thrilled that Julian had finally moved past Raquel, but I was suffering from a gigantic helping of jealousy, since my own love life hadn't worked out so well.

Sitting on the steps with Julian, Trey, and Arianna after school, I shuddered as a gust of chilly wind wrapped around us. We'd be coming into winter soon, the holidays nearly upon us. The ski resorts would be fully open by the end of the month, and my family always made a point to take a break from the holidays and spend a weekend up there. Since the chill didn't bother the undead, playing in the Utah snow was a favorite activity for the vampires in my life. Julian and I enjoyed it, too; we just needed extra layers to stay warm.

When school let out for Christmas, we all usually flew down to California to see Aunt Ashley and Uncle Christian. They had a nice place close to the water. Mom and Dad would spend hours on the beach, regardless of the weather. Julian and I would join them for a little bit before heading back to the warmer, dry land.

Yes, a bunch of fun family traditions were coming up, and I should have been euphoric about them, but I wasn't. This was my favorite time of year, and I didn't have it in me to enjoy it. Not with everything that had happened. Not with so much unknown. Was Hunter alive? Was Halina alive? Was Hunter's dad still breathing? And if he was ... would he come after us? Would we ever be safe?

Starla arrived right on time and stepped out of her vehicle to wave at us. She was wearing a form-fitting sweater dress, warm leggings, and knee-high boots. Her spiky blonde hair was expertly spritzed into place and huge, bug-like sunglasses framed her face. She looked like she'd just stepped from the pages of a fashion magazine.

Trey whistled and bumped Julian's shoulder. "Damn, man, your mom is seriously hot."

Julian exchanged an amused glance with Arianna. "Um, thanks ... I think."

After saying goodbye to my friends, I plodded off to her car. Julian stayed behind, giving Arianna a series of light, adorable, sickening kisses. They were still lip-locked by the time I reached Starla's car. Pulling down her sunglasses, Starla glanced at me. "Want to start a pool on how long it takes them to jump in the sack?"

I grimaced. God, no. I was not ready for that. Feeling Julian's joy when he kissed her was bad enough. Feeling ... *that* ... would be downright horrifying. Understanding my expression, Starla popped a bubble with her gum and looked back at Julian. "Oh, damn, you're gonna feel that too, aren't you?"

She looked back at me, and I glumly nodded. Grimacing, she shook her head. "Father has got to fix you guys."

I frowned at her use of the word *fix*, then nodded. Yeah, she was right, we did need to be fixed ... and soon. Not having to *feel* my brother have sex for the first time would be fabulous.

Starla took us home and surprisingly stayed there until my parents came home. Everyone was on high alert until we learned about Hunter and his dad's fate. I felt pretty confident that Connor was too preoccupied to worry about us right now, but ... I could be wrong.

The evening took forever. I paced the living room, waiting for the cursed sun to go down. I wasn't sure what was going to happen once it did, but I wanted the damn thing extinguished so I could find out. Dad watched me like a hawk. He seemed nervous, like he thought I might zip away to Hunter at any moment. Honestly, I was tempted. Halina was still with him. Or her body was at any rate. It was slim, but there was definitely a chance that Hunter had taken her out ... she'd done it to her maker after all.

My hands were fisted as I watched the last golden rays of sun sink below the mountaintops. I held my breath as I waited ... for something. Halina was so far away from me that I couldn't tell if she was moving or not. I only knew her general direction. It was frustrating, and I murmured, "Come on ... do something," under my breath.

Dad came up behind me and put a hand on my back. "Nika, stressing isn't going to help."

I looked up at him, tears in my eyes. "I need to know."

Dad reached into his pocket and pulled out his phone. "I need to know, too." He turned away from the window as he dialed someone's number. I wasn't sure who he was calling; Halina didn't carry a cell phone, and Dad didn't know Hunter's number. I doubted Hunter had it in him to answer *any* phone call right now anyway. When a detached voice asked, "Hello?" I instantly realized that Halina hadn't run to Hunter alone ... Gabriel was with her, and he *did* have a cell phone.

"How is she?" Dad asked. It annoyed me that Dad had asked about Halina first. I knew that was his main concern, though, and while it was a genuine concern of mine too, I ached to know if Hunter had made it or not.

Thanking my enhanced hearing, I listened for Gabriel's response. "She's fine. Sorry I couldn't answer your call last night. It was a little ... hairy for a moment, but things have calmed."

I looked up at Dad, not realizing he'd called yesterday. He must have done that behind the soundproof doors. Shifting my focus to his phone, I asked, "And Hunter?"

Hearing me, Gabriel answered immediately. "The boy survived his conversion. He was fed well. We could have left him last night, but Halina ... refuses to leave his side. She spent the entire day with him." Gabriel's voice was a little disgruntled.

I was a little bothered by that news, as well, but too overjoyed at the fact that Hunter was alive to really care. I held my hands to my mouth as happy tears blurred my vision. He made it.

Watching my reaction, Dad asked Gabriel, "And his father?"

Gabriel sighed. "Took off the moment his son fed. I followed him for a bit ... but I didn't want to leave Halina alone with Hunter for very long. Last I saw of him, he was headed north, away from town."

Dad nodded. "I'm sure he'll need time to recover from this shock." Pausing, Dad locked gazes with Mom. "But eventually he will recover, and he'll return ... for his son."

"Agreed. We will need to be ever watchful, Teren."

Dad sniffed and closed his eyes for a moment. Reopening them, he asked, "Will you be coming home soon?"

Gabriel grunted. "I do not think so." A rare, irritated emotion laced his voice. "The child refuses to go with us, and Halina will not leave him alone. They seem to be ... at odds for the moment."

Dad blinked. "Isn't he bonded to Great-Gran? Shouldn't he *want* to be with her?"

"Yes, he is ... but he's fighting it ... and ..." Gabriel paused, and said the next part so quietly that I had to strain to hear him, "his bond to her is not nearly as strong as her bond to him. He has only a vague desire to be near her. It's extremely annoying to Halina that he's so aloof about the whole thing."

I exhaled with relief again, glad that my boyfriend wasn't obsessed with my grandmother. That would have made things even weirder for me, and my life couldn't get much weirder.

His voice back to normal, Gabriel added, "He also refuses to eat ... or should I say, bite. He will only drink blood once it's been exposed to the air. Halina is worried that he will starve if she leaves him."

That alarmed me, and I took a step forward. "She has to stay with him then." My wide eyes met Dad's. "She can't let him starve." Starving a vampire wouldn't kill them outright, not after they'd fully converted, but it was horribly painful, and dangerous. A starved vampire would do things they wouldn't normally do ... horrible stuff that the legends and myths were centered around. Hunter would never forgive himself if he turned into *that* kind of monster.

Dad nodded and smiled at me. "She won't let that happen to him, Nika." To Gabriel, he added, "Come home when you can then. And ... be careful."

"You as well."

Gabriel disconnected, and Dad put his phone away. I was happy and unnerved at the same time. They were both alive, but things weren't exactly running smoothly. And Hunter was refusing to eat ... which meant he was disgusted, appalled by what he was. He was hurting, and I couldn't do anything about it. Not from here anyway.

Seeing my expression, Dad pointed at me. "You can't go to him, Nika. Not now. Not yet. He's far too dangerous."

I bit my lip to not snap some rebellious comment at him. I knew he was right. Hunter was a newly transformed, resentful pureblood. He might have been hesitant to kill me before, but now that he'd been forced into a world he didn't want, he might not be so reluctant. And he was supercharged now. Faster, stronger, nearly impervious. If he wanted me dead ... I would probably be dead.

Flopping down on the couch, I nodded my agreement. I wouldn't go to him. Even though it was going to tear me in two, I would stay away from him. For now.

THREE WEEKS PASSED and not much changed. Julian and I continued with school, while my family continued their work at the ranch. Ben flew back home to rest up and try to repair things with his wife. From what Dad told us, his little near-fatal accident while visiting our family had rejuvenated his marriage. Tracey couldn't stand the thought of losing him, and they'd pretty much patched things up. Of course, he was still lying to her on a constant basis. I hoped that wouldn't bite him in the ass again. Ben deserved to be happy.

My brother was finally at peace with himself. I think the fact that he didn't have to hide anything from Arianna helped a lot. Julian was becoming a stronger person by her side; he hadn't had a panic attack since everything with Hunter and his dad had happened. Watching my brother grow into a man was inspiring, but watching his relationship grow was hard on me. Julian's newfound happiness seemed to highlight my emptiness. I was still thrilled for him, though; he deserved someone warm and sweet like Arianna.

Halina still hadn't left Hunter's side, and he still wasn't ready to return to the city. They were getting progressively closer to Salt Lake, but were still just out of range. It was disheartening to feel them getting closer to me when I knew I had to stay away from him. I just wanted to see him, make sure he was okay. Apologize for what happened to him ...

My musings were interrupted by a wet snowball sliding down the back of my neck. I spun to see Julian chuckling at me, his cheeks rosy as the winter air nipped at his skin. He was holding Arianna's hand as our family took a leisurely walk around the neighborhood. Since Connor hadn't made a peep since his son's conversion, our family was falling back into our old routine.

Dad and Gabriel kept an ear to the ground, listening for any word of an attack being made on a vampire, but all was quiet in the area. Connor had moved on ... abandoned his son. It saddened me that he'd fled, but with his beliefs, what other choice did he have? He would never accept what his son was. To him, Hunter had died the day Halina had drained him.

Giving Julian a dry look, I reached down and grabbed a fistful of snow. Quickly compacting it into an ice ball, I chucked it at him. He had to blur a bit to dodge, and Arianna jabbed him in the ribs. "No super powers, Julian," she scolded.

Mom and Dad gave each other an approving glance as Julian dropped his mouth open in protest. "Was I supposed to just let it hit me?"

At the same time, all of us told him, "Yes."

Julian scowled until Arianna leaned up and kissed his cheek. Then the poor sap melted. Happy as I was for them, I wanted to roll my eyes. Now I understood why my parents annoyed Starla so much. A person could only take so much sappiness.

I looked up at Hunter's old house when we walked by it. We didn't usually go this way, not anymore. The salmon-colored home was abandoned. When it was clear that Hunter and his dad weren't going to return, the owner had boxed up all their stuff and put it into storage somewhere. Except his sister's ashes. I'd snuck into the house and retrieved those. I wasn't sure why, just ... if it were my brother in an urn, I wouldn't want him boxed up and locked away somewhere. I would want him to be safe. I would want him to be with someone who cared. And I still cared about Hunter ... try as I might not to.

When we got to the driveway, Dad reached back and grabbed my hand. I smiled up at him, then shifted my eyes to Hunter's house again. It saddened me that someone else was going to be living there soon. Even though Hunter hadn't been here long, the home felt like his, and I would always think of it that way.

Eventually, we made it back to our house. Arianna and Julian disappeared into the kitchen to have hot fudge sundaes before Arianna had to go home. I stayed on the porch, drinking in the chilly night air. Mom gave me a kiss goodnight, then went into the house, respectfully giving me space. Dad stayed outside with me. "It will get easier, Nika," he told me.

I wasn't sure how that statement could possibly be true, but I appreciated the sentiment anyway. I was about to thank him, when I felt something. Or more appropriately, some*one*. Hunter was streaking my way. Well, not entirely my way. He seemed to be heading for his old house, just a few streets away from me.

I took a step in his direction, and Dad moved in front of me. "Nika ..." he said, his voice low and full of warning. He could feel Hunter, too, and he didn't want me running off to him.

Not able to resist Hunter being so close to me, I jumped over the railing, and took off for Hunter's old place. I felt Julian's concern instantly spike, felt Dad following immediately after me, and Mom following just after him. I ignored them all, though; I was too close to Hunter to turn back now.

Mom and Dad were right behind me when I rushed up the steps and twisted the handle to the abandoned house. It was locked, as expected, but I was riled up enough that I did something I normally never would have done. I leaned my shoulder into the wood and easily broke the frame. Dad growled his irritation and grabbed my elbow. "We need to leave, Nika. You can't go in there."

I yanked my arm free and put a foot inside. "It's Hunter," I whispered, well aware that Hunter could hear me, could feel me. "I need to see him, Dad. Please." I looked between my parents, begging them to let me do this.

Dad looked back at Mom, then let out a weary exhale. "Fine, but we're coming with you."

I wasn't surprised, so I didn't protest. Being as quiet as I could be, I walked into the entryway. "Hunter?" Nothing but silence answered me. "Please ... don't leave." My heart thudded in my chest as I turned to the hallway, where I could feel him. One of the bedroom lights was on, but the house was stone-silent.

I took a cautious step forward, but froze in my tracks when the light from the bedroom suddenly snapped off, and the house went pitch-black. My nerves spiked, and I started to tremble. Hunter was in there, I could feel him. I was sure I had nothing to worry about—Hunter wouldn't hurt me—but a sliver of fear went up and down my spine as I inched my way down the hallway toward the bedroom; Julian's mood shifted in response. Like my parents, he didn't like this.

Recalling the empty spot on the mantel where Hunter's sister's urn once lied, I wondered if that was why he was here. If so, I could help him. "Hunter? Are you here for your sister's ashes? Because I have them. I'm keeping them safe for you."

A figure suddenly emerged from the bedroom and stepped in front of me; his bulk blocked my path. Startled at the sudden movement, I gasped and retreated a step. I ran into my parents behind me, and Dad protectively shifted me behind him.

A pair of brightly glowing eyes stared at me in the darkness. The light emanating from them was peaceful, tranquil, and I felt my body relaxing as I stared into the dark eyes behind the glow, eyes that I loved. Hunter's hypnotic gaze broke apart from me to take in Mom and Dad. The glow emanating from my father's eyes highlighted Hunter's face; a small, smug smile was across his lips.

Leaning forward, he met my eyes again. "Your heart is racing, Nika. I can hear it. Are you frightened of me?"

As if to prove to me that I should be, he dropped his fangs. They were shocking to see on the human I loved. But then again, Hunter wasn't human anymore. Realizing his display was mainly an act, I worked my way around my father. Dad clasped my shoulder. "He's dangerous, Nika," Dad whispered.

Hunter chuckled and crossed his arms over his chest. Fangs still down, he raised his eyebrows in question. Was I brave enough to talk to him without my bodyguards around? Looking over at Dad, I paused a moment to let the hypnotic effect of his eyes calm me down. The phosphorescent glow was the one aspect of vampirism that my brother and I didn't have. It was one less thing we didn't have to hide, although, at times like these, it did come in handy.

Feeling at peace, I smiled and patted Dad's stubbled cheek. "I'll be fine. He won't hurt me."

As I stepped forward, Hunter murmured, "Are you sure? You smell ... amazing." He intentionally took a long inhale, closing his eyes as he appreciated my aroma.

Not buying the act anymore, not when I knew the truth about him, I stepped right in front of him, almost toe-to-toe. "Don't act like you're going to bite me. I already know that you won't eat unless blood is exposed to the air." I indicated my scarred shoulder. "And I'm all healed up now."

Hunter opened his glowing eyes. The light narrowed at me as I called his bluff. "Where's my sister?" he immediately asked.

The loss of our passionate relationship made me ache. I never thought we'd end up this way. "She's safe. She's with me."

Hunter sniffed. "I want her back." As an afterthought, he added, "Please."

I nodded. Examining his face, I saw the weariness in his eyes, the haggardness in his features. He really was starving himself. I couldn't imagine the torture he was putting himself through. I couldn't imagine his pain, his guilt, his self-hatred. If he could just accept what he was, we might still have a chance.

He watched me as I watched him, and the light of his eyes lulled me into a complete calm. Even though a warning in the back of my head screamed at me, I reached up and put a hand on his cheek. "Are you okay?" I asked, my voice soft. Hunter froze as his eyes locked onto my wrist. His already lowered fangs grew just a bit longer as the blood pumping through my veins stirred the animal within him. Seeing his eyes dancing with interest, Dad growled a warning.

Remembering what I was dealing with, a newborn, half-starved vampire, I quickly pulled my hand away. Hunter's eyes followed my wrist, but he didn't make any threatening moves so Dad didn't tackle him, and I was sure he wanted to. Shaking his head a little, Hunter grumbled, "No, Nika, I'm not okay." Eyes hard, he added, "I'm a monster. *He* turned me into a monster."

"Hunter, no, you're not a—"

He cut off my feeble attempt to comfort him. "He should have let me die in that church." Clenching his jaw, he shook his head. "He should have done his job and staked me the moment I changed. Instead he ran away ... like a coward." His eyes shifted away from me, the glow softly lighting the bedroom he'd stepped out of.

Not sure if I should, I put a hand on his arm. His eyes immediately returned to mine. "Your dad loves you. He couldn't stand the thought of losing you."

Cocking his head, Hunter absorbed my features as he spoke in a soft voice. "He did lose me, Nika. I'm not human anymore. And Dad understood that. It's why he took off. He left me, Nika. He abandoned me. Because I'm ... a walking disease. A blight on humanity."

His eyes filled with dark red tears. The pain in his silent heart was crystal clear to me, even though he was trying to hide it under his vampirism. This was killing him. Tears stinging my eyes, I grabbed his cheeks again. "No, no, you're not. Being a vampire doesn't change who you are. You can still be that wonderful boy I fell in love with ..." My throat closed as I held him inches from me. I could feel Dad take a step toward me, on high alert since I was so close to him.

Face forlorn, Hunter didn't seem too interested in the pulse pounding right next to his mouth. "I will never be anything but a beast, Nika. She should let me die." A tear of blood rolled down his cheek.

I stepped into his body, needing to ease his pain. I heard Dad whisper my name, but I ignored him. I felt Julian's concern rising, as he wondered what I was doing, but I pushed it back. Hunter was in pain ... he needed me. "She?" I asked, as I wiped the blood from his skin.

He looked down at how closely I was standing to him. "Your grandmother ... Halina." His eyes returned to mine, irritation overriding his despair. "She won't leave me alone." Face twisting into a grimace, he grumbled, "I'm surprised she's let me go for this long. She's always hovering around me, watching over me ... forcing me to feed." He sighed, exasperated. "It's ... frustrating. I just want to be alone, but I'm ... drawn to her, drawn to the monster who made me."

Swallowing the tiny ache of jealousy that flared up, I released my hands from his cheeks. "It's the bond. She sired you, so you're ... linked."

His beautiful eyes got a faraway look. "For how long?" he whispered.

I hesitated, enjoying this fact about as much as Hunter was going to. "The bond is permanent, Hunter." His eyes closed for a moment but his face was still lit by the light emanating from my parents. Seeing his grief, I rubbed his shoulder. "But the desire to be around each other will fade within a year or two. After that, you'll only be aware of her presence in your mind."

Reopening his eyes, he pulled his fangs back up. "It's so odd to know where she is. "He lifted his hand and pointed in her direction without looking. Since I could feel her that way too, I smiled. "It's odd to feel ... where you *all* are." He tilted his head at me, like he was mystified by feeling me *and* seeing me. I could understand why. If I hadn't been born with this bond, I'd probably find it weird too.

"It's the blood ... you share our family's blood, so you're linked to us now. We're connected," I said with an encouraging smile; I wanted him to see the good parts of this, not just the bad. "You're family now, Hunter. Forever."

A genuine smile ghosted his lips, but it was gone instantly. "I never wanted this life," he muttered.

Clenching his shoulder, I nodded. "I know ... and I'd like to help you through it, if you'll let me." Ducking down, I searched his glum face.

"I don't think you can, Nika," he finally whispered. His eyes were guilty when he looked back up at me. "I don't want to hurt anybody ..." pausing, he inhaled a deep breath, and his fangs crashed back down, "but you smell so freaking good."

The sadness on his face broke my heart, and I wanted to reach up and comfort him. I couldn't though. Taking his words as a threat, Dad yanked me back into the safety of his arms. Wrapped in his chilly protection, I felt his chest release a hair-raising growl. Eyes slightly wild, Hunter glowered at my father and let his own rumble fill the night. The tension in the air made Mom grab me from Dad's arms and pull me back a step.

Just as I started to fear that my boyfriend and my father were going to start ripping each other to shreds, Hunter blinked. Shuddering, he closed his eyes and focused on controlling his emotions. When he reopened them, he was more composed. "I wasn't going to harm her."

Dad relaxed when he saw that Hunter was in control again. Shaking his head, he told him, "You don't know what you may or may not do right now, Hunter. You're starving yourself. That makes you unpredictable."

Hunter raised his chin in defiance. "I won't kill."

Dad sighed. Walking over to Hunter, he cautiously extended a hand. "And you don't have to. Nika's right, you're family now, and we can help you live without killing ... if you let us."

Hunter looked down at Dad's peace offering. He started to extend his own hand, but Halina's presence began streaking our way. Hunter's head shot up to glare in her direction. Dropping his hand, he returned his gaze to Dad's. "I'm fine on my own." He looked past Dad to me. "But I do want my sister back."

Tears leaking down my cheeks, I nodded. "I'll get her to you, I promise."

Hunter backed up a step. His face was torn; he wanted to run from Halina and run toward her at the same time. When he backed up to the end of the hall, I jostled around my parents. Dad grabbed my hand at the last minute, but I jerked free. Blurring to Hunter, I tossed my arms around him. "I love you," I whispered in his ear.

He stiffened, then embraced me. His ice-cold body melted into my heat, and a sob broke free from me at the joy I felt being in his arms again. It had been so long since we'd held each other. The simple times, when we were only hiding our relationship because of Hunter's age, seemed like a lifetime ago.

Burying his head in my neck, I heard Hunter take a large inhale, then felt his arms around me tighten. I tensed, immediately remembering that things between us weren't so simple anymore. I was now a source of food to a very hungry animal. Hungry and tormented. His mouth rested near my jugular, and I prepared myself to push him away. Unlike a human victim, I wasn't exactly weak. My vampire-enhanced abilities might not be as strong as Hunter's, but I could put up a decent fight.

Hunter ran his nose up my neck, still inhaling me. Just as I felt my dad move, Hunter released me and fled into the night. I darted to the window he'd escaped from. Leaning my head out, I searched the inky night for him. He was gone, though, already vanished from my vision, and I dropped my head, defeated.

The three of us slowly made our way back home. Halina joined up with us right outside the Bavarian beauty. Leaning against the porch railing, she shook her head of long, wild hair. "That boy is going to give me an ulcer." She grunted and brought her hand to her temple. "I already have a headache."

Mom put a sympathetic arm around my waist as Dad told Halina, "He doesn't seem to want to be around anyone. He thinks he can do it on his own."

Halina sighed and pushed away from the railing. The short dress she was wearing showed more thigh than Mom would ever let me show. I didn't think I'd even be allowed to wear a nightgown that short. "He is stubborn beyond comprehension. He makes raising you seem easy."

THE NEXT GENERATION

Dad smirked at her, then indicated the house. "I'm sure he'll be fine for a while. Why don't you come inside?" Walking up to her, he threw an arm around her shoulders. "It's been forever since you've visited."

Halina's eyes were torn as she looked at Dad, then Mom and me. She clearly wanted to keep running after Hunter. Her gaze swung south, to where Hunter had run off. I searched that direction, wanting to see him, but knowing I wouldn't. He was too far gone, and he clearly didn't want to come back ... yet.

Bringing her eyes back to Dad's, Halina smiled and looped her arm around his waist. "All right. For a time." She grimaced and added, "Gabriel is visiting Starla and Jacen anyway. This will give me an excuse to not have to make an appearance over there." She let out an exasperated groan. "That woman drives me crazy."

I contained my smile. Starla was more like my grandmother than she would ever admit.

After visiting with Halina for a bit, I excused myself and trudged upstairs. Arianna tried to go with me, shooing Julian away and telling him that she needed "BFF time," but I didn't let her comfort me; I just wanted to be alone. How I had gone from being alone and positive that I would *never* find love, to being alone and positive that I would never find love *again* was beyond me.

I heard the tip tap of claws on the floor and looked up to see Spike shuffle into the room. The old pup stopped at my feet and stared up at me with milky eyes. Reaching down, I lifted him onto the bed with me. He curled into my side and was almost instantly asleep. I stroked his fur as he wheezed in my arms. Well, I supposed I wasn't completely alone. Unlike Hunter, who was literally alone tonight, I was surrounded by beloved family members.

Later, after Arianna drove herself home, Julian came upstairs to check on me. I felt his concern for me long before I saw him. Leaning against the doorframe, he crossed his arms over his chest as he watched me. Looking up at my brother, I saw a peacefulness in his features that I hadn't ever seen before. His pale eyes were sympathetic, but happy at the same time. He'd found what he was searching for. I thought I had too, but, things hadn't exactly worked out that way.

He walked over to me, sitting on the other side of Spike. Our pet let out a contented exhale as he snuggled between us. Reaching over him, Julian grabbed my hand. He didn't ask how I was since he already knew I was feeling pretty low and pretty confused. Instead, he indicated the TV tucked in the corner of my room. "Want to watch a movie?"

I smiled at the distraction he presented. "Yeah ... nothing romantic though."

He made a sour face. "That would be about the last thing I'd pick." Grabbing the remote beside the bed, he turned the set on and started flipping through channels. "I was thinking more along the lines of guns and violence." He paused, his face speculative. "On second thought, how about a comedy?"

Relaxing back into my pillows, I nodded my agreement. "Yeah, something funny sounds good." We'd both had enough violence to last a very long time.

Mom and Dad caught up downstairs with Halina, while Julian and I watched an eighties comedy about a girl trying to pass herself off as a boy. We both laughed out loud, and our emotions evened out. I nodded off to sleep long before the movie was over. When I woke up, it was still dark outside, but dawn was fast approaching. I was alone in my bed; Julian was snoring away in his. I was tucked under the covers, probably by my mom. Halina's presence was far away from me, back toward the ranch. She must have finally gone home to visit her daughter and granddaughter. Mom and Dad were in their soundproof bedroom. Even Spike was absent. He had probably plodded after Mom when she'd tucked me in.

Feeling grimy, since I hadn't brushed my teeth or washed my face, I tossed the covers aside and stood up. That was when my tired mind finally realized something I should have realized immediately—I wasn't alone. A dark figure was standing beside the window, a figure I could see ... and feel. Hunter. He was standing in such a way that the streetlamp outside dulled the glow of his vampire eyes, eyes that were relentlessly staring at me.

Startled, I backed up a step. It wasn't every day that you woke up to find someone watching over you as you slept. Recovering quickly, I took a step toward him. "Hunter?" My eyes flashed to the grayness outside; dawn would be here within the hour. "What are you doing here? You should be somewhere safe."

His eyes followed my gaze. "I hate running from the sun," he muttered.

Wondering just how deep his melancholy was, I stepped up to him and put a hand on his arm; his body was like steel under his jacket, cold and unyielding. "You have to. You'll die if you don't." He looked back to me as my voice grew tight. "And I don't want you to die."

A sad expression crossed his face as his eyes searched mine. I wanted him to lean down and kiss me. I wanted to feel the tenderness of his lips, the coarseness of his stubble. But more than all of that, I wanted him to smile. He didn't, though; he merely said, "I already died, Nika."

I brought my hand to his face, caressing the stubble along his jaw that I missed so much. The light from the lamp highlighted his undead features, and I thought he'd never looked more attractive. His eyes drifted to my exposed wrist before shifting back to my face. "I'm so sorry this happened to you," I whispered. "But please don't give up."

He pulled back from me, and looked down at something in his hands. I removed my hand from his skin and looked down at what he held. A black-as-night urn was in his palms. In the faded light of the room, my enhanced sight could see the outline of bloody vampire fangs that extended from the top. Recalling that his sister's urn was a rosy granite color, I felt my heart fill with lead. "What is that, Hunter?"

Sighing, he lifted it up and tilted it so I could see the name engraved on it—his own. "It's tradition in my family, when a hunter dies, their urn is marked with fangs ... in honor of their commitment to the cause." His tone grew harsh, bitter. His hand tightened around the urn, and for a moment, I thought he might throw it through the wall; that would certainly wake up my snoring brother.

Calming himself, Hunter handed it to me. "I want you to keep it. Store it next to my sister's."

My eyes filling, I numbly took the cold marble from his icy fingers. I couldn't speak; I had no words. A trace of a smile drifted over Hunter's features, and he tucked a strand of hair behind my ear. Like before, the smile faded instantly. "Keep my sister safe for me, okay?"

I nodded, then found my voice. "I thought you wanted her with you?"

His eyes drifted to my closet, to where his sister's ashes were resting. "I don't deserve her company," he said in a low voice.

Not sure how to comfort him, or if I even could, I held his urn in one hand and reached out for him with the other. He was through my open window in a flash. A ghost image of him was still in my watery eyes as I gazed at the spot where he'd vanished from me ... again. Not knowing what else to say or do, I whispered, "I'll keep her safe for you, until you're ready to be reunited."

I listened for any sort of response, but I only heard the garbage trucks in the distance. Sighing, I started to close the window. A gust of chilly wind billowed into the room, stirring my lacy curtains. Faintly, in the breeze, I heard Hunter's voice, and hearing it gave me hope—for him and for us.

"I love you, too, Nika."

I smiled as I looked out into the night. Hunter had a long way to go to acceptance, but I would help him get there ... if he'd let me.

THE END

ABOUT THE AUTHOR

S.C. Stephens is a #1 *New York Times* bestselling author who spends her every free moment creating stories that are packed with emotion and heavy on romance. In addition to writing, she enjoys spending lazy afternoons in the sun reading, listening to music, watching movies, and spending time with her friends and family. She and her two children reside in the Pacific Northwest.

You can learn more at:

AuthorSCStephens.com
Twitter: https://twitter.com/SC_Stephens_
Facebook.com/SCStephensAuthor

Also by S.C. Stephens

Dangerous Rush
Furious Rush
Untamed
Thoughtful
Reckless
Effortless
Thoughtless
It's All Relative
Collision Course
'Til Death
Bloodlines
Conversion